ODIN'S FURY

Book Ten in the Viking Blood and Blade saga

Peter Gibbons

Copyright © 2024 Peter Gibbons

All rights reserved

The characters and events portrayed in this book are fictitious. Any similarity to real persons, living or dead, is coincidental and not intended by the author.

No part of this book may be reproduced, or stored in a retrieval system, or transmitted in any form or by any means, electronic, mechanical, photocopying, recording, or otherwise, without express written permission of the publisher.

ISBN: 9798300523282

Cover design by: Erelis Design
Library of Congress Control Number: 2018675309
Printed in the United States of America

ONE

883AD.

The warship Seaworm sliced through storm-tossed waves like an axe blade. Oars bit into the white-tipped waves and hauled the *drakkar* forwards as sixty Viking warriors grunted with the effort. Their muscled backs stretched as calloused hands gripped ash-shafted oars, and its curved beast-headed prow snarled westwards through the swell like a vengeful leviathan. The Seaworm emerged from the fog as though spat from the underworld, racing towards her prey with relentless speed. Clinker-built timbers groaned as the ship lurched into a trough, the planking stretching under the strain so that for a terrifying, fleeting moment, the grey-green sea appeared between the timbers, and only momentum, horsehair, and tar caulking kept the sea from rushing in and sinking the vessel into watery oblivion. An icy wave crashed over the bow, drenching the grim-faced crew,

ODIN'S FURY

By Peter Gibbons

Gudbyrne scan,
heard, hondlocen,   hringiren scir
song in searwum,   þa hie to sele furðum
in hyra gryregeatwum gangan cwomon.
setton sæmeþe   side scyldas,
rondas regnhearde, wið þæs recedes weal,
bugon þa to bence. Byrnan hringdon,
guðsearo gumena;   Garas stodon
sæmanna searo,   samod ætgædere,
æscholt ufan græg.   Wæs se irenþreat
wæpnum gewurþad.

They arrived with their mail shirts
Glittering, silver-shining links/ Clanking an iron song as they came.
Sea-weary still, they set their broad,
battle-hardened shields in rows
Along the wall , then stretched themselves
On Herot's benches. Their armor rang;
Their ash-wood spears stood in a line,
Gray-tipped and straight: the Geats' war-gear
Were honored weapons.

- From Beowulf, a tenth century old-English poem

AUTHOR MAILING LIST

If you enjoy this book, why not join the authors mailing list and receive updates on new books and exciting news. No spam, just information on books. Every sign up will receive a free download of one of Peter Gibbons' historical fiction novels.

https://petermgibbons.com

and freezing water clung to braided beards like droplets of silver. Two young warriors bailed the bilge with red-raw hands, their buckets sloshing water over the side only for another thunderous surge to rain down, mocking their efforts and filling the bilge again.

Hundr tilted his head to drain stinging seawater from the cavernous hole of his dead eye. He stood in the prow and leaned into its dragon head as the ship soared upon the crest of a monstrous wave. Behind him, the crew roared with laughter, intoxicated by the wild dance of wind and sea. The sky above them broiled, malevolent and sombre as an axe blade. Hundr glanced across the waters at the rest of his fleet, spread out in a wide formation. Each vessel appeared too flimsy to survive the sea's violent force, but just as it seemed the ships would disappear into valley-like troughs, they rose again, proud and sleek on the swell. Four warships crammed with Viking warriors, each man sworn to serve Hundr, ready to fight and die at his command. Einar the Brawler waved to him from the deck of the Wind Elk and pointed toward a barely visible promontory to the west, a hard finger of rock smashed and clawed by the sea's fury.

"Land," Hundr called over his shoulder. The warship's shipmaster, Fastbjorn Brokenspear, flashed his teeth in a wicked grin and repeated the call, bellowing in his deep, oak-splintering voice, and the crew let out a clipped roar in response. Men rushed to barrels stored beside the mast post to retrieve weapons and armour wrapped in fleece to protect the iron and steel from the sea's corrosive bite. They had braved the wild winds of Njorth and the pitiless depths of Ran's seas to reach the island, and enemies waited for them there. Hundr rolled his shoulders, loosening cold muscles, wincing slightly at the stiffness of old wounds, almost feeling the icy blades of swords, spears and axes that had torn at his flesh during his long years sailing the Whale Road as a Viking sea jarl. Hundr's swords sang to him as he drew them from their protective fleeces, calling to him for blood. They yearned for the blood of his enemies, of those who served Finn Ivarsson, The Crippled King of Mann.

"Here, my lord," said Fastbjorn, handing Hundr his two swords and *brynjar* coat of chainmail. To wear armour at sea was to risk death, for no man could swim in the heavy coat of interlocking iron rings, which protected a man from neck to knee. It was time for battle. Hundr pulled his *brynjar* over his head. He slipped on the armour that was so familiar to him that it was almost a second skin slithering over his shoulders. He strapped his first sword, Battle Fang, to his back and his second blade, the Ulfberht sword, to his hip. Hundr had taken that formidable blade from a great champion he had fought and killed in Saxony. Men said it was an unbreakable sword, as light and strong as Mjolnir, Thor's mighty war hammer. A sword crafted by dwarves in their home in Niðavellir, one of the nine worlds beyond Midgard, where they carved the mysterious Ulfberht letters into its unmatched blade.

The *drakkar* was alive with movement. The clank of iron mixed with the roar of the wind and the swirl of the sea as Hundr's men prepared themselves for war. Hard men all, Viking warriors traversing the sea from Vanylven in Norway to punish a man for King Harald Fairhair. A king who was also Hundr's friend.

"Are you sure Jarl Bekkr is on this island, my lord?" asked Fastbjorn. The spade of his beard rested against his armour, and he carried a vicious-bladed axe in his fist.

"He's hiding ashore with two crews," Hundr replied. "Soon, he will understand the price for breaking his oath to the king."

"Thorgrim says there is a natural harbour on the island's north shore."

"Let Thorgrim lead the way," he pointed at Thorgrim's ship, the Sea Stallion, and Fastbjorn nodded. Thorgrim, son of Skapti Farsailor, was as renowned a shipmaster as any who sailed the

Whale Road. He knew the inlets, sandbanks, and treacherous waters of those islands, as well as a man knows the curves of his wife's hips.

It was early spring, the time when men emerged from winter like beasts from hibernation. Winter was time for repairs, healing wounds, staying warm beside roaring fires, short days and long nights, stories by the hearth, and longing for warmer skies. Spring and summer were the seasons of war. Einar had argued it was too early to leave the comforts of his hall at Vanylven, where he was the jarl of a bustling fjord-side port and its hillside environs. Einar was the lord of the people who lived in those lands. He was their lawgiver, upholder of justice and the man to whom every farmer and trader paid a tenth of their surplus each year to keep Einar and his warriors in grain, meat, iron and leather. It was early to set sail. Snow was still visible on the mountains around Vanylven's pale blue waters, but Hundr was eager to return to sea and punish those responsible for the death of his great friend Ragnhild the previous summer. Jarl Bekkr had played a small part in the beginning of that conflict, for he had betrayed King Harald and allowed the king's daughter to fall into the hands of Harald's enemies, and those men had used her to start a war which had almost cost Harald his kingdom. Almost. Jarl Bekkr had to pay for breaking his oath to serve

King Harald, and Hundr was the instrument of that punishment. Men had to respect and fear their king. Norway was a land of thousands of islands, inlets, harbours and ports. Each one bristled with warriors, proud men – Vikings who sailed the Whale Road in search of reputation and glory. It was not easy to intimidate a man who lived by the axe and the will of the gods, and his oath had to be earned. Such men had to know the hard hand of their lord to keep their greed and violent thoughts turned away from the king and his family.

The fleet banked around the island of Stronsay, its long coastline and sandy beaches revealing themselves like strips of gold beneath the storm-scarred sky. Hundr had gone first to Bekkr's stronghold on the island of Orkney and found only the jarl's women, children and old folk there. They had gathered on the jetties beside their fortress and shouted to Hundr that their jarl had fled and left them to Hundr's wrath. They had opened their gates upon sight of Hundr's famous banner emblazoned with his one-eye sigil. Bekkr's wife had wept and begged for mercy and pointed a trembling finger towards Stronsay. She was a distant relative of the king, hence her role in finding a suitable husband for his daughter. Hundr followed *drengskapr*, the way of the warrior, and did not make war on women and children. So, he had left the jarl's wife and her people unhurt and set off in pursuit of Jarl Bekkr. The jarl was the oathbreaker, not his wife or the people he was supposed to protect. So, Hundr had followed Bekkr to a neighbouring island in the string of islands of such importance on the route from Norway to the lands of the Scots.

Einar waved his arms at Hundr from across the bows and pointed his axe towards an inlet that curved behind a rocky outcrop to the east of a curling horn of sandy beach. The waters grew quiet there, shielded from the sea god Njorth's wrath by the island's hills and natural harbour. Thorgrim led them in, and his ship formed the tip of a spear as four *drakkar*s fanned out behind him.

"I've heard men grumble that we do the king's bidding," Hundr said, turning to his men and fixing them with his one eye. They were fiercely independent, each one a *drengr*, a warrior of fearsome reputation. They followed Hundr because he had earned their respect in countless battlefields across Scandinavia, England, Frankia, Svearland and further eastwards, where only brave men sail. Hard eyes stared back at him from wind-burned, bearded faces. "We come to punish Jarl Bekkr for stealing King Harald's daughter. That's true enough. But Bekkr started the war that saw Ragnhild killed. She was one of us, perhaps the greatest of us, yet she lies dead, as do many of our shipmates because of last year's bloody war. Bekkr is a friend of our enemy, The Crippled King of Mann, so we come to bring justice to Bekkr and his warriors." Hundr paused, meeting sixty pairs of flinty eyes. His crew chewed their beards and hauled on their oars, not yet convinced that they weren't risking life and limb for a king to whom they had sworn no oath.

"Who do you fight for?"

"The Man with the Dog's Name!" they shouted back at him, for they were his men, his dogs of war.

"Death to our enemies. Death to Bekkr of Orkney and death to the Crippled King!"

"Death! Death! Death!"

Hundr stalked amongst them, clapping one man on the shoulder, taking another's forearm in the warrior's grip. They were his men, there to fight and risk their lives for him. All they asked in return was for him to fill their pouches with silver and lead them to combat and glory. Hundr loved them all. Each scarred face brought forth memories of shivering shields, broken spears, brave deeds and vanquished foes. He returned to the prow, using the rigging to swing himself around the deck busy with men rowing and others preparing themselves for battle. He swerved around a burly warrior testing the handle of his shield and ducked beneath another, trying the heft of a spear above his head. Fastbjorn beat the time with his axe head, hammering it into the bowl of a linden wood shield so that the men picked up the rowing pace, heaving hard for the beach ahead.

"They see us," growled Thatchulf the Frank, pointing his spear to where a line of men hurried from the grass-topped hillside down towards the beach. "Bastards will make their shield wall on the beach and try to kill us as we come stumbling from the tide."

"Then they are braver than I thought," Hundr muttered.

Stronsay was a large island, sprawling and rugged. Its craggy hills and deep gulleys could have easily concealed Bekkr and his men, making it a long and gruelling hunt to track them down. Yet, rather than hiding, they chose to fight instead.

Thatchulf spat over the side. He was a big man with long blonde hair tied at the nape of his neck and the wooden cross of a Christ worshipper hanging from his neck. "Men without honour. Who leaves their women and children and their bent-backed fathers and mothers to face an enemy's wrath whilst they hide in the lee of a neighbouring island?"

"Oathbreakers and nithings," Hundr spat and

turned to Fastbjorn. "Pick up the pace. Don't be last to the beach. Look, Sigvarth is pulling ahead."

Sigvarth Trollhands strode across the deck of the Fjord Bear, another of Hundr's ships, unmistakable with his short stature and barrel chest, howling at his men and gesticulating at the beach.

"It's been a long winter," Thatchulf grinned. "We dragged the ships ashore, ripped out the caulking, boiled the tar and caulked them anew. We scraped the hulls of five ships clean and painted the hulls and sheer strakes. We practised shield wall formations in rain, hail, and snow. We feathered arrows and gathered pollarded wood for spears and axe hafts. Sigvarth sees the enemy and longs for the thrill of battle, as do we all. But I'll be damned to Niflheim if I'll let the little bastard strike a blow before I do."

Fastbjorn threw his head back and laughed at Thatchulf's words. "This is what we live for! We are Vikings, so row you lazy whores! Row for The Man with the Dog's Name."

Oars bit and the Seaworm raced to catch up with Sigvarth's Fjord Bear and Einar's Wind Elk. The ship burst from the raging waters into a gently rolling swell, and Hundr curled his fingers around the familiar feel of the Ulfberht sword's leather-wrapped hilt. His chest heaved with anticipation, and he stared at the enemy as they formed up on the beach in three ranks of overlapping shields. A long one hundred warriors gathered where the sand rose into banks of rolling heather, and they saw that five *drakkar* warships came to kill them. Hundr set his jaw. Saltwater dripped from his beard and hair, and his dead eye pulsed. The freezing water and the whip of the wind had cleansed him after a long winter of waiting, planning, and preparing. Hundr rejoiced at the chance for action, the opportunity to do what he did best. Fight.

The message had come from King Harald two weeks before. A forty-man *snekke* ship slid into Vanylven's harbour, flying Harald's wolf sigil. A droopy-eyed steward had stridden into Einar's hall, all smiles and pleasantries even though the thirty burly warriors he had brought with him waited in Vanylven's square, bristling with spears, shields, helmets and royal power.

"The snows melt, birds are nesting, and soon lambs will bound in the meadows," the steward had said, head bowed and a gleam in his eye. "Men must pay for breaking their oaths, and we must punish our enemies. King Harald bids you, Jarls Einar and Hundr, to sail west. We must conclude the war begun last year by the Crippled King and his allies."

"Why send us?" Einar had replied, leaning

forward in his high-backed oaken chair. His moonlight silver beard jutted as his eyes pierced into the messenger sent north by the most powerful lord in the Viking world. Einar and Hundr had once been free men, sailing the Whale Road in search of reputation and glory, but the Norns weave their tangled threads and laugh at men's dreams. After the brutal sea battle of Hafrsfjord, where Hundr and Einar aided Harald in claiming his throne, King Harald appointed Einar as Jarl of Vanylven in exchange for Einar's oath to serve him as his loyal subject. To rise from nothing and become a powerful jarl was the dream of every Northman who braved the cruel power of the oceans. They chased the chance to become a hero, a warrior of such prowess that Odin All-Father himself would open the doors of Valhalla when their time came. There, they would join Odin's Einherjar, the army who drink, feast and fight until the day of Ragnarök, when they will march against the trickster god Loki, his monster brood and army of the inglorious dead.

Hundr remembered how he smiled at his old friend that day and saw the steward's face lose its good humour as if someone had slapped him. In his heart, Einar still craved the freedom of the sea and the comradeship of a Viking crew, but he had achieved his dream, and the two things made strange bedfellows. Hundr had smiled not just at his old friend's discomfort but because the time had come for war, and its onset was as inevitable as Einar's recent emergence from his decision to hang up his axe and grow old in peace.

"You are Jarl of Vanylven," the steward had said through pursed lips, back straight, and thumbs tucked into his belt. "You rule here at King Harald's pleasure. The work to be done is axe work, sword work and spear work. You and Jarl Hundr are the most feared men in Norway. Is not Jarl Hundr known by all as The Man with the Dog's Name and the Champion of the Northmen?"

"So men say," Einar had allowed, settling back into his chair, a look of resignation on the cliff of his broad, lined face.

"Take your axes and your ships and sail west to Orkney. Punish Jarl Bekkr for breaking his oath and bring war to the Crippled King. Without oaths, we are no better than beasts in the forest. It is our oaths that make us men; they separate us from barbarians, slaves, and cowards. We are men of honour, and all men must uphold the law of a binding oath. There must be punishment, a lesson for all to learn what it means to betray King Harald Fairhair."

The steward left the following day, and now Hundr and Einar brought the king's vengeful justice to Jarl Bekkr of Orkney. A forest of spears awaited on the sands, shifting like boughs in the wind, iron tips dull beneath the storm-darkened sky. There was no guile in the attack, no warcraft or deep cunning. Hundr and his men would attack the beach head-on. They would drive their warships onto the sands, relying upon Thorgrim's knowledge of the waters and trusting that their hulls would not shatter on sandbanks hidden beneath the murky waters. The men waiting on the beach with sharpened blades were ready to kill, to plunge wicked steel into soft flesh and rip men's lives from their bodies with pitiless fury. They were men sworn to serve Jarl Bekkr, hard men tough enough to fight off the countless Vikings who passed through the isles of Orkney every year – slavers, warlords, champions, marauders, and killers who would inevitably try to evade the jarl's port tithe or attempt to steal Bekkr's wealth. Bekkr's men had to stand strong against warriors with enough daring and bravery to sail upon storm-tossed seas in slender ships made of nothing but oaken planks riveted with coarse nails.

"Make ready!" Fastbjorn roared, increasing the drumbeats of axe upon shield to quicken the rowing pace. "Brace yourselves."

The impact was coming, where the hulls would drive up onto the soft sand beneath the white foaming surf, and ships charging like horses would slam to a sudden halt and toss everything on board that was not lashed by rope into chaos. Hundr wrapped his left hand around the bowline's seal hide rope to brace himself. Across the water, Einar's crew broke into a wild cheer as their jarl leant over the side and let his axe dip into the sea and spray them with spume as he roared to them of victory and the chance of a glorious death. The other ships took up the call, and Hundr's crew joined them so that the roar of three hundred warriors drowned out the crashing sea.

Bekkr's warriors levelled their spears, resting the points on the upper edges of their overlapped shields. The shield wall was ready. Their grim faces were set, and their arms, strengthened by years of rowing, hefting shields and wielding axes, were ready to strike.

"Raise oars!" Fastbjorn barked, and the two lines of oars raised in perfect time, dripping water-like droplets of crystal into the rolling sea. Men quickly rested the long ash oars in their crutches and grabbed axes and spears in their calloused hands.

The prow reared up beneath Hundr's feet as though tossed in the air by one of Loki's monster-children. The keel and ribs groaned and creaked as the warship Seaworm rose from the waters like a rearing stallion. Hundr clung to the bowline as everything on the ship flew forward in the sudden impact. Men who had not held fast tumbled into the bilge. Barrels, oars, spare clothing, and coils of rope flew about the ship like storm-tossed flotsam, yet calm descended upon Hundr. His shoulders shuddered at the thrill of it, of the battle calm he craved, the fleeting moment of something higher, where a man lifts above the mundanity of life and soars like an eagle in the half-light between life and death.

Everything around him paused for a moment. The crashing sea fell silent. The roaring warriors stopped dead with their wild eyes and gleaming weapons. It was the time before battle, perhaps the last time Hundr would draw breath in Midgard, the last time he would taste the salt of the sea or feel the wind upon his face. Then it was over. Sound came rushing back, men charged around him, and a spear flung from the beach thudded into the Seaworm's rearing prow and juddered there with a strange undulating trill.

Hundr ripped the Ulfberht sword from her scabbard, and with one hand on the sheer strake, he leapt over the side. His boots plunged into the frigid water, and it was deeper than he had expected, rising above his waist to envelop his legs in its freezing embrace. The cold knocked the breath out of him, and Hundr's boot slipped on tiny shale stones. For a heartbeat, panic flooded his senses as Hundr thought his heavy chainmail *brynjar* would drag him beneath the surface to drown. A spear splashed into the water, a hand's breadth from his face, and Hundr roared in defiance. He surged to his feet and waded through the water. More spears cascaded around him, sending up a spray that mingled with the salt and sweat already stinging his skin. He bared his teeth, rising from the sea as if born from it. Spear after spear splashed around him, the enemy drawn to the unmistakable target of his one eye and the fact that he carried no shield to ward off their missiles. Other men leapt from ships to join the charge, and it was a chaotic flurry of fury and battle lust. Hundr knew that the right thing to do would be to march through the tide together behind a line of shields and then form up into a shield wall in the shallows to charge at Bekkr's men across the sand. But Bekkr's men were outnumbered, and they would not allow Hundr's warriors the chance to form up. Their only hope was to butcher Hundr's men as they floundered in the tide. That unsure footing and the drag of heavy waves gave Bekkr's men a chance to slash and lunge with spears and axes. To stand and trade blows with killers, knee-deep in a sucking, powerful tide was to die. So Hundr held the Ulfberht sword above his head and roared at his men to charge.

A Seaworm warrior raced ahead of Hundr, a tall Vanylven man taking great strides with his long shanks lifting above the water and casting great splashes about him. Hundr followed. His *brynjar* and the wet leather liner beneath it were as heavy as a rock about his shoulders and body. The tall warrior turned and grinned at Hundr, triumphant at his chance to be the first to strike at the enemy, and then immediately died as a spear cast from the beach ripped his throat out. Blood splattered against Hundr's mail, and the spear fell into the murky waters. The tall warrior dropped his axe and shield and crumpled dead into the sea. Anger flared in Hundr's belly, and he snatched up the shield daubed with his own sigil. He rarely fought with a shield, preferring to fight with a sword in each hand as few men could, but the spears were relentless, and Hundr saw his own death in the tall man's gruesome demise.

Hundr slipped his hand into the wooden grip which traversed the iron boss and hefted the heavy shield, holding it before him as he waded through the water. Men from other ships reached the shore; one fell screaming with a thrown axe embedded in his chest, but the rest reached the enemy lines and crashed into them with the fury of men who strive to kill warriors before they lose their own lives on the end of enemy blades. Hundr came from the shallows, and a spear hit his shield with such force that it almost drove him to his knees. Another spear dinged off the shield's boss, and Hundr broke into an outright run. He charged behind the raised shield, heart pounding, blood pulsing in his ears, unable to see ahead of him but aware that Bekkr's men began to charge forward.

Bekkr had held his men back until most of the Vanylven force was in the water, and then he ordered the charge. This was where they planned to kill them, in the ripping shallows, off balance and vulnerable. Hundr's plan relied on pure savagery and fury to shock the enemy with a wild charge and then overwhelm them with greater numbers. His feet pounded on the wet sand as another blade thumped into his shield and stuck there, its weight dragging the shield down. Hundr pivoted, turning at the waist and spinning foot over foot like a dancer. He threw the shield at the enemy and followed it with the Ulfberht sword gripped tightly in his right hand.

Hundr swung his sword at the enemy, and the blade clattered off an iron-shod shield, sending a reverberation juddering up his arm. Before he could recover, a wall of shields came at him, driving Hundr backwards towards the water. Iron met timber, and steel met bone as the two enemy forces crashed together on the shore. The enemy shield wall broke formation, even though their leaders roared at them to hold the line. Bekkr's warriors howled and hacked like wild men, like men who have seen their death approaching from the sea and now struggle to seize the chance to kill those who have come to take their lives. Three big men shoved at Hundr with their shields. He tried to slide the blade over the upper rims, but the enemy knew their business and ducked away. A spear blade came from beneath the shields, yet Hundr skipped aside before it ripped into his groin. Just then, as Hundr feared they would drive him so far backwards that he would drown, a colossal figure came charging across the beach. A monstrous man, swinging a war axe as though it weighed little more than a twig, thrusting men aside with enormous sweeps of his shield. He wore a shining helmet with closed cheek pieces, and Hundr could have laughed for joy because it was Amundr, giant and friend. Amundr smashed into the first man facing Hundr before the warrior turned his head. The enemy flew from his feet like a leaf in the wind, and Amundr hammered his axe into the next warrior's neck with such force that it lopped the head from the man's shoulders. The third man gasped in horror at the fearsome, gory axe stroke, and Hundr killed him, stabbing the Ulfberht sword into his chest and skewering his heart with ruthless efficiency.

The first enemy warrior tried desperately to scramble to his feet, yet the surrounding fighters jostled him, and his boots slipped in the wet sand. He stared up at Amundr with terrified eyes, jaw clenched, and teeth bared in horror. The giant back swung his blood-soaked axe across the rising warrior's skull with the sound of a dog crunching a lamb bone. Hundr clapped Amundr on the shoulder in thanks, but the big man was already on the move again, hurrying to where Einar fought further along the beach.

Hundr advanced on the enemy, fixing his gaze on the line of warriors that now loomed closer. So close Hundr could see brown teeth, greasy beards and red-rimmed eyes behind leather-covered shields. Hundr ran at full tilt, sprinting towards them as spear points levelled and men braced themselves for his onslaught. There was no fear in their eyes. One man charging at a line of overlapped shields was like somebody feeding bloody meat to a starving wolf. These men thought themselves the wolves, but Hundr was the Champion of the Northmen – a seasoned killer. With a swift, low feint, he watched as their shields dropped slightly. Seizing the moment, he drove his shoulder into the gap between two shields, crashing through the bristling spear points. As the impact created a breach, he plunged the tip of his Ulfberht sword into the opening and drove it deeper. A cry of pain erupted from a man as the shield to his left shattered under the force. The wolf was amongst them, rending and tearing with the fingernails on his left hand as he clawed into them. He drew the Ulfberht backwards and sawed the blade through the press of men, slicing arms and faces with the razor-edged steel.

A big man with a beard so thick it began below his eyes and hid his face in its black matted curls spat at Hundr and tried to headbutt him. Hundr leaned away, and a wave of fetid breath washed over him, reeking of stale meat and decay. Surrounded by enemies pressing in from all sides, Hundr found himself trapped, unable to strike a blow. The massive man snapped his rotten teeth menacingly and drove his neck forward for another attempt, but the blow fell short by mere inches. In the chaos, Hundr twisted his body, reaching behind him with his left hand to grasp the antler hilt of his seax, sheathed at the small of his back. But the crush of sweat-slicked bodies encircled him, pinning the weapon in place and leaving him desperate for a way out.

All along the battle line, Vanylven men came from the water and crashed into the enemy, driving them back from the water's edge. Around him, weapons clashed, and men roared in anger and howled in pain, but if Hundr stayed where he was, it would surely only be a matter of time before a rear ranker took his chance to stab his spear over the shoulders of his comrades and kill the Man with the Dog's Name with one well-timed thrust. The enemy shifted, shuffling backwards three steps as their line retreated slightly. The seax came free, and Hundr whipped it upwards, slicing up along the belly of the leather-armoured adversary and into his jaw. Hundr twisted the blade, and the man thrust his body away from the terrible wound. Hundr bullied into the space and stabbed his seax overhand into the eye of the big, bearded man, yanked it free with an awful wet, sickening sound and slashed around him like a madman.

The iron stink of blood and the foul stench of voided bowls stained the air. Hundr's men rallied to his side, driving the enemy back with immense force. He reached over his shoulder to draw Battle Fang, and as his men broke the enemy shield wall, Hundr charged into them with his two swords flashing like lightning as they cut and stabbed at Bekkr's brave warriors.

The fight was over in moments. Half of Bekkr's men lay dead or dying, and their lines gave way to reveal a short, big-bellied and bow-legged man crouched on one knee with Einar the Brawler's axe blade resting at his throat.

"Throw down your weapons," Bekkr said, his voice muffled by a blow Einar had struck against his jaw with the haft of his axe. He gestured to his men and glowered up at Einar. "These are good men. No need for more death."

"You knew the price when you broke your oath

to King Harald," Einar retorted in his granite-hard voice.

"I had no choice. The Crippled King came. Loki is unbound, and the Ragnarök is upon us."

TWO

Einar twitched his blade at Bekkr's throat and spat in the sand at the mention of Finn Ivarsson, The Crippled King of Mann. For a year, talk of Loki had gripped men's hearts. Many worried that Midgard had descended into the long-foretold days of the Ragnarök, the end of days. Loki, bound beneath the earth, tortured by venom dripping from the fangs of a serpent, awaited his moment. His fetters, forged by the Aesir from the entrails of his own son, seemed unbreakable. But the day would come when the trickster god would tear free from that cursed torment and march with his army of monsters, frost giants, and hordes of the inglorious dead to do battle with Odin and the gods of the Aesir. Such talk made men fearful, and Finn spread that talk across the Whale Road like a plague.

"Don't speak to me of Loki. Men came to you with ships and axes and asked you to betray

King Harald. They wanted his daughter. The king trusted you and honoured you with finding her a suitable husband. You broke your oath to the king. You broke your oath, not because you believe Loki is unbound or because Fenris Wolf howls at your gates, but because you feared the Crippled King and his men. As a warrior and oathsworn jarl of King Harald Fairhair, you should have resisted. You should have fought to the bitter end. You know it. That is why you ran when you heard we were coming. You left your women and children to face our wrath. What lord of *drengrs* are you?"

Einar was a *drengr,* a warrior, and he followed the old ways of *drengskapr,* the warrior's code. He was duty-bound to protect his men, his reputation, and the people under his care at Vanylven. To abandon any of those responsibilities was unthinkable and would surely cost a man his place in Odin's Einherjar, the glorious afterlife Einar and all Viking warriors aspired to.

"Oaths are words," Bekkr snarled. "When a dozen ships arrive in your harbour flying the Raven banner with threats of slavery and death, what choice would you make for your people? You and the one-eye are Harald's war hounds. All men know it; all have heard of the men you have slain and the wars you have fought. I expected your arrival. Harald sent Princess Esja here to find a suitable husband, and it was my intention to find her one until the worshippers of Loki came with their fire priests and the Crippled King himself. They demanded the Princess, and I handed her over to save my people. I could not condemn them to death and torture in the name of a king they barely know. What happened beyond that was in the hands of the Norns."

"Then it was the Norns who made you a nithing coward?" Einar knew as well as any Northman that the Norns cackled beneath the roots of Yggdrasil, the tree that holds up the nine worlds. The three Norns weave men's fates into intertwining threads, casting dooms, loves, deaths, births, horrors and joys, and folk pray to them for good fortune. But Einar also believed that despite the weft the Norns make for us all, men have choices. A man can decide to stand and fight or run and hide. He can decide to be a *drengr* or a man who follows no code. Slavers roamed the Whale Road, along with men who desired nothing more than slaughter and summer sailings filled with blood, and every warrior had to make his own choices within the fates the dreaded Norns weave.

A great murmuring sang out from Bekkr's men, and they cast their eyes at the sand at so wretched an insult levelled at their lord. A nithing was less than a coward. Destined to roam the horror-filled cold, ice and darkness of Niflheim after their death whilst the mighty feast and fight forever in the great halls of the gods. Einar stared at the men, meeting the gaze of any who dared look up at him. Einar was there to carry out the king's will, and there was no flinching away from what had to be done. It was Einar's duty, though he did not relish killing men at King Harald's behest. The order had taken him away from his hearth and from the side of his wife, Hildr, whom he loved above all things.

"I am no coward," Bekkr insisted in a stern voice, trembling with anger. He writhed like a beast, bristling at Einar's insult. "For fifteen years, I fought in the front rank, and I always struck with the axe, never shirking from my foes. Men swear their oaths to me willingly because of my reputation and the strength of my arm. I became Jarl of Orkney after The Man with the Dog's Name struck down Jarl Ketil Flatnose, and now Hundr returns to kill me. The Whale Road is stained red with the blood of men you have killed, Jarl Einar and your one-eyed assassin. Kill me if you must, if that is what the king demands, but do not call me a nithing before my warriors and beneath Valhalla where my father looks down upon my deeds with pride."

Einar stiffened. He glanced at Hundr, but his friend showed no emotion at the mention of old Flatnose, who Hundr had indeed killed and whose daughter he had loved and lost. Hundr knew what he was, and many men had died so that Hundr could become a great sea jarl, a lord of five ships and three hundred warriors but without land or title to his name. It was no insult for one raiding jarl to kill another, but the mention of his lost love was something the men in Hundr's crews avoided, refusing to sadden their lord by awakening painful memories best left locked in the old sea chest of Hundr's broken heart.

Bekkr showed the yellowed stumps of his teeth in the tangle of his beard, and his eyes blazed at Einar, full of accusation and anger. It was as though the jarl dared Einar to kill him, challenged him to take his life. The chill wind kissed Einar's neck, and he stared at the warriors surrounding him. Bekkr's surviving men, each bloodied and downcast. Once proud warriors now stood with hunched shoulders and long faces as their fate had led them to defeat on a storm-washed island. The Vanylven men simply waited for Einar and Hundr's order, which they would follow even if it meant hacking Bekkr's men to death and leaving their corpses to rot beneath the shifting skies. Einar did not want to kill Bekkr or his men. He had done what any good lord would do when faced with an enemy of overwhelming numbers. Finn had come to Orkney with his warriors and his malice and forced Bekkr to hand over Princess Esja, and he had done so to save his people from slaughter. One woman's life for the lives of the people under his rule. But that woman had been the daughter of King Harald, and Finn had given her hand to Vigfus Hjorthrimul, a Danish warlord who had married the girl and cast Denmark and Norway into a vicious war. That fight had almost cost Harald his life. It had also taken Ragnhild from Midgard to the hallowed feasting benches of Valhalla. There had to be a price to pay for all of that. There had to be justice.

Einar kept his axe blade at Bekkr's throat, the leather-wrapped haft held firm in his hand. If Einar left Bekkr unpunished, he would incur Harald's wrath, and men would know that Einar the Brawler had gone soft, which could not be allowed in the harsh world of the Vikings. How long would it be before the sea wolves smelled that weakness, like the blood of a lamb separated from its flock, and brought their warships and their axe blades to Vanylven in search of easy prey?

Stronsay unfurled from the beach in a jagged necklace of rocky cliffs and narrow inlets, spattered here and there with golden stretches of warm sand. Sweeping bays like knife wounds cut deep into the landscape, where the sea gnawed relentlessly at the land. The cliffs were not as foreboding as those of southern England or the rugged coasts of Ireland but still rose steep and stern, standing sentinel over the furious ocean. Waves crashed against the ancient stone, sending up misty plumes of saltwater, suspended like ghostly breaths in the cold air. Einar searched the skies for a raven sent from Odin, an eagle, any sign to guide his hand and steer his conscience, but saw only the surrounding warriors. He wished Hildr was with him – his wife, once a proud warrior priestess of the Valkyrie order, now the Lady of Vanylven. Her wisdom had steered Einar through countless disputes, whether it was boundary stones shifted by cunning hands or cattle stolen under the cover of night. With her at his side, Einar had always delivered fair justice, balancing the weight of a jarl's burden. But today, Hildr remained in the hall of Vanylven, and Einar faced the trials of leadership alone, with the fate of a jarl's life in his hands.

Einar sucked in a chest full of sharp, bracing air filled with the tang of salt and the earthy stink of damp peat. The wind hummed constantly, whistling through the rock crevices and rustling in the coarse grass about his boots. The wind carried with it the scent of seaweed and a hint of wildflowers beginning to push through the cold, dark earth after a long and unforgiving winter. Inland, a handful of twisted, stunted trees grasped to the poor soil in a patchwork of moorland and rough pasture dotted with the occasional stone-built wall where men had tried to farm the land and failed long ago. A seagull cawed and soared overhead, but Einar saw no guidance in its white belly or the harshness of its voice.

The sky glinted off the iron amulets hanging around the necks of some of Bekkr's warriors. Vikings often wore amulets depicting the signs of the gods they prayed to. Einar's wife wore a small Gungnir spear for Odin, while others commonly wore a Mjolnir hammer for Thor, a phallus for Frey or a fish for Njorth.

"What is that about your neck?" asked Einar, pointing at a red-haired man.

The man's hand reached for a scrap of iron tied about his neck by a strip of dark leather. "The sign of my god," he answered defiantly, and there was a familiar burr of an Irish accent in the man's voice. That in itself was not unusual. Many Vikings took Irish wives and settled on the Irish coast, founding flourishing trading towns like Dublin, Vedrafjord and Vykyngelo.

"Which god?" The piece of iron was unfamiliar and seemed to Einar as though it resembled a flickering flame.

"The unchained one. Unfettered and loose in the world. Loki, he who will bring victory and glory to those who have suffered too long under the yolk of men like you."

"You worship Loki?"

"I do, as do many here." The red-haired man jutted his chin out impenitently and muttered something in his native Irish tongue, which Einar did not understand. A dozen of Bekkr's men grunted and grinned in agreement at those foreign whispers.

Anger flared inside Einar at that moment. "You are not Bekkr's men. You are things of the Crippled King, are you not?"

"Aye. We serve Finn, son of Ivar the Boneless. A man you once called son, Einar Rosti. Yet you cast him away, left him to rot. Still, he rose like a wolf to lead his pack, and now Loki is at his side. The war is not over, Einar, slave to a usurper king. Last year was just the beginning. You think you sail west to punish us? Fool!" The red-haired man took a step towards Einar, and Amundr sprang from Einar's side. The colossal warrior was a full head taller than any man on the beach, even Einar himself, who was taller than most men. The red-haired warrior snarled at Amundr as the burly giant whipped his shovel-sized hand out, grabbing the Loki follower around the throat. He dragged the man into a savage headbutt, crashing his helmeted forehead into the warrior's nose, mashing the supple gristle to a pulp and sending a torrent of dark blood down the man's face and into his red beard.

"Finn Ivarsson awaits you, king's lickspittle. Are you ready for the Ragnarök?" the red-haired man spat through the blood, grinning like a madman as he collapsed into the coastal grass.

Amundr turned to Einar, eyes glowing in the darkness of the closed cheekpieces of his helmet. Pity fled from Einar like the bird sign he had searched for, flying away to leave only the hardness of a Northman who had once served as shipmaster to Ivar the Boneless. Perhaps Einar was growing soft in his old age. Last summer, he had given up the axe and resigned himself to a fate beyond Valhalla, but the war and Ragnhild's death dragged Einar closer to the man he once was. The man who had hacked and killed his way across Midgard with a vengeful fury. Einar nodded to Amundr, and without hesitation, the huge warrior dragged his axe from the loop at his belt, and in one fluid motion, he cracked the axe blade across the red-haired man's skull, opening his head like a rotten timber to soak Stronsay with a wash of crimson and the sickly grey of brains.

"Are you Finn's man?" Einar growled at Bekkr.

"I am not. He left some of his men with me. To watch me. I like them no more than you. But I did what I did for my people. There are more of them at Orkney, and there's a ship hidden in a northeast inlet. Do not underestimate the

Crippled King. I did, and look what has become of that folly."

Einar sliced open Bekkr's throat with the razor-sharp edge of his axe, and as the jarl choked and blood flowed from the wound like spilt ale, Einar knelt and pressed his axe haft into the dying man's hand. Bekkr's fingers curled around the axe, and he stared at Einar as life emptied from him. "Go to Valhalla, Bekkr, and save a seat for me. I hope to meet you there one day, and we will feast and fight and talk of old fights and fast ships."

Bekkr died, and Einar took back his axe. "Kill the ones who wear the symbol of Loki," Einar shouted to his men, axe held aloft, dripping fat droplets of blood. "Kill the bastards and leave their corpses on the shore as a warning to the rest of their black-hearted ilk."

The Vanylven men gave a clipped roar in response and hacked into the Loki men with pitiless zeal. Einar exchanged a look with Hundr; the one eye of his old friend shone and held Einar's gaze. Hundr had spoken of nothing all winter but the need to end the war with Finn, to sail west and finish the saga once and for all. Hundr had loved Finn's mother once, long ago when the world seemed younger and simpler. She had left him to marry the son of Ivar the Boneless, and Hundr had killed that son and then the father. Finn was the son of that ill-fated woman, Saoirse, who had become the Witch-Queen of Vedrafjord. Einar and Hildr had raised Finn like he was their own son, and Einar could still see in his mind the young boy with curly chestnut hair. Einar closed his eyes as men died around him and remembered throwing skimming stones with Finn into a still lake. He had loved the boy dearly, yet Finn had turned against him, so poisoned by his mother's hatred and black heart that nothing of the boy remained in the man he had become.

Hundr's love for Saoirse ignited a chain of events that had haunted his life for decades. It had cost Hundr an eye, and every woman who had dared to love him had met their death. His own son Sigurd had died, leaving Hundr with one living heir, Hermoth, who sailed now with Prince Erik Bloodaxe, son of Harald Fairhair. The love between Hundr and Saoirse had become a tale of woe and ruin, and Hundr wanted to see an end to it. That end could only come with the death of Finn Ivarsson. It had to be so, Einar knew, even though he had no desire to see the death of the man he had once loved so dearly. But the Norns mock the hearts of men, weaving threads of fate that care nothing for love or loss. Now, off the coast of Orkney, an enemy ship lurked, its sail darkened with the raven banner of the sons of Ragnar, the banner Finn proudly flew because he was the famous Viking's grandson.

And so it had begun, the war to end the saga of Hundr and Saoirse. Einar's heart was heavy with the call of Valhalla. He was an old man now and had once believed his chance to join Odin's Einherjar had passed him by. Yet war beckoned, and like a battle-hardened wolf, Einar followed its call.

THREE

The Seaworm clipped south on the wind. Thorgrim had advised to wait until the storm shifted before making the journey from Stronsay to Orkney. It had been close to midday when they had left, and there was a risk of not making the journey before dark. The men had grumbled at the prospect of making camp on the wind-swept beach beside the Loki men's corpses, but fortune had favoured them. The wind had changed and Thorgrim had beamed with pride as the fleet rowed out of the natural harbour into the wide sea, where each ship had unfurled their heavy woollen sails to fly south before the wind.

Hundr's crew hauled on the rigging, letting out and taking in the sheet and halyard ropes to keep the ship on course. The great one-eye sigil stood proud on the wind-blown sail, and the men sang sea songs and whooped for joy at the thrill of a fast ship. Fastbjorn took the tiller and stood high on the steerboard platform whilst Hundr leant over the side with Thatchulf beside him.

"How will they survive in that godforsaken place?" Thatchulf said, touching the small wooden crucifix he wore around his neck. He was a Christian warrior Hundr had befriended in the fighting pits along with two others, Yazi, the Easterner, and The Crow.

"They won't," Hundr replied without taking his eyes off Stronsay as the island grew smaller in the Seaworm's wake. "Ships come this way every week. Someone will pick up Bekkr's men and return them home. And when they do, they'll speak of how we slew Bekkr and his Loki-worshipping scum. They'll see the bodies, and word will spread along the Whale Road faster than the wind itself. Men will know justice was served – and what fate awaits those who dare follow the cursed one."

"Why pursue this one ship off the Orkney coast? We already know that the Crippled King was here and that he left men to watch Jarl Bekkr. What difference does one ship make? We should use this wind and keep pushing south until we reach the mainland. Out here, there is always the risk of a storm or squall. Why risk it?" Thatchulf pulled his russet cloak tighter about him as though he could already feel the cold of a storm blowing in on the wind. He stared wistfully out at the surging ocean. "My home in Frankia is not so far from here. It seems like a different life now when I think back to when I was a child. Even the time we shared in the fighting pits seems like an age ago, though it has been but a few years. The Vikings defeated my people in a fight beside a winding river, and they dragged me in irons to a ship not unlike this one. I puked my guts up in the crossing to England, and my captors beat me savagely for not doing it downwind. They sold me at the slave markets in Jorvik. You helped me escape from those chains. What hope was there for us before you came to Thrand's fighting pits? Even though he isn't much of a talker even now, The Crow was a husk of a man back then. He lived only to kill; look at him now, free to live his life. Same for Yazi the Easterner. What is it he calls himself?"

"A warrior of the Tolmac people of the grey horses beside the wide river."

"That's it. Who knows who the Tolmac people are? But he has a woman waiting for him at Vanylven, and he knows the sweet taste of freedom. I go where you go, Lord Hundr, as do all of us who left that place of blood and death. What is one ship when we sail to war? Besides, my back aches from rowing. Why row when we have the wind?"

"We should have questioned those men who wore Loki's amulet. Dead men tell no tales, and we do not know what we face when we sail to Mann. We lost a chance to understand our enemy. Finn is a cunning warlord. He will not have been idle since he fled the battle of the Bardarborg with his tail between his legs, leaving his allies to die under our blades."

"Are you saying I should not have killed those men?" said a familiar voice, and Hundr turned to face Einar.

"No, they had to die. But perhaps they had useful information in their skulls, which we could have learned before turning them into corpses."

Einar blew out his cheeks. "You, Hundr, telling me I acted without thinking? I never thought I'd see the day." Einar and Amundr had come aboard the Seaworm so that the two jarls could confer whilst they hunted the ship that flew the raven banner. "The man who charges headlong into enemy ranks without a shield to protect him or men at his sides is telling me I acted too rashly? I must be drunk."

"Bekkr gave in too easily. He should have resisted, sent a messenger to King Harald and held out for the king's men to come. He deserved his fate, as did the men who came from Finn's crews to fester inside Bekkr's hearth troop. They earned the scorn of the Norns. But we must catch this ship if we are to avoid sailing blindly into whatever awaits us at Mann. Finn Ivarsson started this Loki worship for a reason, and it isn't because he believes the chained one is loose. He has bound men to him by kindling the fire of their belief and giving them a reason to fight. Men want to know why the sun sets and why the moon rises. They want to know where we go when we die and why crops fail one year and thrive the next. A man who can offer these answers and give them a god to believe in gains influence and power. Men are wearing a fire amulet for the first time, and Finn the Crippled King fancies himself as Loki's priest. What he offers is exactly what warriors crave – chaos and fury, the promise of war, reputation, and wealth. And all a man has to do is wear that amulet."

"We'll get the ship. Don't worry about that. We have Bekkr's sigil flying high on the Seaworm's mast, and they won't suspect it's us. We all wear amulets. Every man here has a hammer, ship, or some other talisman of the gods around his neck. The fire symbol is new, but so what? Men fight for Finn, so what? Men fight for us. We don't have to say that the chained one is free to persuade men to swear an oath."

Hundr left the argument there. Finn was using Loki to whip up their battle fervour; Hundr was sure of it. He had seen it in the battles the previous year, the fire in men's eyes when they believed the Ragnarök was upon the world. Hundr wanted that ship. He needed to be sure what Finn was up to before he sailed blindly into Mann's waters. He watched as a man hoisted the banner they had taken from Bekkr's ships before scuppering the vessels off Stronsay's bay. It snapped and flew in the wind high above the mast, a badly painted animal on a green background.

"What is Bekkr's sigil supposed to be, anyway?" asked Hundr, pointing up at the banner.

"Amundr?" Einar called down the deck to where Amundr was helping the men to swap their shields, unfastening their own from the sheer strake and securing those taken from Bekkr's men in their place. The big man looked at Einar and waited for the jarl's question. "What manner of banner is that upon the Orkney flag?"

Amundr laboured in a jerkin that finished at his shoulders so that the muscles on his enormous, brawny arms slid over one another like fish in a net. He peered up at the banner and shrugged. "Looks like a weasel," he called over the sound of the sea and the rushing wind. "Or maybe a turd."

Einar shook his head, and the crew who overheard laughed. Amundr shrugged and continued with his work. "What man chooses a stinking weasel as his sigil? Amundr fights with the strength of ten men, but his head is as empty as an ale barrel at winter's end."

"Better a weasel than a turd," quipped Thatchulf with a grin, and he slid between Hundr and Einar to help Amundr with his task.

"It doesn't matter what the beast or symbol is," Hundr said. "All that matters is that the crew of that ship off Orkney believe we are Bekkr's ship, just to lure them close enough. Then we take them."

"I suppose it can't hurt to know what sort of force Finn has at Mann."

"And how strong his fortress is."

"We have five ships and three hundred men. If he outnumbers us, do we sail for home?"

"Sail for home? We have only just arrived." Einar had been reluctant to sail so early in spring; he had asked Hundr to wait a few more weeks for warmer wind and calmer seas, but Hundr knew it was the pull of Einar's warm fire, his comfy bed and the wife within it that delayed him. Einar was no coward. He was one of the bravest men Hundr had ever known, but as the autumn of his years descended, Einar had grown cautious, enjoying the winter months more than the campaigning season.

"For more men. If we face overwhelming odds, we should go to the king at Avaldsnes and return with his fleet. Fight a war we can win rather than charge headlong into certain death and defeat."

"Old friend, we have faced overwhelming numbers before. A king of Mann is little more than a jarl. He only calls himself king because no other great lord has told him not to. Alfred is king of the English, and I do not know who currently rules the Danelaw since we killed Halvdan Ragnarsson." Hundr remembered battling the son of Ragnar inside the walls of Dublin and the ensuing wild fight to escape from the city and its high palisade. A grim battle, followed by a mighty sea fight in a lough in Ireland's wild north. "Men say Bárid mac Ímar still rules most of Ireland. Finn is certainly not as strong as any of those men."

"And yet the Isle of Mann is an important place. We defeated Finn, and he was spewed forth from Ireland's arse like runny shit and landed in a bed made of flower petals. He left with only his oathmen, the men he won alongside us in far Novgorod, and the next we hear, he is a king. Mann sits between Ireland, Northumbria, the lands of the Welsh and Scots. Even in Ragnar's day, Vikings settled there, building ports and markets. The men there grew rich on trade but were forever being raided. I raided there myself as a younger man. It is a hilly place with mountains, woods, and coastal flatlands. Once, a famous shipbuilder lived there, but men burned his hall down and cut off his head to steal a ship he had finished for a great lord of the Danes. It has natural harbours and inlets, perfect to hide a few ships after a good season of raiding. If I remember well, the major town was a place called Eyrrspollr, a trading town built around a sandbank and harbour. Nobody has raided there for years, though; it's too well defended now. Not worth the trouble with easier pickings further south."

"If Finn rules the place, he must have warriors. He escaped the fight at the Bardarborg last year with at least three ships. That could be two hundred men."

"Perhaps he left more at home. Who knows? All I'm saying is that it's better to go in with greater numbers."

"We have to stop Finn, Einar. I remember the boy he once was as well as you. Yet we can never have peace whilst he lives. I killed his father and his mother, and hate has turned his heart to molten iron. He must die, even if we are outnumbered. If there is going to be war, then I would have it now. Not next summer when Finn has had an entire year to bolster his defences and bring more men in to swell his ranks. He lost last year and fled the battle like a whipped dog."

"And what of all this Loki talk? It puts the shits up the men. I've heard them talking and whispering. They fear that what the Crippled

King says might be true. He proclaimed at the Bardarborg that the Ragnarök is upon us. All men know it will happen one day. It doesn't help that we still have Jarl Ravn's *godi*, Fengr Threefingers, sailing with us. The holy man spares no detail when recounting the gory fate of the battle that awaits at the end of days. We know which gods will die, even which of the Loki brood will kill them. It keeps men up at night, eats its way into their thought cages and poisons them with fear."

"Which is what Finn wants. He uses talk of Loki to bolster his reputation. It's nonsense, all of it. He has no more *seiðr* than a crazy old man with a gnarled stick and a grey beard shouting at the sea from a cave. He's a madman, driven out of his mind by hate and fear. The men are afraid to hear of Loki unbound. I understand that. But it's just words, not reality."

Talk of Loki, Finn, and his *seiðr* stopped as the crew fought with the rigging to keep the Seaworm flying before the wind. Hundr and Einar used the time to clean and prepare their weapons, and Einar took the tiller as the rocks of Orkney came into view on the horizon. Einar smiled like a drunken grandfather at yule, and to see the old jarl up on the steerboard warmed Hundr's heart. He remembered Einar as he was when they had first met, a face as stern and hewn as rock, feared and respected by his men, a Viking shipmaster to fear. Now his beard and hair were white, and some of Einar's old muscle had given way to slimmer shoulders and limbs, but he was still a fearsome fighter and knew the Seaworm's lines, her balance, and her capabilities better than any man alive.

Thorgrim kept the remaining four ships in Hundr's fleet out of sight of Orkney's settlements and Jarl Bekkr's hall. For Hundr's plan to work, the folk remaining in Orkney had to believe that the approaching ship was Bekkr's. Off the northeastern coast, the ship bearing the Ragnarsson raven banner lay concealed, but Hundr knew that once spotted, word would race on horseback that Bekkr had returned safely from his refuge on Stronsay. The raven ship would soon prowl along the coast, hungry for news. Its crew, eager to learn what Bekkr had uncovered on Stronsay, would be swift to send word to Mann, warning the Crippled King of any sign of the One-Eye banner. Hundr's trap was set. Bekkr's sigil flew high on the Seaworm's mast, and the shields of Orkney warriors lined her sheer strake. Up close, any man would notice that the Seaworm was not one of Bekkr's smaller, less sleek vessels, but Hundr hoped the ruse was enough to lure the raven ship from her hiding place and bring her close enough to strike.

The day grew long, and the sun fought through heavy clouds in beaming patches to cast a soft, silvery glow over the sea. The storms the Seaworm had braved during the open water crossing from Norway were long gone, but the occasional swell reminded the crew of the Whale Road's unpredictable dangers. The hull cut through breakers, and the wind blew Hundr's hair away from his face as Orkney appeared before him first as a dark, low-lying silhouette, little more than a smudge against the pale sky where the sea met land. The air was sharp and bracing, and as the Seaworm drew closer, the outline of Orkney's wild cliffs sharpened, revealing promontories rising abruptly from the water, their faces punched by centuries of relentlessly crashing waves.

The sound of the sea changed as the *drakkar* drew closer; the hiss of water against the hull became gradually overtaken by the distant roar of waves battering the towering rocks. Cries of seabirds grew louder, gulls and kittiwakes circled above the high places, their harsh calls carried on the wind. Hundr's eye followed the birds, wondering if other eyes watched him from the clifftops. He hoped so. He imagined a rider on a fast pony galloping through the meadows and heather westwards to warn the raven ship that a boat flying Bekkr's banner approached.

Cliffs gave way to stretches of green, rolling hills sloping gently to meet the sea, where short, pebbled beaches offered the opportunity for a safe landing. Hundr had been there before, as

Bekkr had reminded him. He had raided the fortress years ago, landing on such a beach and running across the island's high places to attack the stronghold unawares. Ketil Flatnose had not been there that day, but his daughter Sigrid had met Hundr's raid with defiance, and weeks later, when they met again, Hundr had fallen in love with her. He remembered dashing across the brutal landscape that night. Orkney was treeless, the wind having hewn the landscape into a tapestry of rough grasses and mean shrubs. He, Einar, and Ragnhild had scaled the walls and taken a great treasure from beneath Ketil's hall. But the memory was tinged with sadness, for Sigrid had died in a furious battle deep inside Frankia, throwing herself at an enemy and certain death, hollowed out by grief for their dead son Sigurd. Hundr's surviving son, Hermoth, was so like his mother that her memory lived on, burning bright like a winter fire in Hundr's heart.

Einar banked the Seaworm to come about the island with the wind, cunningly keeping his beloved vessel far enough away to prevent clever eyes from noticing the deception but close enough to show that she intended to come ashore.

"Bring the mast down," Einar called from the steerboard. "We'll row her in from here. But don't tie off the shroud; keep the mast ready."

The men did as Einar ordered, furling the sail but not tying away. That meant the Seaworm could spring to life again when the raven ship approached.

"Row clumsy, lads," Hundr added. "Go slowly. Any man not pulling oars gets weapons ready for the rest. No armour, too easy to spot from shore. Get axes and spears ready. Yazi, ready your bow."

The smell of land mingled with that of the sea as the Seaworm edged closer. The faint, sweet scent of blooming heather, the earthy aroma of peat and the underlying musk of livestock, shit, and piss from behind the hilltop palisade carried on the breeze. The crew did their job well. Oars lowered into the whitecaps, but men only half pulled so that from shore, it looked as though the ship approached with two banks of oars biting and hauling her home, but the ship moved slowly, drifting on the tide like flotsam.

"There she is, my lord," announced Toki, a Seaworm man with a braided beard and his head shaved close to his skull. He pointed a thick finger westward, and Hundr hopped across the deck to clap him on the back. She sailed under oars against the wind, coming about a jagged line of rocks extending out from the island like a skeleton's spine. The raven banner fluttered from her mast post, a white raven daubed on a black flag.

"Let her come closer," Hundr called over his shoulder. "Keep the wind at our backs."

Hundr could make out faces on the high timber ramparts of Jarl Bekkr's fortress and bearded men busy upon the raven ship's deck. For a moment, Hundr thought the ship would bank towards the Seaworm and come to meet her out at sea, but then her sheer strake showed, and the bow came about. He reached for his swords as Yazi, the Easterner, handed them to him. The strange-eyed warrior nodded in acknowledgement as Hundr thanked him. Yazi bent his recurved bow behind his leg, took a string from the pouch at his belt and fitted it to the horn nooks at either end of the bow stave. With a quiver full of white feathered arrows hanging from his belt, Yazi took up a place close to the mast post.

"She's almost inside the harbour!" Einar bellowed from the steerboard. "She'll never be able to come about now before we reach her."

Hundr waved to Einar to show he agreed, and Einar grinned. If the men aboard the raven ship could have seen that smile, they would have leapt overboard in fear.

"Fastbjorn!" Einar roared, "Beat time. Row like your lives depend on it. No need for the sail. Oars will do it. Time to stretch your backs, lads."

The crew grunted as their oars bit, and where the Seaworm had floated gently on the swell, she now surged forwards as though propelled by a giant's hand. Hundr secured his swords to his belt and back, though he did not slip on his *brynjar* and instead wore a simple woollen jerkin. Before him was a chance to cut first at Finn Ivarsson, the man he had crossed the Whale Road to kill. Ahead, the raven ship bustled with warriors; Hundr guessed at least forty. Some of them would have been warriors who fled from the Bardarborg. Others had cut down Hundr's own men during the grim fighting in last year's wars. Einar leant on the tiller, and the Seaworm bore down on the enemy ship.

Aboard the raven *drakkar*, a man frantically waved his arms and ran along its deck, pointing at the Seaworm. Other bearded faces came to look, but it was too late. They recognised that the Seaworm was no ally – the lines, the curve of her prow, none of it belonged to Bekkr's fleet. Her shipmaster tried to bring the *drakkar* quickly about. One bank of oars lifted like a bird's wing, and another bit deep in an attempt to turn and row away from the Seaworm's charge. Panic gripped them. They should have stayed the course, their only hope lying eastward, in outrunning the Seaworm. But fear had them in its jaws, and Hundr was upon them. The moment of battle had come.

FOUR

Panicked voices bellowed orders from the raven ship, and Hundr drew his antler-hilted seax from the sheath at the bottom of his back. The wicked weapon was a perfect fit for the grim fight about to unfold on board the raven ship, where the warriors would be packed together too close to wield swords effectively. It was less than half the length of Hundr's swords, a single-edged weapon for slashing and stabbing. Its thick spine tapered down to a bright point, curving with a broken back. Hundr flexed his hands around the hilt. Men snarled at the effort of rowing whilst a dozen selected men stood with Hundr in the prow. The lovers of battle, the men who would make the leap across the bows and attack the enemy ship with wild fury.

The Crow appeared from nowhere at Hundr's side, a hood covering his horrifically scarred and tattooed face. He was a small man, only reaching

Hundr's shoulder and not big enough to trade blows with champions in the shield wall where enormous men in armour hefted shields and axes to hew at one another and heave at enemy shields. The Crow had been the most fearsome of Jarl Thrand's pit fighters during Hundr's time in that miserable hel, and in skirmishing or quick, brutal fighting, he was without match. The Crow took his leather sling from beneath the folds of his cloak and a handful of thumb-sized stones from a pouch. Two curved knives hung from his belt, and Hundr could almost feel the malevolence radiating from the man, as if violence itself thrummed beneath his alabaster skin.

"We go before the hulls touch," Hundr said, fixing each of the dozen men with his one eye. Scarred men with steely faces stared back at him, relishing the chance to stand and fight on board a moving ship, risking death and terrible injury, all to burnish their reputations and be considered the bravest by their shipmates. "Fastbjorn and Einar will pull the raven ship close with axes and ropes, and then the rest of our men will come. But we go before that. We get amongst them. We rend and tear at them. We spread fear into the hearts with our daring and savagery. Are you ready to fight?"

The men raised their weapons and roared, and Hundr's heart quickened. The churn of fear rose in his belly, the fear that always came before a fight. He relished it and allowed that fear to transform into anger and determination. Hundr was a jarl, a wealthy lord with streaks of white in his beard and hair, and he did not have to make the leap with the boarding party. He could leave that work to other men, younger men with reputations to build. But Hundr was the Champion of the Northmen, and a man does not reach that pinnacle by hiding whilst others do the knife work. Hundr's men loved him for his reputation, and he had to feed it like a waning fire on a chilly night. Fighting fed that reputation, finding the most dangerous of opponents and standing toe to toe with them as weapons swung and men screamed in their death throes. That is what it took to be a Viking warlord, and Hundr did not shy away from it.

The warriors aboard the enemy ship bellowed their defiance, and the Seaworm raced closer. Her oars came up as the shipmaster saw that any chance of escape had gone. The Seaworm was simply too fast. The enemy didn't bother to fit the oars on their crutches. They cast them into the bilge and grabbed their weapons, but two clever men brought their oars to the port side where they would try to pole the Seaworm away. Those men would die first. Hundr's eyes were fixed on the moment the two hulls would collide. The ships had to touch if only for a heartbeat, to give his twelve chosen warriors the chance to leap across. Those reckless fighters, each with nerves of iron, would make the dangerous jump into battle. For the rest, the ships would have to be lashed together before they could board and overwhelm the enemy with their superior numbers. Hundr and his twelve were no strangers to peril. Every year, they hunted ships in the water – Viking, English, Frankish – it mattered little. The sea wolves returning from raiding, their ships heavy with plundered silver, wool, iron, and amber, made the most tempting prey. Hundr had led these strikes too many times to falter now. Speed and shock were everything. As he stood, gripping his sword, Hundr breathed deep, steadying himself for the chaos about to unfold. One misstep, one well-aimed spear or axe from the enemy, and the dozen heroes would tumble into the yawning gap of the sea, swallowed by the icy black depths, claimed forever by Ran, goddess of the drowned.

An arrow whistled from the enemy ship and slammed into the deck below where Hundr stood. Moments later, another flew low and hard across the sea and punched into the warrior behind Hundr. The arrowhead took the man in the shoulder, and he spun away, howling in pain. Hundr's twelve erupted with fury, clamouring towards the sheer strake, desperate to get the enemy who had struck their comrade. The Crow nudged the men on either side of him away and set a stone into the leather pouch of his sling. He whirred the leather thong about his head, and it sang with melodious danger. The Crow loosed his stone. It travelled faster than Hundr's eye could see and found its target with remarkable accuracy. The bowman across the water toppled and splashed into the sea, and the Seaworm broke into an all-out roar of glorious anger.

Einar brought the Seaworm close enough for a man to cast a spear across the gap between vessels. Hundr saw Irishmen on the raven ship, their plaid cloaks thrown over one shoulder. He saw Vikings with tattoos, beards, and braided hair, all armed and ready to meet the Seaworm's assault. Einar leant into the tiller, and the Seaworm came about, angling closer to the adversary's ship, yet he avoided crashing the prow into the enemy's side.

"On me!" Hundr called. He stepped up onto the sheer strake, using the rigging for balance, seax gripped in his right hand. Three spears whipped across the water. One fell harmlessly into the waves, another slammed into the Seaworm's hull, and the third flew too high and passed right over the Seaworm's deck. The ships drew closer, so close that Hundr could see the scars on the enemy ship's hull. Hundr raised his seax and inclined his head to Yazi, who had clambered up the mast and secured himself high in the

Seaworm's rigging. Yazi pulled an arrow from his quiver and let it fly, releasing another before Hundr had turned to follow the flight of the first.

"Spears!" Hundr shouted, and Toki, along with another ten men of the Seaworm crew, launched a barrage at the enemy directly opposite Hundr's boarding party. Yazi's arrows found their mark, and a squat man fell overboard with a white-tipped shaft embedded in his face. The Crow sent stone after stone whizzing into the enemy, and the Seaworm crew cast more of their spears across the water. The deadly rain forced the enemy back from the edge of the ship towards their mast as they sought shelter behind shields and cowered. Men fell screaming with wounds to their heads, shoulders and chests, and more than a few dropped dead to encumber the steps of their comrades.

"Now, fight with The Man with the Dog's Name!" Hundr shouted his rallying cry and leapt towards the enemy ship. Heaving water passed beneath him, and missiles flew in both directions. All sound ceased in that heart-stopping moment, and Hundr gripped his seax tight. He crashed into the enemy, hurling a big man from his feet and sending three others stumbling backwards. Hundr landed heavily and rolled. He lashed out with his seax and sliced a man's ankles before surging to his feet. The Crow made the leap, a wickedly curved blade in each fist, cloak billowing behind him like a dark bird in flight.

An axe haft drove into Hundr's shoulder, and he twisted away before the attacker could drag the axe towards him and rip Hundr's back open with its bearded blade. Ducking low, Hundr plunged his seax twice into the axe man's guts, each cut lightning fast to prevent the weapon from becoming trapped inside the warrior's innards. A knife sliced across Hundr's forearm, and he yanked the limb away before the weapon scored too deeply. Pain lanced through his hip as a knee collided hard against him. Teeth bared, Hundr slashed blindly with his seax, battling not with skill but with raw, savage determination. A hulking warrior with white-blonde hair lunged at him, locking his arm around Hundr's neck while aiming a long knife at his throat. Hundr grabbed the man's wrist, straining to keep the blade at bay. They staggered across the blood-slicked deck, Hundr's feet catching on an injured man writhing beneath them. They crashed down together, the knife flashing dangerously close to Hundr's face. Trapped beneath the fallen bodies, Hundr struggled to free his seax, pinned under his own hip and the injured man, while the blade at his throat crept closer.

The white-haired enemy shifted his position so that his body lay on top of Hundr, and he leaned into the knife with both hands, his entire weight pressing the blade ever nearer to Hundr's good eye. Panic welled within Hundr's chest as the metal came within a handbreadth of his face. Rust tinged its knocked blade, and the enemy grimaced at the effort of trying to kill. Hundr pushed back, attempting to roll from beneath the warrior and release his seax, but the pressure held him tightly in place. A fire pendant dangled from the warrior's neck, and he lifted himself slightly, aiming to slump down and use his weight to drive the knife blade home. The deck was alive with battle; weapons clanged, men yelled in anger and cried out in anguished pain. The light-haired man's slight movement gave Hundr the chance he needed, and the seax blade came free from beneath him. Hundr kept his elbow tight to his body and brought the seax over his face. A look of horror spread across the blonde warrior's features as he saw his inevitable doom. There was no time for him to stop. His body pressed down towards Hundr, and the seax brutally sliced into his throat. The man's eyes bulged with horror as death came for him. Hundr roared in his face, triumphant at killing the man who had come so close to ripping Hundr's life away in the bilge of a fish-stinking boat. Hundr sawed the blade back and forth, and dark blood poured from the wound like a burst dam. It splashed on Hundr's face, hot and grizzly, and he twisted away, pushing the jerking body from him in disdain.

A thin man with a broken nose tried to stamp on Hundr, yet he swiftly rolled away just as a spear thrust followed. Hundr parried the strike with his seax, the ring of steel against steel echoing like a bell. With a vicious kick, Hundr swept the man's legs out from under him. The enemy yelped, crashing onto the twitching corpse of the blonde warrior. Without hesitation, Hundr drove the point of his seax into the man's gut, twisting savagely until a gasp escaped the dying man's lips. Hundr rose to his feet, his breath ragged, shouting incoherently as the madness of battle overtook him. The fury in his veins burned like fire, pushing him deeper into the blood-soaked frenzy. He switched the seax to his left hand, his fingers still slick with blood, and drew the Ulfberht sword with his right. The dozen Seaworm warriors had done their work; the fight aboard the raven ship had devolved into barbarous, one-on-one clashes. Any semblance of organised defence had crumbled under the storm of unrelenting violence. The Crow moved like a shadow, his curved dagger flashing in the fray. He slit one man's throat with a rapid, precise strike, then slashed another across the belly, spilling his guts onto the deck in glistening purple coils. Three men shrank away at the gruesome sight, one of them vomiting uncontrollably, covering his hand with bile as it clutched his axe.

More of Hundr's men boarded the ship as Einar and others dragged it close with axes and rope. Some of the enemy warriors jumped overboard, throwing down their weapons and diving into the sea, preferring to take their chances with Ran's fickle temper rather than suffering the savagery of the Seaworm crew's blades. Yazi shot one of them in the back to leave the body floating face down in the swell. A grey-bearded warrior carrying a sword came at Hundr from around the mast post. He was blue-eyed, broad-shouldered, and his sword blade stained red with the blood of a Seaworm man he had hacked to ruin beneath a tangle of rigging.

"I am Flann, champion of the men of Clann Choinleagain," the warrior growled. He wore a circlet of bronze around his forehead to keep his long hair away from his face and a thick silver chain about his neck. His sword and jewellery marked him out as a successful warrior and a man to fear. Hundr did not know who the man's clan was, but he saw a warrior before him, a brave man willing to risk death. Flann did not flee nor cower away as the rest of his crew died. He sought out the most dangerous among the enemy and challenged that man to one last fight before the end.

Hundr raised his sword in salute of Flann's bravery. "I am Hundr, whom men call The Man with the Dog's Name."

Recognition flared in Flann's eyes, and he came on with a lightning-fast lunge of his long sword. The tip flicked up in Flann's powerful hand, but his eyes gave away the feint as the sword dipped low to tear open Hundr's thigh. Hundr danced away from the stroke and brought the Ulfberht sword down to parry the sword before the lunge turned into a slash. Flann gripped his blade in two hands and came on again, slashing his sword in wild, downward strokes. Hundr dodged the first and parried the second. On the third stroke, he stepped in and stabbed the seax into Flann's unprotected ribs. The Irishman gasped as he stumbled backwards, and Hundr brought the Ulfberht crashing down on the warrior's sword hand, slicing into the tiny bones of his wrist with devastating force. The sword clattered to the deck, and Flann fell to his knees, eyes closed and teeth bared in a pain-wracked grimace.

The raven ship bobbed on the swell, and after the deafening roar of battle, an eerie silence fell over the water, punctured only by the groans of the wounded and the heavy breathing of men who had until that moment been engaged in a fight for their lives. Hundr bent towards Flann, intending to question the man about his Crippled King, but he had slumped forward and died on his knees. Hundr stared at the corpse for a moment as the sea breeze kissed the sweat on his brow and neck. It could so easily have been him kneeling there dead, as bilge water tinged with blood sloshed about his legs. But not today. Today, Hundr had claimed victory beneath the towering cliffs and high palisade of Orkney.

Three survivors knelt beneath the raven ship's prow, and Hundr stalked amongst the dead and the dying to where those men stared at him with frightened eyes. Four Seaworm men stared up from the deck with dead eyes, and another shivered beneath the steerboard, bubbles of blood in his beard, an axe clasped so tightly in his left hand that his knuckles showed white beneath the skin. Thorgrim clasped the dying man's hand, comforting him as life ebbed away. The promise of Valhalla flickered in the man's fading eyes, his face drawn tight with the last vestiges of hope for a glorious afterlife.

"Toss the dead overboard," Hundr said to his warriors, "and put the injured out of their misery. Burn this ship with our esteemed dead upon it in honour of their bravery." Hundr pointed his sword at Flann's corpse. "And that one too."

Hundr slid the Ulfberht sword into its scabbard and reached behind his back to sheath the seax. He clapped The Crow on the back and nodded to Yazi, Toki, and others who had fought bravely. Amundr, his face and hair flecked with blood, was busy hauling bodies over the side.

"Let's see what the bastards can tell us," said Einar. The jarl wiped his axe blade clean on the jerkin of a fallen foe, and he slotted the weapon into its belt loop.

The three men stared at Hundr and Einar and then at each other. They licked dry lips, shoulders hunched, eyes wide with fear. One bore wounds on his forearms, a sure sign that he had fought, but the other two were unmarked and unbloodied.

"Are you Norse or Irishmen?" Hundr asked. Each man wore the fire pendant around their neck. One was bald save for tufts of curly hair around his ears, and the other two had long dark hair and greasy beards.

"Norsemen, my lord," said one of the uninjured men closest to Hundr. He spoke Norse with an Irish twang, and he stuttered his first word with a shake of his head. "Born in Ireland to Viking fathers and Irish mothers. All three of us. From Vedrafjord, lord."

Hundr exchanged a glance with Einar. Vedrafjord was a Viking coastal fortress and settlement on an estuary on Ireland's southeast coast. It was one of many founded by brave Vikings of Einar's generation, which had become thriving ports and markets specialising in the one commodity for which every civilisation in Midgard paid handsomely – slaves. After the death of its old ruler, Randvr Cranelegs, Finn's mother, the Witch-Queen, proclaimed her son Jarl of Vedrafjord. It had been some years since Hundr and Einar had come to Ireland with Finn, only to lose him to the dark, fanatical *seiðr* of his mother.

"There are Irishmen on board this ship. Do they worship the chained one like you fools?"

"No, lord. Most of the Irishers pray to the nailed god."

"So why do they fight for Finn Ivarsson?"

The man shrugged as though the answer was obvious. "Because he is rich, lord. He pays men well to fight for him. This winter, he drew masterless men to Mann – crews without lords, slavers, marauders, and all manner of wicked souls. He despises you, lord, and you too," he added, jutting his chin toward Einar. "The king has built a grand temple in the sacred places of Mann, a temple they say rivals Upsala itself. A flame burns there unceasingly, tended by Loki's priests and *godis*. We were all taken there to be inducted into the ways of the chained one." He paused, licking his parched lips, leaning forward so that his lank hair swayed about his gaunt face. "He has a champion, my lords. Oh yes, a champion to be feared. His hatred for you, Lord Hundr, binds him to the king – and what a hatred it is. It burns hotter than the temple fires. His name is Orm, son of a great warrior who fell by your hand. He is massive, unyielding, like one of Loki's own brood, and no man can stand against him. He fights with two swords, like you, lord, but oh, he is quick. Quick as a hare fleeing the hounds, faster than a hawk upon the wind..."

"He is fast," Einar barked impatiently. "We get the point. Who is this bastard, this champion of a cripple who can't fight for himself?"

"Orm Eysteinsson, son of Eystein Longaxe, whom you killed long ago in Dublin."

Hundr shuddered at the thought of the man who had harboured dreams of becoming king of Dublin. He had ruled the city after Ivar the Boneless' death, having taken the place by force. A berserker with a thick neck, impossibly broad shoulders and a monstrous war axe. He had been a great warrior, and their battle had been brutal before Hundr had bested him. Eystein had died clawing at Hundr, writhing beneath him as Hundr plunged his blade again and again into Eystein's body. That campaign flashed through Hundr's memory like a sea squall. His old friend Sten, whom he had loved like a father, had died in the battle for Dublin, the same city where Hundr killed Ivar in a wild fight on the river Liffey. Memories of dead men from times long since past cast their shadows on Hundr to haunt him and bring forth new enemies born of his lifelong quest for reputation and glory.

"He has a crew, this Orm Eysteinsson?" asked Einar.

The man nodded his head so vigorously that he almost toppled onto his face. "Oh yes, lord. Berserkers, just like his father and his men. Shield-chewing mad men, impossible for any normal man to stand against. The king and his champion await you. He says that Lord Hundr cut off his mother's head and sent it to a *galdr-woman*, which stops the Witch-Queen from passing to the other side. The king had a talisman of his mother's bones, which you destroyed, and all that remains now are a few bones that he wears about his neck on a silver chain. He waits for you, for all of you. He knows you will come, and when you do, he will..."

"Shut your cheese pipe, Rauri!" snapped the wounded man.

"Crow," Hundr said over his shoulder. The small man appeared at his side like a wraith. As usual, a hood covered his tattooed face save for the wings of black hair that hung from beneath it like wings. "Kill that one so that the others understand what fate awaits them if they do not tell me what I need to know."

The Crow slid a curved knife from beneath the folds of his cloak, and Hundr turned away. The injured man's defiance melted away beneath The Crow's knife, and his howls of agony and pleads for mercy made even Hundr close his eye against the horror. By the time The Crow had finished, the blood of their shipmate had spattered the two survivors, and fat tears of terror rolled down their ruddy cheeks. As the raven ship floated on a calm sea, the two men answered every one of Einar and Hundr's questions without hesitation. They spoke of how the Crippled King, terrified of the wrath of Einar, Hundr, and King Harald, had sent messengers to every corner of Ireland, England, and to the lands of the Scots and Welsh. Those envoys promised enough silver to make a man rich until the end of his days if he spent one summer fighting for The Crippled King of Mann. The messengers took with them heavy silver coins minted in far Ispania by the Musselmen, inscribed with strange runes, and coins from England bearing the stern face of King Alfred of Wessex. So, ships had come. Men with no lord and no oaths to bind them, hard men who fought for pay every summer, sailed their *snekkes* and *drakkars* to the Isle of Mann. They carried with them masterless men who raided and fought in the badlands between the Danelaw and England, in the highlands of Scotland and in the endless cattle wars of Wales and Ireland's unconquered midlands.

Finn had the silver to pay them, the captured men assured Hundr, for his island held the largest and richest slave markets in Midgard.

The Crippled King had built those markets up from nothing, and now they even eclipsed those of Dublin, Hedeby, and anything to be found in Jutland or the Vik. Finn profited from the suffering of common folk captured in raids across the coasts of Ireland, England, Frankia, and even further south. His slave markets were so filled with captured women, children, and men that Finn held them in prison ships off the island's coast. Finn collected a tithe from every slave sold, and people said his treasure was so vast that it filled a great hole he'd dug beneath the floor timbers of his hall. Finn's hearth troop guarded that treasure, the Norsemen sworn to his service in a battle long ago in far Novgorod.

"You have earned your chance at life," said Hundr, not bothering to hide his disdain at their cowardice. "Strip them and throw them overboard."

"But lord, we told all we know?" spluttered the long-faced man, openly weeping with fear.

"You did. But you wear an amulet of the Aesir, and our gods do not reward the weak and fearful. Your place in the afterlife will be dark and cold. Náströnd is your destiny, the hel-world of oathbreakers and murderers. There, the fell serpent Níðhöggr will gnaw on your corpses until the end of days, and your screaming souls shall wish that you had fought bravely beside your shipmates instead of cowering like the nithings you are. Swim to shore and live…. if the people of Orkney do not kill you. Or sink and drown."

Amundr grabbed a man in each fist, and before they had a chance to protest, he tossed both over the side like flea-bitten cloaks. They set the enemy ship ablaze to honour their glorious dead, and as the flames licked at the darkening sky, Hundr followed the embers drifting on the wind. Each one brought back a memory of a man he had killed, a woman he had loved and lost, his dead son, a life spent on the Whale Road. One ember burned brighter than the rest, fluttering high on the sea wind, and Hundr recalled himself as a boy, back when his name was Velmud, shivering each night in an animal pen, dreaming of becoming what he was now, a warrior lord. Hundr had cut a bloody path across Midgard since the day he had run away from Novgorod in his youth to escape his father's neglect and seek his fortune. Hundr wondered if it was his destiny to fight forever, to sail the seas and stand firm in the shield wall until some other champion's blade finally claimed his life and delivered him to Odin's hall. He did not fear such a death; it would be a just reward for the path he had chosen. But first, he had to put the ghosts his ambition had created to rest. He had to kill Finn Ivarsson, whether the Crippled King had an army of thousands or not.

FIVE

The Seaworm crew dropped their stone anchor in an inlet close to Orkney's harbour fortress, and the glow of the burning ship warmed the distant hills as Einar drank a horn of ale and ate the last of the ship's oatcakes. To avoid being seen by the raven ship or the people inside the fortress, the rest of the Vanylven fleet had sailed north, hugging Orkney's coastline where Thorgrim would bring the ships around the western cliffs to meet the Seaworm before they journeyed south towards the mainland. Einar cast his eyes eastwards towards Vanylven, where his stewards would prepare Hildr's evening meal. They would fetch enough wood from what remained of the winter store to keep the hearth lit through the night. He could almost smell her hair, and if he closed his eyes, he could see her bright smile and the crow's feet wrinkles at her eyes. He longed to lie beside her, to reach out in the dark of night and hold her soft hand. A hand once calloused by bow, axe, and spear, but now smooth and warm.

A barking laugh snapped Einar from his reverie, and he frowned at the crew who huddled around a brazier set carefully in the bilge where the men warmed their hands and told stories and jokes to one another beneath the hastening twilight. Hundr sat alone beneath the sail, which the men had stretched over the Seaworm's deck to provide cover during the night, sipping a cup of ale. Einar strode across the deck, stepping between the oar crutches, rowing benches, coils of seal hide rope and barrels containing weapons, ale, and what remained of their food supplies. Reaching the awning, he paused, waiting until Hundr noticed his presence. Hundr rose and came to stand with Einar. Together, they leaned on the sheer strake, watching as the men laughed and jested about a time, a few years past, when Einar had led them into the forests of Vanylven to deal with raiders who had attacked farms under his protection.

"...and after we had killed the bandits, we found they'd amassed a small fortune in silver and weapons," said Toki, his round face smiling with fondness as he spoke. "All looted and stolen, of course, but we had no idea who to return the treasure to. We'd left our horses at the bottom of the mountains... their heavy steps would be heard for miles, and we wanted to sneak up on the bandits, catch them unawares, so to speak. Which we did, and the bastards died before they knew what day it was. When it was all done, Jarl Einar needed to find an idiot to drag the looted weapons and silver on his back all the way to Vanylven."

"I carried their weapons and silver back to Vanylven. Nearly broke my bloody back," remarked Amundr in his deep, slow voice, stuffing his mouth with a fistful of salted pork. The men roared with laughter, and Amundr paused mid-munch to stare at them with a confused look on his face. After a few moments of watching his shipmates fall about laughing, the joke dawned on Amundr, and he cuffed Toki around the back of the head, pushing him so hard the smaller man sprawled into a pool of bilge water, sending the men into even deeper fits of laughter.

Einar smiled and shook his head. Hundr had never been one to join with the men's pranks and jokes. He rarely laughed at all, even less so after the deaths of his wife and son, and Hundr had already looked away from Amundr and Toki before the jest played out. His one eye searched the seething, black mass of water over the bows as if the answer to a riddle lay out there on the Whale Road. Einar watched him for a moment, wondering at the sadness festering in his friend's heart. The loss he had suffered was enough to put any man off finding another woman and exposing himself to feelings and closeness. But every man needed a woman, just as every woman needed a man. It was a cold world, harsh and full of suffering, and one of the few pleasures in life was finding somebody to share it with. A kiss in the morning, an embrace on a bad day, watching the sunset together on a frosty night.

Hundr continued to stare out at the seething water, its waves lapping against the Seaworm's hull as stars tried to peek through the shadowed clouds. Einar wondered what thoughts occupied his friend's mind, and then he realised Hundr was thinking about the same thing he always did. War. If ever there was a man born to fight, it was him. Hundr lived and breathed battle, weapons, victory, and glory. Einar had lost count of the times they had fought side by side. So many times, they had faced death together and emerged victorious. They were more than brothers. Theirs was a bond only men who had fought together in battle could understand. Something deeper than trust existed between them, a thing unspoken and yet as strong as the mightiest chain. But Einar knew Hundr would not like what he was about to say. His friend would not understand the simple logic of Einar's proposal. Hundr was like an arrow shot from a bow. Once loosed at a target, nothing could stop him. But Einar had to try for the sake of the three hundred men who sailed with them and the wives and children waiting for them at Vanylven.

All men who set foot upon a fighting *drakkar* knew the risks, and all took them willingly. A warrior goes to war understanding that there is a chance he will die, that he will fall to an enemy blade, or succumb to the Whale Road and its unpredictable fury. That is why the Vikings were so successful in war. They sailed to foreign lands and fought armies made up of men fighting to protect their homes. Most were not warriors; they were farmers, millers, potters, thatchers, or woodsmen called by their lord to fight against the marauding Northmen. Every Viking who took to the Whale Road was a killer. Norsemen, Danes, and Svears who did not wish to fight stayed at home. They farmed the land, became merchants, or tended woodland. Vikings sought combat. They were men who strived for reputation, to be known amongst warriors for their fighting prowess. They fought for that pride and for silver and to burnish their names bright with glory to ensure that after their deaths, men would speak their names with reverence. Yet even amongst those hardened men, perhaps only one in a hundred is a genuine lover of battle, a man who seeks other dangerous men and stands in the front rank to trade blows with the champions. Einar had been such a man in his time and had not earned his by-name for standing in the rear ranks when the shield walls came together. Hundr was different. He had fought and killed champions and warlords most would tremble to trade blows with. Being a Viking was the very fabric of Hundr's being. It was all he had left after a life steeped in blood and death.

Einar knew that his following words would not be welcome, but he owed it to the men to talk sense to his great friend.

"Seems like turning for home is our only option now," Einar said, cutting to the chase rather than trying to draw Hundr in with cunning talk. "Finn has an army gathered about him, an army of slavers and cut-throats. And berserkers. I hate berserkers."

Hundr sniffed and took another pull of his ale. "We go on. We are but a few days from Mann, depending on the weather, of course. Our enemy is close. We cannot turn back now."

"Five ships and three hundred men cannot defeat an army."

"You said it yourself. They are a rag-tag band of cut-throats and brigands. Cut the head off the man who pays them, and the army will melt away like snow beneath the spring sun."

"They are not mere brigands, Hundr. One

cannot simply sail through a fleet of slavers, make port on an island teeming with bloodthirsty warriors, storm a fortress prepared for our assault, and kill the king of Mann."

"I know you miss home, Einar. We all do. But we are here to kill Crippled King, and so we shall. No matter the odds."

"The odds?" Einar's voice sharpened. "We are not playing knucklebones here. Men will die. Our men. We cannot hope to beat an army with five ships. Do not talk to me as though I am some stripling lad who yearns for his mother's tit. War isn't just weapons, bravery, and daring. It is understanding the lay of the land, predicting what an enemy will do, deep cunning, trickery and surprise."

"I know war, Einar."

"Who knows it better than the Champion of the North?" Einar's gaze held steady. "But war is more than that. It's about choosing the fighting ground. You don't fight an army holding the high ground. You don't fight with the sun blinding your men. It's about ensuring food, ale, and water are within reach. And it's about numbers. If we charge blindly, we'll lose men – men we can't afford to lose. You know as well as I that a Viking army's great weakness is our inability to replenish our numbers on campaign. If we do not have enough men to crew our ships, we must leave ships behind. If we lose too many men, men we call friends, then we become a spent force. Limping home with most of our warriors slain leaves Vanylven open to attack. We have been attacked before, and I will not allow that to happen to my people again."

"You can return to Vanylven if you wish. Take the Sea Falcon or the Wind Elk, whichever you prefer, and a crew of thirty men. The rest stay with me. I will kill the Crippled King, no matter how many bastards he rallies to his raven banner."

"How can you speak so harshly to me after all these years? Do you believe I would leave you on the eve of battle? Does our brotherhood mean so little to you?"

"I hold no man in higher regard than you, Einar." Hundr threw the dregs of his ale out into the sea and turned to face Einar. His scarred face was serious but free of anger. "We are here to end a tale that began years ago when we marched with the Ragnarsson Great Army. Finn Ivarsson is the child of that saga, and we cannot have peace while he lives. You raised the boy and loved him; I remember it well. But there is little or nothing left of that boy in the man we seek. What remains is a rabid dog that must be put down before it spreads its disease to others. Already, he has bound men to him with talk of Loki unleashed."

Einar took a steadying breath. Hundr wasn't angry, but Einar still had to fight the tension in his own shoulders, striving to speak calmly. "I agree with all that you say. But let us find a better time to fight when the tides of war are in our favour. We can return to Vanylven and then sail on to Avaldsnes and seek support from King Harald. Finn Ivarsson is as much Harald Fairhair's enemy as ours. With Harald's backing, we can return to Mann with a mighty fleet and thousands of warriors at our backs and finish this thing once and for all."

"We finish it now. I don't care how many warriors Finn has, nor how many ships. We have lived with enemies brooding across the sea for too long, allowing them to plan, fester, and grow stronger whilst we do nothing. If we had killed Saoirse and Finn years ago, we could have saved many lives. Think of all the friends we have lost fighting our enemies. Not just Ragnhild and Bush, but friends long gone. Sten, Kolo, Hrist, Brownlegs, and too many others to mention. It's time to act now. If we sail for home, some other problem will distract us from what must be done. The king will have an errant jarl he wants us to punish, or some raiding sea jarl will fancy his chances and attack Vanylven. We can't make this mistake again. We have waited for too long and allowed other matters to distract us. Finn Ivarsson must die."

Einar looked deep into Hundr's eye and saw the unwavering resolve that went far beyond mere ambition or reputation. This voyage wasn't just another quest for glory. At the heart of Hundr's soul lay the long-standing conflict with the Witch-Queen and the son of Ivar the Boneless. Saoirse had captured his heart in the chaos of an ambush deep in a Northumbrian forest, and that love had endured, even as she turned into something dark and twisted, filled with malice and hate. Hundr would never know peace until it ended – he would never find the kind of solace Einar had with Hildr. Einar's gaze lingered on the scars that marked Hundr's face, each one a reminder of the battles they had fought side by side. He recalled the moments when Hundr had saved his life and how he had done the same in return. It struck him then that there were times when a man had to cast aside all reason and logic for the sake of friendship and honour. What they were about to do was beyond reckless. They were about to sail into enemy waters full of ships and warriors bent on their destruction.

"Very well. We sail in the morning," said Einar, and for once, Hundr smiled. The gesture cast a cloak of warmth about Einar's heart. Hundr held out his hand, and Einar took it, grasping the wrist in the warrior's embrace. He dragged Hundr to him, and the two men held each other, clapping one another's back warmly. Only then did Einar realise that the Seaworm's deck had fallen deathly quiet as the men watched their jarls.

Einar held Hundr close and listened to the sigh of the sea, a last moment of calm before he sailed into the eye of a raging storm. In the morning, they would take five ships and three hundred men to fight an army of warriors bound to the Crippled King by a lust for silver. Every man who came to him, Finn lured closer with his Loki fervour. Einar hoped they faced an army of mercenaries and not a horde of rabid fanatics fighting like madmen, driven by their belief that the Ragnarök itself descended upon Midgard.

SIX

Thorgrim brought the fleet around Orkney's west coast on a warm morning beneath a sky lit red by the rising sun. Hundr waved in greeting to him and to Sigvarth Trollhands, Asbjorn, Harbard, and others as the Fjord Bear, Sea Falcon, Wind Elk, and Sea Stallion came about the crags and cliffs in a triangle formation like a flock of birds on the wing. Hundr had slept well for a change. A calm sea had rocked the Seaworm gently and lulled him into a deep slumber filled with dreams about Sigrid, Sigurd, and happier times. Einar's objections had shaken Hundr, although he had not been surprised. Everything the old warrior had said made sense, and if this had been a campaign based purely on raiding, Hundr would have heeded Einar's advice and either sailed for home or found easier pickings. But this was something else. There was something of the Aesir about it. It was as if Odin, in all his wrath and wisdom, was urging Hundr on to punish Finn Ivarsson for his impudence in using Loki's name to his advantage.

The Seaworm crew rowed gently out to sea before unfurling the mast with the wind behind. A pale morning sun warmed Hundr's face, and the men were in good cheer after their victory. The Whale Road stretched out before the *drakkar* like a shimmering blanket of blue and grey, deceptively calm but with its underlying power never forgotten or taken for granted by the sailors. The Seaworm's dragon-headed prow faced south, beginning the journey to Mann, which Thorgrim expected would take two or three days, depending on the wind and Njorth's good grace.

The fleet sailed past the southernmost point of the Orkney archipelago. The island and its hilltop fortress receded into the distance as the Seaworm's mast caught the wind and pulled the warship out into the open sea. Thorgrim led them confidently along the western edge of Scotland. They kept far enough from the mainland that it remained a faint line on the horizon. Close enough for them to find shelter if Njorth turned on them and the sea suddenly became fierce. The crew had settled into their accustomed rhythm, making the most of the northerly wind which pushed them southwards. The sky above was as vast as the sea beneath the Seaworm's hull, pale blue with clusters of clouds drifting lazily, tinged with gold by the sun. Occasionally, a wandering seabird would glide overhead, its sharp cry breaking the never-ending churn of the sea. Distant shapes appeared on the horizon, small islands or rocky outcrops marking the fringes of the Hebrides, each one a familiar landmark telling Thorgrim that he led the fleet on the right course. They hugged the western edges of the Hebrides, avoiding the turbulent and unforgiving waters of the Minch to the east before turning southwest towards the Isle of Mann. The sea deepened, darkening from blue to near black, and the men began to speak of the creatures that prowled such depths. The waves grew taller and more menacing as they ventured further into the open expanse of the Whale Road. Yet the wind held steady, filling their sails and driving them swiftly towards their destination.

As the first day wore on, the sun sank towards the western horizon, casting long shadows along the deck. The temperature dropped, and the crew pulled woollen cloaks tighter about their shoulders. Fastbjorn led them in a song about how the goddess Freya obtained the bejewelled Brísingamen gold necklace from dwarves, only for Loki to steal it from her, igniting a wrathful war for their recovery. Hundr listened as the men chanted their shanty of Freya and her mighty hall at Sessrúmnir, standing proud in the heavenly fields of Fólkvangr, where she received the souls of half the brave men who perished in battle. On such a voyage, a ship would usually seek shelter for the night in a cove or bay, safe from the sea's fury and any storm that might arise without warning. But Hundr was eager to descend upon his prey, and so Thorgrim led them on through the night, guided by the stars and his own experience.

On the second day, the weather changed. Dark clouds mustered on the horizon, and the wind picked up to whip the sea into white-capped waves that crashed against the *drakkar* and soaked the men with freezing water. The crew fought with the rigging, adjusting the sail and lowering oars as they rode out into the rougher waters. The sky turned an iron grey, and a spiteful rain fell to patter against the deck, mingling with the spray of the sea. By afternoon, the storm had passed, leaving behind it a ship washed clean by the rain and a calm, tired sea. As the men stripped off wet cloaks and dug deep into their sea chests to find dry clothes, Fastbjorn bellowed from the prow.

"Land! And sails!" he called and men's heads popped up like apples in a barrel full of water. The island rose from the sea, its great mountain standing out against the sky like an axe blade. Hundr squinted as his one eye struggled to pick out enemy sails, and as they came closer, he saw half a dozen boats patrolling the seas around the island's northern coast.

"Thorgrim had best take care," shouted Einar from across the Seaworm's deck. "If we can see them, they can see us."

This was true enough, but Thorgrim, son of Skapti Farsailor, was no fool and brought the fleet about, banking like the leading bird in a swooping flock. Hundr peered over the side towards the northern shores of the distant island. The landscape was a mix of rugged cliffs and sandy inlets, the cliffs rising steeply from the sea, streaked with patches of green where grass and scrub clung to the rock. Further inland, the ground sloped gently upwards, scattered with small settlements and distant farmsteads that Hundr could just make out on the horizon. The scent of land – earth, grass, and the faint smell of wood smoke – mixed with the salty air carried on the wind to fill Hundr's nose. The sea around the Isle of Mann was calm, protected by the island's bulk, and the Seaworm glided smoothly westwards, facing Ireland as the crews of each ship glanced warily at the island where the Crippled King waited with his foul god and brigand army.

More ships emerged, like bees from a hive, and at that distance, Hundr could not see from where they came. He paced along the deck and tried to count the sails, which seemed to burst from nowhere as if awoken by Heimdall's Gjallarhorn, the mighty horn which would herald the end of days.

"I count a dozen," said Einar, swinging around the rigging with one hand held against his forehead to protect his eyes from the sun. "Perhaps more. Can't tell from here if they're *drakkars, snekkes,* or something else. Could be anywhere from forty to seventy men on each ship. That's…" Einar's mouth moved as he tried to count silently and then gave up on the impossible number, "…a lot of bastards to kill."

Hundr stroked his beard and nodded thoughtfully. To charge into that many ships with his five was suicide, but he would find another way. "We don't have to defeat the Crippled King's army to win," he said. "We just have to kill Ivarsson. We'll find another way in."

Hundr curled his forefinger and thumb and pressed his tongue backwards. He whistled a long, shrill note to Thorgrim, who turned to look as Hundr pointed out to sea. The fleet arced away from Mann, distancing itself from the enemy ships, and Hundr's brow furrowed while his dead eye pulsed as he sought another way to kill his great enemy.

Hours later, under the cover of a night lit by a thin sliver of moon, Hundr swam through black waters. His shoulders ached, and his hands were as cold as ice on a winter fjord. He carried his seax between his teeth, and its sheath gnawed at the corners of his mouth, stinging and sore. The urge to open his mouth and relieve the pain tugged at him, but if the seax fell, it would sink to the bottom of the deep sea, and he would reach Mann weaponless. If he was to creep through the darkness and find his enemy's throat, he would need a blade. Hundr's arms pulled the water in great sweeps, and behind him, he could just make out the creak and groan of the Seaworm as her oars carried her away from the island and out towards open water. They had waited for patrol ships to pass by the bay on their night watch. Finn had dispatched a fleet to sail around his island, even in the depths of night, to watch for enemies. He was afraid of the wrath of the men he hated and was prudent enough to protect his kingdom from the inevitable retaliation that would surely come after the war he'd started by capturing King Harald's daughter.

Einar had objected to Hundr's plan, of course. *It was madness,* he had said, folly, that Hundr might as well throw himself overboard to drown and have done with it. Hundr's strategy was a simple one. It was impossible to land the five ships on Mann with so many vessels in its coastal waters. Finn was no fool. If he was cautious enough to set patrols and pay his mercenary captains to sail endlessly in his waters, then Hundr assumed he would have beacons set in the high places on every corner of his island. There would be men equipped with warhorns on every deck with orders to blow them long and loud at any sight of enemy ships. The beacons would spark, followed by their neighbours, until all of Mann came alive with blades, bows, spears and axes. If Hundr was going to get ashore and kill the Crippled King, then he had to do it alone. One man could swim unnoticed between the patrol boats and make it to shore. Einar had argued that if one could do it, then so could a dozen, but Hundr held fast. He would not condemn his men to a mission with so many uncertainties. The captured man at Orkney had spoken of Finn's hall and fortress at Eyrrspollr, but Hundr did not know what awaited him when he reached the shore. He hoped to slip in unnoticed, like a fetch, to pass over the walls and into the hall like a cat to slay the Crippled King in his bed.

One thing was true about war – best-laid plans usually turned to ruin, and much of victory relied on shifting with unexpected changes and adapting to the unknown. Hundr was prepared for that. Einar had given way without grace, and with much moaning and heavy sighs, he had guided the Seaworm wide around Mann's northern coastline so that Hundr could approach from its western side. There,

Eyrrspollr perched on high ground beside a natural harbour, which cut into a stretch of sandy beach like an axe blow. That beach was not Hundr's target. It was too close to the town and fortress, and Hundr expected it to be heavily guarded. There was a smaller beach further north, a thin stretch of shale beach Thorgrim recalled using to shelter from a storm when he was a young man. Hundr had dived from the Seaworm wearing only light trews and a simple jerkin. Boots would have weighed him down, and he would have to swim far if he was to reach the beach before daybreak and before the enemy patrol ships returned to that stretch of land on their watchful path.

Hundr squinted over the waves as he swam, straining to see his way. From the ship, the sea had seemed calm, but in the water, the swells rose above his head, dark and relentless. The effort of swimming forward left him disoriented, uncertain of his direction. His target was a pale outcrop of rock on the headland, which almost glowed faintly in the night beside the shale beach. Every six strokes, he searched for it. More than once, he found himself drifting too far south or north and had to correct his course. His breath came in ragged gasps as he kicked harder, the vast sea making him feel like little more than a scrap of driftwood floating in place. No matter how much he pushed forward, the shore seemed no nearer. It was as if he were fighting the water just to stay where he was. Fear gnawed at him – the fear of exhaustion, of slipping beneath the waves to a watery death. His shoulders burned with the urge to stop. But as a sliver of pallid sun crept over the horizon, the white rock loomed closer, and Hundr was sure he could make it before the sun came up.

Einar would wait for two days out at sea. He would wait for the agreed signal: a beacon lit on the northwestern end of Mann. At that moment, Einar would bring the Seaworm close and pluck Hundr from the water like a fish. That was it. Find a way into Eyrrspollr, kill the Crippled King, escape, light the beacon, jump into the sea and sail away. It all seemed so simple when the plan formed in Hundr's mind. Yet now, as he swam through the freezing water, unable to see clearly or tell which way he was headed, Hundr wished he had stayed aboard the Seaworm and paid more heed to Einar's warnings. But he had come too far now to change his mind. The Seaworm was gone, and he was alone in the water with an enemy to kill.

Hundr steeled himself, arms sweeping in wide arcs as he kicked his legs, propelling himself through the cold water. Dawn's light crept over the sea, turning it from tar-black to the ashen grey of a burned-out fire. Lifting his head, he winced as salt water drained from his empty eye socket, stinging as it went. With his good eye, he made out the coast more clearly now – the white rock was closer, and its nearness renewed his strength. The seax clenched between his teeth cut into the corners of his mouth, but he swam on. As his left arm surged through the water, his body rolled with the motion, and he caught sight of something – a hull bearing down on him. The prow, gilded and shaped like a rearing serpent, sliced through the waves, charging towards him. Hundr froze, treading water, heart pounding in his chest, fearing that they had seen him and that at any moment, spears and arrows would come hurtling from the deck to skewer him like a dogfish.

Water slopped about Hundr's neck as he braced for the death blow that never came. Silence hung in the air, broken only by the muffled roar of the sea in his ears. In the dim light of early dawn, he realised the patrol boat hadn't seen him. Hidden in the shadows, he had one chance – to swim for the shore before the hull passed. But the moment he struck out, they would spot him, and he would surely die with a spear in his back. The ship loomed so close that Hundr could make out the scrapes and barnacles clinging to its hull. He could hear a man coughing on deck and the oar blades biting into the undulating swell. Hundr was out of options, so he did the only thing he could. He took a deep breath, grabbed the seax in his left hand and dived.

Hundr pulled himself down into the murky waters, sensing the patrol ship speeding towards him, its size monstrous and oppressive, blocking out the tiny sliver of light from the still-rising sun. He kicked his legs hard and tried to haul himself deeper but could only swim with one hand with the seax in the other. As he tried to clamp the weapon between his teeth, the ship struck his back, the impact jarring him like a warhorse's kick. The force sent him spinning, and the seax slipped from his mouth. Hundr tumbled in the water, and an oar blade slammed into his skull, leaving him dazed. He reached desperately for the weapon, but the water dragged at his hands, making his movements sluggish, and the seax disappeared into the murky depths, lost to the shadows.

Another oar blade crashed into the water inches from his face, the surge of displaced water pushing against him. Hundr curled into a protective ball, kicking away from the ship as froth churned around him. Just as suddenly as it had come, the patrol ship swept past, and Hundr exhaled a stream of bubbles, relief flooding through him. Slowly, he rose towards the surface, his good eye tracking the ship's stern as it glided away, leaving him in its wake.

The iron taste of blood washed the salt from

his mouth, and Hundr could not tell if it was leaking from the blow to his head or the one to his back. His muscles screamed in pain, his back throbbed and stung, and he feared the injury was deep and that his lifeblood seeped out around him, tainting the water as it lapped into his mouth. But there was no time to check his injuries, and he didn't want to know. It didn't matter, anyway; he had to swim for shore, for there was no way back.

After what seemed like an age of swimming, every stroke diminished in strength, each kick like dragging his legs through a bog. Exhaustion weighed down his limbs. He swallowed gulps of seawater, which made him vomit beneath the waves, and Hundr almost cried out for joy when his knees scraped against the tiny stones and soft sand of the rising seabed. He lumbered to shore, glancing about him for signs of sentries and patrol ships, but the beach was mercifully quiet. Hundr slipped, fell, and crawled from the surf, coughing and retching. Blood dripped from his shoulders and down his beard, splattering onto the wet sand like jewels. Hundr rolled onto his back, his chest rising and falling as he stared up at the brightening sky, pale as butter. His seax was gone, leaving him unarmed, wounded, and dressed in nothing but trews and a thin jerkin.

As the clouds shifted above him, Hundr wondered if the gods were watching his daring and if he had done enough yet to catch their attention. Had Odin, Thor, Tyr, Frey, or Heimdall cared that he had swum through Ran's dark kingdom to kill an enemy, one man alone against an army of Loki worshippers? Perhaps not yet, but soon, men would die, and their blood might catch Odin's eye. Odin Bǫlverkr, the betrayer of warriors, lover of battle and patron of the brave – he who lauded courage and laughed at the folly of men. Hundr hoped so, for he would need Odin's luck if he was to stand any chance of killing the Crippled King. He pushed himself to his feet and walked gingerly across the beach, his bare feet crunching on shale and sharp shells. Hundr touched the throbbing pain at the back of his skull, and his hand came away bloody. The patrol ship's hull had cut his back. He could feel the sting and burn of an open wound and the trickle of warm blood down his spine. Hundr found himself injured and in a state of desperation. But he had a man to kill, so he pushed himself to his feet and prayed to Odin to bring him luck.

SEVEN

Hundr climbed the hillside. He used weeds and long coarse grass to haul himself up the steeper sections until he crested its promontory and saw Eyrrspollr for the first time. It sat upon an island a stone's throw from Mann itself. A timber palisade covered that small island, rising from the rock like a jagged crown, connected to Mann by a bridge which the defenders could cut or retract if under attack. The seawater was drying on Hundr's clothes, stiffening them, and the salt made his skin taut. He shivered at the thought of attacking that fortress. If they removed the bridge, there would be no way to attack it except by clambering up the bare rock from the sea or the deck of a ship. The defenders would rain down an iron hel of spears and arrows, along with rocks, boiling water and anything else they could think of to kill or maim an attacking army.

On the Mann side of Eyrrspollr, a harbour bristled with activity even at such an early hour. Gulls cawed and swooped about fishing boats pushing out to sea. Folk thronged the jetties and the sloping land above them. Men carried nets, and women prepared baskets to carry shellfish and other seafood to the town and fortress. The smell of peat combined with the faint waft of smoke filled Hundr's nose, and the prospect of a warm fire made him feel colder, so he stuffed his hands into his armpits to ward off the shivers. He could make out the masts of longships bobbing in the harbour against the hazy horizon. The town on the landward side of Eyrrspollr was a thriving settlement of wattle and daub huts with thatched or earth roofs where tendrils of smoke curled from roof holes. A dog barked, the sound harsh above the braying of sheep. A second, smaller palisade ran around the entire settlement, and two guards lazed at its open gate. That second palisade was little more than a chest-high fence, but it would still cause a significant problem for an attacking army.

Most of the warriors under the Crippled King's service would still be asleep, and yet Hundr counted at least three dozen men inside the settlement, coming from houses to draw water or to piss, strolling along the dirt paths between thatched roofs to find food or report for guard duty. The sound of a man yawning startled Hundr, and he dropped onto his belly. It came from nearby, only twenty paces away. Boots crunched the harsh coastal grass as he approached. A guard patrolling the coastline, Hundr assumed. He held his breath and lay still in the heather and gorse, head pounding and back throbbing. Beyond the wild grass were fields laid out in a patchwork of green and brown where Finn's people grew barley and oats.

The guard whistled a sad tune as he drew nearer, but Hundr did not risk a peek above the grass. If the approaching guard spotted Hundr and raised the alarm, The Man with the Dog's Name would be no more. If they took him alive, Finn Ivarsson would take great pleasure in torturing him. It would be a long, painful death that Finn would see as just revenge for Hundr's killing of his mother and father. Better to die fighting than burned, whipped, starved and mutilated. Hundr was cold and exhausted from the arduous swim and his wounds, but the guard's presence offered an opportunity. Hundr needed boots and weapons. He needed dry clothes, ale, and food. So he waited like a serpent, coiled and poised to strike with murderous venom. A fist-sized rock lay to Hundr's right, and he grabbed it, fingers curling around its hard edges.

Seabirds circled overhead, their cries mingling with the distant sound of waves crashing against the cliffs, and as the footsteps came closer, the whistling grew louder. The man appeared to Hundr's left, his head popping up above the grass as he marched up the slope to where Hundr lay in waiting. A swarthy man with dark skin and small eyes, wearing a hard-baked leather breastplate and carrying a spear resting on one shoulder, he wore a leather cap on top of a round face framed by a thin beard. He whistled his tune and looked out to sea and then paused. He grunted and fumbled with his trews, then sighed with relief as a stream of piss splashed against the grass.

That was his chance, and Hundr burst from the grass like a demon. He charged at the guard, a rock in his right hand and a snarl on his scarred face. The man turned mid-piss, and a look of horror spread across his wide face. In a flash, Hundr crashed the rock into the side of his skull with a loud crack. As the man fell whimpering, Hundr hit him again and again in the face until his features were a bloody pulp. The guard tried to fend Hundr off, his arms flailing, untrimmed fingernails clawing at Hundr's skin, but he was dead before he could cry out. The man carried a skin of ale tied to his belt, and Hundr drank it as though he hadn't drunk for a month. It was sour and thin ale, but to Hundr, it tasted like the ale prepared by Ægir himself, the jötunn giant who brewed the gods' ale. Hundr found a hunk of hard bread in the man's belt pouch and a lump of blood sausage, which he ate hungrily. He stripped the dead man and winced at the pain in his back as he pulled on the guard's woollen tunic and baggy trews dyed with brown and white stripes. Hundr pulled on calf-high boots and the leather breastplate. The guard carried a crude bone-hilted knife along with the spear, and Hundr took them both. He rolled the corpse over the edge of the cliffs, and as the dead guard splashed into the water below, Hundr marched towards Mann's front gate with the confidence of a man who had lived there his entire life.

The gate guards watched Hundr approach with tired apathy. They leaned on their spears with half-closed eyes as though they had woken at the crack of dawn for their turn on duty. Masterless men, Hundr thought. No Vanylven man would take his duty so lightly. Hundr marched through a furrowed field with his new spear resting upon his shoulder and returned the guard's lazy gaze with a look of indifference of his own. He wore the dead guard's cap pulled tight and tilted to cover his missing eye.

"That's my watch over," Hundr said to the guards, followed by an indignant sniff. "No chance I'm walking the entire coast when some other bastard lies in bed scratching himself."

The guards nodded with wry smiles, and Hundr strolled between them and into

Eyrrspollr's settlement. There were more men inside the village than he had counted from the hilltop. Many more. They lolled outside houses, sat on milking stools and upturned barrels, playing knucklebones or tafl and drinking ale. Steely eyes glanced up at Hundr and then looked away when they believed they saw one of their own. Men with gnarled hands and rough faces, braided beards and long hair hung with trinkets and plaited in thin strands. They wore leather and iron and carried axes, knives, and spears. A crew of Irishmen with their long plaid cloaks cast over their shoulders marched down a mud-smeared lane, speaking in their ancient tongue. They carried iron bucklers, the small shields Irish warriors wore on their left arms, some with sharp points where the boss should be. Hundr moved out of their way and bowed his head in deference. He wanted to pass unnoticed inside Eyrrspollr. When men looked at him, they saw a lowly man of no importance, not a *drengr* or warrior bristling with pride. He walked with hunched shoulders and bowed head, hair hanging loose about his face to hide his missing eye. The Crippled King would have undoubtedly warned his men to watch keenly for a one-eyed man.

Hundr avoided the Irish warriors and skirted around a low house with damp grey thatch. A woman came from the doorway, little more than a leather curtain hanging over a hole in the wattle structure. She started when she saw him, placed a hand over her mouth, and looked down in embarrassment. She was a churl, dressed in a homespun smock with her hair tied up underneath a woollen bonnet. The woman backed slowly into the house to avoid what she thought was one of her king's newly purchased warriors. He ducked underneath the low-lying hatch and straightened to find himself face to face with half a dozen warriors gathered about a table where two men arm-wrestled with strained faces and bulging muscles. Hundr kept his head down and moved on, making his way towards the harbour and the smell of the sea, which fought to break through the stink of meat and shit hanging about the settlement like a foul cloud.

A fat man lay beside an empty, shattered ale jug, snoring loudly. Hundr slipped off the sleeping man's belt and took the axe lying next to him. He placed the axe into the belt's leather loop and carried on towards the sea. As Hundr reached the end of the settlement, he discovered that what he had mistaken for an island fortress was actually connected to the main island by a causeway, which had become visible as the tide receded. As he strolled closer, Hundr studied the construction, his gaze tracing the climbable planes of the rock face and noting how many men could march abreast across the causeway. A rope bridge spanned the gap above the causeway, and beyond it, a gate lay open, yawning like a mouth. Hundr paused and watched, leaning against a fence post as guards and warriors came and went. Fishing boats pushed out of the harbour towards their day's work, and Finn Ivarsson was inside the fortress. Hundr could feel it as his dead eye pulsed.

Nobody noticed Hundr. Away on the mainland, men were hammering and sawing, building a grand structure beside the settlement, and Hundr assumed it was Finn's temple to Loki taking shape beneath the watchful eye of its dark priests. A horse poked its head from a stable window, and Hundr stroked its nose. A bent-backed woman, her face mottled by childhood illness, shuffled past carrying a basket of apples. Hundr took one without a word. The woman tutted but didn't stop, continuing on towards the causeway. Hundr followed, biting into the hard, bitter fruit. His wounds ached, but he could no longer feel the ooze of blood down his back, and none had seeped from his head wound, so he satisfied himself that neither was a threat to his life. Hundr glanced about him as he descended onto the causeway and feared that someone would recognise him. If they did, he was a dead man. But the settlement remained calm as its people woke to meet the day ahead.

Three warriors ambled from the open gate, big men in *brynjars,* and Hundr tucked his chin into his chest, ducking lower because he recognised the three as Rus warriors of Finn Ivarsson's hearth troop. Men who had sworn to serve him back when Finn was no older than Hundr's son, Hermoth. It had happened in a fierce battle at Novgorod, far away south beyond the lands of the Rus. To reach the magnificent city where Hundr was born, one had to traverse a fierce, fast-flowing river with treacherous rapids. Hundr had gone there with his crew to recover Odin's Gungnir spear for the Valkyrie order, and he had killed his half-brother, a vile bastard who had made Hundr's young life a misery. Finn had been a fierce warrior then. A true son of Ivar, a lover of combat filled with bravery and a desire to emulate his famous father. The Rus warriors had sworn to serve Finn when he had killed their lord and spared them after a fierce battle. Each of them was a shield wall veteran and a man to fear.

Hundr's boots splashed in pools of water lying between the stones of the causeway bridge, and he remembered the days when he had taught Finn the cuts of the sword – lunge, parry, cut, thrust, footwork, defence and attack. There had been tension between them even in those days when Einar and Hildr had raised the orphan as though he were their own son. Hundr crunched the last bit of the apple and tossed the core into the sea. He should have killed Finn when he'd had the chance, back when he was a boy. But there was no *drengskapr* in that. Such thoughts were foolishness now, and Hundr shook them off as he followed the old woman up the gravel slope towards the fortress's open gate. The three Rus warriors spoke quietly amongst themselves and stood straight-backed with thumbs in their belts. One of them, a man with a crude axe tattoo on his cheek, glanced at Hundr. He looked away, following the woman beneath the palisade and into the fortress itself.

"You there," said one warrior in his Rus accent. "What is your business?"

Hundr carried on walking as though he had not heard.

"You there," the warrior repeated, this time with harshness in his voice. "I'm talking to you. Stop."

Hundr stopped and turned, keeping his head bowed, hand resting close to his stolen axe but not touching its haft. To touch a weapon in front of a warrior was to invite combat. Unless the insulted man ignored it, the challenge could not be revoked.

"Yes, lord?" Hundr answered in a quiet voice. He called the warrior lord not because he was a jarl or lord of warriors but as a mark of respect and deference, from a lowly warrior to another higher up the pecking order.

"What is your business in the fortress? Only the king's sworn men are permitted here. Everyone else camps in the town beyond the water."

"I carry a message, lord, for the king. From my jarl."

"Which jarl?" The warrior took two steps closer, his *brynjar* and weapons jangling as his heavy body shifted. He peered at Hundr, thick brows frowning as though he recognised him but could not quite place him. The warrior had a long, drooping moustache that hung lower than his beard. His neck seemed wider than his head, and even when standing still, he breathed heavily.

"Jarl Muirtach, of Clann Choinleagain," Hundr replied, conjuring an Irisher name remembering Flann, the champion he had fought beside Orkney's high cliffs.

"He's an Irisher. Let him go," grumbled one of the other Rus. "They come and go like rats, scurrying to whisper in the king's ear of shadows and evil *seiðr*. I'm too hungry to bandy words with a nithing. There's beef in the town. Come on." He placed a heavy hand on the first warrior's shoulder and did not care in the slightest that he had offended the warrior Hundr pretended to be. To a warrior's reputation and pride, such an insult demanded combat or apology. But the Rus saw only a cowed man, a mercenary in a poor leather breastplate carrying nothing but a spear. They saw what Hundr wanted them to see, an unsuccessful man, a man who called himself a warrior but who stood no chance standing in the shield wall to trade blows with the dangerous men. The Rus who had questioned Hundr nodded and turned, but after a few steps, he paused, glancing back to stare at Hundr, and Hundr hurried away like a scolded cat.

Fear blossomed in Hundr's chest, a heat which he fought to control. The Rus warrior had recognised him. He was sure of it. It was only a matter of time before the fog created by the sheer strangeness of finding their lord's greatest enemy walking amongst them cleared, and realisation dawned. Hundr clenched his teeth and quickened his pace, shoulders bunched, expecting the Rus warrior to come bellowing behind him at any moment.

The fortress was a simple construction inside its stout palisade. Three long wattle-and-daub outbuildings, their thatched roofs sloping low, bustled with the comings and goings of warriors and slaves. Hundr assumed these were the living quarters. At the centre stood the keep, built like a grand hall, its entrance marked by a heavy oak door beneath a pine lintel intricately carved in the form of a roaring bear – the Crippled King's hall. Hundr made for the oak door, spear resting upon his shoulder and crude long knife at his belt. He was deep inside the enemy's lair, and it had all been so simple. The day was still young, and the sun had barely begun its journey across the heavens. All he had to do was stroll into the hall, slay the Crippled King, and the war would be over.

Hundr marched to the hall, set one foot on its timber steps, and then a figure came shuffling from the doorway flanked by a man in a white robe. A grey-bearded man so thin that his face looked like a skull beneath a shock of pure white hair. He wore a thick iron chain around his neck, heavy enough to fetter a horse, and a large fire pendant hung low on his chest, glistening with amber and silver. A Loki priest. The man next to the priest limped badly and leant upon a black staff. He wore a long black cloak, head covered by a low-hanging hood. The priest stopped and stared into Hundr's one eye.

"What is it?" asked the priest, eyebrow raised in annoyance.

"I have a message for the king," Hundr replied, and as soon as the words had left his lips, the hooded man's head snapped up, the hood slipping back to reveal a face ravaged beyond recognition. One side hung hollow as if the bones beneath had been shattered and left to heal crookedly. His cheekbones sagged, dragging the eye down in a grotesque slant as though dragon fire had melted that side of his skull. His mouth twisted into a cruel slash, a gash of smouldering hate. And Hundr knew why the man limped – the toes of his foot had once been cut off by Hundr's own hand.

A crow swooped over the man's shoulder, its black wings gleaming as it landed on the wooden lintel. It cawed sharply, fixing Hundr with beady eyes, its head cocked in silent mockery. The scarred man gasped, too stunned to speak. The embodiment of his deepest hatred now stood before him. It was Finn Ivarsson himself. The Crippled King of Mann.

Without hesitation, Hundr hurled his spear.

EIGHT

The spear left Hundr's hand like a bolt thrown from the thunder god. Its ash shaft quivered as it left his grip, and a look of horror spread across Finn Ivarsson's scourged face. The Loki priest shot out his left arm in a desperate, reflexive attempt to catch the spear, but the weapon flew too fast. His finger touched the spear and knocked it slightly from its murderous path, just enough to send the iron tip sailing over Finn's shoulder to thump into the oak doorframe behind him. The crow cawed loud and shrill, and Finn recovered from his shock to point his black staff at Hundr.

"Kill that man! It is Hundr, the Man with the Dog's Name! Kill him!" Finn howled. The priest's beard shook with terror, and he wrapped his arms around Finn and bundled the king back towards the hall. Hundr cursed and drew his knife. He ran up the steps towards his enemy, but just as his boot landed on the top step, two warriors charged from the doorway with spears levelled. They were both Rus fighters, gigantic men in heavy *brynjar* chainmail coats and shining helmets. Hundr watched Finn disappear into the hall's gloom. The Crippled King spat curses, eyes wide with fury, spittle flying from his lips. More men appeared as the two warriors charged, and suddenly, all that had seemed so simple had become impossible. Hundr found himself alone and surrounded by enemies.

The Rus warriors roared, and their wicked spear points hurtled through the open door. To fight those two men armed only with a knife was to die, and so Hundr did the only thing he could do. He ran. Hundr leapt down the steps and raced away from Finn's hall. He feared neither death nor pain but could not leave Midgard knowing that Finn Ivarsson lived. The Crippled King would hunt Hundr's son, and Hermoth would know no peace whilst Finn lived. So Hundr had to survive. He had to run and live to fight another day. He sprinted across the open ground before Finn's hall. Warriors came from buildings in their night smocks, groggy from sleep. Some came with axes, and others with nothing but dishevelled hair and questioning looks on their faces.

"Close the gate!" bellowed one warrior chasing Hundr.

If that gate closed, he was a dead man, so Hundr pumped his legs and ran for his life. In ten steps, he would reach the open gateway and the tidal causeway. Heavy boots thumped on the ground behind him as Finn's warriors gave chase. Their armour and bulk weighed them down, and Hundr raced away like a hare from hunting dogs. The big Rus warrior with the drooping moustache stepped into the gateway, huge and hulking. The shadow cast by the gate's frame hid his face, but he stood with his boots planted wide and his axe held in two hands. He now knew the identity of the man who passed him in the gateway and waited there to kill his lord's most hated adversary. The warrior was a Norse-Rus Viking, a man who had sailed and fought across Midgard from Ireland to England, from Jutland to the lands of the Wends and made the frightening journey south to Novgorod, where he had served in its prince's esteemed bodyguard company. He was a killer and a warrior to fear. Yet Hundr charged at him.

There was no time to turn and run in another direction nor to pause and try to fight the moustached man. The very moment he stopped running, the two Rus men behind would drive their spears into Hundr's back like harpooning a fish. So Hundr did the only thing he could do. He launched himself at the moustached warrior. Hundr leapt, knees first. The warrior's axe was already drawn back, his face contorted with tension, neck and shoulders twisting as if to fell Hundr like a tree. The axe blade swung with brutal force, its arc wide enough to cleave Hundr in two – had he not crashed into the man mid-swing. Hundr's knees slammed into the warrior's chest, sending him reeling backwards. The man hit the wooden steps with a bone-rattling thud, his armour clattering as he tumbled towards the rope bridge stretching over the tidal walkway.

Hundr landed sprawling on top of the moustached warrior, and he stabbed viciously with the knife, punching the blade half a dozen times at his torso in quick succession. The quality *brynjar* absorbed the blows, and Hundr had mere moments before the pursuing men killed him. So, he twisted the axe free from the winded warrior's meaty fist and set off running across the rope bridge. It swung beneath him as he ran, and Hundr almost stumbled as he reached the far side to set foot on the mainland and Eyrrspollr's settlement. Hundr turned and grinned at the two warriors, who were halfway across the bridge in pursuit. Flanking them was a monstrous figure of a man, young but hugely muscled, head and shoulders taller than any other man in the fortress. He strode with a sword in each hand, and it was as though Eystein Longaxe had risen from the dead. Hundr swung his axe down hard, striking the thick, coiled hemp rope anchoring the bridge. The blade was keen, slicing clean through with a sharp hiss, and the bridge collapsed, sending the warriors plummeting to the rocky causeway below. The moustached man hauled himself to his feet and stared agape at Hundr across the chasm. In response, Hundr held his stolen axe up in a mocking salute. It was a finely crafted weapon – its haft intricately carved and inlaid with runes, the lower grip wrapped in soft leather. The bearded blade itself gleamed, etched with writhing dragons. The moustached man bellowed with anger and clambered down the hill towards the causeway, followed by Finn's giant champion, Orm Eysteinsson.

"His weight in silver for the man who kills Hundr!" howled a voice from the gateway shadows, and then Finn Ivarsson appeared, leaning on his staff and waving his free arm like a madman. Hundr turned and bolted for the settlement. Stunned folk stared at him as Hundr sped past. Two warriors blocked his path, their feet set firm on the mud-slick pathway. Hundr veered away from them and slipped through the gap between two buildings. He leapt over a pigsty fence but lost his footing in the filth. Hundr hauled himself upright and darted into the labyrinth of wattle buildings and damp, stinking thatch. Turning a corner, he came face to face with a wiry warrior clutching a seax. Without hesitation, Hundr chopped his stolen axe into the man's chest, wrenching the blade free to cast an arc of blood across a whitewashed hovel. Shouted orders rang out around the settlement, and Hundr waited with his back against a wall as a dozen men ran down the lane next to him, weapons jangling and boots slapping in the mud.

"Bastard," snarled a voice on Hundr's blind side. He turned his head to see with his good eye and ducked just as an axe slammed into the building where his head had been. Hundr stabbed his knife into the attacker's thigh and slipped behind him. The enemy howled in pain and tried to cut at Hundr's throat, but Hundr parried the strike with the haft of his stolen axe and plunged the knife into the attacker's soft belly. Hot blood ran over Hundr's fist as he twisted the blade, and a boyish face looked up at him in despair, a face barely fuzzed with its first beard. Hundr pushed the dying man away from him with contempt. A man too young to face a champion such as him. A young man full of ambition and dreams of a warrior's life, dead in the service of a foul king who neither valued nor cared for his wasted life.

A horse whickered, and Hundr ran towards the sound, recalling the stables and horse he had stroked on his way through the settlement. The town was alive with activity – men rushing in every direction. Hundr ducked behind a timber hen house as a line of spear-wielding warriors charged past, their boots thudding on the packed earth. He waited, breath held, as two ruddy-faced men jogged up the lane, then dashed towards the stables. The roan mare was still there, her head poking out from the stall, dark eyes wide and curious, watching the chaos unfold. Hundr stroked her again before slipping into the stall. The mare shifted, nostrils flaring, but calmed as he whispered softly into her ear, running his hand down her neck. Once the horse was settled, Hundr stepped out in search of tack.

The stable stretched long before him, lined with five stalls. Three stood empty; a dappled mare dozed in one, while a chestnut gelding eyed him warily from another. Spotting the tack hanging from a post, Hundr grabbed it along with a heavy riding blanket and returned to the mare. He could ride, though not well – he was a sailor, a warrior, not a horseman. But the mare would carry him faster than he could flee on foot. Without her, he stood no chance. Finn's men would hunt him down and kill him. Even if he reached the outer palisade, he wouldn't last long on the island. Finn would send his warriors, hundreds strong, to scour every crag, bush, and hollow until his enemy was found.

"I've got you now, turd," hissed a deep voice with a thick Rus accent. "Saw you climbing in beside the horse like a thief. You run fast like all cowards do. Nowhere to run now. Just you and me. Come and fight with Alvad. Let me show you how real men fight." It was the Rus with the long moustache. He carried a new axe, no doubt plucked from the hands of another warrior. He grinned at Hundr, brown teeth showing in his maw. "You are going to make me rich, Dog's Name. I will be the Champion of the North, and men will sing my name across the Whale Road."

"A grand boast from a fat man with a big mouth, serving a cripple who fled the battle at the Bardarborg," replied Hundr. "Were you there, Alvad? How fast did you run from the battlefield? Did you shit your breeches when the weapons clashed and the warriors fought? At least Vigfus Hjorthrimul and his men died with honour. They were your allies, and you ran like dogs. Your forefathers look down on you from the afterlife and spit on your soul. You are no warrior. You are the lickspittle servant of a man without honour."

Alvad growled and launched himself at Hundr, consumed with rage, his warrior's pride burning and his axe swinging. Hundr threw the horse's tack at the charging Rus warrior. Alvad tried to bat it away, but the leather reins tangled his axe and gave Hundr enough time to draw his weapons. Alvad tossed the tack away, his face flushed crimson with anger. He swung at

Hundr, and Hundr swayed away from the blow lightly, feeling a twinge from the wound on his back. Alvad kept moving with the balance and skill of a professional warrior, his axe cutting in short, precise chops, feet sliding forward, attacking side-on with strength and a lifetime of battle experience. Hundr parried a strike, blades ringing together to send a shiver up his arm. He calmed himself and forced his mind to ignore the horde of warriors baying for his blood and searching the settlement to take his head. The axe was not Hundr's weapon of choice, but the old weapon master of Novgorod had taught him to use it well. So, he shifted his grip up the leather-bound haft and reversed his hold on the knife to clutch the blade underhand in his left hand.

Alvad grunted as he came on. He feinted low and sliced his axe blade at Hundr's face, so Hundr parried the axe and knocked it high. He cut with his knife, dragging the blade across Alvad's *brynjar*. The poorly crafted knife was no match for the expensive chainmail. Still, the sensation startled Alvad, making him instinctively stagger backwards, and Hundr kicked him hard in the groin. Alvad groaned, doubling over as he fought to steady himself, but the pain overwhelmed him. In less than a heartbeat, Hundr slammed his axe blade into Alvad's forehead. His skull cracked like an egg. Alvad's body shook and throbbed. He toppled, and Hundr wrenched the stolen axe free of its former owner's head.

The horse became skittish at the smell of blood, and Hundr hurried over to calm her. He fitted the tack and threw over the riding blanket.

"Bring me luck, girl," he whispered into the mare's ear. "Carry me as swiftly as Sleipnir, Odin's eight-legged stallion."

Hundr ran and opened the stable door, where two warriors gawped at him with open mouths. He leapt upon the mare's back, clicked his tongue and dug his heels into her flanks. She set off at a trot, and Hundr ducked beneath the door lintel. The two warriors stumbled backwards before the powerful horse, and Hundr kicked his boot at the leftmost man's face. The other warrior shouted to raise the alarm, and the mare lurched. She skittered as men came from paths and alleys, waving their weapons and yelling. Hundr snapped the reins and dug his heels in harder this time, and the mare's muscled legs powered into a canter to throw clods of earth up from her hoofs. Spear points flashed at Hundr, but the wielders were too wary of the horse's power to get close enough to strike. Hundr rode her out into Eyrrspollr's principal thoroughfare as she used the open road to turn her canter into a gallop. The wind whipped Hundr's hair away from his face, and his cap flew off. He leant into the horse and held on tight.

Enemies fled from the horse's path, and the front palisade loomed ahead. The guards frantically tried to close the gate, but the palisade itself barely reached waist height. Hundr leant further into the mare, urging her forward. She charged towards the wall, the cries of men chasing her fading into the wind. Without breaking stride, the mare leapt over the barrier, and Hundr shut his eye, the rush of exhilaration as close to the thrill of sailing the Whale Road as he had ever known. The horse landed, and Hundr slipped on the riding blanket, yet he righted himself quickly and turned to see hundreds of warriors clambering over the walls behind him. An arrow whistled by and thudded into the ground ahead. Another flew wide of the horse's path, but a shuddering pain, sharp as a hammer blow, shot through Hundr's thigh, and he glanced down to see a black feathered arrow buried in the flesh of his leg. He urged the mare to even greater speeds, and she galloped across the open fields and meadows of Mann, leading Hundr towards the beacon on its northwestern point. Then, another blow struck – this time in his back. Hundr leant again onto the mare's neck, gripping the reins with all his strength and hoping that the impact of his wounds did not cause him to fall.

The mare raced up towards higher ground, and white lather flecked her flanks as Hundr reined in and slid down from the riding blanket. He winced as his left leg touched the ground. Pain throbbed about his body, and his head felt as though he could fall asleep at any moment.

"Thank you, girl," he said warmly and stroked her nose.

"Who the bloody hell are you?" a croaky voice demanded to know. A man in a filthy jerkin with long, greasy hair hanging from a balding head sneered at Hundr. He had a spear in one fist and a horn in the other. Hundr glanced down the hillside to where hundreds of warriors streamed from Eyrrspollr. Two riders thundered through the fields ahead of them in pursuit of Hundr.

"You are the beacon guard?" Hundr asked.

"I am. They want you, bastard, and you're mine now. Put down the axe, or I'll run you through."

"Do you have a fire going?"

"What? Put the bloody axe down, scum."

Hundr caught a whiff of burning wood and spotted a thin wisp of smoke beyond the stacked lengths of cut timber which formed the beacon. Hundr staggered four steps, reeling from the arrows stuck in his back and leg. He had to light the beacon. Once Einar saw the flames, he would bring the Seaworm close, and Hundr had to be in the water when he did. He had failed to kill

Finn but had at least escaped with his life. Hundr slipped the axe from his belt, and the beacon guard smiled.

"Good lad," he said, almost laughing. "Put it down. You look like you are about to drop dead, anyway. You might die before the king gets his hands on you. If you're lucky. You got any silver on you, dead man?"

Hundr raised the axe high and gripped the haft in both hands. The arrow in his back tore at his muscles, forcing a groan of pain from his throat. He threw the axe, and it turned head over haft before slamming into the beacon guard's midriff, sending him sprawling onto the grassy hilltop. He screamed and writhed, staring down at the axe embedded in his body. Hundr ignored him and staggered to the beacon, using its woodpile to steady himself. A small fire burned ten paces away, and Hundr hurried to it. He grabbed a burning faggot from the flames and fell. Darkness threatened to overtake him as the sound of approaching hoofbeats thundered over the hillside. Hundr could not stand, so he crawled to the beacon, leaving a shining trail of blood behind him like a snail. He thrust the burning log into the beacon's base, and the kindling caught aflame. Dried twigs and leaves crackled, and then the logs soaked in oil sprang to life with fire. Two horses reached the summit, and their riders leapt to the ground. They ran towards Hundr, and he crawled away, dragging himself forward and fighting the urge to lie down and let the darkness overtake him.

Footsteps and shouting drew closer, though the sounds were muffled by Hundr's lightheadedness. He hurried, crawling desperately, his fingers scrabbling across the stone until they found the cold edge of the cliff. Below him, the Whale Road stretched out beneath the sun, gleaming like a jewelled tapestry as he lay down flat. The arrow stuck in his back snapped, but the wound was numb, and Hundr felt no pain. Hands lunged for him, trying to haul him back, but he shifted and rolled away. The rock beneath him gave way, and a rush of cold air swallowed him as he plunged into the void. Hundr's mind drifted, wondering if this was how it felt to die. The darkness overcame him then, and the sensation of falling faded into nothingness as the depths of the surging Whale Road rose to meet him.

NINE

"Ships, my lord," said Amundr, his heavily muscled arm pointing to the north.

"How many?" Einar replied, squinting. As a younger man, Einar had possessed the vision of an eagle. It had served him well. A lookout with good eyes was as valuable to a captain as a stout mast, and it had helped him rise in importance when he had first taken to sea. Now, he could barely see three ship's lengths ahead of him, and anything too close to his face was as blurry as the thickest sea fog.

"Two sails."

"They'll hang back and raise the alarm. Hundr had better get his killing done quickly because these waters will soon crawl with enemy ships."

Einar waited out at sea on board the Fjord Bear, along with the rest of the Vanylven fleet, keeping far enough away from Mann to avoid being seen by its patrol boats. Einar ordered the fleet to separate into a string of ships, with the Seaworm close enough to Mann to spot Hundr's signal and the rest a horizon away so that they were invisible to Finn's fleet. If Finn's patrol ships noticed the Seaworm off Mann's northwestern coast, they would only see a solitary ship – hardy cause for alarm given how frequently ships passed through Mann's waters. Mann sat at the crossroads of the sea between Northumbria, the lands of the Scots, and Ireland. Fishing boats, merchant vessels and other ships passed across the narrow waterway daily, so one ship far off the coast would not be enough to raise panic amongst the Crippled King's men. But if they saw four ships loitering further out to sea, it would be a different story. Einar knew that Finn would send his fleet to drive them away, forcing Einar into a dilemma: either engage in a fight too soon, before Hundr's signal, or retreat, circle back, and hope to find Hundr alive and waiting, rather than dead in the water.

"Are they making for the Seaworm?"

"No, my lord. Hanging back, just floating."

"Watching, then. Perhaps we should have sailed with the Seaworm crew. Made sure everything goes according to plan."

"Sigvarth has the Seaworm, and Lord Hundr's men are on board. They won't leave Hundr in the water. Even if Finn sends a dozen ships to attack them."

Which was true enough. There had been a lengthy debate between Einar, Sigvarth, Thorgrim, Asbjorn and Amundr about who should captain the Seaworm that day. Fastbjorn, Harbard and Sigvarth knew their business and had made the crossing from Vanylven onboard the Seaworm and believed they should be the ones to fish Hundr out of the water, whilst Einar and the rest remained out of sight. Einar had argued against it, not wanting to idly watch whilst others saved his friend from death. But if Finn sent his fleet, which by Einar's reckoning was at least thirty ships strong, then Einar needed to command the four hidden Vanylven ships and try to take Finn's fleet on a wild chase across open water, buying time for Sigvarth and the Seaworm to pluck Hundr from the waters around Mann.

"Do you think he will come back?" Einar asked wistfully, staring out at the churning waves.

Amundr shrugged. "Hundr always comes back, my lord."

"He's alone inside Finn's fortress. He isn't exactly a man who can blend into a crowd."

"What do you mean, Lord Einar?"

"He has one eye and more scars than a fishing

boat's hull. He'll stand out like boils on an old whore."

Amundr crossed his arms and frowned at Einar's imaginative description. "He always comes back."

"The beacon, lord!" came a shout from the stern. "The beacon is lit!"

Einar raced to see along with the crew, but his old eyes could see nothing beyond the waves.

"Sigvarth has raised the shield. It's time," said Amundr with steel in his deep, rumbling voice.

"To oars!" Einar barked at the crew. "Make ready!"

Einar's heart quickened. The raised shield was the signal to say Hundr was about to enter the water, that the beacon was lit. Hundr had escaped from Eyrrspollr, but they needed to reach him before Finn Ivarsson's warships closed in. Like a fisherman snaring his catch, a boat had to pluck Hundr from the sea. Einar's four ships needed to edge closer to the Seaworm, ready to intercept any of Finn's vessels rounding the headland, while Sigvarth's boat prepared to sweep in to rescue Hundr from the white tips.

Amundr strode from stern to bow, bellowing at the men, encouraging some and scourging others. The wind was not favourable, so the crew grabbed oars from their crutches and set them into the oar holes. The warriors took up position, and on Amundr's order, they rowed. Einar's gaze was fixed sombrely towards Mann. Hundr was his dearest friend, more than a brother to him, and if he had survived the assassination of Mann's king and reached the water, he now faced his greatest peril. Hundr was in the sea, floating and exposed, with no way to defend himself should an enemy ship find him before the Seaworm. All he could do was swim, hoping to outpace the warships that would surely hunt him.

But on the other side of the coin lay Hundr's victory. If Hundr had succeeded, that meant Finn Ivarsson was dead, and despite everything, even after Ragnhild's death and all the ruinous suffering of last year's war, Einar loved Finn like a son. Even after all that had happened between them over the years, even after Finn had cast Einar into Vedrafjord's dungeons and left him to his mother's cruel torture, Einar couldn't forget the boy Finn once was. Whenever he thought of Finn, it wasn't the Crippled King he saw, but the chestnut-haired boy, quick to smile, eager to learn. He could still picture them on the shores of a still fjord, skimming stones together – Einar helping Finn find the perfect flat rock, teaching him how to throw it just right. Those were the best days of Einar's life. The gods had not blessed Einar and Hildr with children, and raising Finn was the closest they had come to having a family of their own. Finn would always be that boy to Einar, the boy who had been perfect before his mother sunk her claws into his young mind and poured all her hate into his thought cage. Finn had become something else after that war in Ireland. A twisted version of himself, so bent and warped by rage and hate. The man Einar and Hundr fought now was the Crippled King, not the boy Einar had loved. At least, that was what Einar told himself, to keep his pity at bay. For there could be no room for pity in Einar's world, in the world of warriors, kings, *drengskapr*, and Valhalla.

"The two ships are moving south, my lord," said Amundr, snapping Einar from his thoughts.

"Head them off. They'll turn back when they see four *drakkars* coming for them," Einar replied.

The Fjord Bear burst to life. Oars bit, men heaved, and the warship lurched forward. Two more pulls and the vessel picked up speed, racing to intercept the two patrol boats before they spotted Hundr in the water or sailed to attack the Seaworm. The Sea Stallion, Sea Falcon, and Wind Elk followed Einar's lead. Einar waved to Thorgrim across the bows, who returned the gesture, pointing south towards the enemy vessels. Einar saw the Seaworm as the fleet grew closer. Her oars rose and fell like wings, and water dripped from them to catch the sun like jewels. She was a beautiful ship, and Einar had sailed upon her since the days before he could grow a beard. He knew her every timber, her speed, and how the ballast balanced her. She was fast and easy to manoeuvre, and Einar knew Sigvarth would get to Hundr before the patrol boats moved in.

"Sails to the west!" shouted a warrior from the prow. Einar hurried, ducking beneath the rigging and dodging about rowing benches and piles of weapons stacked in wait in case it came to a fight. Einar reached the prow and followed the line of the warrior's pointing finger. He cursed his old eyes, for he could see nothing.

"How many?" Einar asked.

"Too far away to be sure, my lord," replied the young warrior, glancing nervously up at Einar. "But I can see at least five sails."

Einar licked his finger and held it up to feel for the breeze. "They have the wind. Get a signal to Thorgrim. Tell him to take the Elk and Falcon and warn off the two patrol boats. The Stallion is to follow us towards the new ships."

"Yes, my lord," nodded the warrior and hurried off to signal Thorgrim.

"Amundr!" Einar roared with his hand cupped around his mouth. "Get this boat moving. We must reach those ships before they get to the Seaworm."

"We can't fight them. There are too many," Amundr replied.

"We don't have to fight them. Just lure them into a chase. Get the flag up, let them see the one eye. They'll follow that. Finn wants Hundr and me dead. Let them see me at the prow. Come on, row, row, row!"

It was a desperate race through the crashing waves as the Fjord Bear and the Sea Stallion's oars pounded the water. The enemy ships came about Mann's west coast with their sails full of wind whilst Einar's men heaved and grunted, every oar stroke stretching their muscles.

"Row, men!" Einar urged them. "Hundr is out there, swimming for his life. If those ships reach him before the Seaworm, then he is a dead man. So row for Hundr!"

The oar blades rose in unison as Amundr beat time, banging the back of his axe upon a shield. Einar rested his hands upon the sheer strake and watched Thorgrim's two ships intercept the path of Finn's patrol boats. They saw two fully manned *drakkars* in front of them and came about to the north, fleeing from battle. That part of Einar's plan had worked, at least. Now, the only threat to Hundr was the ships under sail, but they had the power of Njorth behind them, pressing forward with full sails, whilst Einar's ships had to row. The Fjord Bear passed the Seaworm's stern, perhaps ten ships' lengths away, and Einar squinted, hoping to see Hundr in the water, but he could see nothing. The Crippled King's ships drew closer, sails billowing and emblazoned with the fire symbol of Loki. There were a dozen of them as clear as day, and if their hulls were full of warriors, that could mean nine hundred hardened killers approaching – too many for Einar's two crews to fight.

Einar made his way along the keel and climbed up onto the steerboard platform. He nodded to the man steering the ship and took control himself. The wind buffeted his face and hair, making Einar's eyes water, but he cuffed the tears away with his left hand. Einar changed the Fjord Bear's course, pushing her closer to the island so that the ship came between the Seaworm and the Mann fleet. He turned to look over his shoulder and saw men leaning over the Seaworm's side, and he hoped to Odin they were lifting Hundr out of the Whale Road. The sight gave him hope, but he had to buy the Seaworm time to sail away north. Sigvarth would begin from a standing start. He could bring the Seaworm about under oars and catch the wind, but Finn's ships were too close, and they would close the gap before the Seaworm got her sail up and ran before the wind on a broad reach. The Seaworm could race around Mann's northern coastline and then out to sea. But in order for that to happen, Einar had to draw the enemy off. So, he pushed the tiller again and felt the Fjord Bear shift beneath him.

The *drakkar* came about, and waves crashed against the bow to cover the men in sea spume. Einar charged head-on towards the enemy, and he gripped the tiller tightly. The men rowing glanced over their shoulders at him, fearful of how close Einar brought them to an enemy they could not see as they pulled their ash-shafted oars.

"Ready the sail!" Einar ordered. "Untie the shroud. I'll bring her about beam on – we'll be on a reach and then turn to run before them. We'll lead them north of here, away from the Seaworm. Do it now!"

The crew barked a clipped roar to show they understood, and then every man without an oar in his fist set about preparing the sail. It was a risk. If Einar timed it incorrectly, or the men took too long to haul up the sail, they were all done for. The Crippled King's fleet would envelop them. They would draw the Fjord Bear close with axes and rope, board her, and slaughter the men, surging aboard with overwhelming numbers. Einar glanced across the swell and saw that the crew of the Sea Stallion noticed and understood what the Fjord Bear intended, and they made their own sail ready for the desperate manoeuvre.

Bearded faces glowered at Einar across the water as the enemy ships drew close. Einar wanted to provoke them, to hurt their sailors' pride, so that they broke off from chasing the Seaworm to pursue him. So, he brought the Fjord Bear as close as he could until his chance of escape rested on a knife edge.

"Now!" he bellowed at the last moment, just as he heard the enemy shouting across the water. He leant heavily on the tiller, and the Fjord Bear lurched hard, banking sharply away from the advancing ships. The oars on the port side snapped up while the rest strained to swing the ship around. Men hauled at the rigging, and the sail was hoisted. A roar of excitement erupted from the enemy's decks, warriors brandishing blades, eager for blood. The Fjord Bear's sail cracked as it caught the wind, sending a cold spray of water from its woollen folds, drenching the crew. Then, with a sudden burst of speed, the ship surged forward, fleeing before the wind.

A sixty-man *drakkar* came alongside the Fjord Bear, edging closer, and Einar skilfully steered her away. The Bear picked up speed, and her crew shouted and jeered at the enemy, taunting them, while across the narrowing gap, the enemy captain glowered at Einar. He was a squat, grey-bearded man, seasoned and weathered like Einar himself. A proud seafarer eager for glory and the chance to kill a renowned foe. But pride had made him reckless, and Einar saw it. Grinning, he waved mockingly at the man. The captain's face darkened with rage, and he barked orders at his men, but it was too late – the Fjord Bear had caught the wind. She pulled away, leaving the heavier *drakkar* in her wake. Einar's ship carried only forty men, just enough to row but not nearly enough for a fight. She was built for speed, not combat. But as Einar looked over his shoulder at the approaching fleet, he saw the enemy ships were crammed with warriors – at least eighty on each deck, all eager for blood. They were heavy, slow, and prepared for battle. Einar had come for speed.

"Let her out, lads!" Einar called. The crew carefully let out the seal hide ropes, and the sail was at its maximum, dragging the ship out to sea as the enemy struggled in her wake. The Seaworm was too far ahead, racing before the wind northeast, and Einar's crew howled their defiance at the enemy, who followed like enraged dogs. Only three ships followed the Seaworm, and the rest chased Einar into open water. He had done everything he could. It was down to Sigvarth and Hundr now to make their escape. Einar pushed the Fjord Bear and the Sea Stallion north, where they would sail until the enemy turned back. He had arranged with Sigvarth and Thorgrim to meet off Rathlin

Island on Ireland's northern coast, and there he would wait, hopeful that Hundr lived and that the Seaworm had outrun their foes. He would learn then if Finn Ivarsson was dead, and though that was necessary for the bloody war to end, Einar wished things could have been different. He wished Finn had stayed with him at Vanylven and grown up in peace. Alas, the Norns had willed it otherwise. The way of the *drengr* was of blood and blade, and Einar, Hundr, and Finn had paid that price for a life of reputation and glory.

TEN

Hundr sat upright and violently coughed up what seemed like half the seawater in Midgard. He slumped back down to the deck, and Sigvarth Trollhands' barrel-chested frame appeared over him as the stout warrior lifted Hundr by his shoulders and slapped his back.

"Get it all out," said Sigvarth with professional sureness. "You've swallowed so much that a whale might pop out, my lord."

"I couldn't kill him," Hundr gasped, sucking in great mouthfuls of sea air. "The Crippled King lives." He winced and looked down at his wounded leg. The arrow had snapped during the fall, leaving the arrowhead in his thigh. The pain in his back told him that the arrowhead was also still inside him.

"Never mind that now. Lord Einar saw off most of the enemy fleet, but three of the bastards are chasing us. The wind's changed, and we've no choice but to run eastwards before it." Sigvarth noticed Hundr's wounds then, and a frown creased his already grizzled face. "Bring me a knife and some clean cloth!" he shouted to the crew.

Yazi the Easterner came forth with his knife and a clean jerkin, which he split with the blade. "I will do it," he said, speaking in his thick accent.

"He needs good Norse healing, not the hands of a…"

Hundr nodded, and Sigvarth gave way.

"I have knowledge of the Tolmac people, passed down to us by our forefathers from time beyond time. You Norsemen have forgotten the lessons of the grandsires in your hunt for wealth," Yazi muttered under his breath as he used the sharp tip of his knife to cut Hundr's flesh deep enough to pry the arrowheads out of his thigh and back. Hundr fought to hold in cries of pain, and after the first incision, Thatchulf handed him a finger-sized wooden peg to put between his teeth, which Hundr gnawed on instead of screaming as Yazi's knife probed to free the arrows from his body. Once the grim work was finished, Yazi washed the wounds and bound them tightly.

The day wore on, and the coast of Northumbria came into view. Hundr drank a pot of ale and ate some dried fish with a loaf of black bread, and before long, he felt strong enough to stand with Thatchulf and Sigvarth at the prow.

"That's a river mouth," said Sigvarth, pointing towards a crease in the landscape.

"Can we sail up it?" asked Thatchulf.

Sigvarth shrugged. "We can until we can't. It's probably tidal. Hopefully, in flood. There could be treacherous sandbanks beneath the surface that we can't see. We have to go carefully. Someone will have to lean over the side with a rock on the end of a line to test the river's depth. It could be wide and sweeping or narrow and thin. If we had a man aboard who knows these waters, it would be better. Without that..." Sigvarth held up his hand and rocked it from side to side.

"The three ships can follow us, though?"

"They can."

"Isn't it better to outrun them, then? Head north or south?"

"Could be. But there are more ships out there. The fleet pursuing Einar could break off that chase and come looking for us. The Crippled King could have more coming this way as we speak."

"But how can we outrun them in a river?"

"We aren't trying to outrun them," Hundr interjected. "We must beach the Seaworm and go ashore." He understood Sigvarth's plan, and it was the right thing to do. They had little choice.

"Ashore in a foreign land? Won't they just follow us and kill us on the riverbank?"

"They'll try," said Hundr. "We are light-handed for speed, and there are but forty of us. But we can make a stand on the riverbank if we have to. Or march further inland."

"We are in the wild Northumbrian lands north of Chester," added Sigvarth. "The major fortresses of Northumbria are in Chester and then across the mountains to the east, at Jorvik and Bebbanburg. The folk here are Norse settlers, raiders, and slavers. They won't take kindly to an army from Mann marching across their lands."

"They won't take kindly to us either," Thatchulf grumbled, his brow furrowed.

"We have to try something, Thatchulf," said Hundr, growing tired of his complaining. They had few choices. Hundr's hope of killing the Crippled King had failed, and now he had to do his best to ensure his men survived. The enemy fleet wouldn't catch Einar – the old seafarer knew the ways of the open water too well to be caught by any fleet. But Finn's men would hunt Hundr relentlessly. The reward their lord would place on his head would make a man rich for life. Sigvarth was right; to stay at sea was too much of a gamble, but on land, they might just stand more of a chance of survival.

"Very well, my lord," Thatchulf nodded and left Hundr and Sigvarth alone, staring towards the Northumbrian coastline.

"There are too many of them to fight," said Sigvarth, stroking his beard.

"But we might have no choice. If we run out of river, we'll fight them on the riverbank. If we kill enough of the turds, they might lose heart. If they retreat, then we can march inland to safety. Lead them on a merry dance, circle behind them, and return to the Seaworm to sail away. Like I said, we must try something. I won't try to outrun them only to run into more of their ships. At least on land, we have a fighting chance. I'd rather die on solid ground with a sword in my hand than be lost in the murky depths. Would you not rather die in battle and take your place in Valhalla than sink to the bottom of the Whale Road where your soul will wander forever in Ran's watery hel world?"

"I choose Valhalla, Lord Hundr. As would every man on this ship."

"So we follow the plan, Sigvarth. Make for the river, and when we can, we will go ashore and take our chances fighting the enemy on the bank."

The wind carried them towards Northumbria

until the afternoon waned, and the Seaworm came about a long spit of land jutting into the sea. The three enemy ships pursued them, and Fastbjorn steered the ship beyond the spit. The crew took down the sail so that they could enter the wide tidal river estuary rowed by two banks of oars. Dense forest covered both sides of the low-lying riverbanks. Fisherfolk stared at them from lowly settlements amongst the mud, and in the distance, mountains rose, shadowed and bleak against the setting sun. They kept to the middle of the river, and Sigvarth set a man in the prow, leaning over to dip his stone-weighted length of rope into the water to check its depth. Sigvarth had knotted the rope at regular intervals, allowing the man to gauge if the river became shallower. Slowly, the Seaworm crept around a wide bend where the river narrowed between banks that were heavy with oak, ash, and elm trees.

The crew exchanged nervous glances and rowed in silence. The creak of the trees and the splash of the oar blades were the only sounds as the Seaworm probed through the unfamiliar waterway. Hundr leaned against the sheer strake, the pain from his wounds pulsing. He needed to sleep and recover, but there was no time for rest, not with three enemy ships in pursuit.

"River's growing shallower!" shouted Toki,

standing beside the warrior who was dipping his rock and line into the water. "Down to the third knot!"

"Tide could be at the ebb," Sigvarth remarked, staring thoughtfully at the riverbanks. "Or the river could simply be thinning. We can't be certain how far it runs deep inland. I've rounded blind bends before and found waterways broad as lakes – or others that taper off as thin as a chicken's leg."

"Head for the bank," Hundr ordered. "Don't keep to the middle. If we get stranded on a sandbank, the hull might crack, and we'll have to wade ashore whilst the enemy approaches. If they catch us, we'll need to reach dry land quickly."

"The enemy!" a warrior suddenly shouted from the stern. It was as though the Norns were listening to Hundr's plans as they huddled beside the roots of Yggdrasil and dragged their claw nails across the threads of his life.

Three ships swept around a river bend, warships as big as the Seaworm, oars rising and falling in unison. At the prow of the leading ship, a man stood high above the water, having climbed the wooden carving of an eagle. He perched atop it with his arm curled about its head and a sword held in his right hand. He was a giant of a man, muscled with an impossibly thick neck – Orm Eysteinsson. Orm pointed his sword at the Seaworm, and the enemy roared with bloodthirsty anticipation. They came with the setting sun at their backs, their faces cast in shadow, but the gleam of their blades caught the dying light, shining like stars. The beasts carved into their prows snarled as they bore down on Hundr and his men. They were the Crippled King's warriors, Vikings and Irishmen alike, ready to slaughter their lord's mortal enemy. Hundr felt their hate wash over him like a warm wind.

Death had come for him in the form of another son whose father he had killed long ago. Many men had fallen to Hundr's swords. He glanced up at a red-tinged sky and wondered if that was to be his fate. Was there a price to be paid for his reputation, for the life he had led? Hundr had followed *drengskapr*. He had fought and killed just as Odin urged all warriors to. Was it his destiny to be killed by a man just like himself? Slaughtered by a young warrior bent on burnishing his reputation brightly with the death of an ageing champion? Hundr had killed Orm's father, just as he killed Finn's father. The sons came for vengeance, but as Hundr took his weapons from Thatchulf, he braced himself against the pain of his wounds. He was not ready to die, not yet.

Fastbjorn urged the men to pick up speed, but

Hundr saw the fear etched on Sigvarth's broad face. If they rowed faster, it made it impossible for the man at the prow to test the water's depths. The Seaworm glided gently towards the northern riverbank, where shafts of fading sunlight shone through the trees like sword blades.

"We'll go ashore here," Hundr instructed.

"But, lord?" said Sigvarth. "The river will carry us further east, further inland."

"We'll go ashore." Hundr's gut told him it was the right thing to do, that his men could run through the trees and escape into the wilds of Northumbria where Orm and his men would fear following. They were safe on board their ships, but on land, the local lord would hear of their coming and send his men to kill them. Even so, Hundr would take his chances in the trees – and with the lords of Northumbria.

The enemy ships closed the distance, oars making great sweeps in the gently flowing river, and the warriors chanted war songs to the beat of a drum. Their voices rang loud and clear, and the drum beat in time with the oars to make the sound of Viking war.

"Arm yourselves," Hundr ordered, limping along the deck. "Take as much as we can carry. We'll need ale, food, weapons, clothes. Everything. Anything you can tie to your backs goes with us. The rest we leave behind."

The crew gathered seal hide rope and hemp rope; they cut lengths and made packs of dried fish, pork and beef. They gathered oatcakes and dipped as many water skins in ale and water barrels as they could, and they armed themselves with weapons.

"Save your shafts," Hundr said to Yazi the Easterner when he brought his recurved bow and quiver of arrows towards the stern. "We'll need them in the woods."

The Seaworm's hull scraped lightly on the riverbed and slowed. Fastbjorn brought the bow as close as possible to the riverbank, and as the ship slowed and mud gathered beneath the keel, Toki laid a plank of wood upon the sheer strake. The crew ran from the ship across the plank and onto Northumbrian land. The enemy ships came on faster, their crews roaring like maddened wolves, shaking weapons, desperate for the fight to begin. Hundr waited until last, resting a hand on the Seaworm's timbers.

"I'm sorry, old girl," he whispered. "You have always brought me luck and carried me as far as any man in Midgard has sailed. May the gods keep you safe until I can find you again." He kissed his fingers and touched them to the mast before limping over the plank to join his men in the long, wild grasses.

"Into the trees!" Sigvarth ordered, and the warriors ran beneath the cover of leafy boughs and into the forest's gloom.

"Wait," Hundr said, just loud enough for the surrounding men to hear. "Ready shields and weapons. Leave the supplies behind us."

Sigvarth grinned at him. "I know that look. You mean to fight them?"

"Just enough so that they know what men they face. It might slow their pursuit if they believe we wait for them in the trees. I want them to be afraid of sleeping for fear of our attacks. I want them cautious, marching slowly with the screams and groans of their wounded ringing in their ears. Shield wall on me. When they disembark, we attack them before they form up in proper order. We hit them hard and then we return for our supplies. Kill as many as we can before they can make their numbers count. They'll be too busy making a shield wall and tending to their wounded to chase us. That will give us time to get ahead of the bastards."

"One of their ships lags the others, so we face only two crews."

Hundr smiled. "We can't beat them here. Leave one man in the trees with a horn. Have him count to twenty a dozen times, then blow his horn. Tell the men that when the horn sounds, we break off the fight."

"Yes, my lord." Sigvarth set off to give the orders.

Thatchulf came to Hundr's side with his shield and axe ready, and Toki took up a place on Hundr's left. The Crow and Yazi stood behind Hundr, and the rest of his crew formed in two ranks, shields hefted and ready to charge. Two enemy ships drifted into the Northumbrian riverbank, their prows close to where the Seaworm bobbed gently on the river. Orm Eysteinsson leapt from his ship and landed gently on the grass. He sniffed the air like a wolf and waved his blade to encourage his men to come ashore.

"Wait," Hundr whispered. He wanted more of them ashore so that his charge could have more impact.

Warriors slipped from the enemy ships like insects, advancing slowly with their axes and spears ready. They wore leather armour over russet jerkins, trews of browns and greens bound below the knee in crisscross fashion over naalbinding leggings. Many wore warrior rings on their wrists and arms, and they looked just like Hundr's men, aside from the feral gleam in their eyes. They were grim men, dangerous men, come to slake their thirst for blood and the Crippled King's silver.

"Now!" Hundr shouted, ripping the Ulfberht sword from her scabbard. His men responded with a roar, and as one, they charged at their adversaries. The enemy stared at the charging warriors with gaping mouths and eyes aghast. They paused for five heartbeats, stunned that men whom they thought had fled from their blades now suddenly charged them like demons from the forest.

Hundr ignored the pain in his leg and back. The chance to strike at an enemy who came to kill him imbued him with strength, and a bald-headed man with a broken nose died as Hundr drove the point of the Ulfberht sword into his guts, thrusting the man backwards into his own men. Hundr's shield wall crashed into the unprepared enemy with a crunch like snapping timber. He cut and slashed at enemies who stumbled back from his fury. Men slipped and toppled into the river, and others tried to clamber back onto the safety of their ships. Yazi loosed arrows into their backs, and the Seaworm crew howled with delight as their axes and spears hacked and stabbed at their foes.

For a few precious minutes, Hundr and his men were lords of war. Hundr cut three men down with stabs of his sword and opened the throat of another with the Ulfberht's edge. The thrill of battle surged through Hundr's veins, and when the horn blew in the woods behind him, he had to tear himself away from the enemy.

"Fall back!" he ordered. His men howled like dogs at the frustration of breaking off the fight when their enemies died before them. On the riverbank, a fresh line of hardened warriors, towering figures with shields and axes, had formed – a force far greater than Hundr's thirty. The third ship touched prow to earth and spat her deadly crew ashore to join the rest so that Hundr's men were overwhelmingly outnumbered.

Hundr's warriors retreated with their faces towards the enemy, blades soaked with dark blood. Behind them lay half an enemy crew, slain, and the riverbank was strewn with the wounded, their agonised wails piercing the air. Hundr nodded his head in satisfaction, believing the quick assault would have the desired effect. But then a smell of burning drifted across the wild grasses, and a hand gripped Hundr's shoulder as he slid the Ulfberht sword into her scabbard.

"Odin save us. No," said Sigvarth in a shaky voice.

Hundr's stomach plummeted like a stone sinking into the darkest depths. Orm Eysteinsson stood tall on the Seaworm, a flaming brand in his hand. The firelight flickered across the sharp angles of his face, casting him in a devilish glow. Around him, men scrambled to and fro, their arms laden with twigs and kindling. Orm's lips curled into a wolfish grin – feral, cruel, brimming with malice. His two eyes, full of burning wrath, locked onto Hundr's single, unblinking gaze. Then, with deliberate malice, the son of Eystein Longaxe let the flaming torch fall onto the Seaworm's deck.

"No!" Hundr cried as flames licked about the kindling, and an orange glow grew beneath the darkening sky. The warship Seaworm was as precious to Hundr as anything on Midgard. He loved every timber of that ship, and he could not watch Orm burn the beloved *drakkar* before his eye. Einar would never forgive him, and Hundr would never forgive himself if their beautiful dragon ship burned to ashes beside an unknown Northumbrian River. A ship was impossibly valuable. Owning a ship such as the Seaworm made a man wealthy. It opened up the possibility of raiding, trading, slaving, and binding a crew of his warriors to his name. One did not burn a warship. Hundr had expected Orm to capture the Seaworm and sail her back to Mann as his prize. It would make him wealthy and famous. He could boast that he had taken the ship from The Man with the Dog's Name and Einar the Brawler, for all men knew of the Champion of the North and the ship that bore him.

"We don't have the men to stop him," said

Sigvarth, laying a heavy hand on Hundr's shoulder.

Hundr's anger overcame him. It swamped him like water over a drowning man. He would rather die than see the Seaworm burn. So Hundr did the only thing he could do. He charged. Hundr exploded from the cover of the trees at full sprint, the pain of his wounds forgotten as fury fuelled his strength. The Ulfberht sword remained sheathed at his waist, impossible to draw while running, so he reached over his shoulder and drew Battle Fang instead. A warrior charged at him from the enemy lines and died with a white feathered arrow in his chest. Only Yazi could shoot a bow with such deadly accuracy. In an instant, another man in Hundr's path twisted away as an arrow slammed into his stomach.

Hundr dashed towards the Seaworm. The roar of the enemy about him paled as blood rushed in his ears. He had to save his ship – the *drakkar* that had once belonged to Einar, the ship where Hundr's adventures had first begun. A burly warrior lunged at him with a spear, but Hundr slipped past the thrust, slicing Battle Fang across the man's face in a brutal backhand cut. Ahead, three warriors locked their shields into a wall of linden wood, iron, and muscle, barring his way to the Seaworm. An arrow struck the shield of the man on the left, and Hundr readied himself to charge. Amidst the flames, Orm's laughter rang out like he was the trickster god himself, and Hundr bellowed with visceral rage. An axe whistled over Hundr's shoulder, thrown from behind him, and the bearded blade slapped into the centremost enemy warrior like a cleaver cutting meat. The man quivered and fell, his comrades staring at the gruesome wound in shock.

The Crow darted past Hundr like a racing hound in a blur of speed and leapt upon the rightmost warrior, cutting and hacking with his wickedly curved blades so that all Hundr had to do to reach the ship was jump past the former pit fighter's furious assault.

Yazi peppered the leftmost warrior's shield with arrows, the man crouching behind it as the shafts hammered into the wood like the pounding of hooves. Hundr ignored him and took a great stride, using the shield as a step to propel him up onto the Seaworm's deck. He landed in a crouch and rose to parry an axe strike aimed at his head. Hundr turned the parry into a cut and opened the enemy warrior's bowels. The axe man flailed and gurgled, desperately clutching his spilling entrails, and Hundr spun around him as more of Orm's men came to the attack.

"He's mine!" Orm shouted, the sound of his voice like the roar of a winter storm. Orm

Eysteinsson leapt from the mast and landed behind his dying man. With his eyes fixed on Hundr, he lowered the dying man gently to the deck and whispered softly into his ear. Hundr's eye flicked from Orm to the flames licking at the Seaworm's timbers. He wanted to drop his sword and hurl the burning faggots overboard, but the moment he moved to douse the fire, Orm would strike and hack him to pieces. Slowly and carefully, Orm stood. He reached over his shoulder and pulled a second sword from a scabbard strapped to his back.

"Long have I waited for this moment," Orm said, his voice low and barely audible over the crackle of flames. Hundr's warriors burst from the forest, hurrying to their lord's aid. Hundr regretted his wild charge, realising too late that the men from the third ship had come ashore. They were bare-chested, capering like fools with froth in their beards, howling at the sky as though touched by *seiðr* madness. Orm's eyes never left Hundr, even as his blood-mad berserkers charged at Hundr's outnumbered warriors.

"Take me, and let them live," Hundr insisted, suddenly horrified that his attempt to save the Seaworm could cost his men their lives. For years, he had fought beside them, sailed with them, and bled with them in the fighting pits. His brothers-in-arms were worth much more to

Hundr than a ship.

"Too late for that now, turd. Your men are as dead as you are. They made their choice when they swore an oath to serve a nithing killer."

"It's me you want. My men are warriors all, and many of your fighters will die to kill my thirty. Give me your word, and I'll order them to throw down their weapons."

"That would be simple, wouldn't it?" Orm raised his two swords out wide and took a deep breath as though he savoured the moment. "My name is Orm Eysteinsson. You killed my father, Eystein Longaxe. I am going to kill you, dog. I curse you to Nástrǫnd so that your soul will not see Valhalla. Then, I will hunt your son and kill him, too, so that I wipe your stinking seed from Midgard forever."

Hundr tossed Battle Fang from his right hand to his left, reaching the Ulfberht's hilt with his freed hand. Before his fingers closed around the weapon, Orm sprang forward, moving faster than Hundr thought possible. He kicked Hundr's hand with such power that it crushed against his sword belt and cast him down to the Seaworm's deck.

"When you killed my father, I was left alone. Men came to take his woman and steal his treasure. When those men came, I fled like a mongrel, crawling through the dirt. I was forced to live like a beggar, eating from midden heaps like an animal. But always in my heart, I burned with the fire of vengeance. I whispered your name every night before sleep, and even now, I still do. I rose from nothing and learned to fight with two swords, just like you. I sought the greatest weapon masters and learned until I could learn no more. I became a sea jarl, just like you, and when I heard the call of the Crippled King, I brought my men and my ships to crush you."

The battle raged on the riverbank, and fire spread across the Seaworm, consuming the clinker-built timbers like a hungry Loki beast. Hundr tried to stand quickly, but the arrow wound in his leg screamed, and his thigh gave way. Orm snarled and slashed his sword down with savage power. Hundr barely managed to throw himself backwards, evading the strike by a hair's breadth. He tried to draw the Ulfberht again, but Orm's blades came at him with relentless speed and power. Hundr parried some with Battle Fang and rolled and swerved away from others. The fire had now taken root, roaring behind Orm like the hearth fires of Valhalla. Orm was fast, and it struck Hundr that it was like fighting a younger version of himself, only stronger. Orm's muscles rippled under his skin like coiled serpents, with every strike more potent than the last. Hundr retreated towards the prow, each block a desperate swing as he struggled to keep his footing.

With each blow, Hundr's body weakened. He still couldn't free the Ulfberht, the arrow wound sapping what remained of his energy. He raised Battle Fang to block another brutal overhead strike, but Orm's sword crashed down, biting into Hundr's left hand. His fingers flew to the deck in a spray of blood, and Battle Fang clattered from his grasp. Hundr stared in devastated horror at his mutilated hand, a hand which would never hold a sword again.

Hundr toppled backwards. Death came for him in a mirror image of himself, a savage warrior born of Hundr's own lust for reputation who fought just as he fought. Worse still, Hundr had no blade in his hand. Orm's face twisted, features stretched by euphoria and firelight as he moved to strike the killing blow. A figure dropped between them, a hooded man wielding two curved knives. The Crow. He blocked Orm's strike and forced the towering, muscled warrior back. As they clashed, The Crow's hood fell, and the inky black curtains of his hair tumbled over his scarred and tattooed face.

"Go!" The Crow yelled in his strange accent. Orm's swords flashed like lightning bolts, and the Crow moved with him, the two warriors shifting together like dancers. But then, with a sudden, savage swing, Orm brought one blade crashing down. The Crow's knife trembled beneath the force and shattered, Orm's sword tearing through his forearm. The Crow turned to Hundr, his face eerily calm, a flicker of what might have been a smile twisting his tortured mouth. "I owe you my life. I'll see you again, brother, in the next life. Now run."

Hundr wanted to scream, charge in, and help The Crow fight Orm and his relentless speed. The Ulfberht sword still rested in her scabbard, though the blade yearned to join the fray. But Hundr's left hand was ruined, and his wounds left him weak and unable to fight. All Hundr had was the desire to live. He had to live. To heal, return, and kill Orm Eysteinsson. So he howled his sorrow at the heavens and turned to run. Behind him, blades clashed, and battle raged. He did not see The Crow die, but before he leapt over the side, Hundr hurled himself at the Seaworm's prow. He tore the beast head from its fitting and jumped into the sea, holding the wooden dragon as close as a lover. The frigid water hit him, the cold a brutal shock, and then darkness took him.

ELEVEN

Einar brooded in his hall. Stewards tiptoed around him, placing platters of steaming pork on the table beside cuts of cheese, freshly baked loaves, honey, and a jug of frothing ale. He glowered at the hearth fire, which burned with only the smallest flame because early summer had descended upon Vanylven.

"Eat something," urged Hildr, sitting gracefully on the bench next to him. "You haven't eaten properly since you returned."

"It's been a week, and still nothing. Every day, I walk to the fjord and stare out at the water, hoping to see the Seaworm, but all I see are fishing boats and birds," said Einar. He sighed, took his eating knife from his belt and poked at the meat.

"Hundr has gone missing before. He always turns up in the end."

"He isn't a coin with a Saxon king's ugly head on one side or a set of winter gloves. He is the Champion of the North. The last time he went missing, he ended up in an Odin-forsaken fighting pit. It's like he has a curse, as though it amuses the gods to cast him into danger and watch him fight his way out. I shouldn't have left the Seaworm."

"But you were left with little choice, my love."

"There is always a choice. I could have returned to search for the Seaworm. But the men bleated about the size of Finn's fleet, the danger of capture or death and the need to return home to Vanylven. I listened to those faint hearts, and since the day we sailed north, I have thought of nothing else."

"Their advice was sound, and you know it."

Einar slammed his eating knife into the tabletop and left it quivering. "Of course I know it. I said the same thing to Hundr before he went alone to kill Finn."

"Perhaps you should have stopped him?"

"Stopped him?" Einar nearly fell off his chair. "Have you been drinking the strong stuff today? When has anyone ever stopped Hundr from doing anything?"

"Men would say the same thing about you, and yet…"

"You stopping me from doing foolish things is different. Hundr doesn't have a wife. He only has me. Wives can exert control over a man. It's not the same thing."

"Control, is it?" Hildr sat back and crossed her arms, a wry smile creasing her face.

"You have your ways and means, woman, and you know it. Let's just leave it at that." Einar couldn't help but return her smile. It was a welcome relief from his anguish.

Hildr rested her hand on Einar's forearm. "What if he does not come back? What if Hundr has met his doom?"

"I won't believe he is dead until I see his corpse with my own eyes or have an oath on it from a man who witnessed his death."

"So, your plan is to wait here, staring out at the water forever?"

"No. My plan is to get the fleet scraped and provisioned and return to Mann before the moon waxes."

"Men!" Hildr tutted as she shook her head and balled her fists.

"What's that supposed to mean?"

"You would charge off with four ships to search for a man who could be dead and sail right into Finn's fleet and army? Isn't that the same situation from which you decided it was impossible to succeed?"

"I must do something, Hildr. I can't just leave Hundr to his fate. Finn hates him with a fury bright enough to dim the sun. If Finn catches him, then the tortures Hundr would endure are beyond thinking about." A heavy silence settled between them, both recalling the dreadful imprisonment and unspeakable cruelty Einar had suffered at the hands of Finn and his mother some years before.

"Hard to see anything of the boy we knew in the man he has become," Hildr finally spoke softly and bowed her head.

"Sometimes I think it's easier to believe that the Finn we knew died years ago. That he died fighting in Ireland when we fought against Saoirse."

"Most of him did. Or the best part of him, at least. Finn was lost to us once his mother got her claws into him. All that he could have been, the good life he could have led, perished in the wake of her lust for vengeance."

"Maybe the hate was always inside him. Festering, growing. Still, though, we had some good times with the lad."

Hildr looked up at Einar and smiled again. Her eyes gleamed, wet at the rims, as her lips quivered. "I loved that boy. His laughter, the warmth of his skin, his curls. He was a joy. And yet it was me who shot him with an arrow. There are nights when I cannot get the memory of that feeling out of my head… of hurting a person I had raised from boyhood. How can a mother do such a thing?"

"The circumstances demanded it. If you hadn't stopped him with your arrow, Hundr would have killed him. I shouldn't even think, never mind give voice to such things, but Finn should have died that day."

"What did we do to offend the gods so that they have denied us a child of our own? We sit here talking of the boy we raised as though he is a monster. Perhaps the mistake was ours?"

"We gave that boy everything a lad could want. He learned to fight, fish, sail, ride, and wrestle. We did what we could, but he was the son of Ivar the Boneless. He has cruel, vicious warrior's blood pulsing in his veins. Becoming a warrior was always his fate, but we had hoped he would grow into one of honour, a fine warrior who upheld *drengskapr*, like Hundr's son, Hermoth. Instead, vengeance and hate turned Finn inside out, and now he is a Loki-worshipping thing of black deeds and evil. What part we played in that, Odin only knows."

Einar took a sup of ale, and memories flooded

his thought cage. He recalled the day he and Sten Sleggya had captured the boy in England. They had taken Finn from his uncle, Halvdan Ragnarsson, at his mother's request, believing it was the only way to keep him safe. She had feared that Halvdan, seeking the throne of Dublin for himself, would kill Finn, the rightful heir. In those days, Einar and Hundr had tried to help Saoirse, before she turned on them.

Einar wondered now whether it might have been better for Finn if he had left him with Halvdan. Yet he couldn't bring himself to say that to Hildr, fearing it would only weigh on her conscience and stir darker thoughts of what might have been.

"As for the will of the gods, who can say? We do our best to follow the ways of *drengskapr*, heeding the gods and their signs. Yet our greatest desire was denied us. A whore and a brigand can whelp as many children as they wish and bring them up in the most desperate and torturous conditions. What a life we would have given our child, Hildr."

"It was not our fate." A tear rolled down her cheek, and Einar wiped it away with his thumb.

He swallowed the lump in his throat and paused for a moment to let those thoughts drift away, dreams evaporating like clouds on a summer day where rain turns swiftly to sunshine. "The older I get, the more I believe that vengeance is a curse inflicted upon the world by Loki. It spurs men on to fell deeds and kills warriors young. Ivar burned with the desire for vengeance after Hundr killed his son Hakon. That led to Ivar's death. Saoirse and Finn both became consumed with that same quest for revenge. Rollo the Betrayer brought fire and blood to Vanylven in his thirst for vengeance. We, too, have killed for revenge. A man we captured told of Finn's new champion, a man named Orm, who is the son of Eystein Longaxe."

A shiver ran across Hildr's shoulders. "I remember Eystein. He was a fearsome man. This Orm, too, seeks vengeance, then. It is a cycle that will never end. One killing begets another. There will be no end to war and death. But then Odin is a god of war; he is the betrayer of warriors and the god of battle. What would our world be without war? Would we all be farmers and merchants? Who would rule? There would be no need for warriors in that world. But such talk has no point. We live in Midgard, and as long as there are gods and men, there will be war, vengeance, axes, death, rape, slaves, and suffering. All we can do is fight for our own place in that world. Which is what we have built at Vanylven."

"Everything you say is true, and the folly of sailing back to Mann with four ships is plain enough. But I must go, Hildr. I must leave this home we have built for ourselves, which we won by our axes and our daring. Even if it means my death, I must look for Hundr."

Hildr stared into his eyes, her jaw set firm when she saw the determination and steel in the look he gave her. "Very well, husband. But what if there was another way, a way where we don't go back with just four ships? What if we sail to Mann with an army?"

Einar stood and walked around the table. He knew where she was going, and Einar had to walk to keep his temper. "I will not crawl to Avaldsnes and beg King Harald for men, Hildr. We can't run to Harald every time we come up against a powerful foe."

"We don't need to beg. This was Harald Fairhair's war. It was his daughter captured by the Crippled King and Vigfus Hjorthrimul. We fought at the king's bidding, so he has skin in this game, Einar. Rognvald will understand. He is our ally and the king's most powerful advisor and friend."

"Pah!" huffed Einar, waving a hand in annoyance. "Even if we sailed to Avaldsnes, and the king agreed to send a few crews, it won't be enough. Finn has gathered an army. His slave markets are the largest in Midgard. Any slaves captured in England, Ireland, or the lands of the Scots are sold there. Men flock to his markets from as far south as Ispania and as far east as Miklagard. The folk in the south and east pay handsomely for blue-eyed girls with milk-white skin. And you don't want to know about the children sold in those places. Finn is as rich in silver as Odin is in wisdom, and he has bought himself an army. He could have thirty warships or more. That's two or three thousand warriors. He has enough silver to pay them and buy food to keep them. Harald will not send his entire army west to kill the Crippled King. Mann is miles away from Norway, and the king's forces are still recovering from last year's war. Harald nearly died fighting Vigfus. His great ship, the Ormrinn Langi, was captured and only recovered at the Battle of the Bardarborg. He will not take such a risk again."

"And yet Harald must have vengeance upon the man behind his daughter's capture. That man was Finn Ivarsson, and all know it. The king's daughter married Vigfus. She is dishonoured. What prince or lord would want to marry her now? As we said, vengeance makes the world go round. Harald will fight."

"Very well. For argument's sake, let's say Harald grants us three ships and crews. That's only two hundred more warriors to add to our three hundred. It's not enough."

"I left the Valkyrie temple at Upsala with Ragnhild many years ago to fight alongside the sons of Ragnar. That was the high priest's order and the will of Odin. I met you during that war, and I thank the Norns for that blessing in the weave of my life every day. In our time together, we have sailed across the Whale Road, far and wide. We have fought many battles and made many friends. Now, it is time to call upon those friends and allies to come to our aid. How many warlords and warriors are there in Midgard who owe their lives to you and Hundr?"

The oars of Einar's mind began to row. He took a loaf from the table and bit off a chunk, chewing slowly as he considered Hildr's plan. "We would have to sail far and wide, visit many ports and talk to dangerous men."

"And women. For after we visit Avaldsnes, we shall sail to Upsala and the Valkyrie temple. The high priestess would know of Ragnhild's death, and the order owes us a favour. We were the ones who sought Odin's Gungnir spear when it was stolen from Upsala, and we returned the gods' weapon to their care. My old sisters will join our fight."

"You say *we*, as though you mean to come along?" Einar swallowed his bread and frowned at his wife.

Hildr nodded, her face set and sure. She stood from the table, walked calmly to the corner of the hall, and removed a fur blanket from an old oak chest riveted with black iron. She lifted the lid, its leather hinges creaking, and Hildr lifted out her old Valkyrie *brynjar*, her eastern recurved bow and a quiver full of arrows. "I will sail with you this time. If Hundr is dead, then perhaps we shall find our destiny together in the halls of Valhalla."

"Thor's balls... there cannot be another woman like you in all of Midgard." Einar beamed at her, pride swelling in his chest. They were both old, heads full of grey hair and faces wrinkled with age, but Hildr had once been a fierce warrior, and if Einar was going to die in battle, he would be proud to die by her side.

"I will talk to the Valkyrie order, and they will help us."

"After that, we sail to the lands of the Svears and to Bjorn Ironside. Refil, his son, and I were imprisoned together in Ireland. Refil, his brother Eric and Bjorn might support our quest once they know we are sailing to find The Man with the Dog's Name."

"And what of Haesten, the wily old fox of the Whale Road? Has any word of him come through Vanylven lately?"

Einar's mouth turned down, and he nodded respectfully upon hearing the name of the old war dog Haesten. "Not that I have heard, but we shall ask. Haesten would make a formidable ally.

Crews will flock to join us once they hear an army sails with Bjorn Ironside, a son of Ragnar Lothbrok and one of the greatest heroes of our age – alongside Valkyrie warrior priestesses, King Harald Fairhair, and Haesten. Haesten who sacked Paris and sailed with Bjorn further south than any man had dared to before. It shall be an army for the ages, a warrior's dream, fodder for bards for generations to come."

"So you think it's a good idea, then?" Hildr said, and she laughed as Einar swept her up into his arms.

"You aren't just a pretty face, my love."

"I have my moments."

"You also have a rump worth dying for and…"

"Einar!" Hildr punched him on the shoulder, and they laughed together. Einar kissed her, and they embraced. The skin of her cheeks was soft against his beard and the cliff of his broken nose and sharp cheekbones. They pulled apart, and Hildr caressed the scars upon his face. Einar stared deep into her pale blue eyes. He thanked the gods for his luck in having the love of such a fine woman.

"You are as wise as you are beautiful. So we shall sail the Whale Road together once more, my love?"

"We shall. And let our enemies tremble when

they hear of our coming. The Finn we knew is dead. The man we fight is the Crippled King with his twisted Loki worshippers. We'll find Hundr, dead or alive. And if he is dead, then his killers shall feel a wrath so fierce that they'll believe Surtr the fire giant has risen against them."

Hildr had kindled hope in Einar's heart. With renewed purpose, he strode from the hall, his voice booming as he commanded his men to hasten their preparations. The ships were to be scraped, caulked, and ready to sail within a week. He ordered his warriors to sharpen their axes and polish their mail, for war was on the horizon. Einar gathered the folk of Vanylven, telling them what must be done. Provisions were needed – smoked meat, dried fish, freshly brewed ale, and oatcake – enough to sustain his warriors on a long and perilous voyage. He told his warriors of the army they would build, and their fear of Hundr's demise transformed into the thrill of war. This would not just be a raid or a fight with some two-ship jarl. This was to be a war of champions, a fleet of heroes most men had only heard tell of at firesides on dark winter nights.

All Einar had to do was persuade two kings, Odin's holy order of warrior priestesses, and the greatest raiding jarl of their age to join their forces with his. It had all seemed so simple when Hildr had proposed the expedition, but as Einar coiled rope, sharpened his weapons and made ready, he realised the enormity of the task before him. Men like Harald, Bjorn, and Haesten were not easily talked around. They were wealthy men in the winter of their lives, enjoying their hard-won glory. All Einar had was his and Hundr's reputation and hope that the greatest warriors in Midgard remembered what Hundr had risked for them, how he had bled and suffered for their causes. It was a dream, Hildr's idea, that they could build an army worthy of fighting Odin's Einherjar itself. Einar hoped that dream would come to pass, for his friend was out there somewhere, and Einar would not leave Hundr in the hands of his hate-twisted enemies.

TWELVE

Hundr lay on his back, staring at the sunrise with one arm around the Seaworm's dragon prow. The paint had cracked and peeled from the timber, but the wood was smooth beneath his rough fingers. The rest of his men, the mere eight who had survived the fight with Orm Eysteinsson, lay asleep. Hundr had not slept since Thatchulf and Sigvarth had pulled him from the river, still clutching the prow beast he had taken from the Seaworm. The beloved ship was gone now, along with most of Hundr's men, three fingers of his left hand, and Battle Fang. It had been over a week since the fight beside the river, or so he thought. The days and nights blurred into one. Fever and waking nightmares plagued him, faces of the twenty-two dead men, once sworn to him, gone to the afterlife because of his inability to lead them to safety. Hundr refused to let anyone touch his wounded hand.

The stumps of his fingers festered, as had the arrow wounds in his leg and back. The gash on his skull was now a scabbed crust, and he lay on the coarse grass and wondered why Odin had forsaken him.

They had spent the night sleeping in the open, huddled in the lee of an arching crag a week's slow march southeast of the river where they had fought Orm. The land around Hundr wakened in a gentle, golden glow in contrast to the black, icy fist which enveloped his heart. The sky shifted from the colour of a sapphire to a lavender hue. To the east, shades of pink and orange heralded the sun's arrival, the beginning of the sun god Sol's race across the skies pursued by a ravenous wolf. The last few stars twinkled faintly in the pre-dawn sky and faded as the sun's light chased them away. A few wisps of cloud, like the breath of a god, delicate and tinged with gold, stretched across the sky, and a morning wind chilled Hundr's flesh. He had sold his *brynjar* and arm rings two days ago. It had been an enormous sum to pay for a few loaves of gritty bread, a haunch of lamb and four skins of ale. Sigvarth had wanted to kill the farmer and take whatever supplies they chose, but Hundr had refused. They were nine desperate men who did not need to incite the wrath of the local lord by killing one of his churls. Hundr had marched in only his boots and trews since that day, letting the harsh rain, wind, and occasional bursts of sun whip and burn his flesh as penance for his failures.

The warm light of the rising sun fought with the wind to bathe the rolling hills and sweeping valleys beneath Hundr in a wan golden glow, casting long shadows from crooked trees and white rocks. The surrounding land was a patchwork of lush green meadows and fields, bordered by dry stone walls that crisscrossed the terrain and marked the boundaries between one portion of land and the next. Heather-covered moorlands shone with morning dew and took on a soft, silvery sheen whilst the wild grasses swayed gently in the cool morning breeze.

Hundr tore his eye away from the sky and looked instead at the mangled remnants of his left hand. The stumps of his missing fingers were scabbed and leaking pus. They ached like no pain Hundr had felt in his life, not since Hakon Ivarsson had taken his eye with a red-hot knife. Orm had been so fast, so strong. Hundr was shaken. He had lost Battle Fang, the blade gifted to him by an old warrior jarl, a sword that had brought luck and fame. Hundr had prided himself on his ability to fight with two swords, a rare skill that gave him an advantage in battle. Yet now, his ruined hand would never hold a sword again. Hundr felt hollow, just as he had when Sigrid and Sigurd had died, as though something of himself had perished in his defeat by Orm on board the burning Seaworm.

The nine survivors had camped on high ground overlooking a sweeping valley leading down from the lofty mountain peaks that halved Northumbria like a monster's skeletal spine. After they had saved Hundr from the river, it had been a desperate flight eastwards away from the men Orm sent in pursuit. Twelve of Hundr's men began that flight, and three had died on the road before they had lost Orm's men in a desperate dash through a rain-soaked night that Hundr could not remember. Yazi told him that Thatchulf and Sigvarth had carried him on their backs, taking turns with his weight, and throughout it all, Hundr had refused to leave the dragon prow behind. He kept it close, holding it to himself like he had once held Sigrid. If one part of the Seaworm lived, then perhaps the spirit of the *drakkar* did, too.

Copses of oak, ash, and hawthorn littered the slopes, standing tall and sturdy, their leaves a vibrant green, rustling quietly as the wind whispered through their boughs. Bluebells, foxgloves, and buttercups splashed colour between the mountainous rocks. Hundr could smell damp soil and wildflowers amongst the stench of his own blood and sweat. Blackbirds, skylarks, and curlews heralded the new day with melodious song, their voices echoing around the valley. Hundr listened closely, hoping to hear the caw of a raven, one of Hugin or Munin, the two ravens Odin sent out into the world to report to him of the goings on in Midgard. But he heard no raven calls. A sheep bleated somewhere out of sight, and cattle lowed. Farms lay close by, which meant food and ale, but also people who would report their presence to their lord and alert the local warriors that ragged fighters stalked their lands.

"I swear a fox or a badger bit me in the night, grumbled Eyolfr, sitting up. He lifted his jerkin to check his side.

"You haven't been bitten since that whore's tavern in Frankia a few years back," quipped Gunnulfr, a sturdy warrior who wore his beard in two long braids.

"And I paid good silver for that. The only price to be paid here is a wet arse and an empty belly."

The rest of the waking warriors chuckled except for Yazi, who took up his bow and quiver and went to check on Hundr's wounds.

"I must help you today," Yazi said in his broken Norse. "If you let it get worse, you'll lose your whole hand, perhaps."

Hundr stared at his wounds and shook his head. "We keep pushing southeast. It can only be a few more days to Jorvik from here."

"I'm sorry to say it again, my lord," said Toki, "but I still think we should loop back westwards towards the coast. Einar and the lads might be looking for us. We don't know what awaits us in Jorvik. I know it's inside the Danelaw, but there has been no king there since Halvdan Ragnarsson. Many have taken control of the city and even dared to call themselves king, but few have lasted more than a year before some other ambitious Viking took it from them, usually with an axe to the skull. It's a shit pit of wicked folk. A man can take anything he wants in Northumbria – land, silver, women. All he has to do is snatch it from someone else. Every farm has a palisade and men to guard it; every valley is owned by a warlord with a hearth troop of a dozen hardened warriors. My cousin Hrafn came here, won a vast estate for himself, and was back home two years later with nothing to show for his troubles but a missing right arm and his tongue cut out."

"We go east," Hundr ordered. He would say no more. Something tugged at him, drawing him towards the old city of Jorvik, though he wasn't quite sure what. He had landed close to where they had fought Orm when Hundr had arrived in England years ago to fight for the sons of Ragnar Lothbrok. That war had led Hundr to the walls of Jorvik and his first great battle. He hoped the Norns and Odin urged him to that city of the Rome folk because it would bring him luck, but he could not say that to his men. They were already half-starved and downcast at the loss of so many friends and sword brothers. Hundr hoped to find something of his old self in Jorvik, a desire to be a champion and a hunger for reputation. If he was going to fight Orm, he would have to do it without two swords. It was all he could think about. Orm had bested him easily. He was bigger, faster, stronger. Hundr had to face him and defeat him, or else lose himself to madness.

"I like the idea of Jorvik," said Sigvarth. He stood and stretched his back, coughed up a gobbet of phlegm and stared out at the valley below. "We haven't seen them, but we can be sure Orm's men are following us. Ever since King Alfred and Guthrum made their peace and Alfred granted everything above Watling Street to the Danes and Norsemen, the north of England has almost been like a new Denmark or Norway. It is full of our people and brimming with battle and chaos. We can easily slip into that chaos. Are we not each of us children of the storm? We are warriors, sailors, fighters, and Vikings. There are nine of us, and nine is a good number for our people. Odin's stallion, Sleipnir, has nine legs. Odin hung himself from a tree for nine days to gain wisdom. Nine worlds spread from the branches of the world tree Yggdrasil. We are down on our luck. That's true enough. But we have the strength to change that. We have axes and swords, no shields, but our blades should be enough for us to lose ourselves in these wild lands until we can get back to Vanylven."

Harbard stood and joined Sigvarth, tucking his thumbs into his thick leather belt and puffing out his chest. He had small, flinty eyes set in a dark, wind-burned face. He wore his hair in a braided topknot with the back and sides of his head shaved bald. "To Jorvik. Kill some bastards and take what we need. Get back to Vanylven and return to strike at Orm and the Crippled King with full hearts and stout warriors at our backs. I like this plan."

Hundr rose and bit his lip to stop a whimper from escaping his mouth. His thigh screamed at him to stop and rest, and his hand and back burned like fire. But there could be no rest, not whilst the Crippled King and Orm lived. Hundr bent and picked up the Seaworm's prow dragon and put it on his back. He wrapped his sword belt around it, and Thatchulf fastened the buckle for him, though he frowned and shook his head at the burden Hundr insisted on carrying despite his suffering. Hundr set off down the valley; his shoulder and back muscles ached, and his legs wobbled, but he gritted his teeth and ignored the pain.

One foot in front of the other. Head southeast to

Jorvik. Live. Survive and rise to fight again. Finn must die. Orm must die.

Hundr repeated the mantra to himself as the heavy timber prow scraped the skin from his back, and his wounds threatened to turn his mind over into madness.

They kept a steady heading southeast, and the land fell gradually into a vast, flat expanse of country. Hundr's pace slowed, and he lagged behind the group as they strode ahead. He shuffled, back bent under his load, tottering and veering from side to side. The land here was much more difficult to manage than the mountains and forests behind them. There, the terrain had been firm, with cliffs and trees to hide them from any on their trail. They had entered a pathless wilderness at the roots of the high places. Soon, they would find settlements, farms and people. But here, there was nothing, with few signs of animals or birds, as the mountains turned to flatlands. The ground beneath Hundr's boots became damp and, in places, boggy. The nine splashed through shallow puddles and avoided deeper-looking pools of foul, stagnant water. Great stretches of reeds and rushes emerged as the morning went on, and the warbling of small birds hidden beneath them filled Hundr's ears. There was no obvious trail to follow, and the men cursed as they plodded through the shifting quagmires.

Swarms of flies tormented them, tiny fiends buzzing in relentless clouds, and Sigvarth roared in frustration as he chased a horde of them from around his head.

Hundr lost his footing and fell face-first into a muddy puddle. His good hand squelched in the filth, but it was not strong enough to support his body and the prow, and Hundr's face mashed into the mud. He came up gasping and rolled onto his side.

"Let me help you, my lord," said Thatchulf. He hurried towards Hundr, but Hundr held his good hand up in warning.

"No," he insisted. "This is my burden and mine alone." Hundr had to make this journey himself, including the penance of carrying the dragon prow. He was wounded and delirious, weakened, and defeated. But he still had his warrior's heart and would carry the last remnant of the Seaworm back to Einar. With luck, he would find a new *drakkar* to place the Seaworm head upon. Hundr tried to rise, but his feet slipped again in the mud. He pushed down with his hand and rose halfway, but the arm buckled, sending his head slopping back into the filth. Sigvarth, Harbard, and the rest of the warriors turned away, unable to look at their lord whilst he slipped and struggled like a pig. Eventually, Hundr dragged himself to his knees and stood, though each step was a battle. The day passed in a blur, and Hundr fell more times than he could count. Their camp that night was damp, cold, and uncomfortable, and the insects prevented the men from sleeping. Creatures haunted the reeds and hillocks, creaking and clicking, tormenting the warriors in the darkness.

Hundr slept fitfully, tossing and turning until the early hours when exhaustion finally claimed him. But his sleep was fevered, and he awoke drenched in sweat, his body burning as if he'd waged a battle in his dreams. His teeth chattered, and his stomach was sour. As he tried to rise, his legs gave way beneath him, and he stumbled, reaching for the prow beast.

"Leave the thing, my lord," pleaded Sigvarth, kneeling beside Hundr and offering his hand. "Let Yazi treat your wounds."

"No," Hundr growled, though he could not hold Sigvarth's gaze.

"Another day, and you'll lose that hand. Perhaps your leg as well. What good will you be, then?"

"Quiet, Sigvarth."

"How will you fight our enemies if you have no hand or leg to do it? You might even die here in this foul place. Is that to be the end of Hundr, The Man with the Dog's Name, Champion of the North? Dead in a swamp from the wound fever, denied Valhalla? Odin's Einherjar will be the poorer for the lack of your blade."

"You go too far!" Hundr seethed with anger that his oath-sworn warrior would talk to him so – not just an oathman but a friend.

"Perhaps not far enough. The Crippled King wins if you let yourself die in this place. I love you, my lord; we all do. You are our leader and our champion, and we are proud to fight beneath the banner of the one eye, honoured to say we fight beside The Man with the Dog's Name. But we have lost good friends, shipmates – men we have spilt blood beside. They perished in the battle at the river, and if you die, then Orm Eysteinsson has truly bested you. You must live, Lord Hundr. You must fight. For us, if not for yourself."

Hundr struggled in the slop, but he hauled himself to standing and once again took the prow beast burden upon his back. He winced as the heavy wood rested against the open sores caused by days of rubbing and banging against his flesh. That day, they left the last of the pools and mire, and the land began to rise steadily again. Away in the distance, Hundr could see a line of hills, jagged like wolf teeth. Yazi loped ahead of the marching warriors and returned in the late afternoon with a brace of rabbits and three birds. They made camp that night beside a huddle of elm trees set in a deep defile, and they lit a fire, risking its glow because the tree and the low ground would hide them from any pursuing force. The fire warmed their spirits, and the warriors shared a laugh as they ate the meat from Yazi's catch.

Hundr sat alone and watched the flames. In the dancing flickers of yellow and gold, he saw Loki laughing at him, taunting him as if he were Odin's pet, and the trickster god had struck a victorious blow against the father of the Aesir on the day Orm defeated him. The fire crackled, and with it, something changed within Hundr. Sigvarth's hard words had milled about his mind all day, and now that Loki himself taunted him, something stirred in Hundr's heart. Sigvarth was right. If he was to rise and strike back at his enemies, he would need what remained of his hand and his leg. He would need to become something new. He might not fight with two swords anymore, but he could fight with one better than any man alive. Hundr realised beneath the trees and before the fire that he must forge himself anew in the flames of his rage. He had to practise and learn just as he had when he was a boy in far Novgorod. Hundr closed his eye and saw himself again as he once was, a small, shivering boy named Velmud, sleeping with the animals but spending every waking hour practising with sword, spears, axe, shield, and bow. It had to be so again. To defeat the Crippled

King and Orm Eysteinsson, Hundr realised he had to walk that road once more.

"Yazi!" he called. The Easterner looked up with fat from rabbit meat dripping into his beard.

"Yes, my lord?" he said, eyes flicking from Hundr to the rest of the men.

"It's time to heal my wounds. Time to begin anew."

Yazi grinned, and the rest of the eight warriors around the fire nodded and set their jaws firm in stoic happiness to see that their lord had emerged from the darkness of defeat. Yazi took his hunting knife and placed it in the glowing sticks and twigs in the fire's heart. He came to Hundr and washed his hand, thigh, and back carefully with water from the skin fastened to his belt.

"Once I have sealed the wounds," Yazi said, frowning at the stubs where Hundr's fingers had once been, "I must find some things to help healing. Honey and leaves. Special leaves."

Hundr nodded and sat with his back resting against the Seaworm's prow beast. "Do what you must."

Yazi washed the wounds as best he could and cut a strip of cloth from his jerkin. He mumbled about how dirty it was and took his knife from the campfire. Its blade glowed red like the morning sun before a storm, and as Yazi brought the hot blade closer, Hundr instinctively jerked away. A memory of the pain of his lost eye came back like a spike in his mind. Hakon, son of Ivar the Boneless, had burned Hundr's eye away with a blade much like the one Yazi now held. Hakon had slashed Hundr's chest and face, leaving him horribly scarred and disfigured. In that moment, the image of Hakon's cruel, sneering face came back to him, full of malice.

Ivar the Boneless had been a great warrior, both feared and revered in equal measure, but his son Hakon had been weak, consumed by bitterness over his failure to live up to his father's legend. Hundr had fought them both. Ivar's malevolence was matched only by his mastery of the sword, yet Hakon had been nothing more than a shadow of the man who had sired him. The ache behind Hundr's ruined eye had never truly faded. Whenever fear or unease crept in, the hollow where the eye had once been seemed to throb with the memory of that pain.

"Take this, my lord," said Harbard, offering Hundr a stick from which he had stripped the bark. Hundr bit down on it, the rough wood firm between his teeth.

"Ready?" Yazi asked.

Hundr steeled himself and nodded. How could a man ever be ready to have his wounded flesh burned by a red-hot blade?

The knife touched his severed fingers, and Hundr grunted, sawing his teeth into the stick to stop from crying out.

Live. Survive and rise to fight again. Finn must die. Orm must die.

Hundr repeated the words over and over in his mind, a litany against the pain. He welcomed this suffering just as he had savoured the agony of dragging the prow beast across Northumbria's wildest country. The blade pressed into his thigh, sealing the wound with fire, and the acrid stench of his own burning flesh filled the air. This was his penance. This was the tribulation he had to endure in honour of his fallen oathmen. For The Crow, whose tormented face haunted his dreams. A man who had lived in the grip of pain, a slave, a pit fighter, but also a warrior of extraordinary courage and skill. The Crow had saved Hundr's life aboard the burning Seaworm, dying a warrior's death so that Hundr might live. He would never forget that sacrifice.

Odin, do you see how I suffer? Grant me fortune, give me strength, and I will strike down the worshippers of Loki with vengeance and fury. Hear me, Odin!

THIRTEEN

Einar left Asbjorn to rule Vanylven whilst he was away, and he sailed the Wind Elk out of Vanylven's fjord with a heart buoyed by the task that lay before him. He would assemble the greatest force of Northmen since the Great Ragnarsson Army had conquered most of Saxon England. To achieve it, he was accompanied by Amundr, Hildr, Thorgrim, and sixty of Vanylven's finest warriors. Einar chose the Wind Elk in honour of Ragnhild, for she had been its shipmaster, and the Valkyrie priestess had died fighting against the Crippled King.

The journey to Avaldsnes would take three or four days, depending on the wind and the weather. It was not a treacherous journey like crossing the open sea to Orkney, where a ship could face malevolent storms and waves higher than the mightiest hall. The Wind Elk was a *drakkar*, just like the Seaworm, built for speed and endurance with a hull carved to slice through the whitecaps and a large square sail bearing Hundr's famous one-eye sigil. Einar, Thorgrim, and the crew knew the route to Avaldsnes well, for it was King Harald Fairhair's capital, and they had visited the king at his home many times. The voyage began under oars, and Thorgrim led the crew in fearsome war songs. These chants, filled with tales of battle and glorious deaths, stirred the men's spirits, fuelling their resolve as they embarked on a mission to assemble an army powerful enough to challenge the Crippled King and his mercenaries. They all knew that they did so to seek Hundr, their lord of war, and the men pulled their oars with grim determination.

Once the Wind Elk reached open water, Einar gave the order to raise oars and stow the long ash shafts in their crutches. Men hauled on seal hide rigging until the yard lifted to cross the mast post and then untied the reef lines and unfurled the sail. The sail was a patchwork of wool dyed to bear Hundr's sigil, and it filled with the summer breeze to carry the *drakkar* forwards. A favourable wind blew from the north as though Njorth himself lent them his aid. The sea rolled calmly beneath the Wind Elk's keel, though the occasional swell rocked the ship gently. Einar stood at the tiller with the wind in his hair and beard. He still worried about Hundr and hoped that his friend was alive, but at least now he had a purpose. The sharp tang of saltwater and seaweed filled the air, blending with the leathery scent of the crew's sweat.

Hildr came to stand with Einar. She wore woollen sailing clothes trimmed with fur for warmth and a naalbinding cap. Her *brynjar* and weapons were stowed safely inside barrels wrapped in wool and lanolin to keep out corroding seawater. She slipped her arm through his and rested her head on his shoulder. It wasn't so long ago that Einar had worried for his soul, fearing that his chance to die in battle and secure his place in Valhalla had passed. Einar had even feared fighting in the last campaign but had found courage again in the arduous war against Vigfus Hjorthrimul. Ragnhild's death had imbued him with some of his old strength, and he was as eager for battle as he had ever been.

The Wind Elk sped past towering cliffs and rocky promontories and camped in sheltered coves with small, pebbled beaches. They skirted too many islands to count, for that part of Norway was as thick with islands as fleas on a churl's dog. Some were nothing more than rocky islets, others larger, boasting verdant hills, scattered settlements, and timber longhouses surrounded by pastures and crop fields. Einar and Thorgrim kept a sharp eye on such islands, constantly wary of bands of jarls, whose ships might spot the Wind Elk and seize the chance to attack a lone vessel. A ship like theirs was a glorious prize. Any warlike jarl would see the *drakkar* and know it was laden with weapons, armour, helmets, captured silver, and heavy purses. Yet they passed by unchallenged, thanks in no small part to Hundr's flag, a clear warning to any would-be raider that the men aboard were fierce warriors, not to be trifled with. The islands also served as landmarks, each headland, oddly shaped rock, and fjord acting as a signpost on their journey to Avaldsnes. In the distance, the jagged peaks of the Sunnmøre Alps loomed, shadowy and majestic, watching over the land with ancient, implacable grandeur.

The crew had prepared the ship with all haste. Heeding Einar's orders, they had scraped the hull and replaced the horsehair tar between the clinker-built timbers where needed. They brought hard bread, smoked meat, dried fish and barrels of fresh water and ale, all gathered about the mast and lashed together with thick hemp rope. The Wind Elk drew close to Avaldsnes, gliding past the island of Karmøy, where the sea narrowed, and the water became as calm as a fjord. The scent of pine and spruce from the forests came as a welcome change from the ship's smells, and on the third day, Einar spotted the silhouette of Avaldsnes on the horizon where its fortress guarded the entrance to the Karmsund strait. Einar led the warship slowly towards King Harald's port. Thorgrim had the men take down any shields from the sheer strake and remove the carved elk's head and her fearsome antlers from the prow to show they came in peace.

Avaldsnes commanded a shipping strait, a mandatory passage for traders journeying from northern Norway south towards Denmark. It was the gateway to the east for most of King Harald's northern subjects, and he collected taxes from merchants wishing to pass through and trade in his kingdom. The surrounding port bustled with fat-bellied trading *knarrs*, *drakkar* warships, and smaller three- or four-man skiffs rowing busily about the harbour as Harald's port stewards collected the coin or silver required for a man to dock his ship at Avaldsnes. At the central jetty, the king's own ship, reputed to be the largest and fastest warship in all of Midgard, held pride of place. Folk gathered in awe around the famed Ormrinn Langi, marvelling at its splendour.

"You can't meet the king dressed like that," said Hildr, frowning at Einar's worn sailing clothes, soaked and dried stiff from rain and sea salt.

"We'd both better change," Einar replied, "because you're coming with me."

Einar had men bring up his finest clothes

and weapons, along with Hildr's *brynjar* and axe. Amundr and Thorgrim also donned their war finery, ready to march with Einar up the wooden steps towards the stout palisade encircling Avaldsnes. Einar pulled a leather jerkin over a fine hemp undershirt and then shrugged on his fish scale armour, which one of the crew had polished to a bright sheen. He wore green trews and naalbinding leggings wrapped tightly about his ankles and lower legs. His thick silver and gold chain adorned his neck, and his arms and wrists jangled with warrior rings. Hildr pulled on her *brynjar*, tied back her silver hair, and then helped drape Einar's heavy fur cloak over his shoulders. He fastened the cloak with a horse-headed pin, fully ready to meet the king of Norway.

Einar paid the harbour steward two silver coins and rewarded the haughty little bastard with a sour frown for his troubles. He marched along the jetty followed by Hildr, Amundr, and Thorgrim, and the gate guards waved them through the throng of merchants and churls waiting at the gate. The guards nodded respectfully at Einar, and he returned the gesture. Beyond the palisade, farmland spread across the island in a wash of green grass and stone walls. Sheep and cows chewed lazily at the lush grass. All around the settlement, folk hurried about their daily business. Bearded faces peered down at Einar from the palisade's fighting platform, and Amundr glowered up at them. The giant insisted on wearing his shining helmet with the cheekpieces closed. It made him look like a fearsome frost giant because only the whites of his eyes showed through the helmet's darkness. They entered a bustling square where churls sold eggs, baskets, fresh rushes, and loaves of bread in a multitude of different shapes. A woman with a squint and a mouth bereft of teeth screeched at a dirty-faced boy who snatched an egg from her basket and ran away barefoot, darting through the crowd like a hare. Stewards in King Harald's livery carried armfuls of wood towards his hall to burn on the always-lit hearth fire.

Harald Fairhair's hall loomed above Avaldsnes, towering like a mighty hall of the Aesir. It was twice as long as Einar's at Vanylven. It sat upon a raised hill, and timber steps led up to a large platform where two great pillars of painted wood rose, one topped by a snarling bear and the other with a wolf. Each pillar, carved from a single oak trunk, was thicker around than Einar's body and etched with intertwining whorls, dragons, axes, and war hammers. Braziers burned before the pillars, and the hall stretched high and wide behind them. Its door was open, vast and cavernous, and above it, two long planks curved upwards to meet above the roof, their ends cut into savage dragons painted blue, red, and green, which seemed to snap at each other high above the settlement. On the eastern side, lower, wattle-walled buildings extended the hall where the king and his family could live away from the main feasting area and sleeping platforms. The roof shone like a carpet of gold, thanks to the thatching of gloriously fresh wheat and oat straw.

"The last time I was here," Einar said, "Prince Erik ran the oars before a thronged quayside, and the Crippled King came with a raven upon his shoulder."

"Let us hope this time is a little less dramatic and ends with the king deciding to support our request," Hildr replied.

"Lord Einar," called a thin-faced steward in a green tunic embroidered with Harald's wolf sigil. He came bustling through the square, dodging around the folk busy with their daily duties. Einar recalled the steward and nodded to him in greeting. The steward stopped before Einar and his party, straightened his tunic and blew out his cheeks. He bowed deeply to Einar, Hildr, Thorgrim, and Amundr and gawped as he drank in Amundr's enormous size, made fiercer by his obscured face. "Welcome back to Avaldsnes."

"Is King Harald at home?" Einar asked.

"Yes, my lord. He is receiving petitions in his

hall at this very moment. I shall tell him you are here. But I must warn you, the king is very busy and has a line of people waiting for him to judge disputes and hear their requests. Please, follow me."

He led them up the steps towards King Harald's imposing hall and through its huge, oaken doors. Guards in heavy helmets and green cloaks stood inside the doorway, and they banged iron-shod spear butts onto the paved flooring to announce a new arrival into the hall. The sound of each thump echoed around the open space like a bell. Braziers on each stout roof post lit the inside of the hall, and rush lights hung from the ceiling in iron cages. A fire burned at the centre, and the smoke escaped through a hole in the high thatch. Silver birch planking framed the hall's interior so that it shimmered and shone in the firelight. Raised platforms lined the walls above and around the hall, providing space for Harald's warriors, slaves, and stewards to sleep. Fresh rushes lay thick upon the floor to soak up spilt ale and food, and every eye in the hall turned to stare at Einar and his companions.

Harald's guards stood in a line through the hall's centre, effectively separating two groups of petitioners and wisely preventing those with grievances from clashing as they awaited the king's judgement. Einar encountered similar claims weekly in Vanylven – land disputes, murder accusations, arguments over inheritances and unpaid dowries; the list seemed endless. Each week, he and Hildr did their utmost to deliver sound judgements based on the cases presented by both parties. Einar had no envy for the king; these proceedings were the most taxing part of his duties as jarl. People implored him for justice, each side passionately laying out their arguments and swearing to Odin that their version of events was the absolute truth. Hildr often remarked that both parties genuinely believed what they said. Over time, such disputes became entangled with hearsay, and individuals were inclined to convince themselves of a version of the truth so firmly that they would solemnly swear oaths, convinced they were not lying. As Einar met the piercing gazes scrutinising his stature, his fur cloak, chain, rings, and the scars etched upon his face, he recognised the wisdom in Hildr's words. After a battle, men recounted the same events in vastly different ways, causing the truth to become muddled by a haze of distorted memories. In the end, the only certainty lay in the tapestry of stories and recollections woven from those fractured truths.

King Harald sat upon his throne on a raised dais, and he, too, stared at Einar across the vastness of his royal hall. Harald's beard was a mix of chestnut and silver, and he wore it braided, hanging over a green tunic. Harald's long, handsome face was accentuated by a gold circlet that rested upon his creased brow. His hair, closely cropped to distinguish him from the other men in attendance, marked a stark contrast to the flowing locks that had earned him the epithet of 'Fairhair.' As a younger man, he had sworn never to cut it until he was King of all Norway, and after the battle of Hafrsfjord, Einar had watched in silence as Harald's tresses were shorn, a symbol of victory after years of bloody war. He was a clever man, brave and ruthless, and Einar held his gaze for a moment before raising his hand in greeting. Harald returned the gesture, as did his queen, who sat on an identical throne beside him. Queen Snæfríðr Svásadóttir cradled their one-year-old son in her arms, Sigurd Haraldsson, younger brother of Prince Erik Bloodaxe. Snæfríðr was a beautiful woman with a long, elegant face and hair so blonde that it shone almost white.

The steward bowed again to Einar and then hurried off in a strange bent-backed lope towards the king. He clambered up onto the dais and whispered something into the king's ear. Harald nodded. Two men stood before the king, petitioners who were likely in mid-argument before Einar strode into the hall and interrupted proceedings. King Harald inclined his head slightly and whispered to his steward, who then hopped down from the dais and repeated his peculiar walk back to where Einar waited. Harald beckoned to the petitioners, and they resumed their arguments in earnest.

"The king will receive you in his quarters, Lord Einar," said the steward, and he led Einar through the hall and out through a side door. He took them to a set of rooms attached to the hall, a room furnished with a large table and benches, tapestries on the wall and a hearth fire at one end. Whilst the king's warriors and their families lived upon the raised platforms within the hall, these were the king's living quarters, and a door to the south of the room led to the royal bedchamber. "King Harald will be with you as soon as he can." The steward left, and within moments, three maids brought two jugs of ale, horn cups, and a platter of meats, bread, and cheese.

"The cheese is good," muttered Amundr as he stuffed a slice into his maw.

"You can take your helmet off now," Einar replied. "The king might be a while, and you don't want to get cheese on those cheekpieces."

Amundr shrugged. He pulled off his prized helmet and set it down carefully on a lintel above the fire. He returned to the platter, grabbed a fistful of cheese, and took a bite large enough to make a bear proud. He stared at Einar as he ate, raising one eyebrow as if to let Einar know he was right. It was easier to eat the cheese without his helmet. Einar sighed and rubbed his eyes.

"No sign of Rognvald in the hall," remarked Hildr. "We shall miss him if he is not at court."

"Aye," Einar agreed. "And his cunning."

Rognvald Eysteinsson was King Harald Fairhair's closest advisor and friend, and he was the Jarl of Rogaland, perhaps the largest and wealthiest land in Norway. Rognvald was a friend to Einar and Hundr, and they had fought side by side many times. He was a shrewd man with the valuable knack of being able to pour honeyed words into Harald's ear and convince him of a particular course of action.

"So we shall need to convince Harald ourselves."

"We aren't asking for a few fleeces or a lend of his prize bull. We need ships and men. It's a lot to ask of the king."

The door to the quarters swung open, and a burly guard donned in the king's green, carrying a spear and shield, stepped in and held it open. The king and queen swept in with their cloaks billowing behind them, followed by the bent-backed steward, who took those cloaks and poured two cups of ale for the royals.

"Lord King," said Einar, bowing his head in

respect, "Queen Snæfríðr."

"Jarl Einar," Harald replied and gripped Einar warmly by the shoulder. "I did not expect to see you in Avaldsnes so soon. Lady Hildr, you are dressed for battle and yet still look radiant. I hope Einar here has not pressed you to return to your bow and axe?"

"It is good to see you, Lord King," Hildr said, bowing deeply. "May I?" she asked the queen, then reached to touch the baby prince. Snæfríðr smiled, and Hildr cooed and stroked the baby's soft head.

"Amundr, I think you have got bigger since the last time I saw you," quipped Harald. "We must arrange a wrestling match against my best man whilst you are here."

"Yes, King Harald, thank you, Lord King," nodded Amundr. A piece of cheese fell out of his mouth, bounced off his *brynjar*, and hit King Harald's soft leather boot. Amundr stared at it, and for a moment, Einar thought he was going to pick it up and eat it. But the king laughed before turning to clasp forearms with Thorgrim and then turned back to face Einar.

"Did you go to Orkney and punish Jarl Bekkr for me?"

"Yes, Lord King. Bekkr is dead, and his people have felt your justice."

"Good. Then I shall need to appoint a new jarl. Orkney has value. We can't have any old marauder running the place. And what news of the Crippled King?"

"Grave news, I am afraid. We sailed to Mann. Hundr was intent on taking his head, but we found an army waiting for us."

"An army?"

"Yes, Lord King. The Crippled King has amassed a great mercenary force of ships and men, paid for by his slave markets. Hundr went ashore to kill him, but he sadly failed. He and the Seaworm became separated from the rest of the Vanylven fleet."

Harald frowned and took a drink of ale, his eyes never leaving Einar's. "Where is Hundr now?"

"Lost. We do not know if he is dead or alive."

"And what does the Crippled King intend to do with this army of his?"

"He builds a temple of Loki to rival Odin's temple at Upsala, and he is forcing men to worship the chained one. As to what he intends to do with his army, who can say for sure?"

"He hates you, Einar, does he not?"

"He does. Though I raised him like he was my own son. He hates me because I am a friend to

Hundr, whom he hates beyond all things."

"I remember the tale. So the Crippled King will bring his army to Vanylven to kill you both?" Harald set his cup down and fixed Einar with a flat stare, no emotion showing on his handsome face.

"He might. But either way, he must be stopped."

"I agree. He was the father of all our troubles last year. He is a pox on our arses, and as long as he lives, we must keep an eye watching westwards." Harald paused as though waiting for Einar to speak. He glanced at Snæfríðr, who talked quietly with Hildr, still fussing over the swaddled prince. "Is there something else, Einar, or did you come to relay this news to me personally?"

"Hundr is dead or missing, Lord King. And the Crippled King..." Einar's mouth flapped open as he searched for the right words. Harald was not a big man nor a particularly fearsome warrior. But he was a man who had won a throne by his own hand, his ruthless determination, and over the corpses of any who had resisted his rise to power. He was a powerful man to fear, a clever man, and Einar could not hope to engage him in a test of words. Einar wished Rognvald were there with his silky words and honeyed tongue to help him convince the king of what must be done. "The

Crippled King must be stopped, but I do not have enough men to do it alone."

Harald nodded and pursed his lips. "So you have come to me to ask for warriors?"

"Yes, Lord King, warriors and ships to…"

Harald looked away, raising a finger in warning, and Einar's words died in his throat.

"You came to me once before, or rather, Hundr came for you when you had lost Vanylven to your enemies. I remind you, Einar, that you rule Vanylven as my vassal. You are my oathman, and I am the king of Vanylven and of all Norway. I make a man jarl and trust him to protect his lands in my name from all enemies. You receive one-tenth of the surplus from every merchant, farmer, woodsman, shipwright, and thatcher in your lands. With that silver, you feed your family and your hearth troop of warriors. Those warriors protect Vanylven under your command and are to fight for me whenever I call. Is that not the nature of our relationship?"

"Yes, Lord King." Einar fought to keep the anger from his face. He chose a wrinkle on Harald's forehead and focused his attention on that, quashing his desire to reach out and snap the king's throat for speaking to him like a child.

"I sent men to your aid last time and ousted Rollo the Betrayer from your lands. Now, you require my ships and my warriors once more?"

"Not to save Vanylven. To find Hundr and to bring the Crippled King to heel."

"You said Hundr could be dead. And you raised this Crippled King, taught him how to fight, how to sail, how to be a Viking." Harald drained his ale and placed the cup carefully on the table. He waved his fingers absentmindedly over the food and tore a piece of bread from a loaf. Harald examined the bread, dipped it in honey, and took a bite. He seemed no more vexed than if he and Einar discussed the weather.

Hildr came to Einar's side, and her *brynjar* reflected the hearth fire's glow. She cleared her throat and smiled at the king, though there was a steel in her eyes that Einar knew all too well. "I am going to speak plainly now, King Harald. I believe I have earned the right and hope that you will not hold it against me."

Harald stared at her, and his eyes narrowed, but his mouth was too full of bread and honey for him to stop Hildr from saying what she was about to say. Einar's stomach turned over inside him, just as it would before battle or as mountainous waves tossed his ship about during a storm.

"I do not need to speak on my husband's behalf, for his name and reputation are well known. He is a jarl, warrior, warlord and shipmaster. But Hundr is not here, and so I will speak for him. Hundr and the warriors of Vanylven have more than played their part in your rise to power. I myself fought at Hafrsfjord, as I am sure you remember. Hundr fought that day, too. I do not think many would disagree when I say that he was the greatest warrior that day as we fought, and friends died in a sea battle to make you king." Harald swallowed his bread before it was adequately chewed, his face reddening as he rushed to interrupt Hildr, but she kept on talking. "Then, we took to the seas to recover the Yngling sword, the blade of the first kings who claimed descent from the Aesir themselves. Hundr and Einar fought to recover that blade for you. Yes, you sent aid when Rollo attacked Vanylven. But you are our king, and when a force invades a jarldom with vast numbers, should the king not send his own army into battle to protect his own lands? You talk as though you did Einar a favour. Yes, he is your oathman, but that relationship works both ways."

"Careful, Hildr," Harald warned.

"I speak as I do with nothing but respect for you, Lord King. But we have embarked on a quest. Hundr is not just a warrior and a sea jarl who has been of service to you. He is your friend, is he not? He is lost, perhaps dead, but we who have stood beside him in the shield wall and who follow the ways of *drengskapr* should take up arms and find him or discover what has become of him. We sail to gather a warband unlike any other. We shall gather the greatest heroes of Midgard. Every warlord, king, and jarl who has fought with The Man with the Dog's Name, an army of champions to match the Einherjar of Valhalla. We come to you first, Harald Fairhair, because Hundr calls you a friend as well as his king. His own son, Hermoth, was fostered at your court to learn how to become a man. You entrusted Hundr with that same honour by having him foster your son Prince Erik in return. What a man Erik has become. Erik Bloodaxe. Feared and respected in his own right. A warrior of reputation yet to see twenty summers. So I ask you now, not as King Harald, but as Harald Fairhair, the greatest warlord of our age, will you join your sword and your cunning to the army we shall take west in search of Hundr?"

Harald's back straightened, and his chest puffed out. Einar held his breath, unsure if the king would fly into a violent rage or embrace Hildr.

"Hundr is my friend. You have stirred me, Hildr," murmured King Harald. He nodded his head slowly, and his jaw jutted. Harald held out his hand, and Hildr took in the warrior's grip. Then, he repeated the gesture with Einar, Amundr, and Thorgrim. "Sometimes we need to get the attention of the gods, to let them know we are here and thrill them with our deeds. I spend too much time in my hall these days, listening to men complain about hedges and dead men's wishes. I will summon Rognvald and his berserkers. I cannot march to war and leave my kingdom undefended. But if you can raise an army to challenge the Crippled King, then I shall support it with ships and men. You have my word. Return to me when you have built your army and when you have gathered the champions and the lovers of war. I shall join you, and together, we shall show Odin how Northmen fight!"

Harald lifted the entire jug of ale and drank so deeply that the golden liquid poured down his beard. Snæfríðr laughed, and Harald handed the jug to Einar, who followed his lead. They slapped each other's backs, and the king seemed lighter, excited like a boy about to take his first sea voyage.

Einar glanced at Hildr. She winked and held up her index finger. "One," she mouthed and folded her arms. For they had the first of their champions. King Harald Fairhair of Norway.

FOURTEEN

Darkness still veiled the land when Hundr woke. Dew clung to spiderwebs like crystals, and a full moon lit the meadow with silvery half-light. He took the Ulfberht sword in his right hand and went through the basic movements first, lunge, parry, sweep, and guard. Then, he moved through the advanced combinations he had learned as a boy, repeating them until his torso became sheened with sweat. After pausing to take a drink of ale from a skin, he repeated the exercises three times until his lungs heaved and his arm and shoulder muscles screamed in pain.

Live. Survive and rise to fight again. Finn must die. Orm must die.

Hundr repeated those words to himself, and they flooded his body with strength. He sheathed the Ulfberht sword and stared down at the ruin of his left hand. It had been four days since Yazi had seared the wounds closed with his knife, and every morning, Hundr's strength increased. But the missing fingers and his injured thigh wound were still raw and painful. They had spent those days hunting and marching ever closer to Jorvik, leaving the wild mountainous country and entering a prosperous land of tilled fields, farms, and dense forests. They had kept to the forests to avoid the locals – nine ragged-looking men marching through the countryside would soon attract unwelcome attention.

Hundr bent and tried to pick up an axe with his left hand. His three remaining fingers curled around the haft like a claw. He lifted the weapon, but his grip was poor, and it fell. Hundr winced and glanced at the sleeping forms of his men, relieved that they had not witnessed the shame of him being unable to hold a weapon. He tried again but could not hold the axe upright, let alone swing it in anger. Frustrated, he attempted a spear but fared little better. They had taken all of their weapons from the fight at the river, and though low on food, they had weapons aplenty. Finally, Hundr picked up a shield. He gripped the heavy boards with his right hand, threading his left arm through the loop. His remaining fingers clutched the grip, the raw, scabbed stumps pressing painfully against it. Yet, he found he could hold it. Testing its weight, he shifted it, feeling most of the strain fall onto his thumb, but it stayed firm in his hand.

Moving cautiously, Hundr worked through a series of shield wall formations. His movements were passable, but the nagging worry persisted – would his mangled hand be able to withstand the brutal clash of enemy blades? That, he knew, would only be proven in combat. Letting the shield fall aside, Hundr took up the heavy prow of the Seaworm upon his shoulders and began his strengthening exercises. He bent low, using his legs to drive his body upwards with power. Each deep stride, every twist of his waist, sent burning aches through his neck, shoulders, abdomen, and thighs. But with each movement, Hundr felt his strength growing.

"Shall we practise together, lord?" said Sigvarth in his gruff voice.

Hundr had not heard the warrior wake, and he was nervous about testing himself against another warrior so soon after sustaining his injuries. Nevertheless, he beckoned Sigvarth forward. Sigvarth, known as Trollhands because of the unusually large size of his hands, gathered up his axe and rolled his neck from side to side to loosen the muscles. He was a short man but barrel-chested, stocky, and as stout and hard to shift as an oak tree stump.

"Are you ready?" Sigvarth asked.

Hundr nodded and flexed his hand around the grip of the Ulfberht sword. Sigvarth came on tentatively, taking light sweeps with his axe, which Hundr easily batted aside with his blade.

"Come on. Harder," Hundr ordered.

"You have lost a lot of weight, my lord. I wanted to start off slowly."

Hundr sprang at him, feinting high and then tapping the Ulfberht sword's tip against Sigvarth's belly. The warrior frowned, shrugged, and came on with his axe. Hundr parried with his sword and wove his body around the cuts and slashes, but he soon found himself out of breath after so many days spent stumbling and suffering through the mountains. Sigvarth's attack grew in strength, and as Hundr darted away from an axe thrust, Sigvarth drove his knee into Hundr's shield. The thumping collision forced the boards back onto the stumps of Hundr's missing fingers, and he could not stop himself from crying out in pain. Sigvarth's blood was up, and he hacked his axe down hard. His oarsman's strength ripped the shield from Hundr's hand as easily as if a child held it.

Hundr stared at the fallen shield, horrified that he could not even hold it steady against one single axe blow.

"I'm sorry, my lord," said Sigvarth, raising his open hand.

"Do not be. I must push myself if I am to learn

how to fight with this cursed left hand. Perhaps a wider strap over the forearm to take the weight of the shield there?"

"If you can't grip a heavy shield, why not try a buckler like the Irishers use? You know, the smaller shield with the spike at its centre?"

"I have to find a way to protect my left side. With two swords, I defended by attacking. But if I can't hold up a shield or carry a weapon with this hand, how can I fight?"

"You will find a way, Lord Hundr. You still fight like a demon with your right hand. Faster than a stray dog after hot leftovers."

Hundr smiled and clapped Sigvarth on the shoulder. The rest of the men rose from their slumber, huffing and groaning about damp arses and sleeping in the open.

"No more hiding in the woods and scurrying over barren hillsides," Hundr said as he cleaned the Ulfberht sword's blade and slid her into her scabbard. "I have sold my armour and my arm rings for food already. All we have left are our weapons. Let's march through open country and see if we can't attract some attention."

"If it's a band of angry churls, we'll have no problem," piped Thatchulf. "But if a warband comes after us…" he blew out his cheeks.

"You have your breastplates and your

weapons. We are hungry and tired, but we can still fight. Jorvik can't be far away now, so let's see if we can kick a few sleeping bears into action. I'd rather take from warriors than simple folk. We'll need something to trade, or silver, if we are to find a crew or a trader who can take us north. They won't do it for free. We'll have to pay to sail back to Norway."

The men didn't argue with Hundr's reasoning, and so the nine fugitives set off to seek some of the unwanted attention they had been avoiding. Hundr marched with the prow strapped to his back, its rough timbers still chafing the sores and scabs it had rubbed into his skin with every step, but he felt more awake, closer to his old strength than he had on any day since the fight with Orm. They found a meandering river, which Hundr believed was one of the two wide rivers that came together at Jorvik, the course of which he remembered well from his time fighting in the region as a younger man. They followed its flow westwards, marching through tilled fields and meadows. More than one nervous face peered at them across the wheat and barley fields, and a squint-eyed shepherd in filthy rags made the sign to ward off evil before he hirpled away over the hillside as they passed his herd of goats.

Yazi killed a goat, so Hundr ordered Thatchulf, Toki, Harbard, Eyolfr, and Gunnulfr to build a large fire from green wood to roast the meat.

The damp, fresh wood sent a towering column of smoke into the sky, visible for miles around. Hundr and Sigvarth bathed in the river to wash the worst of weeks of grime and filth from their bodies. Hundr washed his wounds carefully, and Yazi reapplied his poultice of honey and leaves, which he gathered at every opportunity from the woods on their journey south. As the nine men ate roasted goat, which was tough and stringy and tasted of smoke, they kept their eyes on the hills and dales about them. Sure enough, when the sun had reached halfway across the sky, ten riders came over the hills from the direction in which the shepherd had fled.

"Our guests have arrived at last," said Sigvarth, winking at Hundr.

The nine warriors did not get up. They continued to eat the roasted goat and pretended not to notice at all as the riders drew close. Horses snorted and whickered as the ten strangers reined in their mounts five paces away from Hundr and his men. Hundr did not look up, but he ate his meat and listened as the men spoke of old voyages and the deeds of fallen friends.

"Stand up, brigands!" shouted one of the riders eventually. He spoke in Norse with a Danish accent, and Hundr continued to ignore him.

"Bastards!" cursed another, dismounting and striding towards the seated group, a spear clenched in both hands. Hundr waited, patient as a coiled viper, until the man was nearly upon them, his spear raised to crush Eyolfr's skull. Then Hundr struck. The warrior was tall, his face twisted into a sneer. His blue eyes gleamed beneath a stained leather breastplate, and his filthy trews were stiff with dirt.

Hundr's hand shot out, gripping the spear's shaft, and with a swift motion, he drove his knee hard into the man's gut. The warrior wheezed, doubling over, and Hundr sent him sprawling to the ground, where he curled up and retched into the grass. Rising, Hundr seized the spear, pointing it at the mounted warriors as his own men, eight in all, slowly got to their feet, drawing their weapons.

The riders all carried spears and either axes or seaxes at their belts. They wore their hair long and their beards braided, for they were men of the Danelaw and not Saxons from King Alfred's kingdom south of Watling Street.

"Throw down your weapons," ordered the rider at the centre. He was a grizzled man with a bald head covered by a naalbinding cap. He had a ring on each of his wrists, and though he was fat and red-faced, Hundr picked him out as their leader. "You're on my lord's lands without permission. You are robbers and bandits. If you go now and swear to leave this place, we shall let you go in peace."

"What if we like this place?" Hundr asked belligerently. He smiled, and the fat warrior sneered at Hundr's travel-stained tunic, lack of armour, and wounded hand. He did not see the Champion of the North standing before him but rather a traveller wet from the river surrounded by ruddy-faced warriors. He thought them most likely masterless men turned out by their last lord for thievery, insubordination, or laziness. "Perhaps we'll stay."

The fat man ground his teeth, cheek muscles shifting behind his beard. He had thought to drive off a group of bad men with threats and a shake of his weapons, but now realised it would take much more than that. The riders didn't want to fight; they weren't shield wall warriors. They were hedge guards and tithe collectors for some backwater jarl of lands Norsemen had taken from Saxons back in the days of the Ragnarsson army conquest of Northumbria.

"All right then," the fat man huffed, and he spat over his horse's head. "Hurt a few of them, lads. Then drive the rest off."

The riders laughed mirthlessly. Four clambered off their mounts, and three urged their horses forward. Fighting on horseback was difficult, and Hundr, like most warriors, preferred to fight on foot. Hundr had seen warriors in Frankia who rode monstrous war horses with stirrups and stout saddles, and those men could fight from the backs of their horses with terrifying force, but Hundr doubted the men before him were of that calibre, nor did he believe that their mounts were trained for war.

Hundr roared like a madman and brandished his captured spear at the first horse. It shook its head and tried to turn, and when her rider sawed at the bit, the horse violently reared up on her back legs. As it thudded down, the rider pitched forward and clung on desperately to avoid being thrown to the ground. Hundr took three quick steps forward and stabbed the spear point into the man's throat. A guttural sound escaped as the rider clutched at the weapon, and Hundr ripped it free to send a gout of blood splashing across the horse's long neck. The beast panicked at the smell of blood and bolted, throwing the injured man to the ground. The other horses grew agitated, eyes wide and nostrils flaring. Two of them bolted for the hills, their riders powerless to stop them. Hundr hurled the spear at the fat man, but he threw himself from his horse, crashing heavily to the ground as the weapon sailed over the mount's head.

Sigvarth killed the first enemy with a savage axe strike to his face, leaving a ghastly wound. Yazi shot two men with his bow, and the rest of Hundr's warriors set about the fat man's company with brutal efficiency. Hundr drew his sword and found the fat man crawling away from the fight. He placed the blade at the leader's heavy jowls, and the crawling man stopped still. He turned slowly and stared at Hundr with frightened eyes.

"Who do you serve?" Hundr asked.

"Jarl Stigmarr is the lord of these lands, and we protect his farmers from those who would raid and steal from them."

"You are his hearth troop?"

"No, we are his reeves. He has thirty men inside his hall, each one a warrior. They'll come for you when we don't return."

"Good. Now, give us everything you have."

They left the fat man and five of his men alive. The rest died in the fighting. Sigvarth and the others laughed as they sent the defeated men scurrying naked across the hillsides, their white skin deathly pale against the surrounding greenery. Hundr and his men took three good knives, seven axes and spears, four seaxes, pouches of hacksilver, skins of ale and sacks full of biscuits, flatbread, dried beef, and cheese. Hundr took a worn leather breastplate from a dead man. They captured five horses, and so for the rest of that afternoon, they took turns riding and marching with full bellies, drinking fine ale from full skins. Even Hundr felt his mood lighten at the small victory, and it seemed they had put Orm and his berserkers behind them with hopes of Jorvik and a change in their luck ahead.

It was a grey, calm dusk when Stigmarr and his warriors came. Hundr and his men had halted beside a great hollow in a sloping valley. It was as though a giant spoon had gouged a section from the land, and inside, it grew silver birch trees around thorn bushes, ferns and strange pale rocks cloaked in green moss. They sat beside a warm campfire, eating what remained of the goat and supplies taken from the fat man and his riders. From the descending darkness, men approached like shadows, their forms shifting in the failing light. Yazi saw them first and took up his bow, and Hundr led his men to form a line on the upper edge of the hollow, facing the advancing warriors.

"At least thirty," Yazi proclaimed. "Maybe a few more."

"We cannot fight thirty men and live," complained Thatchulf.

"It's too late for that now," said Hundr. He had not expected the local lord to rally his men so quickly. Hundr had thought the fight would not come until tomorrow, if it was to come at all, because he'd planned to be gone by then. He wanted to follow the river to Jorvik with his plundered weapons and silver and use them to find a berth home. There, he could recover and take the fight to Orm and his Crippled King. Now, a much larger force faced the nine before the hollow, and Thatchulf was right. They could not stand against thirty men.

A man on a white gelding rode before the advancing column, his black clothes and beard in stark contrast to his pale mount. He urged the horse forward so that it cantered along the line of warriors as he glared at Hundr and his men. Bald and thick-bearded, he wore a black cloak and carried a sword belted at his waist.

"I am Jarl Stigmarr!" he called across the field. "You were warned to leave my land, and you killed my men. Now, you cannot leave."

"We want no trouble here," Hundr replied. "We'll be gone come morning. Just passing through, you won't see us again."

"You killed my men. What do you think happens if I don't punish men who attack me? Soon, every bastard with a blade will believe that Stigmarr is weak and that if you have no master and no honour, you can come here and take whatever you wish. That cannot be. Men must fear stealing from me, or what kind of jarl would I be?"

"Your men fought like old women," Hundr replied, his anger rising because Stigmarr was right. He dragged the Ulfberht sword free from her fleece-lined scabbard and firmly set his feet. His mangled left hand longed to hold a blade but instead hung uselessly by his side.

"I want that one alive," Stigmarr barked at his men, pointing his sword at Hundr. "Keep three or four to take to the king at Jorvik. He'll want to make an example of them. Kill the rest."

The warriors came on slowly as though they marched to work in the fields. Blades caught the sun whenever it appeared between shifting clouds, and Stigmarr's warriors spread out in two ranks so that the line could wrap around Hundr's meagre force, ready to cut at them from all angles.

"We must stand and fight," said Hundr. "There's no time to flee, no chance to run. We must kill three men each. We are all dangerous bastards in a fight. Kill your share, and then we can find a ship to take us home."

They readied their weapons and formed a circle so that no matter which direction Stigmarr's men came from, they would face a hardy blade. Yazi had only five arrows left in his quiver, but he used them well. In the time it would take a man to eat an apple, he loosed all five shafts, and five of Stigmarr's men fell, either crying out in pain or dropping dead in the darkness. The enemy roared in anger, and their indifferent march became a wild charge full of rage.

"Don't die easy!" Hundr called as he readied the Ulfberht sword. "If they want our blood, let them come for it over the corpses of their brothers. Kill three men each, or save a place for me in Valhalla!"

The enemy closed the last few steps in a flat run. They came with spears, axes, and mouths wide open as they screamed their battle cry. Hundr's guts tightened as the clash closed in. Not because he feared Stigmarr's men, he had fought adversaries far more fearsome than these, but because of his wounded hand. He was not yet ready to fight. He could not wield weapons with his old skill and speed. But Hundr steadied himself. If it was his time to die, then so be it.

The first enemy charged at him, howling like a fetch, and Hundr lashed out with his sword so that the point tore into the man's open mouth. The blade sliced through both tongue and cheek and splashed dark blood beneath the blackening sky. The enemy crashed into them with a sickening crunch and then fell back two paces to hack and slash with their weapons. Eyolfr went down in that first clash with a spear driven deep into his chest. He twitched as his lifeblood pooled out beneath him while Hundr and his seven remaining warriors fought for their lives. Hundr batted an axe blade aside with his sword and sliced open the attacker's throat with a flick of his wrist. The enemy avoided him then. Two of their number had already fallen to his shining sword, and Hundr felt that perhaps his injury wasn't as significant a dent to his warrior prowess as he had thought. Gunnulfr swung his axe into an enemy shield, but the weapon stuck fast. As he struggled to free it, the enemy stabbed beneath the shield's rim with his seax and the wicked blade tore at Gunnulfr's groin. Blood spurted from that grievous wound as Gunnulfr collapsed, making a sad, mewing noise as he died beneath the clashing blades. On Hundr's blind side, Sigvarth roared his defiance while Yazi fought behind him, still holding his ground. Hundr trusted that no man amongst Stigmarr's force could cut the Easterner down.

Stigmarr himself appeared amongst his men, heavy-paunched and strong-faced. He came on clutching his sword, flanked by two giant warriors, flint-eyed men with axes and shields. These were the jarl's real warriors, and they barged through the circle of their own men to get at Hundr. Hundr struck hard with the Ulfberht sword, and Stigmarr's face twisted in horror as he barely deflected the blade meant for his throat. One of the giant axe men slammed into Hundr's left shoulder with his shield. Hundr slashed back, but the second man was on him from the right. They moved to trap him, shields raised, aiming to crush him between them. It was the right strategy. Hundr was the leader and clearly a skilled fighter – why risk a fair fight when they could pin him down and hack him to death?

The shield pressed him on his useless left side, and though Hundr tried to heave the man away with his left elbow, he did not have the strength to drive him backwards. Stigmarr swung down at him, and Hundr parried the blow, but the second axeman smashed into his right shoulder, trapping him like a beast for slaughter. Hundr thrashed, attempting to swing his sword, but he was pinned. With brutal force, Stigmarr struck him across the face with the hilt of his sword. Hundr sagged but found the will to surge upright, spitting, writhing, and kicking at his attackers as chaos erupted around him.

Stigmarr sneered, and once more, he attacked with his sword hilt, this time driving it into the side of Hundr's head. A flash of blinding light enveloped Hundr's vision, his strength ebbing away like water from a broken vessel. As the world dimmed, the cackling of the Norns rang out in his ears. Just when he had thought he was growing stronger, when hope had seemed within reach, the Norns spat in the face of his hope and turned the threads of his life to ruin.

FIFTEEN

Hundr swam in the nothingness. Darkness and despair swarmed him, engulfing his senses like seawater over a drowning man. His ill luck had condemned more of his men to death. The sounds of battle were gone, replaced by the rhythmic dripping of water. Hundr realised he was conscious, yet not in a body of his own. His good eye would not open, and panic seized him as his hands pawed at his face. But these were not his hands – they were whole, big, strong, and uninjured. He had two eyes, yet despite being open, he could see nothing. Fear and confusion churned inside him like a fish thrashing on a quayside. He was blind.

He was not Hundr but somebody else, somewhere else. Hundr tried to calm himself, recognising the sensation and realising that he was experiencing one of the dream visions that had come to him throughout the saga of his life. He had been

Völund before, the smith of the gods who had killed the children of his captor, Niðhad, and fashioned goblets and jewels from their eyes and skulls before flying away on cunning wings crafted in his mighty forge. He had been Loki, and even Odin, racing a giant on Sleipnir, his eight-legged horse. The visions were always tales of the gods, cruel and glorious tales meant to teach men lessons of old, and whilst Hundr feared the terrible brutality of seeing the world through the eyes of such powerful beings, he welcomed the wisdom. He needed Odin to grant him luck. Hundr hoped he was not dead but perhaps existing briefly in the realm between life and death. He had to return to Midgard. His men needed him, and his enemies could not be allowed to prevail.

Live. Survive and rise to fight again. Finn must die. Orm must die.

Hundr repeated the words in his mind, and the mouth that was not his gave voice to them, echoing as though he were trapped in a vast, damp cave.

Hundr felt around him, and his fingers touched wet, rough stone. He crawled in a circle, probing with his hands because he could not see. Hundr was in a place without a door, without windows, or any means of escape. He was in a prison. His hand found a rough rope dangling from above, and tied to it was a bucket. Inside the bucket was a pot of warm ale, an apple, and a chunk of hard bread. Hundr, who was not Hundr, drank the ale and took a bite of the apple. The taste of the fruit stunned him. It was like eating golden sunshine or tasting water dripping from a star. It was an apple of Iðunn, the fruit that gave the gods eternal life. Awareness came to Hundr then, an appalling understanding of who he was in his ethereal vision. He was Höðr, son of Odin, brother to Baldr the Golden One, and the most hated being in all the nine realms on Yggdrasil's mighty boughs.

Hundr, now Höðr, sagged, and the magical apple rolled out of his hand. Hundr felt the despair inside the god. It was overwhelming, consuming, like a knife in the imprisoned god's heart. A memory came to Höðr, unbidden and unwelcome, but there nonetheless. He found himself transported away from the prison to Asgard, the home of the gods. The air was no longer damp and grim but crisp with fresh smells of pine, sea salt, and smoke from distant fires. Höðr stood amongst giants. He could not see them, but he could feel the malevolent presence of Loki, his foster brother, and the masterful, powerful aura of his brother Thor, the mightiest of all the sons of Odin and the master of thunder.

The magnificent halls of Asgard loomed before him, clear in his memory even to blind Höðr. Stone walls rose vast and shining with a light that seemed to come from the walls themselves. Though Höðr could not see, he could envisage the halls from the descriptions of his fellow gods and from the feel of his fingertips. Golden beams stretched upwards to meet high ceilings carved with ancient victories and prophecies yet to come. Torches the size of pine trunks lined the walls, their flames casting flickering shadows over tapestries woven with the tales of the Aesir. At the centre of it all sat the great hall of Valaskjálf, Odin's high seat of power with its silver roof and wide doors.

Höðr drank in the memories of those glorious old days before the dreadful events which would cast him into eternal imprisonment. He remembered the presence of the gods around him. The weight of their steps, the air shifting as they moved, the rustle of their garments, the mesmerising scent of Freya, Frigg, and Sif. Odin All-Father sat upon his throne, tall, imposing, his one cunning eye ever watchful. Höðr recalled Odin's presence feeling like storm clouds before the rain, an unworldly force contained within the form of a man-shaped father of the gods. His beard was thick, like the roots of an ancient oak, and his cloak was a deep, shadowy blue embroidered with the runes of power. Ravens flew about Odin – Hugin and Munin, the messengers of thought and memory, and the beat of their wings cut through the vast hall's silence with a soft fluttering. Hundr had once owned swords named after those ravens, long ago, before the Crippled King, before Orm. So long ago.

Höðr smiled at the memory of his brother, Baldr. He remembered how it felt to be close to Odin's favourite son. Though Höðr could not see him, Baldr radiated light and warmth. The gods spoke of his beauty, as did any mortal lucky enough to glimpse the god so fair. His golden hair flowed like the sun breaking a dark horizon, his eyes a piercing blue to peer into your soul. He wore white and silver, his armour shining like polished steel. Though Baldr did not need his armour, for nothing in the nine realms could harm him. His voice was gentle and yet carried strength. He never shouted, for there was no need. When Baldr spoke, all listened.

Hundr shivered as Höðr recalled a different presence standing to his left in the great hall of his father – Loki, the trickster and deceiver. Unlike the others, though still godlike, he was no son of Odin but the offspring of a frost giant, fostered and reared by Odin as a brother to Höðr, Thor, and Baldr. There was something about Loki's presence that felt slippery and elusive. Höðr could sense his smile, joyless and dripping with both charm and malice. Loki's hair was black as pitch, long and unbound, and his eyes flashed with a cunning that made Höðr uneasy. A blood-red cloak draped him, shifting with his movements, never staying still, as if even the fabric he wore could not be trusted.

Hundr saw Asgard through Höðr's memories, but the god felt alone. His world was one of descriptions, sounds, sensations, and vibrations, but never light. There was a veil which surrounded him, and though Höðr was a god, he could not escape the shadow cast over his existence. His senses were heightened, attuned to every subtle shift in the hall of his memory, but he could not see the glory the other gods spoke of. He could hear the awe in their voices when they spoke of Baldr, the way they called him the golden one. But to Höðr, his beloved brother was just another presence in the darkness.

Höðr finished his apple and drank the ale to slake his thirst. Then, a cruel memory stung the imprisoned god's thought cage, and Hundr felt it, too, like a whip. Laughter echoed through the halls of Asgard as the gods played their favourite game— throwing spears and stones at Baldr, testing the strength of the protective seiðr their mother, Frigg, had placed upon him. Each weapon and object bounced harmlessly off Baldr's body, falling to the ground with a dull thud. The gods roared with joy, taking turns to see if they could hurl anything that might harm the invincible Baldr. Höðr stood apart from the crowd, listening. He knew his brother's laugh. It was bright and full, ringing like the peal of a bell. To Höðr, it was a beacon, a point of light in his otherwise endless night.

Then Loki's presence sidled up to Höðr; the memory of that moment made the god's shoulders shudder. Loki's voice came like a whisper in his ear, smooth and persuasive.

"Why do you stand here alone, brother?" Loki asked, taking Höðr by the hand. His touch was cold and unwelcome. "Why not join them? Why are you always left out of the fun?"

Höðr had hesitated at that moment. He had wanted to be part of the celebration, to play and laugh with his fellow gods. He wanted to feel what the others felt, to hear their laughter directed toward him, not just at Baldr. Loki squeezed his hand, his thumb caressing Höðr's knuckles.

"Here," Loki had said, his tone filled with sly encouragement. He placed something in Höðr's hand. It felt like a bow. "I will guide your aim."

Höðr's heart had raced. He had trusted Loki. Yes, he was the master of mischief, but he was also a god and his brother. Loki would not lie. The string was taut under Höðr's fingers, and Hundr felt the tension in Höðr's arm as he pulled the bowstring back. The weapon felt light, almost too light. He hadn't known that Loki had placed an arrow made from mistletoe in his hand, the one thing in the world that had not sworn an oath to spare Baldr. When he had been a child, fell dreams had plagued Baldr's nights, dark visions of his own death. Night after night, he would wake in terror, the shadows creeping closer, threatening to take him. Frigg had panicked and had sought to protect him. She had gone to every creature, stone, and plant and extracted a promise that they would not harm her beloved son. But in her haste, she had overlooked one thing, the humble mistletoe.

Höðr knew now, lamenting in his damp prison – Loki had known about the mistletoe. And with that knowledge, he had crafted a terrible plan. Höðr's memory flicked back to that horrendous day in the hall. Höðr's breath had caught in his throat. He had hesitated, but then, Baldr's bright, warm laugh echoed across the hall. It had reassured him. Höðr had reminded himself that Baldr was invincible. What harm could the arrow do? He had released the string.

Silence.

Then, a sound Höðr would never forget – a soft gasp and the thud of a body hitting the ground. Baldr's body. The light of Asgard had been extinguished. The laughter had died instantly, replaced by gasps of horror and the clamour of gods rushing to help their fallen brother. Höðr had stood frozen, confused. What had happened? He could not see. He remembered his hands still outstretched; the bow had slipped from his grip.

Frigg's wail tortured Höðr's immortal soul. A sound so raw and full of grief that it had been as though Yggdrasil itself had splintered and toppled. Odin's voice had come low and trembling, filled with sorrow and rage. The other gods had whispered, their voices a murmur of disbelief, of blame. And then one voice had cut through them all.

"Loki?" Höðr had said.

But Loki had already vanished, slipping away like the shadow he was. Höðr was left standing alone, the weight of his actions pressing down on him like the wildest of storms. Though he could not see what he had done, he had felt it in his bones and in the broken anguish that had filled the hall.

Baldr was dead. And Höðr, blind Höðr, had been the unwitting instrument of that death.

The gods had imprisoned him, many had cursed him, and others pitied him, but none had ever understood. None would know what it meant to be Höðr, to be led by the cruel hand of fate itself. None of the gods had ever asked how it felt to be used, how it felt to know that he had been Loki's pawn, or how deeply he had mourned his brother's death. Even Odin had said little to Höðr in those dark days. His silence had been worse than any punishment, for Odin saw more than any of the gods. He had foreseen the Ragnarök, the end of all things, and Höðr had seen in Odin's cruel single eye that he believed Baldr's death was just the beginning.

Hundr, living inside the god's pain-wracked mind, felt that suffering. It lingered in the air, a tangible grief coiling around his heart. The Höðr vision finally faded, and Hundr felt himself slipping away like a bird tumbling from the sky. As he fell, one truth of Höðr's vision remained – even the gods cannot escape the cruel threads of fate.

SIXTEEN

The Wind Elk left Avaldsnes laden with fresh provisions, food, ale, cloaks, and blankets woven from the fleeces of the king's own sheep. King Harald himself waved them off, and Einar left the king's high seat, confident that Harald Fairhair would provide warriors to support his war with the Crippled King. The Wind Elk made the journey south, passing the endless fjords, islands and inlets that formed Norway's west coast. She flew on a fierce sea wind that whipped the sail taut, proudly displaying Hundr's one-eye sigil emblazoned in black upon the heavy grey wool. The *drakkar* cut through the white-tipped swell like an arrow, and her proud, antler-headed prow rose and fell with the surge of the sea. Einar left his grey hair unbound, savouring the warship's thrilling speed and the cold sting of sea spray on his face as waves pounded the hull. Thorgrim leaned on the tiller at the steerboard and whooped with joy as the ship raced beneath them.

Njorth blessed them for two days, carrying them on their journey with full sails and tranquil seas. Then, on a morning when sheeting rain poured down from a low sky, they rowed south in search of a favourable wind. They found it near the coast of Fensfjorden and quickly sailed southeast, skirting Norway's southern shores towards the land of the Svear. King Bjorn Ironside, ruler of Sweden and an old acquaintance of Einar, reigned there. As they neared his kingdom, Einar debated with Hildr and Thorgrim whether they should first visit the old warrior king who was famous for his feasting and the hospitality he extended to his friends. The furthest destination on their journey was the Valkyrie temple at Upsala, and to get there, they had to sail around Bjorn's kingdom and come about it to the northeast. Upsala lay on the east coast of Svearland, and while travelling overland or by horse would be quicker, Einar hesitated. He did not want to risk falling foul of a local Svear jarl who fancied testing his warriors' mettle against theirs, enticed by the Wind Elk crew's *brynjars* and weapons. So, Thorgrim led the Wind Elk south, running along Jutland and around Sjælland. He knew the way, and as shipmaster, he kept the Wind Elk at a safe distance from the coast, spending nights in secluded bays and rarely going ashore. More than once, curious *drakkar* or *snekke* ships followed them, sniffing them out like prey. The lone ship would seem like easy pickings for the Danish jarls of the mainland and the countless islands around Sjælland. Even Hundr's famous sigil might not be enough to ward off the hard men of the Vik, so Thorgrim ensured they steered clear of the sea wolves.

The sun shone, and men stripped their heavy sailing clothes to enjoy the warmth on their skin as they sailed close to the great trading port at Birka. Its waters were thick with fat-bellied *knarr* trading ships heavy with amber, iron, beads, spices, and slaves. Hildr made eyes at Einar at the prospect of trading some of their silver for some new jewellery, but Einar kept his gaze on the sea ahead and drove the crew hard as they turned north for Upsala. The rawest crew members, the young lads with little more than fluff for beards, bailed the bilge. They knelt in the hull between the thwarts with buckets, scooping out the seawater and tossing it over the side. When two of them carelessly threw water upwind, drenching the crew, Amundr clashed their heads together in reprimand. Einar chuckled, knowing they wouldn't repeat that mistake. They shivered with red, raw hands and cut knuckles from where their hands became caught between their buckets and the ship's timbers. It was backbreaking work which every seafarer worth his salt knew and remembered, a rite of passage necessary to earn the respect of the older crew members. Einar watched them from the steerboard and remembered Finn Ivarsson bailing on a similar journey east many years ago. He was different then – a good lad with a warrior's heart who was hardworking and eager to please. Thorgrim had taught Finn the tricks of the tiller, and Hundr had taken the time to teach him swordplay. They were happier times, yet how the Norns must have laughed, knowing as they did the blood and carnage that lay ahead for the son of Ivar.

Ships came to look at the Wind Elk from afar as she banked west to enter the river approaching Upsala. The men rowed with long, powerful strokes around the wide bends until the great temple loomed large in the distance. The golden wood of the temple's structures reached above the treetops like a glorious crown. Einar shivered as he remembered the tales of the great tree at Upsala, where the sacrificed corpses of men and animals hung from sacred boughs in honour of Odin and the Aesir. He had seen it for himself on their last visit to Odin's temple, and he found Hildr standing at the prow, staring at the massive structure with glassy eyes.

"It is strange to think I grew up here with Ragnhild and Hrist," she murmured, leaning in to rest against Einar's chest. "Stranger still that our parents left us with the high priest as offerings to the All-Father. Given that you and I weren't blessed with children... it feels so sorrowful."

"Do you know who they were, your mother and father?" Einar asked. Hildr had never spoken of it before, and Einar had never pressed her on the subject. After so many years together, Einar knew by her mannerisms which things she did and did not wish to discuss beside the fire or warm in bed.

"No. We were all the second or third daughters of jarls who trembled at the prospect of paying three dowries. Unwanted and unloved, we were babies raised to be warriors in the service of Odin. It is hard to remember one's childhood. The days and weeks pass into a mist. I remember only the laughter and the tears, blisters, aching muscles, and cruel punishments."

"Was it hard?" Einar rarely thought of his own upbringing, scrapping and battling his peers and vying for his warrior father's attention. He had grown up tough, like most Northmen, because it had to be so. A man had to be as hard as oak and as tough as Frankish steel if he was to brave the Whale Road and fight in the shield wall.

Hildr sighed and gathered her cloak about her shoulders. "No. We had good times, sisters together, learning to fight. Becoming masters of bow, axe, spear, and shield. We prayed and learned the stories of the gods, and we ran in the fields. There was always not quite enough to eat and just enough trouble to make. It was a life better than many young girls can hope for in Midgard. We have seen some dark places, you and I. Slave pits, hovels. There is cruelty in the world, and though the temple was harsh, I fared well."

Einar, Hildr, Thorgrim, and Amundr went ashore, leaving the Wind Elk and her crew docked at the worn-looking jetty where two old women in white priestess robes took three pieces of hacksilver as a mooring tax. The women gave the crew freshly brewed ale and baked bread, and so Einar left them smiling as they marched through the dense forest surrounding the temple. Warrior priestesses in *brynjars* and white cloaks lined the road at twenty-pace intervals. Standing perfectly still, each held a spear at a slight angle, their faces expressionless as Einar and the others passed. The forest path snaked through the tall trees, which stretched overhead like veins on the back of a frost giant's hand. The heavy canopy and damp, rotting leaf smell made the place close and oppressive.

They marched in silence until the golden timbers of the Odin temple rose above the tree canopy like the rising sun.

"It's a fine thing to see," remarked Thorgrim, gawping up at the vast structure. "A hall fit for the gods themselves."

A high gabled peak towered above ancient oak, fir, birch, aspen and alder. Hildr reached for the spear amulet at her chest and whispered a silent prayer. The air was thick with a palpable curious atmosphere. Einar felt it, too, his boots crunching on fallen pine needles as they moved through the forest's darkness. A shiver ran through him. Birds sang, and the woodland creaked and groaned. It was as though they passed over the Bifrost itself, the shimmering bridge linking Asgard, the home of the gods, with the mortal realm of Midgard. Amundr took a step closer, his huge shoulder brushing Einar's as he walked next to him.

"Any closer, and you'll be able to draw my axe," Einar hissed at him, but the big man lumbered on, glancing furtively left and right into the blackness beyond the ferns and briars. "You look like you've seen a fetch wandering yonder. What's got into you?"

Amundr stayed close to Einar and swallowed so hard that his Adam's apple bounced up and down like flotsam on the tide. "I can feel them," he muttered in his cavernous voice, bending to speak into Einar's ear. "The Huldufólk, the hidden people. In the trees, watching us."

"The elves and faeries won't attack you. They'd be hanging off your arms like cobwebs. Pull yourself together, man. There may be Huldufólk, trolls, or dwarves hiding in the woods, but the only giant here is you." Einar gave his shoulder a gentle bump, but Amundr shook his head like a stubborn child and continued to walk so close to Einar that he almost trod on his foot.

"When Ragnhild came here last time, she came as an outcast," said Hildr softly. "We had not returned to the order after the fighting for the Ragnarsson army was over. She had broken her solemn vow of celibacy, and they did not greet her kindly. She fought a holmgang here, and only when she recovered Odin's sacred spear were her sins forgiven. I, too, broke that oath, and I, too, should have returned after the war in England was over."

"They forgave you both. The high priestess said it herself. We returned the spear, and all was forgiven. Do you feel guilty even after all these years?"

"A little. I can feel Odin's eye upon me. There is a weight to it. A judgement."

"You have sent many a warrior's soul to Valhalla, my love. If the All-Father looks upon you, it is with thanks. You've always followed *drengskapr*, as have I. A warrior either dies in battle or lives on. We have lived on whilst most of our friends and brothers have died. We have grown older and should not be denied the simple pleasures in life. You are a woman who took a husband. There can be no sin in that."

"I broke my oath."

"Aye, you did. And I'm glad you did. It was a good oath to break, or I would have lain alone these years and never known the warmth of your..."

"Einar!" she snapped and punched him on the arm. "Not here."

He smirked at her, and she merely smiled, shaking her head. Einar reached for his own amulet and touched the cold iron. He feared the gods, and like all sailors, he avoided the bad luck of haft words. It was not uncommon for Einar to whisper prayers, beseeching the gods for their help and favour. Yet he doubted Odin begrudged Hildr for taking a husband and laying aside her axe and bow. With that thought, Einar tucked his thumbs into the wide belt at his waist and strode through the forest, even as Amundr clung to him like a frightened child.

The forest grew thinner, the sun breaking through the canopy, and the heavy foliage disappeared to reveal a high gate of dark timbers between two thick pine trees. Before that gate waited two figures in long robes and hoods the colour of old blood. They stood still like carved prows with bowed heads, and beyond them, the temple itself loomed, vast and majestic. Einar gazed up in awe at the magnificent structure and wondered how the skill of men could build such a thing. It was not like the great, dressed stone of the Rome folk he had seen in Frankia and England, which no man knew the secrets of their crafting. But the temple before him, though made with wood, iron nails, squared joints, and thatch, was no less impressive, and he could scarcely fathom the sheer scale of its construction. It was as though the giants of Jotunheim had laid vast feasting halls on top of one another, each smaller than the one below as they rose higher than the tallest boughs. Its timbers, though ancient, appeared to be of the freshest cut wood, shining bright as though coated with precious gold. The priestesses had painted other timbers red, black and blue, with swirling images of dragons, horses, boars, and scenes from well-known tales of the gods.

Einar approached the hooded figures, and Hildr cleared her throat. Both hoods snapped up to reveal ivory-white faces with sunken eyes like skulls. Amundr gasped, and Hildr quickly placed her hand on his forearm.

"It's just white face paint," she whispered, but

her words seemed to have no effect on Amundr, who sidled behind Einar.

The two figures were tall, and their faces were long, lean, and thin, with cheekbones as sharp as spear points.

"Lord Einar, Lady Hildr," uttered one in a slow woman's voice, devoid of welcome or geniality.

Einar inclined his head in solemn greeting. "We seek an audience with the high priestess," he said. He hoped his visit was a welcome one and that some goodwill remained with the order for his recovery of Odin's stolen spear. The two pale faces stared at him, and for a moment, he thought they might refuse entry and send him back to the Wind Elk without even a chance to ask for their support. Upsala was a place of worship, of the old ways, sacrifice, honour, and blood. He had not anticipated a warm welcome, for it was not a place a man went expecting to receive the honours of guest friendship. There would be no feast thrown in his honour, no casks of ale broken open, no songs sung or tales told. Upsala was a serious place, one to be feared, revered, and treated with respect.

The two white faces simultaneously nodded as though they thought and moved as one being. Einar looked closer at those deathly pale visages and saw that Hildr was right. The otherworldly paleness came from a chalk paint daubed onto their faces, flakes of it cracked and visible on their cheeks. The darkness around their eyes, which gave them a skull-like appearance, was a paste of powder, smudged and gloopy at the corners of their eyes. They wanted to appear like the dead, risen from the afterlife to administer Odin's will and receive sacrifices in their honour, but seeing the paint and paste reminded Einar that they were just people and not spirits of the realms beyond Midgard.

The two figures turned, and the gates opened behind them. Double doors made from tightly packed pine trunks creaked on their hinges and moved inwards to open the way into the sacred temple. Einar and the others followed the pair through the high gate, and the temple itself towered before them, its vastness soaring over the walls. The grounds surrounding the temple were immaculate and tranquil, and they appeared to Einar as close to Asgard as men could achieve on Midgard. Gravel pathways wove between strips and hillocks of grass so green that it seemed like someone had painted each blade with the same care as the priestesses' faces. The paths meandered like a river, forming huge whorls which reminded Einar of the swirling beast heads carved upon their ships and on the door lintels of their feasting halls. Perched on the grassy knolls between the pathways sat smooth stones carved with strings of winding runes and the snarling faces of gods, beasts, and monsters. Some of those rocks had bright colours daubed on them, while others were coated with what looked like dried, flaking blood. A rhythmic chanting flowed around the grounds like the wind, a low hum of song pulsing from inside the golden temple.

The hooded guides led them through the labyrinthine pathways, and Einar could not help but stare at the ancient snarl of tangled trees to his right. A mighty oak stood at the centre, with sprawling branches as thick around as a man's waist. Smaller, but no less ancient, trees surrounded the oak in a small grove. Their boughs twisted and clawed around one another, their trunks cast in shadow, gnarled and misshapen. Einar's jaw tightened as he noticed something sinister. Many of those trunks bore grotesque carvings – faces contorted in pain, others grimacing with the hardened resolve of battle-worn warriors. Yet the true horror of that grove lay not in the carvings or the wild tangle of branches but rather in the bodies hanging from the oak. Pale and rotting corpses of men, women, horses, dogs, and other animals dangled as sacrifices to Odin and his dark, malevolent power.

"Wait here," said the leftmost guide from beneath the folds of her hood.

"The gods," Amundr whispered, and Hildr placed her hand gently upon him once more. The giant warrior, whom Einar had seen charge into shield walls packed with champions, clashed with frothing berserkers, and faced down countless men in holmgang duels, stared upon the tree of sacrifice and trembled. "Are those people in Niflheim?" he asked.

"They are slaves and livestock whose lifeblood has been offered by their owners in sacrifice to Odin. Their blood honours the All-Father, and the folk who donated the flesh may ask something of Odin in return."

"These Svear folk have murderous ways of honouring the gods," Thorgrim muttered.

"What's wrong with pouring a libation, offering a prayer to the wind, or even cutting a beast's throat to spill the blood on a new ship for luck? To hang people naked from a tree seems like a strange way to honour the gods if you ask me."

"This temple has stood longer than anybody can remember," Hildr replied. "Its existence stretches back into the mists of time, and who can say that it wasn't here when the Aesir themselves walked amongst us, in the world's youth, when humanity was newly born to Midgard? The ways of the temple are ancient and wicked, but so is Odin himself. These traditions come down to us through the years longer than a man can count, so fear them, Thorgrim, but do not question them."

The shipmaster cast his eyes down and stared at the path, chewing his beard but unwilling to ask any further questions about the dark ways of the Odin temple. The guide marched towards the temple doors – two great oaken slabs set back on a long, blood-red wooden porch carved with intricate, intertwining designs. New acolytes in white robes stepped forward, pressing the heavy doors open with effort. They groaned on massive iron hinges, and smoke billowed out from within, carrying a putrid, decayed stench that made Einar wrinkle his nose.

From the smoke emerged a woman in a pure white robe that drifted around her. Her iron-grey hair was braided and draped over one shoulder, framing a round, deeply lined face that held a look of stern authority. Her lips were thin and tightly pursed. She paused on the porch, her steely gaze sweeping over each of the visitors. Amundr recoiled under her piercing stare while Einar jutted his chin, shoulders squared. A warrior and a jarl, he would not be cowed, even by a priestess of Odin All-Father.

"High Priestess Helgi," said Hildr, and she bowed her head solemnly.

"Sister," Helgi replied, her voice a rasping sneer. "I see you come dressed for war once more."

"War is upon us, High Priestess. And this is no skirmish between warring jarls or a king's battle waged to bring more land under his control. This war we fight concerns us all. There are strange goings on in the west. Men worship the chained one. They wear his totem and build temples in his name. They are openly worshipping he who should not be named within these walls, he who tricked blind Höðr into slaying the golden one. They talk of the Ragnarök, and foul men flock to the banner of the chained one's champion in Midgard."

Helgi leaned forward, her face shifting from cold aloofness to squint-eyed concern. "Who is this man who would unleash the chained one upon us all and cast Midgard into the flames of the Ragnarok?"

"The Crippled King of Mann. There must be war to stop the spread of his foulness before it consumes us all. So we come to you, High Priestess, to ask for the blades of the Valkyrie to join our army. Our friend, Jarl Hundr, who fought so bravely to recover the Gungnir spear for this temple, has become lost while fighting this Crippled King. We are building an army to fight for the All-Father, to fight for us all and stave off the wicked end of days this enemy would gladly unleash."

"Then we have much to talk about." Helgi turned to her acolytes. "Find them food and drink, and make sure Lady Hildr is honoured as a former sister of this temple. Einar Rosti, please, follow me."

The Valkyrie sisters bustled through the enormous oak doors, Helgi following close behind. Einar looked towards Hildr, but she merely shrugged, joining Amundr and Thorgrim as the sisters guided them away. Why him? Einar wondered. Surely, it would be better for Hildr and Helgi to speak together about the war and their need for warriors. Einar frowned and followed the high priestess through the lofty curving gateway of the temple and into the darkness beyond. The pallid smoke flooded his senses with its scent of decay, and Einar breathed it in. He knew not what awaited him inside the Odin temple, but he needed Valkyrie warriors if he was to fight the Crippled King and find Hundr, so he steeled himself for whatever lay within those walls, where the high priestess spilt the blood of those marked for sacrifice, and the rites of murder and death were commonplace.

The heavy doors closed with a thunderous slam, sealing him inside. Now, Einar was alone with the Valkyrie – and with Odin himself.

SEVENTEEN

Hundr swayed; sweat drenched his brow and stung his dead eye. Sigvarth had to press his shoulder into Hundr's to keep him on his feet. His one eye fluttered, mind drifting in and out of consciousness. He could not fall, would not fall. Hundr was a *drengr* and would not show weakness before his enemies. He bit his lip to startle himself to alertness and his one eye peered out from the bruise of his face. He found himself in a king's throne room, cold and fashioned from hard, ancient stone. Heavy tapestries draped the high walls, an empty throne loomed at one end, and a hearth fire crackled and burned on the western wall. Four alabaster-white skulls adorned the top of the throne, with one at the end of each armrest. A score of men stood in the room, warriors all, and a gaggle of stooping slaves lingered in a corner by a table filled with jugs of ale, cheeses, roasted pork, and bread. The warriors wore leather armour patched here and there with chainmail, and Hundr noticed the orange flashes of rust spotting their spear points and shield rims. They stank of unclean leather and old sweat – far from the proud, polished warriors who preened with the arrogance of status. These were men with dark eyes and stooped shoulders, rotting teeth, unkempt beards, and little care for their weapons. Men whose ambitions were as corroded as their steel, hungry for easy silver and battles with weaker foes.

The place reeked of death and festering, thick with corruption and the musty stink of beasts. Four dogs lazed around the throne, enormous hunting hounds with spiked collars and paws the size of a man's head. Flensed bones lay uncleared around the animals, picked clean of meat but left like carcasses to give the place the feel of a death god's underworld. The floor was cool beneath Hundr's feet, and the icy stone soothed the cuts and scrapes on the soles of his feet. Those feet had stumbled, run, marched, and tottered over nettles, grass, briar, and mud, traipsed through freezing streams, and waded through rivers to reach the throne room in the ancient city of Jorvik.

Sigvarth and Toki flanked him, with Harbard and Yazi the Easterner just behind. As Eyolfr and Gunnulfr had fallen in the fight with Stigmarr's warriors, and Arne had died days later from his wounds on their gruelling journey, their warband now numbered only six. Hundr vaguely recalled holding Arne when he wept in the night as they lay barefoot and bare-chested beneath the night sky. Stigmarr's men had woken Hundr one morning with a kick to the ribs, and they had laughed to find Arne stiff and dead, curled up next to Hundr like a child. They had left Arne's body on the road, a fine and brave warrior, a Vanylven man discarded like carrion for beasts and birds to feast upon. Stigmarr had stripped Hundr of his boots, his breastplate, and his prized Ulfberht sword, binding his hands with coarse rope. To lose the Ulfberht, a blade unmatched across Midgard, to a backwater jarl and his so-called warriors was a wound to Hundr's pride that gnawed deeper than the rope burns on his wrists. Hundr's head bowed as he remembered they had also taken the Seaworm's prow. The monstrously heavy wooden prow Hundr had carried on his back across half the Danelaw to preserve the memory of the proud warship Seaworm. Now, it was gone – taken by men unworthy of its majesty. For the first two days, Stigmarr rode, dragging Hundr behind him like a cur, the rope pulling taut with every stumble, his raw and half-healed wounds reopening as his body struck rock and scree. Eventually, when Stigmarr grew bored of this sport, he left Hundr to struggle along on foot, reeling from pain, to join the other captives. The days after Arne's death blurred into a fevered fog – his wounds festering anew, his body wracked by sweat and sickness, sinking in and out of consciousness.

Hundr knew that when his fever had nearly taken him, his men had borne his weight, and he would never forget what they had suffered to keep him alive. It was as though the Norns had taken his life and turned it on its head, draining the luck from him like water from a bucket. As he stood there swaying in what he assumed was a king's hall in Jorvik, Hundr wondered what he had done to offend the gods so. That worry had plagued his mind through every lash, every kick and punch, as Stigmarr's men dragged him starved and battered across the land all the way to Jorvik. What if Finn was right, and they stood upon the yawning chasm of the Ragnarök? Hundr raging against that, fighting against the Crippled King, might earn him the enmity of a force more powerful perhaps than the Aesir themselves. Who was he to steer the course of fate?

"All bow to Veggr Kolbeinsson, King of Jorvik!" shouted a shrill voice. Heavy boots thumped upon the stone floor, and a large man climbed onto a raised platform and slumped into the skull throne. He wore a *brynjar* beneath a blue cloak and a circlet of gold on his furrowed brow. Every man in the hall bowed to King Veggr, whom Hundr had never heard of, and Veggr snarled at them. He had long blonde hair tied away from his face, a thick golden beard, blue eyes, and a face more scarred than Hundr's own. A slave hurried up to the platform, a young girl in a torn woollen smock with sad eyes and bruised arms. She carried a horn of frothy ale, and just as she reached the king, she stumbled and slopped the ale onto his boots. The king's hand rested on the skulls fixed to the arms of his throne, and he drummed his fingers upon them as he stared down at the spillage. His lip curled in disgust, and he cracked the girl around the head with the back of his hand. She fell to her knees, whimpering, and scrambled away from the platform. Another girl ran to the king with a replacement horn of ale, which he drained in one gulp whilst every person in the hall looked on. Hundr could feel the fear emanating from the gathered warriors like a foul stink. They were all afraid of King Veggr.

"Well?" King Veggr demanded before belching so loud it almost shook the high rafters. His voice was a harsh bark in thick Danish-accented Norse. "I was in bed with two Frankish whores. Why am I here?"

"My king," said Stigmarr, stepping forward from in between the clutch of his men. He bowed deeply and gestured towards Hundr and his men. "We captured men on the road and have brought them before you for judgement."

King Veggr leaned forward, curling his lip at Hundr and the captured Seaworm men before slumping back onto his throne. He beckoned for more ale, which the slave girl hurried to serve him. "They look like beggars and stink like pig shit. You should have killed them on the road. Why waste my time with brigands?"

Stigmarr swallowed hard and bowed again. "Forgive me, my king, but you ordered your jarls to bring any masterless men found wandering in the kingdom of Jorvik to you for punishment."

King Veggr grunted and rolled his eyes. He drained a second horn of ale and did not care that a substantial portion of it dripped from the corners of his mouth, down his beard, and made a small puddle beside his boots. "They do not look like warriors. I could fight them all at once and not suffer a blow. If these scruffy whoresons are what passes for warriors in England, then I could take Alfred's throne in Wessex with fifty men."

The warriors in the hall stamped their feet and crashed their spear butts against the stone floor at that comment. It was unusual for a lord to allow his men to bring weapons into his hall. Ale and mead do not mix well with proud, armed men hubristic with a warrior's arrogance and reputation.

"They were not in this state when we found them, King Veggr. In fact, they killed some of my men, good men. We found weapons on them, and I offer you the finest of them as a tribute to your greatness." Stigmarr nudged one of his warriors, and a bandy-legged man hirpled forward and handed the Ulfberht sword to King Veggr.

Veggr turned the scabbarded sword over and examined the hilt work. He stood, eyes wide with wonder, and drew the blade. It shone like a glinting star in that hall, and the sound of it scraping from the scabbard's wooden mouth plucked at Hundr's heart. It was his blade. Hard-won in battle. Battle Fang was lost along with his fingers, and now the dwarven-forged blade he had carried to victory across so many battlefields lay in the hands of another man.

"A fine gift indeed, Stigmarr. You have done

well." He tore his eyes from the etchings upon the blade and squinted at Hundr and his men. "Which one of these whoresons carried the sword?"

"The one eye." Stigmarr turned and kicked Hundr as though he were a lazy dog.

"Bastard must have stolen it from a better man. Stabbed in the back," King Veggr scoffed and spat derisively in Hundr's direction.

"He can wield it well enough, Lord King."

"Is that what you did, turd? Sneak up on a *drengr* and stab him in the back, or cut his throat?"

Hundr kept his head bowed. Veggr was no *drengr.* Hundr had encountered men like him up and down the Whale Road. He was a warrior; that was plain enough. But there was no honour in the man. The way he treated his servants and the fear in the eyes of his vassals told Hundr all he needed to know. It was hard enough to stay on his feet, so Hundr chose not to bandy words with Veggr, a man of no honour who had somehow made himself King of Jorvik.

"Answer the king!" Stigmarr hissed, and he kicked Hundr again. Sigvarth reared up in anger, and the warriors laughed as one of Stigmarr's men forcefully prodded his spear shaft into Sigvarth's belly. They'd tied him at the wrists, just like Hundr, leaving him unable to defend himself. Sigvarth doubled over, winded, and Hundr winced as the men of low reputation scoffed at Sigvarth Trollhands, a mighty warrior worth ten of their kind. Hundr stared at the stone wall behind the king, wondering how far northern England had fallen since the days when Ivar the Boneless, Bjorn Ironside, and Halvdan Ragnarsson had taken the city from King Aelle the Saxon. Hundr had scaled the city walls, fighting his way over to battle inside the city beside Ivar himself. That had been the day he had earned his first arm ring and when men had begun to look upon him with respect.

How far the mighty have fallen.

"They also carried this with them, Lord King," Stigmarr said, quickly changing the subject before Hundr's insolence embarrassed him further. One of his men dragged forth a heavy piece of carved timber. Hundr's heart sank with sorrow, but then he rejoiced because it was the Seaworm's prow. Seeing the dragon head in this wretched place pained him deeply, yet it stirred hope within him. The Ulfberht sword and the Seaworm's prow were together, and as long as he drew breath, they bore witness to his former glory. "They won't say much, but I believe they are a shipwrecked crew, raiders or warriors run afoul of Njorth off our coast. Why else would they carry a prow unless to remind them of a lost warship? These are no wandering brigands who have found themselves without a lord to feed and pay them. They are more than that, and their capture honours you, Lord King."

"You're right, for once, Stigmarr. I can see the defiance in their eyes. These dogs fancy themselves, but yet here they are in rags stinking of their own piss. The one-eyed bastard has some spirit. Perhaps he thought to come here and make himself rich at my expense. He'll learn to answer when I speak," Veggr sneered, leering at Hundr and his men. "I can see they have suffered upon the road. You have not been gentle with them, Stigmarr. But neither will I." Veggr pulled a silver arm ring from his wrist and tossed it to Stigmarr, who caught it, chest swelling with pride. Veggr held up the Ulfberht sword as though he had won the blade himself. He stared around at the warriors gathered in his hall and fixed them all with his pale blue eyes. "Stigmarr speaks true. I commanded my jarls to bring any masterless men they find on the road here to me. I am king in Jorvik, the crown taken from Hardacnut by my axe and my will. This is our world. Only the strong can hold lands and titles in the Danelaw. I cannot have hungry jarls recruiting masterless men to their banner or sea wolves landing their ships on my shores. Men must know what it means to challenge King Veggr. Every man with an axe in Jorvik must fear me." He pointed the sword at Hundr and shifted the blade slowly across each of the Vanylven men before it finally came to rest, pointing at Thatchulf. "Take this one and hang him from the city gates. Leave him there for three days for the crows to feast upon his eyes and tongue. Then, cut off his head. Boil the skull until the flesh falls off, and bring the bones to me. I shall add it to the others. I shall chain the rest of these dogs in my hall beside Guthred Hardacnutsson. I will chain them here for all to witness their disgrace so every man will understand the price of defying Veggr, King of Yorvik. Take him!"

"Remember me, brother," Thatchulf

whispered. He leaned into Hundr and pressed a cold metallic object into Hundr's shackled hand. Thatchulf rammed his shoulder into the nearest guard, then swept his leg out to topple the man behind him. He bent to snatch up a spear, and though his wrists were bound, he thrust its point into the face of one of Stigmarr's warriors. Blood sprayed as shouts erupted around the hall, chaos spilling through its ranks.

Sigvarth charged another of Stigmarr's men, and the hall came alive with drawn weapons and cries of alarm. A thick-bearded man with an axe raised above his head charged at Thatchulf. Burdened by his bulk, he was slow – a flaw Thatchulf, the former pit fighter, exploited with ease. Holding the spear mid-shaft, hands bound together, he drove its point into the man's round belly, piercing the leather breastplate. The man gasped, collapsing to his knees, as Thatchulf tore the spear free, splattering fresh scarlet blood across the cold stone floor.

The hunting dogs growled, bright white fangs showing beneath snarling maws. Hundr stumbled forward, anger rising inside him, needing to protect his friend from Veggr's cruel punishment and the blades of his warriors. Fever and weakness quenched that anger like water thrown on a fire, and he could only stumble forward on unsteady legs. He had not the strength to charge, nor could he fight or help Thatchulf. Hundr's anger gave way to shame as a circle of men gathered about Thatchulf. Veggr's warriors hefted shields and used them to bully Hundr's men, shoving them backwards to corral them like cattle. Hundr, Sigvarth, Harbard, Toki and Yazi shoved back at the guards, but in their shackled, weakened, and unarmed state, there was nothing they could do for their shipmate and brother, who stood alone amongst a multitude of baying enemies.

"I won't die on the end of a rope," Thatchulf roared, teeth bared and eyes fierce. "I am a warrior and will not go to God shamed by backwater nithings like you!" He was a Frank and a Christian, though he spoke in Norse so his enemies could understand him. "Fight me! Fight me!" Thatchulf was shouting, and he jabbed his spear at his enemies, daring them to attack.

"Get back!" King Veggr bellowed. He leapt down from his thrown, vast bulk landing heavily. He still held the Ulfberht sword in his hand and he tested the weight, swinging it about him in wide strokes. His men fell away, sidling backwards with weapons held ready in case their king ordered them to strike. "He's mine now. I'll add your skull to my throne, turd, and feed your corpse to the pigs."

Thatchulf lunged at the king, and Veggr swerved aside just as the spear point flashed past his face. Thatchulf brought the spear back, but his movements were made clumsy by his tied wrists, and his grip on the weapon was in its centre, off balance, making it impossible for him to do anything but stab with the weapon. Veggr held the sword in two hands, and he jabbed it at Thatchulf. Hundr staggered forward, his mind and heart crying out for him to rip the blade from Veggr's hands and drive the point into his foul heart. The king held the sword like a child, like a man unaccustomed to the weapon of elite warriors. He moved like an axeman, all muscle and brute force. Veggr brought the weapon down in a short chop, and it smashed through Thatchulf's spear, severing the point and leaving Thatchulf clutching a length of broken haft. Thatchulf advanced like a starving bear. He kicked and stabbed at Veggr, bellowing incoherently as he fought to die a warrior's death. Veggr chopped and slashed at Thatchulf like a butcher, opening a gash in his thigh and shoulder. Blood flowed freely from Thatchulf, and it smeared on the stone floor beneath his feet. He ducked beneath the wild swing of the Ulfberht sword and came up with the litheness of a dancer and cracked the broken spear across Veggr's skull.

The king stumbled, dazed, and the Ulfberht sword clattered to the floor. Thatchulf grinned like a madman and lunged at the king, thrusting the jagged wood toward Veggr's throat. Before it could reach its mark, one of the king's men blocked the strike with his shield, shoving Thatchulf back. Another drove a spear into the back of Thatchulf's thigh, forcing the former pit fighter down on one knee. The first guard then swung his axe, slicing into Thatchulf's forearm with a sickening crunch. Hundr heard the snap of bones.

Thatchulf's arm was a mangled mess of blood, flesh, and splintered bone, but he forced himself back to his feet. Veggr snatched up the Ulfberht sword, his face red and twisted with fury. He raised the blade high, bringing it down with both hands. Thatchulf, eyes closed, lifted the broken spear in a futile defence, accepting his fate. He died like a warrior. The sword cleaved into his neck with a spray of dark blood, and Thatchulf fell to the stones. Veggr stabbed and hacked at his corpse in a crazed frenzy, and a tear rolled down Hundr's cheek. His friend had died, and there was nothing he could do to help him. The scrap of iron Thatchulf had passed to Hundr was the crucifix he wore around his neck. Hundr's friend was gone, another Vanylven man lost, and Hundr wondered if there would ever be an end to the suffering of the Seaworm crew.

EIGHTEEN

The heavy temple doors creaked closed behind Einar, and he followed High Priestess Helgi into the darkness inside the vast, ancient Odin temple. He swallowed as he breathed in air thick with fragrant smoke that reeked of fungus and dried plants. Einar coughed to clear his throat, and a deep chanting sprang up from the temple's recesses, the sound reverberating around the high roof, throbbing in Einar's ears. There was a foulness to the air, a reek of death, and the smoke seeping into his lungs made Einar's mind gloat. He fought to maintain control of his senses and swallowed down the urge to vomit.

Einar's weathered leather boots thudded softly against the wooden floor, which was worn smooth by the passage of countless feet over many generations. Wooden beams spanned the space above him, carved with serpentine dragons and runes of power. The wood, aged and soot-darkened, gleamed in the flickering light cast by rushlights and torches placed along the walls. Those beams supported the towering structure, and as the smoke bled into Einar's lungs, the carving seemed to move and shift around him, filling him with dread. For this was the temple of Odin, and the All-Father was cruel and cunning, the benefactor and betrayer of warriors.

Helgi halted abruptly, and Einar almost collided with her, so captivated was he by the closeness he felt to Odin All-Father in that foreboding place. She raised her pale arms and whispered a prayer to Odin, which Einar could not hear above the rhythmic chanting. She clapped her hands twice, and the chanting stopped as suddenly as it had begun, leaving Einar and Helgi alone in smoke-ringed silence. Before them loomed a towering, vividly painted totem, taller even than the mast of the Ormrinn Langi. It was hewn from a single, massive oak trunk, its surface etched with intricate runes of ravens, axes, ships, and wild-eyed beasts entwined in twisting patterns. At its peak, a monstrous, bearded face with a single eye gazed down – the piercing all-knowing eye of Odin himself, seeming to peer into the depths of Einar's soul.

Other vast totems flanked the All-Father, smaller but no less awe-inspiring. They spread around the temple walls, bearing the bearded faces of the gods, soft faces of beautiful goddesses, and ever more ravens, boars, axes, and dragons. Smoke coiled around them as Einar's gaze fixed upon Thor's hammer, Mjolnir, beneath the face of the thunder god. He saw

Njorth's fierce countenance above churning sea monsters and Frigg grieving for her son Baldr's death in her marshy hall of Fensalir, mistletoe twining around her carved hands. Helgi shed her heavy cloak to reveal a long, woollen robe dyed in rich hues of red, brown, and black. Silver-threaded runes glimmered along her sleeves, and plush fur lined the neckline. Her head was shaved except for a single, lengthy braid hanging from the crown. Silver necklaces and arm rings jingled as she moved, and she grasped a yew staff from beneath a flickering torch. Intricate carvings of wolves and ravens, symbols of mighty Odin, adorned the top of the yew staff.

"You bring ill-tidings, Einar Rosti," said Helgi, turning to fix him with her stern face. "Hildr spoke of men worshipping the chained one, he who shall not be named in this temple to the All-Father. Who is this Crippled King of Mann, and what has become of The Man with the Dog's Name?"

"Midgard is changing," Einar replied. "The nailed god grows in power, and as our ships sail further south, east, and west, we find new peoples with strange beliefs. In our quest for glory and silver, our people move away from the old gods, the gods of our fathers. The Crippled King is full of hate, and he uses the chained one to bind men to him with fear. He brought war to King Harald Fairhair last summer and even came to the king's hall with a cawing raven perched on his shoulder. He spoke of the dawn of the Ragnarök and how the chained one is loose from his fetters."

Helgi shook her head and leaned closer, peering deeper into Einar's eyes. "But there is more to this tale, is there not? I can see it broiling inside you like a mountain ready to erupt. Tell it all, Einar, tell me what has become of The Man with the Dog's name, he who was so favoured by Odin? And why does this Crippled King seethe with such venomous hatred?"

Hooded figures shuffled into the hall, each holding a long, slender rod that trailed a stream of fresh smoke. The scent – pine resin, sharp and clean – pierced the air, pushing back the fouler stench. Einar shook his head to steady his senses before recounting to Helgi the tales of Ivar, Saoirse, Finn, and Hundr. He spoke of the Witch-Queen and her dark *seiðr*, of Hundr's lost wife and son, of Hrist, Ragnhild, and the other Valkyrie priestesses who had sailed on the warship Seaworm. Einar painted for her the battle at Hafrsfjord with Harald Fairhair and detailed all they had seen and done in the reaches of Ireland, England, Frankia, and Novgorod. Helgi silently absorbed every word with stoic patience, yet when Einar spoke of the temple the Crippled King was raising in Mann, she shuddered with a tremor of dread. As Einar described the fire amulets worn by Finn's warriors in homage to the chained one, Helgi's hand instinctively reached for her own Gungnir spear amulet to ward off the ill-omen of Einar's words.

"Dark times," she whispered.

"Which is why we come to you now. We come for warriors, Odin's own Valkyrie priestesses.

Join your warriors to ours and to those of Harald Fairhair. We shall sail to Mann and bring war to the Crippled King. We must find Hundr. It was he, above all, who fought to retrieve the sacred spear of your temple, stolen as it was by renegade priestesses."

"How many men can the Crippled King bring to war?"

"Thirty crews, we think. Perhaps more."

"That's two or three thousand warriors, Einar. How many do you have?"

"Three hundred warriors sworn to fight for Hundr and I."

She raised an eyebrow. "You need more warriors."

"Three hundred less the crew lost with Hundr and the Seaworm. But King Harald has pledged to join the fight, and when I leave here, I go to King Bjorn Ironside. Hundr and I rescued his son from the Witch-Queen of Vedrafjord in Ireland. Bjorn is Ragnar Lothbrok's last living son, and he will join our army. Then I shall seek Haesten, he who has sailed further and sacked more cities than any man alive. I am certain he shall stand with us. Our numbers may be few, but we will gather the mightiest warriors in all of Midgard. Our army will be as if the Einherjar itself has marched from Valhalla's gates to battle the Crippled King. Can your order pass up the chance to join such a cause? To proudly fight a war that will echo in song and legend until the end of days? What have you been doing since the Great Ragnarsson Army marched upon England?

Fighting in minor wars between petty jarls? Your order exists to fight in wars of legend and send the finest warriors to honour Odin's hall. So will you join us, Helgi of the Valkyrie?"

"Words fit to stir the heart of any warrior before battle, Einar Rosti. Though I serve as High Priestess of our order, even I do not possess the power to command our warriors to war. For that, I must seek Odin's will. Do you seek an army of warrior priestesses for your war against the Crippled King?"

"I do."

"Then we shall augur the All-Father and see what our fate shall be."

Helgi drove her staff down twice into the floorboards. A door opened at the temple's eastern wall, and a line of acolytes came in, holding flaming torches. They gathered about an altar at the centre of the temple, a massive stone slab hewn from the bedrock and stained dark with the blood of countless sacrifices. Suspended above it, the silver spear Gungnir hung by slender threads of silver, appearing to float amidst the smoke. This was the spear of the All-Father, fated to slay the monstrous Fenris Wolf on the day of Ragnarök. Its head was vast, gleaming fiercely in the torchlight. The blade was as wide as a man's head, and the shaft, crafted from smooth wood, bore intricate runic engravings with silver threads winding along its length. It was magnificent. Einar had not seen it in years, not since he and Hundr had recovered it from Novgorod. Back then, Hundr had used the spear to kill his half-brother,

Yaroslav, Prince of Novgorod, offering his life to Odin as a *blót* sacrifice for victory. They had sailed the broad Volkhov River to do so. With all that had happened since then, the journey felt like a lifetime ago. In the smoke and the heady atmosphere inside the temple, Einar recalled the friends and brothers he had lost since that wild fight inside Novgorod's high walls. He remembered Ragnhild and hoped Odin did too, for if there was ever a warrior who honoured the All-Father, it was her.

Einar stared at the altar, his eyes lingering on the dried blood of hundreds of souls sacrificed upon its ancient stone. He hoped that Hundr's *blót* had meant something to the All-Father, that all the souls he and Hundr had sent to join the Einherjar would grant him favour with the father of the Aesir. Two large Valkyrie priestesses garbed in *brynjars* entered through the side door, and between them, they dragged a wiry man with a head of wild, brown hair and a bushy, unkempt beard. He struggled between them, staring at the altar, terrified by his surroundings. Einar closed his eyes, bracing himself for what was about to happen, for he understood the price Odin demanded of the priestesses.

"Odin, hear us!" Helgi called, and the Valkyrie inside the temple let out their blood-curdling, undulating battle cry, which Einar had heard Hildr and Ragnhild scream so many times before. "We offer you the soul of this man, a nithing cur caught stealing food from fields meant to feed your Valkyrie shield maidens. We offer him to you, a sacrifice to Nástrǫnd, a man of low honour for Níðhöggr the corpse ripper to gnaw on and keep the mighty serpent at bay. Show us your will, and grant us guidance in return for this offering!"

Einar kept his eyes closed as the Valkyrie fought with the man to drag and heave his writhing body onto the altar. He could not look as an acolyte passed a ceremonial dagger made of jet-black, wickedly sharp stone to Helgi. He heard their chanting, growing wilder and quicker as the man screamed and begged for his life. In a heartbeat, the chanting suddenly fell silent, as did the man's screams, and only then did Einar open his eyes to see blood pouring down the altar and into grooves etched into the temple's wooden floor. Helgi bent over the sacrificed man, hands busy over his still corpse. She gasped and turned to Einar, placed her hands upon the altar, and then smeared blood across her pale face. She grinned, teeth showing white amongst the dark blood, and stalked towards Einar. He tried not to flinch away from the horror of it all and stood still as she wiped the blood across his forehead like paint. Einar was no stranger to death, and there was honour in standing toe to toe with a warrior, trading blows until one overcomes the other. The same honour was not in the sacrifice before him, but he needed to find Hundr. He needed to end the war with the Crippled King, and so Einar held his tongue and let the Valkyrie do their work.

"Odin favours you," Helgi proclaimed, eyes wide with fervour, blood staining her hands and dripping down her pale arms. "War, Einar. Odin shows me war in the blood of our sacrifice.

Can you feel his presence?" So caught up was she in the moment, in the blood, death, smoke and the atmosphere inside the temple, that her voice dropped to a breathless whisper. "Odin is amongst us. His will speaks in the blood we have offered to the Corpse-Ripper. We shall join you, Einar the Brawler. The Valkyrie shall send a force to join your army of heroes. Odin wills it! Odin's fury broils with ardour. Those who have taken up worship of the chained one must be stopped, and their leader must be punished for leading them on this path. Worshipping the chained one gives him power – it aids his struggle against the mighty fetters that hold him tight. Should he break free, the Ragnarök will begin. It has been foretold since the dawn of time. First, the Fimbulwinter shall descend, a harsh and unrelenting winter lasting three long years to freeze the world. The sun and moon shall be swallowed by monstrous wolves, Sköll and Hati, plunging Midgard into eternal darkness. Midgard itself shall shudder, mountains shall crumble, and the seas shall rise. The giant serpent Jörmungandr will burst forth from the depths, poisoning the sky and waters as it thrashes, whilst Fenris, the monstrous wolf, will break free from the chains placed upon him by Tyr, and his jaws shall gape wide enough to devour Midgard itself.

"The skies will rend like a split log as Surtr, the fire giant, marches from Muspelheim, his flaming sword scorching everything in his path. The chained one, freed from his fetters, will lead his brood of giants and monsters into battle against the Aesir. The fell ship Naglfar will come from the Whale Road, crewed by the souls of the inglorious dead, and the battlefield, Vigrid, will be the stage for the last battle. Odin will face the monstrous wolf but will be swallowed whole, though his son Vidar will avenge him by tearing the wolf's jaws apart. Thor will slay Jörmungandr yet succumb to its venom. Loki and Heimdall, eternal enemies, will slay each other in a brutal duel. Fire will consume the world as Surtr unleashes his flames, reducing all to ash. So it shall be, Einar, if we cannot bring this Crippled King to heel."

Einar knew the tale of the Ragnarök, as did all who grew up worshipping the Aesir, but to hear it recanted inside the great temple of Upsala sent a shiver down Einar's back.

The Valkyrie feasted Einar, Hildr, Amundr and Thorgrim later that day, and the priestesses were jubilant at the prospect of a glorious war and a chance to fulfil their vows to Odin. When it was over, and the sun crept behind the pines, Hildr took Einar walking in the fields and groves where she had played as a girl and learned to fight beside Ragnhild. She wept at those memories of Ragnhild running through the wild grass in their childhood. Hildr told Einar of days full of laughter, but there had also been hardship, for the Valkyrie weapons masters were not gentle in their instruction. At last, they lay down beneath soft furs in the Valkyrie barracks, and Einar listened to his wife sleep, conflicted by his hopes for his glorious death in battle and a desire to live on forever by her side.

The barracks were empty when Einar awoke the following day. He dressed and walked out into a sun-drenched morning where dew glistened on spiders' webs like tiny diamonds. Einar found Hildr dressed in her *brynjar*, weapons beside her, and a Valkyrie sister shaving the sides of her head clean with a sharp knife. Hildr sat with her eyes closed until the sister finished her work. Then, she plaited Hildr's remaining hair into a thick braid, into which she wove threads of red-dyed wool.

"You look the way you did the day we met," Einar said once the sister left them alone.

"I cannot fight beside my old sisters without becoming who I once was. And I don't look the same. I am older, weaker, grey-haired and wrinkled."

"You have never changed, my love. You might have put down your axe and bow and taken to wearing a dress instead of battle armour. But you have always been a Valkyrie warrior priestess and the woman I love. You look as beautiful as you did all those years ago, with the sun in your hair and a snarl on your face."

"Einar!" she chided as he grabbed her and pulled her close. "The sisters will see. They are sworn to a vow of celibacy."

Einar let her go, and she punched him playfully. He did not remind her that she, too, had once taken that vow, and he could not count how many times they had lain together, but he was glad for that broken vow all the same. Acolytes led Einar, Hildr, Amundr, and Thorgrim through the first path until they reached the river, and Einar emerged from the trees to the sounds of war horns blaring long and loud. Six *drakkar* warships glided along, their sleek, narrow hulls cutting through the water with ease. It was still morning, and a mist clung to the water, rising in ghost-like wisps as the sun climbed higher in the eastern sky. The river was wide but slow-moving, deep and black, reflecting the towering pine and birch trees lining each bank.

Einar walked to the shore, his heart swelling with hope. He marched through marshy reeds down onto a small patch of sandy shore where the roots of old trees twisted into the water. Birds whistled and sang in the treetops, their cries piercing the stillness between horn blasts. Longships came swiftly as their oars dipped into the water, prows carved with Odin's favoured beasts, ravens and wolves. The Valkyrie had painted each prow beast in bright colours, so that the animals seemed to have a life of their own. Their eyes glowered along the river, fierce and unblinking, as though daring any unseen enemies to show themselves. Above the decks, the rigging hung loose, striped sails furled tightly against the yard. Valkyrie warriors crowded each ship, some pulling oars, others staring ahead. They chose not to dress for the sea but instead wore their shining armour with bows across their backs and axes at their belts. Their shields, each bearing the spear symbol of Odin All-Father, were lashed to the sides of each warship.

The Wind Elk waited beside a small jetty, the crew staring at the six ships and their magnificent crew in awe. It was rare to see so many warriors in *brynjar* chainmail, and they shined as though they had ridden from Asgard like Odin's actual Valkyrie, the choosers of the slain. The Valkyrie fleet came to a stop, and amidst more blaring of war horns and the beating of drums, High Priestess Helgi went to each ship and daubed a stripe of sacrificial blood onto the brow of each of the four hundred warriors the order sent to crush the Crippled King. Once that ceremony was complete, Einar and his party boarded the Wind Elk, and seven ships left the temple at Upsala. They rowed around a bend in the river where dense forest gave way to open meadows, where grass grew tall and golden beneath the warm sun. They rowed in determined silence, the Wind Elk crew grim-faced and ready for the next leg of the voyage. Einar stared out into the rippling river. Next, he would sail to King Bjorn Ironside, son of Ragnar, the last rightful Ragnarsson entitled to fly the dreaded raven banner, though Finn Ivarsson flew that famous standard in honour of his dead father.

In the distance, the faint silhouette of Upsala's great temple rose above the trees like a shadow on the horizon, and Einar gripped the tiller so hard that his knuckles turned white. He had Harald Fairhair's warriors and now four hundred Valkyrie warriors at his back. Einar closed his eyes.

"I am coming for you, brother," he whispered into the wind, hoping Njorth would carry the message across Midgard to Hundr, wherever he was. "I am bringing an army to you. Live."

NINETEEN

The moon waxed and waned, and Hundr remained chained in King Veggr's damp throne room. It was a cold, dark place of stone from which droplets of moisture clung to the walls, slithering between the dressed stone in curling rivulets. Thick manacles around Hundr's wrists held iron chains fastened to a rust-covered ring set within the old Roman-built wall. The chain was long enough to allow him to piss and shit in an overflowing, stinking bucket which he, Toki, Sigvarth, Harbard, and Yazi shared with Veggr's other prisoner, Guthred Hardancnutsson. He had a quiet demeanour, with a face of sharp angles and greasy golden hair that he braided, even though it was caked in filth.

Guthred marked the days by scratching a pebble upon the stone on which he slept, and he told the other prisoners stories of the gods and of his father Hardacnut, whom Veggr had killed to win Jorvik's throne.

"My father was a weak man," he said more than once. "The crown of Jorvik passed through many hands since Halvdan Ragnarsson died. It landed in my father's lap because his warriors won the throne with knives in the black, dark deeds and whispers behind closed doors. So it was with Veggr, who was my father's oathman. He killed my father in front of me and chained me here to mock my inability to protect my inheritance."

Guthred was a devout follower of the nailed god, and four times each day, he would kneel and quietly utter his prayers. He prayed for Hundr and his men and for the folk he knew outside of their grim imprisonment. He was, perhaps, the kindest and most unselfish man Hundr had ever met. Hundr and his men bristled with warrior's pride and arrogance, but Guthred thought of others before himself. He was the true heir to the kingdom of Jorvik, and though he had seen his father slaughtered by Veggr, there was no vengeance in Guthred's heart.

"I have already forgiven him," Guthred would say whenever any of the Seaworm men asked him how he planned to avenge his father's death. "The lesson is well taught by the life of St Cuthbert, who was mocked and rejected as he preached the word of god. He responded with kindness and grace, and when his tormentors fell on hard times, Cuthbert came to their aid, and through the example of his mercy, they repented."

"I'd slit open Veggr's belly, cut off his head and throw his body in a midden heap if he killed my father," remarked Toki, which the Seaworm men agreed was a far better punishment for Veggr's usurpation of the throne than forgiveness. They coughed and wheezed through freezing nights with nothing to cover their naked torsos, for Stigmarr had left them nothing to wear but their trews, which quickly became foul and infested with lice. Over the six days following their imprisonment, both Hundr and Sigvarth fell ill. Hundr's wounds festered anew, while Sigvarth succumbed to a gut sickness. Hundr watched the sun and moon trade places through a narrow window high in the opposite wall, each cycle blurring into the next as he lay shivering, vomiting, and sinking into the filth around him.

Toki, Harbard, and Yazi did their best to tend to Hundr and Sigvarth. They fed them more than their share of the slop and leftovers King Veggr tossed to them once his hunting dogs were full. But for many of those days of sickness, Hundr could eat nothing at all. Yazi bathed his wounds with drinking water, foul water, which made Sigvarth even sicker. The men huddled together and kept each other alive, though they grew thinner and weaker than Hundr thought possible. They were like nithings drifting in the afterlife reserved for the inglorious dead.

"Did we die without our weapons?" Sigvarth whispered one night as he and Hundr huddled together for warmth, gaunt faces close to one another, ragged beards stained with vomit.

"No," Hundr replied. "We are alive, though where we are is worse than Niflheim. The Norns have twisted a cruel thread into the story of our lives. Odin has forgotten us, but we cannot allow this to be our destiny. I will not die like this."

Warriors who do not die in battle are condemned to spend the afterlife in Niflheim, the realm of cold and darkness ruled by Hel. It is a land of perpetual frost, cloaked in mist, with jagged mountains and frozen rivers. The sky remains an unyielding grey, and the earth is lifeless, entombed beneath snow and ice. Hel, the goddess who is half-living and half-dead, presides over the souls of those claimed by illness or old age. Her hall, Eljudnir, looms grim and vast, its walls cast from ice and shadow. The dead who drift there exist in bleak, joyless shadows, far from the honourable halls of Valhalla. Though Niflheim was cold, desolate, and unforgiving, Veggr's throne room was worse. The king and his men taunted Hundr and the few battered survivors from the Seaworm's crew, parading them like trophies to warn all who visited of the fate awaiting masterless men in his kingdom. On feast nights, Veggr's warriors would beat them, piss on their shivering bodies, mock their stench, and toss scraps of meat for them to fight over against Veggr's hunting hounds, whose snarling contempt matched that of the king.

One night, deep in a fever, wounds throbbing with pus, Hundr thought he was going to die. He shuddered at the horror of it, hearing the laughter of his dead brother and harsh father as they stared at him from beyond the grave as though they had always known this would be his fate.

"No," Sigvarth had said, draping his thin arm around Hundr's trembling shoulders. "You are going to live. We are going to live. We are warriors, and we shall rise again to strike at our enemies."

Live. Survive and rise to fight again. Finn must die. Orm must die.

Hundr clung to his mantra, drawing strength from Sigvarth's words, and he lived. The infection passed, as did Sigvarth's sickness. They grew stronger and battled Veggr's hounds for meat to keep themselves alive. With nothing to pare his nails, Hundr's hands became clawed like a beast's. He endured the taunts, Veggr's savage kicks, the humiliation, and the sorrow – all of it hardening into a seething hatred that fuelled Hundr's strength. By the light of the moon, watching it wane to a sliver of hacksilver and swell back to full brilliance, he waited, yearning for a single chance to break his chains and fight his way to freedom.

Sorrow and hardship amuse the Norns as much as pride and glory, and Hundr's chance came on a day when rain hammered through the small window, and Veggr's bedraggled slaves dashed about his hall. They dragged feasting benches from the edges of the throne room and swept away the dog shit and food scraps. A wide-hipped woman with weary, downcast eyes, who Hundr has seen Veggr rape in front of his men more than once, emptied their shit pail and washed away the foulness beneath their thin bodies.

"Does Veggr have visitors?" Toki asked, speaking Saxon, for the woman was a slave who spoke only a little Norse.

She glanced around nervously, checking that none of Veggr's warriors would hear her speaking to the imprisoned men. "Yes," she whispered. "Some important prince of your people. We must make the place clean. There will be a feast tonight." Her head sagged at the prospect, for on feast nights, a belly full of ale made Veggr particularly malicious and cruel. He would strip his slave women and pass them around his men, beat Hundr and the Seaworm crew, and more than once, Hundr had seen him kill a man for a perceived slight or insult.

"These Northmen who have settled in the Danelaw have forgotten what it means to be a *drengr*," Sigvarth tutted and spat in disgust. The rest of the Seaworm men murmured in agreement, and the slave woman left them in the cold corner of Veggr's throne room.

Slaves filled the feasting benches with jugs of ale, loaves of bread, pots of honey, and platters of apples, pears, and berries. As the afternoon wore on, they added logs to the hall fire and set up spits with roasting pig, duck, and trout. Hundr and his men salivated at the smells, and Hundr's belly pinched with overwhelming hunger. More slaves bustled into the throne room, scattering fresh rushes on the floor to soak up spillages, and rushlights were lit to brighten the dark space. For once, the place seemed like more than a dungeon, and warriors drifted in to take their places on the benches according to their rank. The more important men sat closest to Veggr's throne, with lesser men keeping to the back.

"That is Faxi, one of Veggr's allies and once a warrior in my father's service," Guthred said, pointing to a swarthy man who took a seat close to the front. "He is a jarl now, with lands and horses. He led my father to the room where Veggr waited to kill him."

It was a nest of vipers, and Guthred spoke every man's name as they entered the hall one by one. As the benches filled and the throne room hummed with the rumbling echo of quiet chatter, slaves brought in steaming bowls of onions, leeks, and cabbage. Moving among the warriors and lords, they poured frothing ale into wooden mugs as men used eating knives to consume the bread, honey, fruit, and vegetables. A red-haired warrior in a patched *brynjar* marched from the rear, his boots thudding on the top platform upon which Veggr's throne stood, skulls casting dark, hollow stares over the crowded room.

"King Veggr of Jorvik!" the warrior shouted, and he banged his spear butt three times on the wooden platform to announce the king's arrival. Veggr marched in through the same door, and the hall erupted into cheers and clapping to acclaim the usurper's entrance. He wore his *brynjar*, a black cloak, and the Ulfberht sword in its scabbard at his belt. Bile rose in Hundr's throat to see his magnificent sword on the hip of so vile a man. Veggr lifted a hand to quieten the crowd and slumped into his throne. He yawned and clicked his fingers at the slaves by the fire, who began to slice cuts of roasting meat and distribute them amongst the crowd from large wooden platters.

Two benches close to the front were empty,

and Hundr wondered what noble lord could attract such honour from the foul Veggr. His answer came in a storm of pushing and shouting at the back of the throne room. Hundr strained against his fetters, unable to see properly, but a crowd leapt up from their feasting benches. Men jostled each other, shouting in outrage as some were thrust back and others rushed to join the commotion. King Veggr stood, face gurning with growing anger. He gestured to the warrior who had announced his arrival, and the man jumped down from the high platform and thrust men out of his way with the butt of his spear. The throng surged like the sea; men shouted and heaved at one another, and then it parted as a tall warrior with flame-red hair barged through, laughing and tossing men out of his way. Veggr's spearman tried to stop him, but the red-haired warrior grabbed the spear, twisted it savagely out of his hands, and used the stave to trip the man over. The men in the hall paused, staring at the fallen man and then at King Veggr, who could do little more than gape at the insult to his herald.

The red-haired man tossed the spear to a seated guest and guffawed. He threw his head back, laughing raucously, and it was so infectious that the rest of the hall joined him. Even Veggr's fury softened. The red-haired man leapt up on a feasting bench, swiped a jug of ale and drank it until it spilt into his beard and down onto the table. Hundr sat up straight, and warmth enveloped his heart like a lover's embrace. He could not help but laugh at the sheer madness of fate because the wild, red-haired warrior was Erik Bloodaxe, Prince of Norway and Hundr's foster son.

"That's Erik," gasped Sigvarth. "The mad little bastard is almost as tall as Einar now."

"I am Erik Bloodaxe!" Erik bellowed, throwing his arms out wide. "Well met, King Veggr. Your men wanted me to wait outside the hall, but I do not wait." He made an exaggerated bow and leapt down from the table. A dozen warriors followed Erik, all big men in *brynjar* coats of chainmail, men with scarred faces and strutting, arrogant strides. They were warriors all, *drengrs,* bristling with pride and confidence.

"And look!" Sigvarth said, grabbing Hundr's arm and pointing towards Erik's men.

There was another familiar face amongst Erik's warriors. A man with golden hair and a short beard yet to reach the thickness of full manhood. He was straight-backed and broad-shouldered, and Hundr almost wept for joy. It was his son, Hermoth, there in his war finery at the side of his friend, Erik, the son of Harald Fairhair. Where there had been only bleakness and suffering, when Hundr had been sure that Odin had forsaken him, a ray of hope clattered into Veggr's hall like a thunderbolt.

Erik swaggered between the benches, wearing a heavy fur cloak which shimmered as he moved. He wore shining mail and carried two axes tucked into his belt, upon which he rested his hands as he walked, shoulders back, rolling with each step as he met every man's eye, daring them to meet his champion's gaze.

"Do you know these men?" asked Guthred, sliding over to sit next to Hundr.

"One of them is my son," Hundr replied, unable to conceal his smile. "The leader is Erik Bloodaxe, whom I raised and taught to fight. He is brave and daring. Like a hero of old. But he is also a killer, ruthless, and ambitious."

"Then God has answered my prayers, Hundr, for he has sent men to liberate us."

Hundr doubted Erik had come at the nailed god's behest. Erik had killed his first man when still a beardless boy and earned his byname with the blood spattered upon his axe that day. Hundr had been there, just as he had seen Erik fight and kill savage warriors up and down the Whale Road. Erik had run the oars of a *drakkar* outside Avaldsnes while the entire court was watching. He commanded a warband sworn to him alone and owned his own *drakkar* warship. Hermoth sailed with Erik, for they had grown up together like brothers, and now they sailed the Whale

Road seeking reputation and silver. Erik would be king of Norway one day, and to be a king of a land full of brutal, ruthless Viking warriors, a man must command respect.

Erik and his men reached the space below King Veggr's high platform, but Erik did not bow.

"King Veggr, we thank you for your hospitality," Erik said, speaking loudly so that every man in the hall could hear his voice. "We come from Ispania, where the sun burns hotter than the flames of Surtr's flaming sword. We saw vast sea monsters, men with skins as dark as night, women of such beauty they take a man's breath away. We raided and fought in wars and won so much gold and silver that we had to leave most of it behind or risk our ship sinking into the murky depths with its weight."

"We throw a feast in your honour, Prince Erik," replied Veggr, slouching in his chair as though he did not care about the famous prince's adventures. But the splendour of the feast and the uncommon cleanliness of his foul throne room told Hundr differently. Veggr paused as though he wracked his thought cage for something eloquent to say, something profound to match Erik's boast. He cleared his throat and said, "Sit. Eat. Drink."

Erik and Hermoth took their places at the feasting benches and tucked into Veggr's food.

The hall settled down whilst men ate and drank their fill. Once the food was over, the entertainment would begin. Perhaps a bard with a song, or a challenge of wrestling, axe throwing or some other test of strength and skill.

"We should call out to Erik and Hermoth," urged Toki, pulling at his chains. "Have them release us from this place."

"No," said Hundr. He wanted nothing more than to call out to Hermoth, to have his son and foster son cast off his chains and free him from Veggr's malice. But Veggr did not know who his captive was. He thought Hundr some masterless brigand whom he kept as a pet to warn others what became of men who threatened his authority. If he knew he held The Man with the Dog's Name, things could go differently. Seeing their father treated so poorly would anger Erik and Hermoth, and that could only result in violence in a hall where they were vastly outnumbered.

"But they are right there, a stone's throw away from us? This is no accident. It is the will of the gods, my lord. Please, cry out, or let me call to them in your stead?"

"No."

Toki stared at Hundr, his mouth moving up and down, but no words came. Despair showed upon his once-hard face, and Hundr lay back against the wall, keeping to the shadows as Veggr's dogs growled at him, smelling the food and hoping for the first share of the scraps. Erik and Hermoth ate with their men under Veggr's suspicious gaze, and Hundr watched his two sons. He slunk back into the darkness even further, ashamed that they might see what had become of him. Hundr was maimed, filthy, with matted hair and beard, wearing nothing but ragged trews. He looked like a beggar, not like the Champion of the North. The feast went on, and men's voices grew louder as more ale flowed. Veggr threw a pork bone towards his dogs, and Harbard leapt for it, beating the hounds who growled and snapped their jaws at him. Moonlight poured in through the window to illuminate Hundr's wretched face, and in that split second, as Harbard grabbed the bone, Hundr caught Hermoth staring straight at him. Hermoth leaned forward, mouth open, just staring into Hundr's single eye, and Hundr stared back. A lump welled in his throat, and Hundr swallowed it. A man at Hermoth's table made a joke, and Erik's warriors laughed. Hermoth joined in, and Hundr was sure that his son had not recognised him. How could he? Hundr was supposed to be pursuing Finn Ivarsson in the Irish Sea, not here, chained like a thrall in Jorvik. Hermoth laughed and leaned close to Erik to whisper something into the prince's ear.

"How is the food?" King Veggr roared, slopping ale from a curved horn as he staggered up from his throne. His men shouted their approval and banged their fists on the table. "Shall we have a song? A tale of Thor, perhaps, or the story of Ragnar Lothbrok's siege of Paris?"

Veggr's men shouted back, calling out which of their king's suggestions they most approved of.

Prince Erik stood up, and the hall fell silent as men waited to hear what the brash young prince had to say. He swayed, and his ale spilt onto his boots. Hermoth stood and took the cup from Erik's hand, and the prince belched and held on to the table to steady himself.

"How about a challenge?" Erik said, staring at Veggr.

"What sort of challenge, young prince?" Veggr replied warily. "Wrestling? Axe throwing?"

"What are we? Maids? A fight, King Veggr. A little blood to honour your feast and the grand old city of Jorvik." Murmurs ran about the hall, and Erik turned, smiling at his men, his blue eyes catching the torchlight. He wobbled and steadied himself again. "Would you like to see a fight?"

Erik's men shouted their approval, and the rest of Veggr's guests took up the roar until the throne room shook with drunken bellows, thumping fists and stamping feet. Veggr waved for calm, and the hall fell silent again.

"Do you make a challenge yourself, Prince Erik?"

"Why not? I have been long at sea, and my axes are thirsty."

"Whom do you challenge? We have many great champions here in this hall who would be honoured to fight you. Shall we say that the first to draw blood is the winner?"

Erik shrugged. "If you wish. Do you have a man in mind?"

"Sigolfr, will you fight for Jorvik?" Veggr said with a gleam in his eyes. A gigantic man stood from a bench three seats down from Erik. His head was enormous and framed by curly black hair and a beard so thick it was like a bear's pelt.

"I'll fight him," Sigolfr declared and he raised his shovel-sized hand as the warriors in the hall shouted their support, red-faced from ale and the promise of a fight to entertain them.

Sigolfr strode forward, towering over Erik, thicker in the chest and broader across the shoulders. Men could carry weapons in Veggr's throne room, and Sigolfr carried a seax at his belt.

"And what about a wager?" Erik chirped, smiling up at Sigolfr. "Our fellows here can wager their silver on one fighter or the other. But we are royalty, King Veggr. So our wager should be something a little more… substantial."

"Like what?"

"I'll wager my ship that I can beat your man here." Hermoth and Erik's men tugged at the prince's arms to calm him, to stop their lord from his drunken, prideful gamble.

The crowd gasped, for a warship was worth a fortune. Only a jarl or wealthy merchant could muster the silver to own such a magnificent vessel and pay a crew to sail her. She required a berth, constant repairs, supplies, rigging, and a sturdy sail. To own such a ship was to command great wealth.

Veggr licked his lips nervously. "And if you win?"

"It must be something as precious to you as my ship is to me. An arm ring or a bag of silver will not suffice. I like your slave girls, King Veggr. They serve well, and they are pretty for Saxon wenches. So if I kill your man, I shall take every slave you own. How about that?"

Veggr squinted and dragged his hand down his greasy beard. "Slaves are expensive."

"Not as expensive as ships. But listen, I won't have it said that Erik Bloodaxe is not a fair man. I have a reputation, and you are a new king, so I understand your... hesitation. Let's make it fair. I'll fight three of your best men. Including your giant."

Veggr smiled then. "So be it."

"He is drunk out of his mind," said Sigvarth beside Hundr.

"Wait," was all Hundr would say, for he knew the prince well – Erik was no boaster and certainly no fool.

Veggr's slaves pushed back the feasting benches to clear a space for the fighters. Sigolfr and Erik stripped to the waist, for a fight to first blood demanded that the opponents wore nothing that might stop a blade, and the crowd needed to see blood to determine the victor. Sigolfr was a mountain of muscle. His shoulders were like boulders, and his arms were as thick as oak trunks. Erik was tall and broad-shouldered but slim at the waist. Writhing beasts were tattooed on his chest and back, and he held an axe in each hand. Two large men came to join Sigolfr, a shorter man with a harelip beneath a thin beard and a man not much smaller than Sigolfr with a long face missing his front teeth. The three men looked dangerous, big men carrying axes, confident that together, they could fight one arrogant princeling. But Erik was no ordinary man.

Hundr clenched his fists, and the chained

Seaworm men gathered about him with a mix of hope and fear etched upon their drawn faces.

Erik swung his axes in broad arcs around his body, loosening his muscles. He grinned at the crowd pressing in, pushing close to form a rough circle amidst the feasting benches. Any signs of drunkenness had vanished, leaving his face set hard and ruthless. From his skull throne, Veggr remained seated, but he now leaned forward, hands clasped and smirking with confidence. It was no holmgang circle, no hazel rods or any of the other ritual elements required for a lawful duel, but Erik faced three men, and all four carried sharp axes.

"Do you think Erik understands that the fight is to the first cut?" asked Toki.

"How can he defend against three men at once?" Sigvarth said, shaking his head as dreams of freedom and revenge sparked and died before him.

"He knows," Hundr uttered, "but I doubt he cares." Hundr had seen the look in Erik's eyes before. The prince saw a chance for reputation, for men to tell the tale of the day they saw Erik Bloodaxe fight three warriors inside Jorvik's Roman walls. Erik was everything a *drengr* should be: dangerous, ambitious, and skilled. Hundr had been such a man himself, hungry, desperate to fulfil his ambition. Perhaps he still was that man, or at least he could be if he survived the horrors of Veggr's throne room. Hermoth approached Erik and spoke into his ear. The two young warriors clasped forearms, and Hermoth glanced at Hundr once more, but only for a heartbeat before looking away. Hundr again wanted to cry out to his son, to let him know he was there and that fate had brought them together. But the Norns were cruel, and Hundr did not trust their malevolence because Erik and Hermoth could sail away just as quickly as they'd arrived, leaving Hundr to die in the filth and gloom.

Erik raised his axes and turned to face every corner of the crowd. They shouted their challenge back at him, faces twisted with bloodlust as they wagered slivers of hacksilver and small coins on the fight. Veggr's warriors circled Erik, axes held tight in their fists. They shared knowing grins and spread out, positioning themselves to attack the young prince from all sides. Erik spun his axes, the bearded blades flashing as they carved arcs through the air around him. With a sudden toss, he sent them both whirling upward; every eye in the hall followed their glinting dance in the firelight. Then, as they spun back down, Erik caught each one deftly. The crowd erupted in cheers, and where they had despised the man bold enough to challenge three of their own, they now laughed and clapped in awe at his skill with the axe.

"Begin!" Veggr bellowed from his throne, and the hall suddenly fell silent. The only sounds to be heard were the shuffle of the fighters' boots on the floor rushes. Erik stood between three adversaries, and every soul in the throne room held their breath, including the Seaworm men.

Sigolfr struck first, his bare belly quivering as he swung his axe in a powerful overhand arc meant to cleave Erik in two. From behind, the warrior with the harelip lunged forward, not to kill the prince but to score a quick cut on his back and claim the honour of first blood. Should that strike land, the duel would be won, and King Veggr would be the proud owner of a *drakkar* warship. In that instant, the warrior saw his own future unfold – royal favour, land, arm rings, and respect. But then Erik moved, and while Veggr's men seemed to wade through honey, Erik darted as quickly as Sleipnir himself.

Sigolfr's axe came around in a wide arc, and Erik made a half-turn. Only his shoulders and upper body moved, and the curve of his axe blade sliced open the big man's belly with a line of crimson. At the same time, Erik's left-hand axe parried the blade of the harelipped warrior with a loud clang. Erik spun in the opposite direction, his feet adjusting so that he pivoted in an arc, feet surging strength up through his hips and broad shoulders and into his muscled arms. Axes flashed in a rapid blur, and then Erik stopped, crouching with one blade raised high above his head, the other poised low, ready to pounce like a cat eyeing a field mouse.

The three men staggered back, faces twisted in shock. Sigolfr whimpered, his axe slipping from his grip as he pressed desperately at his belly, trying to hold in his spilling insides, blood streaming from the wound as though from a burst barrel. The harelipped warrior swayed before dropping to his knees, mouth working soundlessly in disbelief as blood seeped from his gaping throat. He collapsed, lifeblood pooling across the stone floor. The third man, his axe arm slashed across the tendons, watched his weapon clatter to the ground. He glanced from his injured arm back to Erik in horror.

"First cut!" Veggr shouted in fury from his throne. Erik picked up the third man's axe and pressed it into the man's left hand. He took it and shook his head slowly, lip trembling and tears rolling down his bearded cheeks as he understood what must happen next. Erik swung his axe in a ferocious overhand cut, and the weapon chopped into the third man's forehead with an audible crack.

"Yes!" Sigvarth whispered, and he clasped Hundr's shoulder in celebration.

The three men thought themselves warriors, but they were simply Veggr's hired muscle – big men who believed that holding a weapon made a man a warrior. Erik had been trained to fight since the day he first walked. He was a killer, savage and pitiless, a man who would one day become king of Norway. The warriors in the throne room stared at the dead and dying men with looks of horror on their faces. They had hoped to see a prince humbled and their men victorious but had instead witnessed brutal violence, fast and uncompromising. Erik turned in a full circle, letting them see his blood-spattered face. Then, he bent and tugged his axe free of the third man's skull, and those nearest flinched away from the awful death wound.

"I won," said Erik, pointing a bloody axe at King Veggr. "Bring the slaves to my ship at once."

"We said the first cut," Veggr growled.

Erik shrugged. "Would you like to fight, and we can let the gods decide who has the right of it?"

Veggr glowered at Erik, and the prince met his gaze. Veggr looked away, and Erik sniffed. He slid his axes slowly back into the loops at his belt.

"Very well. Have the slaves brought to my ship before midnight. All the slaves. But I'll take those slaves with me now." Erik pointed at Hundr,

Guthred, and the Seaworm men.

Hundr's heart leapt, and it was all he could do not to cry out with joy.

"You broke the terms of the fight. First cut only. The wager is forfeit." Veggr waved his hand at Erik as though he were one of his thralls to be dismissed.

Erik touched his axes and took a step closer to the king. Hermoth and the rest of Erik's men sprang from the crowd and lined up behind him, facing outwards towards the throng. They were outnumbered, but each of Erik's men was worth four of Veggr's curs. "I made the first cut, but I always fight to the death. Do we need to have a serious disagreement, King Veggr?"

Veggr licked his lips, glanced at the shackled men, and then back at Erik. "Take the filthy bastards and begone."

Hermoth strode over and beckoned to one of Veggr's slaves, who quickly brought the tools to remove the prisoner's shackles.

"Father," Hermoth said quietly, bending and staring into Hundr's eyes. "Though I do not know how you ended up in this place, it's time to go."

Hundr felt as light as a bird as the shackles slipped from his wrists, and Hermoth helped him to stand. He had to struggle not to laugh for joy. Stigmarr glared bitterly at Hundr from within the crowd, his eyes dripping with disgust. Hundr marked that look and stored it away with the beatings, torture, and humiliation he had suffered in Jorvik.

"Not that one," Veggr growled as the slave removed Guthred's fetters.

"All of them," Erik insisted. Veggr stamped his foot like a petulant child and stormed from the throne room. Guthred followed Hundr towards the door where Prince Erik waited, beaming at Hundr as though they met for Yule feast.

"Lord Hundr," Erik smiled and clapped Hundr on the shoulder. "It seems you found a spot of bother on the Whale Road."

"Get us out of this place," Hundr said. Erik draped his own cloak around Hundr's shoulders, and they left Veggr's fortress with hurried steps, followed all the way by Veggr's warriors.

Live. Survive and rise to fight again. Finn must die. Orm must die.

Hundr glanced back at Jorvik's walls as they hurried to Erik's ship moored on the banks of Jorvik's twin rivers. He was free. Hermoth, Erik and his crew gave Hundr clean clothes, food and ale. They asked him what bad luck had befallen him to end up in such dire circumstances, but their voices were like the sigh of the sea in the night because his own thoughts screamed at him, drowning everything else out. He could not sail away without the Seaworm's prow, not after all Veggr and Stigmarr had put him through. There must be a reckoning, and he would need the Ulfberht sword to kill Orm Eysteinsson and the Crippled King.

TWENTY

Einar sailed the Wind Elk away from Upsala with six Valkyrie warships at his back. Gunnr sailed on board the Wind Elk. She was a Valkyrie war leader and fierce warrior whom Hundr and Einar had fought alongside in the battle to recover the Gungnir spear. The High Priestess remained in Upsala, though she had given orders for Gunnr to act as the leader of the Valkyrie contingent, and so she sailed with Einar and Hildr to discuss the voyage and their plans for the war to come. The Valkyrie spoke of Bjorn Ironside's great fortress on the Island of Munsö, on the east coast of Svear land, or Sweden as some called it, and so Einar followed Gunnr's recommended course to reach the home of the great king, and only living son of Ragnar Lothbrok.

They left Upsala and sailed along the Fyris River, rowing through its meandering waters until the fleet came to Lake Mälaren, a vast inland sea where the wind blew strong enough to hoist the sail and give the crew a rest from their oars. They glided alongside marshy banks and dense forests of pine and birch. Smaller vessels around the lake sculled quickly away from the seven-ship fleet, and Einar knew that word of his ships would fly south to Bjorn just as fast as the Wind Elk could sail. So, he flew Hundr's one-eyed banner high on the mast so that men would know who sailed through Bjorn's lands.

At the mouth of the lake, the waters opened up to reveal a wide swathe of shimmering water dotted with islands. Einar stood tall upon the steerboard platform, feeling the eyes of the coastal jarls and island warlords staring at him unseen from across the water. He was a warrior jarl with seven ships under his command. Einar sailed without fear of attack. It would take a fleet of ten or twelve ships to attack his force, and few men could put to sea with an army of that size. They passed larger islands crowned with imposing fortresses with spiked walls, Sigtuna and Adelsö, both islands where kings once lived and ruled. Gunnr spoke of dangerous jarls who now brooded there, with hearts full of their ancestors' deeds. Powerful men ruled by Bjorn, who raided east and south, braving the Baltic Sea to attack Finns, Slavs, Krivichs, and Khazars. Beyond lay the Byzantine Empire, a land of great wealth ripe for trade and raiding.

Gunnr guided them around rocky islets and skerries, and even Thorgrim, son of Skapti Farsailor, was glad to have her aboard in waters in which he was unfamiliar. They reached Bjorn's fortress at Munsö on the second day after a quiet night camped on a stony beach beneath a sprawling forest. Munsö was one of many islands of varying sizes in this vast waterway, a natural labyrinth of rugged shores and forested land. Einar looked around at the landscape – rugged yet fertile, with rolling hills, meadows, and dense forests of oak, pine, and birch. It was a land far more prosperous than his own harsh home at Vanylven, with soil rich enough for farming and an abundance of timber for sturdy ships and strong halls. Bjorn had done well to conquer such a kingdom, which he had ruled now for many years.

Bjorn's fortress dominated Munsö like a heavy crown upon an old king's head. He had built the stronghold on the island's highest point, commanding a view of the surrounding waters and adding to older, more ancient defensive works so that new, golden timbers mixed with darker, older wood. A stout palisade, complete with a fighting platform, ditch, and bank, surrounded a keep, hall, and settlement from which smoke rose in great columns and the bustling sounds of a busy town blew across the water on the wind. From the steerboard, Einar saw longhouses roofed with earth or thatch alongside smaller workshops for smiths, leatherworkers, and shipbuilders. Sheep, goats, and cattle grazed in the meadows, and all seemed peaceful. But two dragon-prowed warships eased from behind a promontory, and the sun caught the glint of spear points atop King Bjorn Ironside's fortress. The dragon ships were a reminder that despite the green fields and lowing cattle, this was the realm of Vikings – home to jarls who took their axes and daring to foreign shores and returned rich and glorious, or not at all.

The two dragon ships slid across the calm water, and the dreaded raven banner flew from their masts. That banner was a warning. It was the banner first flown by Ragnar Lothbrok, the most famous of all Viking warriors. Ragnar had flown that banner from the walls of Paris after he had sailed a vast fleet up the river Seine to sack the wealthiest city in Frankia. Later, Ragnar's sons had all flown it in honour of their father, most famously when they invaded Northumbria to exact vengeance upon King Aelle for throwing old Ragnar into an *orm-garth,* a pit of snakes. The sails of those two *snekke* ships would also show the white raven on black wool so that all men knew that the warriors on those ships were Bjorn Ironside's oathmen.

"They know your banner?" asked Gunnr, making her way from the prow to the steerboard platform.

"They know it," Einar replied.

"If they don't recognise us, we could have trouble."

"Bjorn knows us," said Hildr, peering out at the warships across the water. "But we should remove the prows out of respect. To show we come in peace."

Einar nodded, and Gunnr passed a signal back to the Valkyrie fleet so that every ship, including the Wind Elk, took their prow beasts down. The ships came closer, and hard faces peered at Einar from across the bows. They gave no greeting but also made no threats. Einar kept the Elk on course for Munsö whilst the two ships made wide turns under oars and followed Einar's fleet at a distance.

Gunnr guided Einar along the safe approach to the island, for the temple at Upsala sent regular delegations to Bjorn to augur for him and provide gifts of silver as tribute to the king of the Svear lands, which extended far beyond Upsala into the cold north. The waterways were calm that day, but she warned they could be treacherous, with sudden winds from the north whipping across the lake. She led them through the narrow channels, and Einar saw rocks and skerries lurking beneath the surface of the water, waiting to scupper any unsuspecting ship's hull. Birka became visible in the distance, with its bustling slave markets filled with captives from Svear raids in the east.

Einar steered the Wind Elk into Munsö's harbour, drifting slowly between the merchants' ships and skiffs moored against long jetties or anchored just offshore. The island bustled with life. Women sold shellfish and bread from the docks, calling above the tumult of seamen, soldiers, fishermen, and common folk who strolled along the seafront wearing brightly dyed clothes of green, red, brown and blue. A small faering waved them onto a mooring between two wide *knarr* trading ships, both lying low in the water, heavy with goods to trade at Bjorn's busy port. A steward wearing a black hooded jerkin emblazoned with a white raven asked Einar to instruct the Valkyrie warships to drop anchor just outside the moorings, which they did without objection. The harbour sat within a sweeping cove that would protect any ships from the worst of any sudden storms.

Einar went ashore with Hildr, Amundr, Thorgrim and Gunnr, each clad in their war finery. Einar wore his heavy bear fur cloak over his fish scale armour. Hildr and Gunnr gleamed in their Valkyrie *brynjars*, while Amundr and Thorgrim wore their own polished mail, each with an axe looped at their belts. Amundr insisted on bringing his helmet, which he carried under his arm like a woman might carry a baby.

"Please, follow me, my lord," said the steward. He scrambled up from his small boat and bowed to Einar. He was a clever-faced man with a hump over one shoulder, which made him walk as though he danced a jig. The steward led them along the jetty, clearing the throng out of their way with his walking stick. The fisherman and sailors shuffled aside and bowed their heads in respect once they saw Einar and his companions in gleaming armour and gaped up in surprise at Amundr's monstrous size.

"I'm hungry," Amundr rumbled as they passed a stall at the end of the jetty where a woman sold cuts of fried fish on small sticks. The fish sizzled on hot stones, and the smell drew a crowd to pay her with small scraps of hacksilver.

"We are here to see a king," Einar snapped, "not buy scraps of fish from the quayside."

Amundr shrugged, and they followed the crooked-backed steward into a labyrinth of open-fronted booths where people sold food, rope, fishing hooks, knives, amulets, good luck charms, and anything else a traveller across the Whale Road might waste his hard-earned silver upon. High above the harbour, the fortress loomed, with a brown, well-trodden path snaking up to its gate. Around the harbour and alongside the path, wattle houses topped with earthen roofs billowed smoke from their hearth fires. To the west, the bustling settlement gave way to pastures, where livestock grazed, indifferent to the hustle and bustle of Munsö's daily life. Suddenly, a commotion rippled through the crowd in the busy harbour. A chicken flapped its wings and flew just above the people as they parted like water crashing against rocks, and beyond them, a huge man, taller than everybody in the crown by a head, waved his arms, shouting in a booming voice and tossing folk aside like a farmer walking through a field of wheat.

"Einar the Brawler!" the big man bellowed in a deep voice. "Einar, is that you, you old rogue? Have you killed anybody since you came ashore? Einar, don't hide behind your womenfolk. Where are you?"

"Bjorn Ironside," Einar beamed, unable to keep the smile from his face. Bjorn was a simple man to like. He was brave and had earned a reputation as a fighter, yet he was also kind, full of laughter, and loved nothing more than drinking and wrestling with his men. He was one of the most feared men in all Midgard, a son of Ragnar, who had won a kingdom for himself and had become a legend in his own lifetime. Six men followed the king, all enormous and adorned in shining armour, carrying tall spears from which hung the raven banner.

"Einar, you are the son of a thousand fathers," said Bjorn, stopping before Einar with his hands on his hips and an angry look upon his broad face. "You have grown old. Why have you not come to visit me sooner?"

"King Bjorn," Einar replied, and he bowed respectfully to a king who deserved it. "It does my heart good to see you after all these years. Though for a moment, I thought you a lack-witted, toothless grandfather searching for his piss pot upon the quayside."

Bjorn's jaw moved, his bushy beard shifting back and forth, and he glowered at Einar with a stare that would make even the iciest fjord boil. But then he threw his head back and guffawed loudly. "Come here, you old sea dog!" Bjorn opened his arms as he strode towards Einar and then embraced him so tightly that, for a moment, Einar thought his back might break. Bjorn wore a tunic of soft eastern cloth over dark trews, a thick fur cloak hanging from his shoulders and a circlet of gold resting on his furrowed brow. He was broad in the chest with hugely muscled arms, and the heady scent of yesterday's ale and roasted beef clung to him. "Where is The Man with the Dog's Name?" Bjorn peered over Einar's shoulder at his companions. "I remember the day he and I fought back to back outside that church in Frankia. We faced an entire army, he and I. The bards sing of it even now, and I swear we killed a hundred warriors each that day."

"That is why I am here, Lord King. I do not bring good tidings, I am afraid. There is war in the west, and we must talk if you can spare the time."

"Spare the time? By Thor's hairy arse, but we shall have ale and food and talk of old times, and you can tell me what brings you to my kingdom. I have not seen you since that business in Ireland with my son Refil. I have not had the chance to thank you for that. Erik and Refil told me everything, and I know you and Refil had it hard in the Witch-Queen's dungeons."

"You remember Hildr, my wife?"

"Who can forget a woman of such beauty and so swift an axe? You are welcome, Lady Hildr." Hildr smiled and then yelped in surprise as Bjorn pulled her into an embrace with the same gusto with which he had just held Einar. Einar laughed, and the onlooking folk also laughed at their king's exuberance. "A Valkyrie," he said to Gunnr once he had released Hildr from his bear hug. "Where is Ragnhild?"

"In Valhalla. I shall give you the tale of her

death when we share some ale," Einar answered.

"Aye." Bjorn paused for a moment and dragged an enormous hand down the springy bush of his beard. "Another hero gone to the Einherjar, and yet we remain, old friend." Bjorn stared into the distance as though lost in thought, and then, after a heartbeat, he caught himself and took an exaggerated step back. "Frigg's tits! I thought a Frost Giant had entered my kingdom, but it's just you, Amundr, you big bastard."

"Lord King," Amundr replied with a bowed head.

Bjorn grabbed Amundr's biceps and squeezed them, appraising them with a shake of his head. "I think you have grown skinny since the last time I saw you. I have a wrestler for you to try. He's as big as you, I think, but your arms have grown as thin as willow rods. I think he can beat you. Perhaps I can beat you, though it is many years since I last wrestled. Come to my hall, and we can talk, all of us, and see if we can find some meat to put some strength back into poor Amundr's arms."

Amundr frowned, staring down at his massive biceps, and Einar grinned. Bjorn took Thorgrim's arm in the warrior's grip, and they followed Bjorn's broad back up the pathway towards his hilltop fortress. All along the route, Bjorn called to his people by name. He kicked a stooping blacksmith up the arse and took an apple from a wizened grandmother. A fat man pressed a pie into Bjorn's fist, and two young girls ran to kiss him on the cheek. The people cheered and clapped as he passed, and Bjorn did not hurry. He shared jokes with them, admired new thatch, and tested the edge of a newly forged axe blade. By the time they passed through the palisade gate, the morning was half over, and the steward took their weapons with a promise that he would keep them safe. Amundr held onto his helmet and growled when the steward tried to take it, so Einar soothed him and promised that he could twist the hunchback's head off if anything happened to it.

"He looks old," Hildr whispered as they followed Bjorn into his opulent hall, a dragon prow keel poking through its golden thatch, towering above a space with enough feasting benches to fit Einar's hall thrice over.

"He is old. So am I," Einar replied. Bjorn's hair was silvery white, and though his beard still showed black around his mouth, it, too, was as white as fresh snow. He was slightly stooped, and Bjorn's shoulders and chest had lost some of their old thick muscle.

"Do you think he will fight?"

"Let's find out."

Bjorn blustered about his hall and introduced

Einar and Hildr to his three wives, who were all young and voluptuous. He showed Amundr off to his hearth troop as though he were a bull at a Yule festival. Those hard-bitten men nodded appreciatively at Amundr's giant frame and asked where he had fought. Bjorn's men were no ordinary hearth troop, no backwater gaggle of paid bullies with spears and cudgels. These were the true hard men of the Whale Road. *Drengrs* who prided themselves on their honour and bravery in battle. Each one had a reputation that could make most jarls blush with shame. Their weapons, beards, hair and armour were immaculately kept, and the pride in their profession was palpable. There were no beardless boys amongst them, nor rich men's sons granted position by favour. They'd earned their place in Bjorn Ironside's hearth troop on the battlefield. They spoke respectfully with Amundr, those dangerous men with grizzled beards and wind-darkened faces. Bjorn's men were veterans of his own campaigns, voyages to the edges of the Whale Road where they had fought men of every colour and god under the sun. Others came to him from his brother's forces. They were all Ragnarsson men, as Einar himself had been once, long ago.

Bjorn ordered his stewards to bring food and ale, and an impromptu feast sprang up. Einar sat with Bjorn and Hildr beside the fire and ate roast pork from a silver platter. All the usual feast day formality was foregone, and Bjorn's top platform and throne were left empty. The men sat and ate where they pleased. Thorgrim and Gunnr spoke to Bjorn's captains about the waters they had sailed, of current, wind, and tide. Amundr struck up a friendship with the biggest of Bjorn's warriors, and they sat together eating heaped plates of meat and drinking fine ale from curved horns.

Einar told Bjorn about the Crippled King and about how Hundr had become separated from his fleet between the Isle of Mann and Northumbria's western coast. At first, the king of the Svears was all for leaping to action, eager to set sail at dawn to search for Hundr. But when Einar revealed why they fought the Crippled King, and who he really was, the king's enthusiasm wavered.

"You come to ask me to kill my nephew for Harald Fairhair? You raised Ivar's son. I remember him when he was young," he said and tossed the last third of his ale from his horn into the fire, where it hissed on the flames. "Harald bloody Fairhair. That bastard who stole a kingdom? Whose ships raid my coastline and kill my people?"

"He isn't all bad," Einar replied with a shrug.

"Norway wasn't even a kingdom until he killed

the old kings of smaller countries and declared himself the king of all Norway. I warned Hundr about him when he came to my trading port at Lödöse."

"I know, and then we fought for Harald at the battle of Hafrsfjord."

"Where he won his kingdom."

"Where he won his kingdom, and I became Jarl of Vanylven in reward for the part we played in that fight."

"I won't fight for a usurping marauder."

"If you don't mind me asking, King Bjorn," Hildr interjected, leaning forward and smiling. "How is it that you came to be king of Svearland?"

"It's funny you should ask, because it's a good story. We should save it for later on when the ale is properly flowing. The short version of a long tale is that I killed the old king. It was said that my father, Ragnar, had a claim to the throne through one of his wives, and I wanted to ensure the kingdom stayed in the family. So we had a battle, and I won. They were good days. Ivar ruled in Dublin, and Halvdan was in Northumbria. My brothers and I were always trying to outdo one another. Funny, really."

"So you took the throne by force?"

"Of course I did. What can a man get in this

world if it isn't taken by force? More ale!" He raised his horn, and a steward hurried over to fill the vessel with frothy ale.

"Which is how Harald won his kingdom."

Bjorn was mid-gulp, and he stared at Hildr with one wide eye over the rim of his horn as her cunning comparison dawned upon him. He swallowed and then nodded slowly. "True enough, my lady, true enough. From what I hear, Harald is a stripling with less strength in his arm than a poxed grandmother."

"Then what threat is he to a great king like you?"

Bjorn laughed and shrugged to acknowledge that Hildr had the right of it. A tumult of cheering erupted inside the hall, and Einar sighed as he turned to see Amundr stripped to the waist, wrestling with one of Bjorn's oathsworn warriors. The man was hugely muscled with the drooping moustache of a Novgorod Druzhina warrior.

"Here we go," Bjorn grinned. "My man is a fine wrestler. He won a fistful of silver last year wrestling champions from across my kingdom. I'll wager you three Musselman coins that my man wins."

"Done," Einar replied. The coins minted by the men who worshipped a god called Allah were renowned for their quality. Einar had held some in his purse from time to time. "I'll match the weight in hacksilver. But I warn you, this could go badly for your man. Don't be angry if it goes too far."

"Too far? What are we? Washerwomen fussing over a ruined pair of trews?" Bjorn guffawed and slapped Einar on the back so hard that he nearly fell over. The wrestling began, and Einar had to admit that Bjorn's champion was lightning-fast. He sprang at Amundr's legs like a leaping salmon. Bjorn whooped for joy, sensing a quick victory as the warrior tried to haul Amundr from his feet. Amundr staggered but rapidly bent down, seized the champion by his thick belt, and lifted him off the ground as if he were a sickly pup. The warrior's arms and legs flailed, and Amundr wrapped his tree-trunk arms around the man's torso, driving him into the ground with such force that Einar winced at the impact. The champion groaned, struggling to push himself up, but he collapsed again, crawling feebly and clutching at Amundr's ankle in a dazed attempt to recover. Amundr growled and reached for the warrior's head with both of his shovel-sized hands.

"Amundr! No!" Einar roared, recognising the feral look on his friend's face and fearing that he might break the champion's neck like a chicken's. Amundr stared at Einar, then glanced back at the champion. He bent again and then thought better of it. Amundr rubbed his hands together and helped the crushed warrior back to his feet. Bjorn's hearth troop grumbled and tugged their beards, so sure had they been that their man would win. The defeated champion shook his head and then raised Amundr's arm in respect as the hall erupted into raucous cheering. The warriors drank their ale and gathered about Amundr to acclaim his strength. So mesmerised were they by Amundr's size and strength that they did not complain when Thorgrim went among them to collect his and Amundr's winnings.

"I should have remembered the wrestling," Bjorn grumbled as he fished into a leather pouch at his belt. He found the coins and pressed them into Einar's hand. "Frigg's tits, but I thought Amundr was going to twist my man's head off."

"You and me both. I'd have to hide behind Hildr to get out of here alive."

"Do not jest about such things. I have seen the Valkyrie fight, and they are as formidable as any warband in Midgard. You have six ships full of them anchored off my island."

"Are Refil and Erik far from your lands, Lord King? I should like to see them."

"They are off raiding. Refil is forever at sea. Even in the winter months, he longs to take ship and travel the Whale Road. Erik has become a fine warrior with a reputation of his own. They will be saddened to have missed your visit. All men know what you did for Refil and what you endured together in Ireland. But if you think to use my sons to persuade me to fight alongside Harald bloody Fairhair, you've got another thing coming."

"We did not come here to use a son to persuade a cantankerous father to lend us a plough or grant watering rights for our cows at his stream," said Hildr. "We sailed from Vanylven to the land of the Svears to seek the mighty Bjorn Ironside, the greatest living Viking in Midgard. We came with news of war and to ask the king of warriors to come and fight beside us. This is a battle sanctioned by the Valkyrie high priestess herself. We fight on the side of the Aesir, and men will talk of this war for generations long after the light of our lives has been extinguished from this world. We seek Bjorn Ragnarsson, whom men call Ironside because he is so hard to kill and so strong in battle. So what say you, Bjorn, son of Ragnar?"

"Einar, your wife has the deep cunning of a starving weasel. If I keep talking to her, I fear I shall end up marching my warriors to the ends of Midgard. Come, let's walk the battlements together, you and I."

Bjorn winked at Hildr, and she raised her

horn in salute. Einar followed Bjorn out of his hall and up onto the fighting platform that ringed his fortifications. The wooden platform was supported by a raised bank above a deep ditch encircling the hillside. Any man seeking to attack Bjorn's stronghold would first have to sail past his longships and make landfall on the island. From there, he would face a steep climb up the hill, cross the ditch, and assault the palisade – all while Bjorn's men hurled whatever terrors they could devise from the spiked timber walls above. Einar shuddered at the thought, knowing that even if an attacker managed to reach the top of the palisade, they would find Bjorn and his fearsome warriors waiting for them with axe and shield and a lifetime of battle experience.

"I like it up here," Bjorn said as they reached a west-facing portion of the walls. A brazier burned there to keep the guards warm, but the men patrolling the fighting platform left Einar and Bjorn in peace, pulling their cloaks closer about them to keep out the cold. Night had fallen, and the sea lapped gently against the island shore. Birka glowed orange in the distance beneath a starless sky. "I can think here on the walls. Nobody bothers me. I can hear whispers of the old days on the wind. Old friends, old fights, good ships."

"I think that's the curse of old men," Einar

replied, resting his hands on the palisade and peering out at the black waters below. "As our lives stretch out behind us, the faces of those we've lost and the deeds we've done come back to haunt us, echo to us. I am forever reminded of my friends who wait for me in Valhalla, some of whom I fought beside more than a score of years ago."

"Valhalla. I fear my chance to join my father and brothers in Odin's hall has long passed, Einar. It has been two years since I fought in the shield wall or sailed upon a fast ship to raid. Is it my fate to be the only son of Ragnar to die in his bed?"

"I carry the same burden. I see my friends die glorious deaths, assured of their place in Odin's Einherjar. But no matter how many times I fight, I remain alive, living on in Midgard. I feared I'd lost my chance, that I was too old – that was until I saw Ragnhild die in battle. I fought again that day and killed skilled warriors, but still, the blow would not come to send me to Valhalla."

Bjorn bowed his head, his mouth turned in an upside-down smile. "Do you remember my brothers, Einar? When we were young men?"

"I do. I doubt we shall see their like again."

"Sigurd was a cunning fox, and Ubba a grim beast but a great fighter. Ivar – has there ever been a greater swordsman or battle commander?

He could be cold and hard, but there were times when you could drink with Ivar."

"No, there weren't." Einar smiled, and Bjorn laughed. Einar didn't mention that Hundr was the greater swordsman, and it was Hundr who had killed Ivar on the River Liffey beside Dublin's high walls.

"True, he was a horrible bastard. I don't think I ever saw him smile, not even when we were children." Bjorn breathed in a chest full of night air, and his face became solemn. "Niflheim cannot be my destiny. It keeps me awake, Einar, the thoughts of it. My sons are out now with my fleet; they will both be pleased to see you again. What if they cross to the halls of the Aesir before me? We have all seen old men withered and toothless. Their minds fuddled by age. They live on in other men's halls, telling stories of their former glory. That cannot be us, old friend." Bjorn stood tall and fixed Einar with a fierce stare. "I can feel it on the wind, Einar, that perhaps this is our time. Why not let Odin's fury for his foster son's betrayal fuel your war with Finn Ivarsson? Loki betrayed Odin and killed his favourite son, and Finn has betrayed everything he was to you. There is battle luck in the All-Father's wrath. We can take up the war of the Aesir, get their attention, and show Odin that two old men can still swing an axe and do him honour. That can be our own luck. We can make ourselves worthy of Valhalla again."

"Then sail with me, Bjorn Ironside, son of Ragnar Lothbrok. Let us seek Valhalla together. Stand with me in the front rank, where the champions clash – where we have always fought. Perhaps we shall meet the glorious death stroke, holding our weapons tight. We can wake together in Valhalla and meet our old friends, drink with the brave men we have slain, and fight a fresh battle each day for Odin's pleasure."

"Aye," Bjorn answered, grabbing Einar's wrist in a powerful grip. "I will summon my sons to return from their voyages. We shall sail beneath the raven banner and bring red war to this Crippled King. Refil and Erik will bring my fleet, and I shall follow you with twenty warships full of Ragnarsson fighters. Look for my arrival within a dozen sunsets."

Twenty longships and one and a half thousand warriors. Einar gripped Bjorn's forearm with both hands and stared deep into the old warrior's eyes. He could return to King Harald with an army at his back. With the Valkyrie and Bjorn Ironside's warriors pledged to fight against the Crippled King, Harald would have no choice but to match Bjorn's force or lose face before his kingly rival.

Now, there was only one more warlord to find, one champion to seek. A legendary warlord who

Hundr and Einar had known since their days fighting in Frankia. Haesten.

TWENTY-ONE

Hundr leaned against the mast post aboard Erik Bloodaxe's *drakkar,* the Hábrjótr, the Whale Breaker. A fast, warrior ship named after the black and white killer whales found far to the north of King Harald's kingdom. He watched as Yazi the Easterner struggled to string a bow, his neck and cheeks hollowed by starvation in King Veggr's court. Stigmarr and their captors had taken Yazi's recurved bow. So he took one from Erik's weapons store and now bent the stave around the back of his leg and struggled to stretch the string over the horn-topped nock. Yazi eventually strung the bow and slumped to the deck, exhausted. Hundr, Sigvarth, Toki, Harbard, and Yazi were thin, weak, and lucky to be alive. The last remaining crew of the Seaworm, they had been dragged and beaten close to death before Erik's men had carried their frail bodies from Jorvik like children.

"I can cut that for you, my lord," said one of Erik's men, pointing at Hundr's matted, filthy hair and beard. Hundr hadn't realised he had absent-mindedly crushed a louse between his finger and thumb as he watched Yazi struggle with the yew bow.

"It must all come off, I fear," Hundr replied quietly. His hair was beyond the help of a comb or a wash. It was thick in rope-like strands, crawling with lice and stinking. "Cut the hair as close to the scalp as you can and the beard short."

The warrior sucked his teeth, nodded, and took a knife from a sheath at his belt. He ran a whetstone along the blade in long, smooth strokes. Hair and beard were a crucial part of a *drengr's* dress, an integral aspect of what identified him as a member of the warrior class. A Viking would braid and comb his hair and beard with the same care he applied to his weapons. Men hung talismans, bones, and the amulets of slain enemies in those braids. To have his hair and beard cut short to his scalp was the final humiliation, the last assault upon his status as a warrior and a champion. Hundr sat on a barrel and stared out at the night-dark sea, where torchlight and fires dotted the Northumbrian coast like distant stars.

Erik and Hermoth had sailed Erik's two ships along the river Ouse and into the wide Humber estuary before rowing out to spend the night on a gently rolling sea. Erik's men had fed the survivors oatcakes, honey, dried fish, and freshly brewed ale bought from Jorvik's riverside merchants. Toki had jumped overboard and whooped for joy as he swam in the sea, ducking beneath the surface and sticking his legs out like a hall entertainer. Sigvarth had followed him, cleansing himself in the sea and then happily shivering after the crew hauled him back onboard.

"Here, I can do that," said a familiar voice. Hundr turned and saw Hermoth smiling down at him. His son had grown tall, taller than Hundr himself. He was broad-shouldered and carried battle scars upon his hands and forearms, as all warriors should. He looked so like his mother in the moonlight, golden hair glistening and kind eyes smiling, that it brought a lump to Hundr's throat. Hermoth took the knife from the warrior and cut Hundr's rancid hair away from his scalp. "You shall look like a hairless baby when this is done."

"Better than a head crawling with lice," Hundr replied.

"It was good fortune to find you in Veggr's stronghold."

"It was. But ill-luck to end up there in the first place. Perhaps Odin has decided to look favourably upon me once more."

"What happened, Father? How did you end up in that Thor-forsaken place?"

As Hermoth trimmed his father's hair close, leaving only a fine fuzz, the sea breeze kissed Hundr's newly bare scalp. Hundr recounted to his son the tale of the Crippled King – how he had tried to kill Finn on the Isle of Mann and their frantic escape to the Seaworm. He spoke of Orm and the burning of his cherished warship, the Seaworm, and Hermoth listened with quiet patience.

"Shall we return to Vanylven, Father? Back to Einar and the rest of your ships?" Hermoth said once the tale of woe was over.

"No. There must be a reckoning with Veggr and Stigmarr first. They do not know the man they had chained all this time. I must remind them of it. Besides, they have taken things which are precious to me, and I would have them back."

"Forget Veggr and Stigmarr. They are nithings. There will be a new king in Jorvik within the month. They haven't had a king there longer than a year since Halvdan Ragnarsson."

"Aye. Perhaps the next one is on board this ship."

"You talk in riddles, Father. I do not understand."

"Guthred," Hundr pointed to where Guthred stood, staring out over the water with a wool cloak draped about his narrow shoulders. "He is the son of the old king, Hardacnut. He is a Christian. Veggr killed his father. Guthred is no warrior, but he has a sharp mind, and if he tells it true, then there are many Christians in the Danelaw who would like to see a worshipper of the nailed god restored as ruler of the Kingdom of Jorvik."

"Sounds like you already have an idea in mind?"

"I have had time to think. Long days and endless nights. Now, it is time to strike back at my enemies. If we can get Guthred to the Christ priests, or Bishops as he calls them, then we might have an army of Christ warriors at our backs as we attack Jorvik."

"Attack Jorvik? We have two crews, Father. That is not enough. Even for you."

"We shall talk of his tomorrow, you and I, with Erik, Sigvarth, and Guthred. Veggr has my sword, and he has the Seaworm prow. I carried that thing on my back across Northumbria, from the western sea, over the mountains, through bogs, rivers, and marshes until we reached the eastern part of that old Saxon kingdom. Whilst it lives, so does the Seaworm. I want it back."

Hermoth finished cutting Hundr's hair, and he stood back with a frown. Hundr ran his hand over the stubble, and he felt cleansed – as if the bad luck and humiliation had fallen from him with the hanks of his cut locks. Hermoth knelt in front of him and began to cut at Hundr's beard with the sharp knife.

"Your mother would be proud of you, son." Hundr looked at Hermoth and wondered what his twin brother Sigurd would have looked like had he reached the same age. "Just as I am proud of the man you have become."

"Hush, Father, the men are listening."

"Let them listen. All my life, everything I have fought for, that burning ambition and hunger for glory, came from a hole my father left inside me. He was a prince, and he hated me. He loved my mother, but she was a Norse slave in his Rus palace. My father and my brothers showed me nothing but cruelty and hate. I was like a dog to them. That is where my name came from, Hundr. I cast off my old name, Velmud, and became a man named for a dog. But my father did give me one gift – the lessons of his weapons master. I passed that gift on to you, Hermoth, and I taught you myself. But I hope that I have also given you something else, the thing I never had and wanted more than anything in this world – the love of a father." Hundr stared into his son's blue eyes, and the ship rocked gently beneath them, waves lapping at the hull. Hermoth smiled, drawing his father into a warm embrace, and Hundr could have stayed like that until the end of days. Hundr had survived, and in the darkness of his infected, sweat-soaked nightmares, he had feared dying without telling Hermoth what he truly meant to him.

Hermoth pulled away and continued to cut Hundr's beard short. "Thank you, Father, for your words. I shall carry them with me like a Frankish forged blade. I suppose you have also formed an idea of how we can attack Jorvik's Roman walls?"

"I might have a thought or two on that riddle."

"Only Ivar conquered those ancient walls, and he had the Great Army at his back."

"I know. I ran up the ladder behind Ivar and fought beside him inside the walls."

"I forgot, though I have heard Einar tell that tale a hundred times."

"But there are more ways to get at Veggr than climbing his walls."

They remained at sea for two weeks as Hundr and the Seaworm survivors ate, drank and grew stronger. Erik and Hermoth went ashore with their warriors to find food and ale, and they sailed north to where Guthred believed his people waited for their nailed god to show them a way to restore their stolen kingdom.

"There is a Bishop there named Eadred," Guthred had said. "He is the Bishop of all Northumbria. A man from the west who has visions of the holy Saint Cuthbert."

Hundr neither knew nor cared who Cuthbert was, but he understood the power of priests and bishops over men who worshipped Christ. So, north they went, and fisherfolk who wore crosses at their necks showed them the way. Hundr rose early each morning. He used a sword belonging to one of Erik's men, and he continued to practise the cuts of the sword, just as he had before Stigmarr's attack. An Irisher aboard Erik's second ship gave Hundr a small buckler shield after a promise from Hundr that he would pay the man ten times its worth once he had his vengeance upon Veggr and Stigmarr. Hundr fastened the small shield to his left arm using a leather belt riveted to the linden wood boards, and he could hold the grip with his remaining three fingers. Though he would likely never hold a sword again with that ruined left hand, he could grip the buckler well enough. He practised until his muscles burned, and whenever it was time to row, Hundr, Sigvarth, Yazi, Toki, and Harbard took double turns until their backs screamed with exhaustion. They grew stronger, and at last, Erik's dragon ships reached an unnamed river where they sought Bishop Eadred.

They found the Bishop preaching to a crowd of Danes and Saxons atop a hill, beyond which a stream curved and babbled over little islets and slick rocks. The people stood and sat upon the sides of a sloping valley, churls dressed in rough browns and greys, ruddy-faced children in ill-fitting smocks, women with pregnant bellies, and warriors with missing legs, arms, and scarred faces. The people stared at the Bishop with hopeful faces, hanging upon his every word, enthralled by the promise that the Christ-God might deliver them from lives of toil and hardship to a golden afterlife. A priest in a coarse brown robe dipped folk in the waters, from which they emerged weeping.

"He is baptising them," Guthred explained as Erik's Vikings questioned why people were lining up to be washed by a man in the river.

"He is washing them," Toki insisted. "Are they children with dirty arses who cannot wash themselves?"

Guthred smiled, patient as ever. "The people here receive the word of God from the good Bishop Eadred, and then the priest baptises them to purify their souls."

"You spoke of this Christ heaven often in Jorvik, of angels and harps and peace. But what man wishes for that over the glory of Valhalla, Thruthvangar, or Fensalir? How could a warrior turn down an afterlife of battle, feasting, and resurrection for harps and a god who could not defend himself against his enemies?"

Guthred spread his arms wide as if to envelop the folk gathered in the valley below them. "Because of the life you live, you only think of warriors, their wives, jarls, kings, queens, and princesses. But most of the people who inhabit the world are people such as these. They are churls and thralls who till the fields and grind the wheat. They suffer sickness and misery in darkness, living in cold hovels with only their loved ones to keep them warm and share their pain. If they worship your gods, what awaits them after death? Yet more misery. Niflheim guarantees cold, darkness and suffering until the Ragnarök descends. My God is a god for everyone, for all people. He offers forgiveness for sins, and we are all sinners, and he offers hope for something greater, something warm and peaceful after death where our loved ones who have passed before us await with welcome embraces."

"Feasting and battle for me," piped Toki, sticking out his bottom lip. "What say you, Sigvarth?"

"The worshipers of the nailed god are timid folk. Our gods are for the brave men, fighters –

people like us. Leave them to their Christ and washing each other in the river."

The people below saw Hundr and Erik's men and panicked as one hundred and fifty warriors armed with axes and spears stared down at them. But Guthred strode down the hillside with open arms, and Bishop Eadred rejoiced to see the prince alive and well. Eadred was a small man with protruding teeth and a patchy beard, yet he had a voice that could fill an entire valley. He ignored the Vikings and knelt at Guthred's feet until the prince raised him up, and the two men walked through the crowd to stand atop the Bishop's preaching hill.

"Behold!" Eadred called to his flock. "A miracle! The Lord God had delivered Hardacnut's son to us alive. I saw it. Saint Cuthbert sent this glorious day to me in a vision which I dared not share until this day. We shall recover Jorvik and its Minster for the Holy Father's worship. Go now, bring your weapons, hasten to your homes and bring your kin, for we march upon a holy war. We shall restore the word of God to Jorvik and its Minster. God wills it!"

Hundr left Guthred with Eadred, promising to meet him outside Jorvik's walls in seven nights' time.

"That rabble couldn't assault a midden heap," Erik growled as they marched back to their ships.

"Never mind the walls of Jorvik."

"They won't have to scale the walls."

"We don't have enough men to do it. So how do we get to Veggr?"

"Leave that to me. Did we release the slave girls yet?"

"Not yet. They seemed happy to stay with my men for a while. They like the ale and the food. We can leave them here if you wish?"

"Not yet. I have a job for them."

TWENTY-TWO

"Why do we have to fight for him?" grumbled Gunnr. She tutted and tightened the leather laces of the brace she wore on her forearm to protect from the thrum of her bowstring. She was tall and hawk-faced, and her lips pursed sourly as she fixed Einar with a stern look.

"Because we need his warriors," Einar replied. He picked up his shield and stared out at the army of Franks assembling across the golden sands.

"He has six ships?"

"He does, and warriors to fill them. That's a long four hundred warriors to add to our force."

"We might lose precious warriors today fighting a battle which is none of our concern."

"We need Haesten's cunning and his warriors. He isn't some backwater jarl with a few ships to his name. Haesten sailed to Ispania with Bjorn Ironside and has fought more battles than your warriors have had hot meals. He has won victories against the Danes, Franks, Saxons, Jutes, Angles, Musselmen, and the Rus. He has forgotten more about sailing and fighting than we shall ever know. Besides, we can hardly ask him to fight for us and refuse to do the same for him?"

"I'll ready the Valkyrie." She curled her lip and stalked off to join her warrior priestesses, shaking her head and muttering as she went.

"She doesn't want to lose any of her sisters here, that's all," said Hildr. She tested the string of her bow and loosened the arrows in the quiver hanging from her belt.

"Which is fair enough," agreed Einar. "But we need Haesten, so this is now our fight. The years haven't softened Gunnr's temper."

"Where is the old fox, anyway? The enemy is here."

"Here he comes," Einar jutted his chin to where a horde of warriors tramped down a scree-covered bank from the headland onto the beach. At their head strode Haesten, walking with the same easy confidence as always, and his hatchet-sharp face creased in a lop-sided grin as his eyes found Einar's. He wore a shining helmet to cover his hair, which was now completely bald atop his wide head but had grown long, grey, and lank around the edges. His gut pushed his *brynjar* outwards from his midriff, and he clutched a finely crafted axe in his right hand. He had once been a straight-backed, proud *drengr*, but now he walked with the hunched shoulders of an old man.

"Good day for it, Einar," Haesten chirped, and he winked at Hildr. "Your Valkyrie captain over there has a face that would turn milk." His eyes flicked towards Gunnr before tucking his thumbs into a thick belt studded with silver buttons and stretching out a mighty hand to clasp Einar's forearm.

"Bastards want to fight?" asked Einar.

"They do. I've sailed my ships up their river, raided three of their churches, and killed a princeling and his warriors. Now they've come to stop me. My ships are behind them in the mouth of a river beyond the beach, and they think they have me trapped. But they didn't know you were coming, Einar."

"Neither did you."

"True," Haesten allowed.

"Would you have fought them if we had not come?"

Haesten thought about that for a few heartbeats. "We marched overland to take a fort over the southern hills there, and I left my ships in this river until we returned. The Franks found them and think they have cut me off. I wasn't going to fight them until you came, truth be told."

"So, how would you get back your ships?" Hildr asked. A Northman's ships were his life, how Vikings sailed their shallow draughted hulls along rivers to raid and plunder where least expected, and to lose them meant death. If Haesten's crews became stranded in Frankia, they had no means of escape, and the Franks would cut them to pieces as they tried to retreat across that vast country rolling with hills, pastures and wild forests. As Haesten's numbers shrank and he had to forage for food and drink, the Franks' numbers would increase as local lordlings brought their warriors to the fight, and so it would be a long, sorry march to death.

"I had leather tents made when I was in England for a time before I fell out with King Alfred and King Guthmund. I have dozens of them. We were going to fill them with wood, hay, and anything that floats. Then, just cling on to them and float down the river at night, right past the blustering Franks, onto my ships and away before sunrise. But Odin sent you to me, Einar Rosti, so now we can kill the fools and take their weapons, armour and silver and sell them for a fine price. Which I will split with you, of course."

"Of course," Hildr shot Haesten a wry grin, and he laughed. "So, these men want to kill you for raiding their lands?"

"They do."

"And if we defeat them, you will sail with us to Mann to find Hundr and kill the Crippled King?"

"I will. We swore oaths on it last night, did we not?"

"We did. I just wanted to be certain that our bargain is clear."

"Lord Haesten!" called a voice from within Haesten's ranks. "They are forming up."

"Bjarki, is that you?" asked Einar.

"Lord Einar," the warrior replied and bowed his head respectfully. He was a stocky man with a copper beard and clever eyes. Einar had met the captain of Haesten's forces many years ago. He was a friend and a fine warrior. "I missed your arrival last night. I was busy preparing to leave this place. But it does my heart good to see you so well, and you, of course, Lady Hildr. Now we get to kill these Frankish bastards. Is there anything better in life than slaying men who have to come to rip your life away?"

"We shall fight beside one another once more, old friend."

"It is my honour."

"Shield wall!" Haesten shouted abruptly, lifting his axe high. His four hundred warriors moved into the centre, with the Valkyrie on the right, matching their numbers, each one equipped with bow, spear, and axe. Einar aligned his men on the left flank, the ebb tide lapping beside them. Amundr bullied his way into the front rank with Thorgrim. Amundr had his precious helmet's cheek pieces closed and was huge and baleful in his *brynjar,* with an axe in his right hand and a shield in his left. Thorgrim hefted his double-bladed war axe while Hildr took a place in the third rank, recurved bow at the ready.

Einar rolled his shoulders, picked up his shield, and drew his axe. The Franks faced overwhelming numbers on the beach, but they still organised themselves into ranks to fight against the Norsemen who had invaded, killed their men, and stolen their wealth. Haesten had taken relics, killed priests and burned churches. He was the enemy of their Christ-God and everything they believed in. But Einar felt no pity as he prepared to fight in his fine fish scale armour. This was the life the gods urged all Norsemen to – battle, courage, death, and war. It honoured Odin, Tyr, and Thor, but the worshippers of the nailed god could never understand it. Theirs was a god of peace and harsh rules, and now Einar would fight them to bind more warriors to his army.

The beach stretched northward, curving out of sight behind towering crags. Wide, pale sands lay beneath a bleak, unsettled sky, dark clouds looming over northern Frankia like a *Völva's* cursed brew. A chill breeze brushed Einar's neck, carrying the briny scent of waters linking the lands of the Danes, Saxons, and Franks. To Einar's right, the sea churned relentlessly, its icy waves flecked with white foam.

Before him stood the Frankish forces, raised from local levies to protect their lord's lands and wealth. They were churls, thralls, and the lord's professional retainers, summoned to repel the Viking threat. Most were hardly warriors – farmers and labourers, hastily armed with spears thrust into their hands. In the centre of the Frankish line, however, stood true fighters. These men wore conical iron helmets with nasal guards to shield their faces. Some were clad in chainmail, others in hardened leather. All bore wooden shields in a strange, elongated shape, painted with the sigil of their lord, a swooping bird of some sort that Einar could not identify. The front rankers carried heavy shod spears and axes, and the wealthier amongst them brandished swords. They wore woollen cloaks dyed in dark hues, fastened at the shoulder by bronze brooches, and the sea wind whipped them mercilessly about their legs.

The commoners wore only leather jerkins or padded gambesons. They held spears before their frightened faces or clutched simple axes, clubs, or farm tools. Einar spotted a few hunting bows towards the rear. Their shields were smaller and rougher than those of the warriors – patched things of wood and hide, which Einar doubted would stand up to a solid axe blow.

The wind picked up, rustling through the ranks as it stirred the long, wild grasses on the dunes. The sea's rhythmic crashing onto the shore grew louder, ominous and unrelenting as if reflecting the tension that hummed among the gathered men. A distant gull screeched, its harsh trill carried on the wind. The Frankish nobleman came before his men on a white mare and barked commands at them, his voice hoarse from the cold as he ushered his fighters into a closer formation. Then Haesten barked an order, and four hundred Valkyrie warriors loosed their arrows. The shafts raced high into the dull sky, casting fast-moving shadows upon the beach, and before the first volley struck, another was already thrumming from their powerful bows.

The arrows struck like murderous rain, slapping into the Franks, thudding into shields and tearing into soft flesh like fangs. The Franks roared their anger and surged forward. Their leader's horse became skittish at the shouting, clearly not trained for war, and an arrow thumped into its rump. The beast bucked and sent the Frankish lord tumbling to the sand. Arrows flew without respite, and the Franks' march left a trail of corpses and writhing, injured warriors behind it. The middle of their formation came quicker as the braver, experienced warriors pressed forward, and the flanks made up of the churls and local levy marched slower, so they advanced in the shape of a spearhead.

"Where are we from?" Einar shouted, axe raised above his head, battle rage kindling inside him.

"Vanylven!" his men roared in response.

"Are you ready for war?"

"Kill! Kill! Kill!"

At that moment, Haesten stepped out before the army, grey hair blown by the wind, and he, too, raised his axe aloft. "Charge!" he roared, and so they did.

The Vikings hurtled across the beach. Valkyrie, Haesten's veteran army of reavers, raiders and killers, and the Vanylven men.

"I'm too old to bloody run," Einar huffed, out of breath after ten paces. His shield, *brynjar*, and axe weighed him down, so he let his men stream past him and marched towards the fight instead. As a younger man, he had led his men from the front, but those days were long gone. Einar marched forward, shield heavy in his left hand and axe comfortable in his right. A year ago, he had feared battle, that he was no longer able to trade blows with the evil men, with the killers and warriors of the Whale Road. But he was Einar the Brawler, and he now welcomed battle like cool fjord water after a day of hard labour.

"Then let's march to the fight with dignity, my lord," said Thorgrim, winking at Einar as he fell in alongside him. Ahead, the armies came together with a crack like thunder; weapons struck, and men died. Shield walls heaved at one another, and the Frankish line bowed out towards its flanks. Einar joined his company and barged his way to the front to find a line of Franks pushing at his men with their shields.

"Break them!" Einar bellowed.

Thorgrim surged forwards, ducking beneath a Vanylven man's shield arm to kick an enemy's shield at its lower rim. As it dropped, Thorgrim drove the haft of his axe into the Frank's face, crushing his nose to a pulp. He followed with a ferocious swing of his double-bladed war axe, severing the Frank's leg cleanly below the knee. The Frank fell backwards into his own men, howling, blood spurting from his ruined limb. The sight of the severed leg lying in the sand sent dread rippling through the Frankish ranks, forcing them to retreat. All men fear such a wound, the pain, and the days of suffering before infection took their lives in a weeping, shivering fever.

Amundr crashed into the space with his shield, throwing three of the enemy backwards. The giant's axe flashed like sparking tinder, the bearded blade caving in a Frank's skull like rotting fruit. Gore spattered the Frankish front line, and they winced as the brutality and savagery of battle washed over them. Hildr loosed three arrows into the space in quick succession – one struck a chest, the next a shoulder, and the third embedded in a Frank's open mouth. Einar charged into that horror with axe and shield, laying about him like a demon from Niflheim. He smashed his axe through a spear stave and into the chest beyond, battered another man down to the sand with his shield, stamped on his throat and left him for the warriors behind to finish.

In moments, the fight for the right flank was over. The Franks turned and ran from the beach like children from an angry father. Einar ceased his onslaught once the enemy broke, and he let his shield fall, resting his hands on his knees, chest burning from exertion. Hildr knelt beside him and emptied her quiver into the Frankish lord's warriors, his experienced men in the centre who held firm against Haesten's men.

"Amundr, Thorgrim," he said. The two

warriors turned to him, bloody and wild-eyed with rage. "Form the men up and charge the Franks from the flank."

Amundr bellowed at the men, halting their pursuit of the fleeing enemy. They formed up quickly in ranks and charged. The battle raged, Hildr's bow twanged, and from the other side of the beach, the Valkyrie's familiar undulating war cry resounded as they, too, streamed into the Frankish foes. The centre held for twenty heartbeats as Franks fought against raiders they hated, against men who had burned their holy places and sacked their lands of wealth. Yet the Franks lacked the skill to withstand the Vikings, and soon, their lines wavered, breaking under the assault. That was when the slaughter truly began – when the enemy turned their backs and ran for safety. In the shield wall, men are protected by the ranks and the barrier of heavy shields, but in retreat, men die badly. So it was that day on the beach.

Thin rivers of blood ran along the sand flowing into the sea, and Haesten's men stripped the dead of anything of value. The Frankish lord died with Bjarki's axe in his stomach, and Haesten led his men to their precious ships.

"Time to set sail and kill this crippled bastard on the Isle of Mann," Haesten said, his blade of a face staring out into the wind. "We'll find Hundr and put your enemies to the sword. I hear Mann is rich in slave gold and silver. Maybe we'll be lucky, kill your foes and make our ships heavy with plunder."

"Bring your ships and your men, Lord Haesten," Einar replied. "Follow our sails westwards, and when the Crippled King is dead, and we have found Hundr, then you can have your fill of Mann's treasure."

"What are we waiting for, then?"

"First, we go north. My ships await at Vanylven, and King Harald Fairhair has promised ships and men. Then we go west as one fleet. Bjorn Ironside follows."

"Bjorn," Haesten uttered wistfully. "I have missed that old bear. Men will talk of this war for generations. You have brought the warlords of the north together, Einar. Let's give the bards something to sing about."

TWENTY-THREE

A week later, Hundr stood with Erik and Hermoth on the edge of a forest to the south of King Veggr's city of Jorvik. They had sailed their ships into the Humber and along the Ouse, anchoring in the shelter of a broad river bend where it divided into a smaller stream. There, they beached the warships, concealed them with branches, and left a dozen men behind to stand guard.

"We have our men, and we have brought the slaves," said Erik Bloodaxe, hands resting on the axes at his belt. "Now, are you going to tell us how we are going to kill that bastard Veggr?"

Hundr told them. There would be no great assault like there had been when Hundr scaled the walls almost twenty years ago. This time, he would use guile to enter Jorvik and then fury to kill its usurper king.

"What if Guthred and his priest's army don't come?" asked Hermoth when Hundr had finished.

Hundr shrugged. "Then we'll have to fight our way out."

"Veggr has three, maybe four hundred men?" asked Erik.

"And we have one hundred and twenty," said Hermoth.

"I'm going in there tomorrow to kill that bastard Veggr and his nithing servant, Stigmarr. Guthred will arrive with an army, perhaps not an army of warriors, but an army of Christ worshippers who want their god restored to the old Roman city. Four hundred men cannot stand up to our warriors and army of churls."

"An army of churls and thralls is no army," warned Hermoth.

"And yet we must do it," insisted Hundr, and Erik laughed at the madness of it.

Jorvik sat on the confluence of the River Ouse and River Foss. The two rivers not only made the city a perfect place for the Romans to bring in trade and sail their legionaries deep into northern Britain's lands, but they also provided natural defences. Any army wishing to assault the city had to cross those rivers first, giving the defenders a chance to kill them as they swam or tried to bridge the waters. The Ouse ran through the heart of the city itself, and its slow-moving waters allowed ships to transport goods, provisions, and people into the ancient settlement. The smaller Foss formed a protective boundary on Jorvik's eastern side, where it was dammed to create a barrier around the city.

The walls were a mixture of decaying Roman grandeur, monstrous blocks of chiselled stone and modern wood, wattle, and mud. Built from stone and rubble, the walls had crumbled in places, and the Saxon and Viking inhabitants had repaired those sections with stout oak and pine timbers and filled the spaces with rubble and wattle. A wooden palisade and rampart encircled the entire fortification, while towers – some remnants of Roman craftsmanship and others built by Saxons – stood vigil over gates facing east and west. Hundr had considered scaling the walls, knowing Veggr lacked enough warriors to guard their entire span. But his strength had not yet returned enough to make the climb and still face the coming fight.

Within the city walls stood an old Roman fortress and stone buildings that had been repurposed as houses. In the six hundred years since the Romans abandoned the island to the native Britons, who were later conquered by the marauding Saxons, Angles, and Jutes from lands south of Denmark, the roofs of these buildings had rotted and collapsed, patched over now with thatch. The Minster, which Bishop Eadred so longed for, was a small stone church once topped with a bronze cross. Ivar had used it to store his looted treasures. It had thick stone walls, small arched windows, and a wooden roof. To Bishop Eadred, it was more than just a building; he spoke of it with deep conviction, claiming it as the seat of his Christ-God in Northumbria – a place he was determined to reclaim for his faith. And so, the Bishop and Guthred would bring an army of Christ worshippers to Jorvik's walls to take the city and the Minster from Veggr the Usurper. However, scaling the walls demanded champions, men favoured by Odin – warriors like Ivar the Boneless and his fellow Ragnarsson kin, and indeed, Hundr himself. Thus, Hundr's task was to force the gates open and hold them long enough for Guthred's ragtag army to surge inside and overpower Veggr's warriors.

Hermoth brought up a wagon led by a stocky-limbed cart horse. Six of the slaves liberated from Jorvik alongside the Seaworm survivors huddled in the back, staring at Erik and Hermoth with sad eyes. They were the women of Veggr's throne room, slaves taken from Northumbria and elsewhere and subjected to the rape, beatings, and servitude of Veggr's court.

"You shall be free," Hundr said to them warmly as he climbed into the wagon. "Do this one service, and I shall set you free, each with a pouch of silver to find a new life. All you must do is stay in the wagon. Do not run. Can you do that in return for your freedom?"

The women glanced at one another, and all but one stared down at the wagon's timbers. They shivered in thin, woollen shifts and bare feet, but Hundr needed them if his plan to take the city was to succeed.

"We can do it," nodded a young woman with deep brown eyes and a long nose. "We'll stay in your wagon and do what we must."

"Good."

"Are you going to kill Veggr and his men?"

"Yes."

"Then we shall gladly do as you ask."

Toki and Sigvarth climbed in beside Hundr to sit amongst the women. Thin and gaunt from their imprisonment, they looked like slaves, and they cast dirty cloaks about their shoulders to hide the axes, seaxes, and knives held close to their emaciated bodies. Hundr carried a buckler, and hidden in the folds of a filthy blanket lay a sword he'd borrowed from one of Erik's warriors. He had left Hermoth and Erik waiting, concealed beyond Jorvik's walls and between the twin rivers, as the wagon rumbled slowly along the path to the city's western gate. Hermoth drove the wagon, clicking his tongue and urging the horse onwards with the leather reins. Hundr glanced over his shoulder and watched as Erik, Yazi, and Harbard waited with the rest of Erik's warriors hidden in the forest's shadows. They were good men, and Erik would bring them howling through the gates with menace and axe blades. All Hundr had to do was get inside the walls and hold the gate long enough for Erik's men to get inside. Then, they would hold it until Guthred and Bishop Eadred marched with the Christians of Northumbria.

Hundr's dead eye pulsed, and his shaved head was cold in the evening breeze. The moon appeared early in a clear sky, hanging there like a great silver coin whilst the sun had yet to set. He took that as a good omen, a sign from Odin that his luck had changed. Hundr straightened his leg inside the wagon, testing the thigh muscles beneath the wound that had now healed. There was no pain. He flexed the three fingers on his mutilated hand, and they moved well, though he longed to hold a blade in that hand, to fight with two swords as he always had – a skill that few men possessed. Yet it was unlikely he would ever feel that joy again. Nevertheless, he was alive, and for the first time since his defeat by Finn and Orm Eysteinsson, he was moving towards his enemies and not running away from them.

"Heads down," Hermoth called over his

shoulder to the pitiful figures in the wagon. "We are almost there." Hermoth wore a long, brown cloak over his *brynjar* and weapons. He left his hair loose so that it hung about his face, and he kept his head bowed, not straight-backed and proud like a warrior, but stooped and furtive like a slaver should be. The wagon rattled over one of the bridges that crossed the River Foss and then came to a creaking halt. Hundr kept his head down and could not see the walls or the gate before them. The stink of shit and burning wood drifted on the breeze from the city. Hundr prepared himself, breathing slowly, hoping that his strength would hold up long enough for him to strike at Veggr and Stigmarr. He was strong enough to wield his sword and buckler, but it would not last. It would have to be enough. He needed the Ulfberht sword and the Seaworm's prow. They were part of him, what made him The Man with the Dog's Name. As he waited there beside the sad-faced slave women, he knew that once the dwarf-forged sword and dragon prow were his, he would grow stronger. He would be the Champion of the North again, ready to rise and strike back at the Crippled King and the son of an axeman he had killed long ago in Ireland's green country.

"Ho there!" Hermoth called in Norse, the language spoken by men throughout Jorvik and the Danelaw.

"What do you want?" shouted a voice from the battlements.

"Slaves for King Veggr's hall."

"Piss off. It's too late. Come back tomorrow."

"I was ordered to bring them today. They are needed for the king's hall."

"I said piss off, slaver."

"The king will be angry. Furious. He is not a man to forgive foolishness lightly."

"Foolishness? Careful, turd, or I'll come down there and throw you in the river."

"Alright then. Tell the king I was here and that you turned me away. He has no slave girls to warm his bed or serve his ale. I will come back tomorrow. I'll see you then, if you live the night. Perhaps your head might be on a spike above the walls, or Veggr might take pity and only geld you for disobeying his orders."

"Annoying little bastard!" the guard roared from the battlements, and moments later, the gates creaked and scraped as the guards heaved them open.

Hermoth had played his part well. He clicked his tongue and led the wagon beneath the hulking stone walls. Hundr kept his head down, and the wall's shadow passed across the wagon, which became lighter as they entered the city.

"Now then," said the guard, his boots thudding on the wooden steps as he descended the battlements. "We've left our nice warm brazier and our ale to open the gate. It's time for the gate tax." Three men came from the summit with the guard, sniggering at their captain's words.

"Gate tax?" Hermoth asked.

"The king is going to pay you for these scrawny Saxon wenches, and you've no doubt already had your way with them."

"Even the boys, Bolli, he's even had his way with those men," piped another voice to more laughter.

"Even the boys," said Bolli, the captain. "So we want a silver coin each for our trouble."

"I don't have silver until after I've seen the king," Hermoth replied.

"Then we'll take one of your stripling wenches each, and when we're done, you can be on your way."

"Maybe I do have a silver coin for each of you. Hold the reins whilst I look."

The bit and bridle jingled as Bolli, or one of his men, took the reins from Hermoth. Hundr dared not look up to see who in case one of the gate guards recognised him from Veggr's throne room.

"Good boy," drawled Bolli.

"Yes, here it is," said Hermoth cheerfully. Hundr heard the sound of an axe blade sliding from its belt loop and the sing of steel through the chill night air. Then, a chop like a butcher cutting meat, and Hundr sprang from beneath his cloak like a pouncing cat. Hermoth had smashed his axe into a guard's face and leapt down to face the rest, axe in one hand and knife in the other. Hundr gripped his sword and buckler and jumped after him, closely followed by Toki and Sigvarth.

"Die!" Sigvarth roared, and he disembowelled a short, fat man with a sweep of his axe. Hundr winced at the noise, for it would surely bring more of Veggr's four hundred warriors charging to the gate. A lanky guard with a lop-sided jaw thrust a spear half-heartedly at Hundr and then turned on his heel to run. Hundr drove the point of his sword into the small of the man's back, feeling the crunch of his spine through the hilt. The sword was ill-balanced and of poor metal, but it was still a sword, and Hundr's heart raced with the thrill of combat.

The gate guards lay dead or dying, and Hundr took a flaming torch from its iron crutch and ran to the open gateway. The evening was turning into night, and Hundr waved the torch back and forth to signal to Erik Bloodaxe that the fight for Jorvik had begun. Moonlight glinted off iron and steel at the forest's shadowed edges, and Hundr turned back to the city, knowing that Erik and one hundred and fifty Vikings came charging towards the gateway with weapons drawn, ready to kill.

"Trouble," said Toki, pointing his bloodstained axe up the straight, cobbled pathway leading into the labyrinthine streets and paths inside the old Roman settlement. A dozen warriors strode up the cobbles, spears in hand, peering into the falling darkness to see what had caused such commotion.

"Get the women to safety, Toki," Hundr ordered. "They must be kept safe."

"Yes, my lord," Toki replied. He helped the slave women down from the wagon, and they stared at Hundr with frightened faces. Toki led them through the gate, towards the river, which shone beneath the night sky like the Bifrost bridge.

"Loose the horse," Hundr said. "Turn the wagon over. They'll have to come around it to fight us."

Hermoth and the Seaworm men heaved at the wagon whilst Hundr cut the horse's tack. He slapped the cart horse on the rump, and it whinnied, bolting up the cobbled street, shaking its head. The Jorvik warriors shouted in alarm and darted away from the horse. Two men came on before the rest, men in leather and carrying spears. Hundr checked the straps on his buckler and clutched its grip in his ruined hand. He held the sword in his right and went to meet the foe.

Can I still fight? Am I still the man I was?

Veggr's warriors saw a thin man with an egg-bald head coming towards them with a cheap sword and a small shield. They grinned at each other, showing rotten teeth through their greasy beards, and Hundr brought the hilt of his sword to his mouth and kissed the cold steel.

Odin, see me. Look upon me as you did the first time I attacked this place. Grant me your favour, restore my luck, and I shall send you souls and kill the men who would unchain Loki, the foster son who killed your beloved Baldr.

A spear point lunged at Hundr. He deflected it with the buckler and darted low, stretching out with his sword arm to pierce the spearman in the groin. Hundr pulled back, his blade tip bright with blood. The spearman yelped, dropping his weapon to clutch his wound in that most vulnerable of places. A second warrior, enraged, roared and lunged his spear at Hundr's face. Hundr parried with his sword and slammed the iron-rimmed edge of his buckler into the man's chest, forcing him back.

The enemy gasped, seizing Hundr's buckler with his left hand. He was strong. Much stronger than Hundr in his starved state, and he would have ripped the shield from Hundr's hand but for the leather strap that fixed it to his left forearm. He barged Hundr backwards with his shoulder and then lashed out with his spear. Hundr ducked, his breathing laboured and limbs heavy. Hundr dropped to one knee and brought the buckler down hard on the warrior's foot. He yelped, leapt backwards, and died with Hundr's sword in his throat. Blood trickled down the sword's fuller to wet Hundr's hand, and he gritted his teeth against the exhaustion.

Ten enemies regrouped on the cobblestones, their faces hardening as the horse trotted away. When they saw the bodies of their fallen comrades, rage darkened their expressions. With shouts of war and weapons raised high, they charged at Hundr.

Hundr stood firm, bracing himself. Behind him, a wagon toppled over, scraping and grinding against the cobbles. It formed a crude barricade – a makeshift palisade that the attackers would need to cross if they wanted to drive him out and close the city's wide gates.

The first to approach was a young man, quick and reckless, charging with fierce determination. But in the shadows, he could not see the night wraith waiting for him on the stones of Jorvik. Hundr's face was a mask of ruin, the scars of battle and hunger carved deep. A jagged red line ran from his forehead to the cavity of his dead eye, where malnutrition in Veggr's dark throne room had hollowed his cheek into a pit of shadows. His features, twisted by old wounds and ravaged by the pursuit of glory, were barely visible in the night – but they were a warning, had the young man been able to see it. Naïve to the danger, the young warrior pressed forward. Hundr swept his borrowed sword low, catching the man's legs and sending him sprawling across the cobbles. His head struck the stones with a dull crack. As he struggled to breathe, Hundr brought his buckler down upon the young man's throat, crushing his windpipe. His face flushed red, eyes bulging, and he spluttered, dying, unable to catch his final breath.

Before Hundr could rise from his crouch, another enemy hit him with a shoulder charge, throwing him onto his back. Hundr sprawled on the cobbles and tried to thrust to his feet, but from the corner of his good eye, he saw an axe blade coming for his neck, as swift and sure as a raven on the wing, and Hundr thought he would surely die. But a figure leapt over him like a horse clearing a hedge. The figure landed nimbly in front of Hundr and killed the axeman with a brutal chop of his own axe. The figure was tall, golden-haired, lithe and full of a Norseman's savagery. It was Hermoth, and in that fleeting moment of pride, Hundr remembered his son as a boy, timid and afraid of battle, paling beside the brutish wildness of his friend, Erik Haraldsson. That boy was gone, and the man he had become cut open a second enemy's thigh with his knife, ending the foe's life with a bearded axe blade to the chest.

The enemy warriors halted their charge, forming a baying line before Hermoth. They were young men who thought themselves warriors. They believed that Veggr's favour made them strong, that by carrying a spear and wearing hard-baked leather, they had become warriors. But in Hermoth, they faced a true warrior, a *drengr* taught to fight by The Man with the Dog's Name, taught to sail by Einar the Brawler, foster son to King Harald Fairhair of Norway, a warrior raised to the axe who spent his summers sailing Midgard with Erik Bloodaxe in search of the most dangerous wars, the most brutal fights to burn their reputations as bright as a blacksmith's forge.

Hermoth clashed his knife and axe blade down on the cobbles, crouching like a wild beast. The weapons sparked on the old Roman stone, and he stood slowly, rising to his full height with his weapons stretched out wide in a defiant challenge.

"Come and fight with Hermoth, son of The Man with the Dog's Name!" Hermoth bellowed, his voice no longer soft but hardened and cruel – the voice of a ruthless Viking. "Come and die!"

Hermoth passed his axe to his knife hand, picked up a spear and hurled at the line of enemies. It struck one in the shoulder, sending him staggering back, screaming like a child. The enemy line faltered, and Hermoth shouted at them, goading them to come and face his axe. Half of them turned and ran from the gates, but two scores of their comrades emerged from alleyways and paths, men with helmets, axes, and shields. The first few of Veggr's men found their courage now that more came to swell their ranks. They smiled mirthlessly at the four men attempting to hold Jorvik's mighty gateway behind an upturned wagon, confident that four hundred of King Veggr's warriors would soon follow those already come to bolster their ranks.

They came on tightly packed together, wary of Hermoth, his blood-drenched axe and knife. Kneeling beside a corpse, Hermoth seized an axe and, taking two steps forward, he hurled it overhand. The weapon struck an enemy warrior in the chest with a sickening crunch, knocking him off his feet. Hundr stood, strengthened by his son's bravery, and gripped his buckler and sword.

"Let the bastards come," Sigvarth growled, appearing at Hundr's side with an axe in his hand. "They must all die for what we suffered in this place."

King Veggr himself marched from behind a thatched building, clad in armour that made him appear huge amongst his men. He carried the Ulfberht sword, and the glinting blade sang out to Hundr as though it longed for his hand around her leather-wrapped hilt.

"Kill them!" Veggr bellowed, pointing his sword at Hermoth. "Kill them and bring me their heads!"

More of Veggr's men appeared, thronging the street until there were too many to count. Their numbers emboldened them, and the enemy charged like wild horses, filling Jorvik's night air with their threats and war cries. Hundr, Sigvarth, and Harbard ran for cover behind the upturned wagon. That created an obstacle for Veggr's men to manoeuvre whilst Hundr and the others struck at them with their weapons. But with such vast numbers, it could only be a matter of time before they dragged the wagon out of the way and slaughtered the four impudent attackers.

Something flashed past Hundr's blind side, a man sprinting at top speed. He came in a coat of chainmail with an axe held in each fist, roaring his hate and challenge to Veggr's warriors. It was Erik Bloodaxe, young and fearless, his long red hair unbound and the colour of blood beneath the full moon. That blood-red hair streamed behind the prince like a horse's mane, and he charged at the enemy, one man against overwhelming numbers. The men at the front of Veggr's force stopped and tried to push back against those behind who shoved them forward. They knew Bloodaxe from his brutal fight in their king's hall, and they also knew no man within their ranks could stand before his fury. Without breaking stride, Erik charged into them, his axes whirring like a wolf's gnashing fangs. Hermoth joined him, and they cut at Veggr's men like gods. Blood spattered, men soiled themselves in fear as death came for them, and they watched their friends die from terrible injuries. Young men listen to bards and scops and believe war is all glory, shining swords, princesses, and hordes of treasure. Hundr knew different, and he saw the horror dawn over Veggr's men as their friends and brothers died with axe wounds to their necks, faces, and chests. Bones, organs, and bloody flesh showed in those wounds upon men they had laughed with, lived with, ate and drank with.

Erik's men charged through the gateway behind Hundr like water rushing into a dried-up river. They followed their prince and the sound of Erik's men hitting Veggr's warriors was like thunder meant for the end of days. Hundr waited, holding Harbard and Sigvarth back from the charge. They were not yet fit to join the fray where men pressed close together to hew and claw at one another. Toki was in the gateway, returned from taking the slave women to safety, and the cart horse appeared from an alleyway, eyes wide and terrified by the ferrous stench of blood.

"Toki!" Hundr called above the din. "Take the horse and ride north. Find Guthred and have him hurry here. If he's camped for the night, wake him. He must come now, even in the darkness. Veggr's men will rally, and we don't have the numbers to kill them all. Guthred must come tonight."

"What if I can't find him, my lord?" said Toki, taking careful steps to the frightened horse and gently grabbing its bit and what remained of the cart's reins. The horse whickered, but Toki stroked its long nose, whispering to the beast whilst the deadly battle raged in the streets beyond.

"Then we are dead men. So find him, Toki."

TWENTY-FOUR

Toki galloped on horseback and crossed the River Ouse to seek Guthred's army of churls Hundr needed if he was to take Jorvik and kill King Veggr. Erik and Hermoth led Erik's men in their violent charge against Veggr's forces, and they outmatched the King of Jorvik. They hacked into his forces, filling the night with their war din while the injured and dying screamed and wept for mercy. Hundr hefted his buckler and sword and found Harbard and Sigvarth at the rear of the fighting. Their earlier enthusiasm had waned, their strength weakened, and they now looked at Hundr with drawn faces and shamed eyes. Even Yazi could only fire his bow sparingly.

"Our weapons are red with the blood of our enemies," Hundr said to the Seaworm survivors. "We have all struck a blow, and there is no shame for us this day. Let the others fight until we grow stronger. Then we shall rise and fight in the front rank like we always have." It was small consolation for men of reputation, but before they could argue, Veggr's men broke. They ran away from Erik and Hermoth's fury and the organised shield wall attack from Bloodaxe's crews. Veggr led the retreat himself, lumbering through the darkness, taking his men to the safety of Jorvik's inner keep.

"We fight for the Bloodaxe!" shouted one of Erik's men.

"Bloodaxe! Bloodaxe! Bloodaxe!" the warriors responded as one, raising their weapons in salute to their bold leader.

"They'll be back," said Sigvarth, sliding his axe into its belt loop. "Veggr has lost maybe thirty men here, perhaps more. He still has three hundred or so of his bastards to send against us."

"They'll come, and we must be ready," Hundr replied.

"We haven't seen Stigmarr yet," growled Harbard. "I want to see that bastard suffer."

"Veggr has more men," Sigvarth uttered. "He should surround us and come at us from the ramparts above the gate, from the streets around us, and from the front. He has enough warriors to do it. A score of archers could keep us huddled behind the wagon whilst his men charge at us."

"But you are Sigvarth Trollhands," said Hundr, "experienced in battle and in the ways of war. Veggr is a backstabber. He has not seen the combat you have seen. Let us hope he finds the answer to this riddle slowly. It is night. Men don't enjoy fighting in the darkness. So let's see what happens."

"Let's storm the keep," piped Erik, striding through his men, his eyes wide with battle joy.

"We have beaten them, but they still outnumber us three or four to one," Hundr replied. He understood Erik's lust to finish the fight. When he was a younger man, he would have felt the same himself. But Hundr had been lucky in those days. He had experienced warriors like Einar and Sten Sleggya to temper his rash youthfulness. "Storm the keep now, and we shall all die. Veggr and his nithings will cut at us and stick us full of spears and arrows as we try to fight our way in. I want him dead, Erik. And I want Stigmarr dead as well. To do it, we need Guthred to come with his Northumbrians."

Erik licked his lips, glanced at his warriors, and then back to Hundr. The warp and weft of the prince's cunning played out upon his youthful face. His eyes shone, his taut mouth softened, and his bunched shoulders suddenly relaxed. "You have the right of it, foster father. We shall wait." Erik smiled as though they were picking apples at market and not standing spattered with blood inside Jorvik's Roman walls. Erik sucked in a chest full of night air and looked up at the ancient defences. He stamped his boot on the cobbles and nodded appreciatively. "I like this place. Maybe I shall come back one day." He winked at Hundr and went to his men, laughing with them, congratulating them on their bravery.

They pulled Veggr's dead and dying men into the middle of the cobbled street to create another obstacle for the defenders to overcome when they returned. Erik had his men make two lines of shields in front of the upturned wagon where they would form the shield wall when the attack came again. To keep warm, the men used braziers and chopped up a guard shed for firewood, building a blaze beside the gate. The men were jubilant after their victory, and they shared the remaining supplies from their belt pouches. They warmed blood sausage over the fire, shared bread, and drank ale. Hundr and Erik set men to watch the lanes and alleys leading to the gate in case Veggr tried to spring a surprise attack. They set men atop the gate and stared into the night, hoping to see Guthred's army approach.

The attack came late when the moon had travelled almost its entire journey across Midgard. There was a hint of light in the east, a sliver of pallid yellow beyond Jorvik, seeping over distant hills like spilt honey. Veggr's warriors came not in a wild charge but slithering from the keep like spiders. Hundr, Hermoth, and Erik watched them from behind the wagon, spears passing through the city like a shifting forest, and the Bloodaxe warriors observed them in grim silence. They appeared on the walls carrying bows but stopped short of the gatehouse where Hundr had placed six stout men to keep the enemy from getting behind their backs. Veggr and Stigmarr did not show themselves, but the enemy came quietly. No drums, horns, or shouts of anger, just a slow, tired march. Hundreds of warriors filled the streets and winding paths as the nervous eyes of the common folk peeked from closed window shutters and doors.

"Shield wall!" Erik ordered, and his men took up their positions in front of the wagon. They made a roof of shields over the wagon's rear to shield the fighters from the onslaught of arrows. Those missiles came without fanfare or orders. A single arrow tonked off a shield boss and flew wildly over the rooftops. Then the arrows came in twos and threes, slamming into shield boards and skittering from the cobblestones. Hundr crouched beneath the roof of shields with Harbard, Yazi, and Sigvarth. Erik and Hermoth stood in the shield wall lines beyond the cart, waiting to meet any headlong attack with their Viking fury. But that attack never came. The defenders continued with their barrage of arrows and then threw spears and even rocks at the attackers. Masonry shattered on the cobbles, and arrows and spears thudded into wattle buildings. Some men suffered wounds, but no men died in that assault. Yazi loosed his own shafts at the enemy, and he dropped five men from the high walls before he collapsed, exhausted from drawing the yew bow.

As the sun rose above the distant horizon, casting warm summer light over the city, the missile attack continued in a strange, silent stalemate. The Bloodaxe warriors atop the gatehouse erupted in joyous cries as the barrage abruptly ceased, sending Veggr's men into a panic. Hundr peered out from behind the shields and saw the enemy on the western walls pointing away from the city. Filled with exhilaration, he dashed from cover and beneath the open gate.

Guthred and Bishop Eadred had led the people of Northumbria to Jorvik, and they emerged from the trees and meadows in their hundreds and thousands. They flowed across the land like wheat in the wind, chanting prayers and songs to the Christ-God as they advanced. Eadred, Guthred and Toki rode at the head of the army, and Bishop Eadred held an enormous crucifix on a long rod. The cross shone like the necklace of Brísingamen in the morning light, encased in silver and studded with gems.

"Guthred has come!" Hundr called. He ran back to the upturned wagon, gathered up his sword, and strapped the buckler to his left arm. "The rightful heir of Jorvik is here. Erik, Hermoth!" Hermoth and Erik came to the wagon, weapons drawn and hungry looks on their young, wolfish faces. "The army of the people has arrived. Veggr cannot stand against so vast a force, even though they carry only scythes, knives, and staves. We must attack before the coward flees."

Erik laughed and grabbed Hundr's shoulder. "To the keep then, foster-father, for vengeance."

The prince charged with Hermoth at his side. They led one hundred and forty warriors along Jorvik's main street, and the enemy melted away before them. There was no battle for Jorvik, no bloody combat where Hundr and Erik would need to fight for every street, killing dozens of foes to gain a mere ship's length. The defenders just ran for their lives as news of Guthred's arrival spread through the city like a torrent. So Hundr, Erik, and Hermoth marched shoulder to shoulder towards the city's inner keep whilst the men whom Veggr paid to guard his city and protect him fled into the alleys. They cowered in pigsties, beneath dog shelters, and inside the common folk's houses.

Upon entering the city, Eadred planted his shining cross before the Minster and led his people in a rapturous song to honour the glory of their god. Guthred joined Hundr and marched behind them, wearing no armour and carrying no weapon. He came to war dressed as a simple man, in a plain jerkin and trews, with nothing to mark him out as nobility but the straightness of his back and the confidence of his stride. Four gigantic churls flanked him, big men with short, ruffled hair, hands dirty from field work, broad faces and unkempt beards. These were Guthred's people, the Danes and Saxons of the Northumbrian Danelaw, who had suffered at the hands of rotten kings since the death of Guthred's father, Hardacnut, and now came to place their prince on the throne. Guthred was one of them, a man without arrogance or pretension, a godly man who had rallied his people to give Hundr the vengeance he required to heal his fractured warrior's soul.

"Veggr the Usurper!" Hundr called when they reached the walls of Jorvik's inner keep. "The true king is here to take his throne."

"Piss off, you piece of weasel shit!" a man shouted from inside the walls.

"If you come out now, we shall let your men go free."

Hundr waited for a response, but none came.

"He can't have many men still loyal to him in there," remarked Erik, an axe held in each hand.

"Take it, then," said Hundr. "But I want Veggr and Stigmarr alive."

Erik grinned and led his men in a wild charge against the keep. It did not take long. They hammered the door to firewood with axes and sent men to rip up the thatch from the roof. Erik and Hermoth stormed the front door behind stout shields whilst a dozen men dropped in through the hole cut into the roof. Hundr waited outside as weapons clanged and men died. Before the attack could turn to slaughter, Veggr and Stigmarr stalked from the front door. Their weapons and armour were unmarked by battle. They came with Erik's warriors' spear points prodding their arses to guide them, and Bloodaxe's men mocked their shame.

"I curse the day I met you," sneered Stigmarr, spitting at Hundr's feet.

"You did not know it then," said Sigvarth, "but you had The Man with the Dog's Name as your prisoner, the Champion of the North. And you treated him like a beast."

Stigmarr and Veggr stared at Hundr, but they had no time to respond because Sigvarth Trollhands threw his axe underhand, and the heavy blade turned as it sailed through the air and thumped into Stigmarr's chest. Stigmarr staggered, grabbed the haft which had crushed his chest bones and fell to his knees. Blood bubbled at his mouth, and he stared at the weapon which had taken his life and then slumped dead at his king's feet. Hundr sighed, releasing the foul humours which had lived inside him since the day of his capture.

"You can fight for your life," said Hundr, pointing his borrowed sword at Veggr.

"And if I win?" Veggr smirked, pointedly staring around at the enemies surrounding him.

"If you win, you can go free. My men won't lay a hand on you."

"Come, then." Veggr slowly drew the Ulfberht sword and swung it about him, its dwarven-forged blade singing its war song to Hundr as it sliced through the air. "You might be old and finished, but men will know that I, Veggr Kolbeinsson, killed The Man with the Dog's Name, Ivarsbane, Champion of the North."

Erik and Hermoth pushed the crowd away from the keep to make a fighting circle, and as Hundr checked the strap on his buckler, Veggr charged. He attacked without skill or swordplay but came on with brutal strength and savagery. Donned in his *brynjar* and blue cloak, he roared like a bear as he swung the Ulfberht sword overhand like a cleaver. Hundr lifted the buckler to catch the blow. The power in Veggr's arm drove Hundr's weakened body downwards. The buckler caught the sword, but the small shield crashed into Hundr's skull. He shook his head to clear his vision. Veggr kneed him hard in the face, and Hundr tumbled backwards, rolling to come up with his sword still clasped firmly in his hand.

Not like this, Odin All-Father. Give me the strength to kill this man, and I will offer you the blót, the sacrifice of he who would free Loki from his fetters.

Hundr closed his one eye, and strength flowed into his ravaged body – a belief in his skill and strength nourished by the return of his Odin luck. Hundr rose and growled. He kept low, stalking around the fighting circle like a wolf, sword and buckler held wide, dead eye throbbing with wrath. Veggr came on again with the same monstrous overhand stroke of a blade forged for better warriors than he. Hundr darted forward and drove the buckler's edge into Veggr's gut. The big man doubled over, and Hundr danced away from him. He was fast again, lithe and wicked, and Hundr slashed the sword across Veggr's hamstrings. Blood sprayed bright in the morning light, and Veggr fell to his knees. He vomited and cried out in abject fear, turning to Hundr with wet eyes and a mouth twisted in terror.

"Now you know what it means to fight a

warrior," Hundr said. "No glorious afterlife for you, raper, murderer, backstabber. Before you die, I want you to know that *Níðhöggr* will gnaw on your corpse until the end of days. I condemn you to *Nástrǫnd,* that corpse shore for wolfish murderers and oathbreakers."

"No!" Veggr screamed, openly weeping. The warriors turned away from his shame, and Veggr crawled on the cobblestones like a nithing beggar.

Hundr sliced open Veggr's forearm with a flick of his wrist, and the Ulfberht clattered on the stone pathway. Hundr laid down his borrowed sword and picked up his beloved dwarven-forged blade. The leather grip fitted his hand perfectly, the sword balanced as though forged for his hand alone. Hundr turned at the hip and whipped the blade around. It cut through Veggr's neck like a knife through butter, and the usurper's head fell to the cobbles in a gout of arterial blood. Hundr stripped the bloody silver chain from Veggr's headless corpse and tossed it to Erik's man who had lent him the buckler and sword. He claimed the dead king's *brynjar* for himself.

At last, justice. After all he'd endured – imprisoned, starved, beaten, humiliated, and fighting now with a mutilated hand – Hundr had proven himself once more as The Man with the Dog's Name, feared across the seas. Now, all that remained was to retake the prow of the Seaworm and see the end of the Crippled King and Orm.

With Veggr defeated, Guthred's people praised their Christ-God and rallied around their new king, placing him on the throne. In gratitude, Guthred handsomely rewarded Erik and Hundr with silver from Veggr's horde.

Hundr left Jorvik with his sword and new armour. He sailed with Erik and Hermoth with a heart full of violent glory and restored luck. They had found the Seaworm prow in the corner of Veggr's throne room, along with Yazi's bow, and Hundr took the dragon head with him aboard Erik's Whale Breaker. Two *drakkar* warships left the Humber, and they turned north to follow Northumbria's crags and headlands before turning west. For that way, the Crippled King and Orm Eysteinsson awaited, and Hundr had made a promise to Odin that he must keep.

TWENTY-FIVE

The Whale Breaker sped south, her striped sails filled with favourable wind. Erik Bloodaxe's two ships had sailed around the northern tip of the wild lands where tribes of Scots fought to protect their coast from Viking settlers. They turned south where the northeastern tip of Britain reached out towards Ireland, so close that a ship could cross the distance in one day. Ships bearing the fire symbol of Loki patrolled the seas, the small *snekke* warships scudding close to the shore. Hundr was sure they had spotted Erik's proud symbol of two crossed axes flying high from the mast, for they did not hide it. Hundr had attempted to infiltrate Finn's fortress and kill him. He had failed, and that chance was gone. Finn was no fool. Now it was war, bloody war, and so Erik led his ships towards Mann without care of the Crippled King's patrol boats.

Finn had recruited an army, which Hundr

guessed was somewhere close to three thousand men strong. He had a vast fleet to protect the coastline of his island and the rich slave markets that made his army possible. In contrast, Erik could bring only one hundred and fifty warriors to battle. Hundr had considered sailing north to Vanylven to rally Einar and the remainder of his warriors, but the end of summer was fast approaching, and he could not risk waiting through another winter to avenge his enemies. Orm Eysteinsson had taken Hundr's fingers and burned the warship Seaworm, all at the behest of the Crippled King. Too many of Hundr's men, friends, and loved ones had died. There had to be a reckoning, though he had yet to discover how to triumph against such staggering odds. But his Odin luck had returned, and he trained daily with sword and buckler. He rowed and ate and grew stronger so that by the time they came into sight of Mann's coastline shimmering beneath the sun, he was ready to fight.

"He has a lot of ships," noted Erik Bloodaxe, hand on the tiller of the Whale Breaker, hair whipped away from his face by the wind. He stared towards Mann, where a dozen warships were drifting lazily around the island's northern coast.

"Which begs the question, why are we sailing towards them?" asked Hermoth. He wore a simple jerkin at sea, his fair hair tied in a tight braid. "We have but two ships, and if he can afford to send twelve to protect his northern shore, then he must have many more protecting the rest of the island."

"He has ships and men, bought and paid for in silver. Finn has his own men, the core Rus warriors of his hearth troop." Hundr said. "The rest are hired blades."

"Those twelve ships could hold seven hundred warriors, Father. Who knows how many more lie in wait? Paid blades or not."

"And yet the Crippled King must die. His man, Orm Eysteinsson, burned my ship. Even if I came here on a three-man faering with nothing but a dull blade and a maimed hand, I would still try to strike them down."

Erik laughed. "Which is why I love you, foster father. We'll fight the bastards. We don't have to meet them in the shield wall. There is more than one way to skin a boar."

"So, we find a place to get the men ashore."

"And then we kill the turds until we can lure out the leaders."

"That's it?" said Hermoth, throwing up his hands. "That's your plan? We sail around Mann and look for a hidden bay or cover and make landfall? Then, with our two crews, we fight against the Crippled King and his three thousand warriors and hope to kill the king and his captain?"

Erik shrugged and glanced at Hundr. "Yes, that's it."

"If we don't scupper our ships on unseen rocks or sandbanks beneath the water, we go ashore and hit them like bandits until we can find their king, hoping that three thousand warriors don't surround us and hack us to pieces?"

"We make landfall, and a skeleton crew takes the ships back to sea to keep them safe," said Hundr. "The ships sweep the island until we light a beacon to signal that we need their return."

Hermoth stared incredulously at Hundr and Erik. "Why do I feel like the stupid one here? But if you two are convinced, then so be it."

Erik laughed again and clapped Hermoth on the shoulder. "You worry too much, my friend. We sail, we fight, and perhaps we shall die. That is the way of things for men like us. If we fail, we shall laugh about it in Valhalla. If we win, men will know that few stood against many and that Erik Bloodaxe killed The Crippled King of Mann."

Hermoth shook his head and went to tie off a loose rigging rope. Hundr watched him go and knew that despite his son's misgivings, he would fight as hard as any man aboard the Whale Breaker. Erik grinned and closed his eyes, enjoying the speed of his ship and the fresh sea wind in his face. He cared little about the odds facing them, only of the reputation and glory to be found on Finn's island kingdom. Hundr recognised that daring, that fearless bravery. It reminded Hundr of himself as a younger man. After all, what does a Viking warrior fear in death? Die well, and Valhalla is your reward. The real fear lies in the maiming wound. It's the one that doesn't kill but takes away a man's chance at glory, leaving him crippled or dying in his bed from the injury days after the battle's end.

Hundr's enemies were close. The two men who had tried to take everything from him waited on the island, and he would go ashore to find them. The curse of his young love for an Irish princess had cast a dark shadow over Hundr's life, and Finn Ivarsson was the last remnant of that foul stain. It was time to end it, or die trying.

Erik's ships approached a narrow cove on Mann as night crept over a churning sea where white-tipped waves crashed against the Whale Breaker's hull. They had sailed out into open waters during the afternoon and returned as the sun set, running before the wind towards a small beach. Half a dozen patrol ships had sailed by the cove. Once they had passed, Erik's two ships came about and raced at full speed to make landfall unseen. Twilight hung over the cove, casting it in a purple and grey hue. It was a secluded inlet, the narrow entrance marked by rugged cliffs that sloped into the sea and tooth-like jagged rocks jutted out from the shoreline. As the *drakkars* drew closer, the water stilled. Erik gave the order to take down the sails and man the oars. They approached carefully, men leaning over the prow with rope and stone to test the depths and search for unforeseen hazards below the dark water.

Hundr peered over the side at the looming island where his enemies awaited. The salt air hung thick with evening damp, heavy with the smell of seaweed and wet stone. A chill wind swept in from the open sea, making the men shiver as they gathered their armour and weapons, preparing to disembark. A heavy splash echoed around the cove as the stone anchor plunged into the shallow water, its rope pulling taut as the Whale Breaker slowed to a stop. Hundr scanned the darkening clifftops with his one eye, but he could see no sign of any enemy spearmen. The warriors about him did the same, knowing they would be easy prey if the enemy attacked as they clambered ashore, burdened by weapons and sodden clothes, and could be cut down from above like lambs led to slaughter. Erik's second ship mirrored the manoeuvre and anchored ten paces away, hull timbers creaking and bearded faces peering at

Erik, waiting for the order to slide over the side. The ships rocked gently for a moment, beast heads snarling at the Isle of Mann.

Erik raised and dropped his hand, and one by one, the men slung heavy shields over their backs, gripped spears, swords, axes, and seaxes and climbed over the side. Hundr grabbed his buckler and the Ulfberht sword and held both above his head as he dropped over the side. The cold seawater took his breath away for a moment as he sank up to his chest. He jumped on his tiptoes, and his boots sank into the soft seabed. He waded slowly towards the beach as more men plopped into the water behind him. Erik came last, and the men he left to crew his ships raised the anchor and rowed the warships out into the darkness, leaving their shipmates to whatever fate awaited them. The shore rose abruptly, and within ten paces, the chill water lapped at Hundr's knees as he tried not to shiver. Stinging seawater drained from his dead eye, and he lowered his weapons, clasping them close to his chest.

The beach was a narrow strip of sand covered with shale, rock, and dark seaweed. Beyond it, the island rose into steep hills, thorn and briar scrub clinging to the slopes. A handful of stunted trees, misshapen, bent, and gnarled by relentless sea winds, seemed to beckon Hundr closer. Sigvarth and Toki grumbled at the cold but flashed wild grins at Hundr as he stamped his feet to shake off the worst of the wet. More men came ashore, their boot steps muffled by wet sand as they clamoured together for warmth, coughing, sniffing, and checking their weapons. Hermoth trudged up the beach with a dozen men to scout the surrounding land for any sign of enemy patrols. Hundr strapped the Ulfberht sword to his belt and slung the buckler shield across his back. It was time for war.

TWENTY-SIX

Twenty-six ships rowed into a gaping river estuary on the western tip of the kingdom of Alba. Einar had led the Wind Elk in first, for Thorgrim knew the waters. The other Vanylven ships came with them, followed by the rest of the fleet. He knew a place where one thousand four hundred warriors could camp safely for the night without fear of attack. The ebb tide had withdrawn, exposing muddy flats and glistening sandbanks under the fading summer light. The estuary lay still, its banks untouched by dwellings or hostile eyes. Further inland, Thorgrim explained, there were many fishing villages; however, the coast here was too wild and harsh for anyone to live so close to the sea during winter's grip. They beached the ships on dark sand and came ashore to camp for the night, safe knowing that the flood tide would raise them up and provide safe passage come morning light.

The air was warm despite a sea breeze, and Einar called a war council of the fleet's leaders to gather around a campfire of driftwood where a sheep roasted over the crackling flames.

"I know these people," said Haesten, glancing inland towards sweeping marshland and green meadows. "Used to be good raiding here before Domnall mac Causantín became king of the Scots and Gaels hereabout. He bound the tribes together, killing any of the bastards who objected to his rule. They worship the nailed god now and fight like demons."

"Let's hope they stay in their beds this evening, then," Gunnr uttered. She shrugged out of her *brynjar* and hung it on the branch of a nearby birch tree.

"Just so," nodded Rognvald, Jarl of Rogaland. "I would hate to lose any of my king's ten ships before we have even reached our destination."

"We are glad to have you, Jarl Rognvald," said Einar. "We thank King Harald for sending so many men to do battle." Einar sipped at a wooden mug of ale. He had hoped Harald Fairhair would provide more men and ships from the jarls of Norway. But Rognvald was a cunning warrior, and his crew of *Úlfhéðnar* warriors were unmatched in battle. Seven hundred warriors were not to be sneered at.

"King Harald regrets he could not come in person, but the demands of court keep him at Avaldsnes. We are here now, Einar, and shall be within sight of Mann tomorrow. But we have a dual purpose. Do we search for our friend Jarl Hundr, or do we strike at the Crippled King?"

"This army comes to find Hundr, a man who is a friend to us all and has fought for and beside each of us. But this is a riddle to which I do not have the answer. That is why I have called you together this evening. Our voyage stands at a crossroads. The last time I saw the Seaworm, she sailed away from Mann towards Northumbria, and yet our great enemy lies upon Mann. Each one of you has brought ships and men to this fight, so we should all have a voice as we decide what to do with our army."

"Very noble of you, Lord Einar," remarked Rognvald. "You lead our force, and yet you have brought only four ships to the fight. So, there is more at stake for some of us should we choose unwisely."

"Come now," said Haesten, "we all risk our lives on this venture, no matter how many ships we have brought. At least Einar's men are his own, Lord Rognvald."

"I haven't come all this way so that you grumpy old whoresons can measure your puny manhoods beside the fire," hissed Gunnr, and

Einar winced.

"Whoresons?" said Haesten, stiffening. He fixed Gunnr with his hatchet-like face.

"Enough," Einar blurted, and he rose from the log on which he sat. "Our choice is simple. We can either sail our ships up a Northumbrian River and seek news of the Seaworm, or we can attack Mann. Gunnr, what do you say?"

She pursed her lips and sighed. "If we bring a thousand warriors into Northumbria, we could start a war. The search is a task for one, perhaps two crews. We don't want to lose half of our warriors fighting a war we did not come to fight."

"She has the right of it," agreed Rognvald. "Though she has obviously not seen my manhood, for such a sea monster could never be called puny."

Gunnr tutted whilst Einar and Haesten chuckled.

"We should kill Finn Ivarsson first," said Haesten. He stretched his back, then reached to cut a slice of lamb from the spit. Haesten blew on the smoking meat and then stuffed it into his mouth. He chewed, blowing out a gust of steam as the meat burned his mouth. "Use our forces to crush him once and for all. Then we can search for Hundr. We cannot search with an enemy at our backs. We must beach our fleet somewhere, which is always the vulnerability of our Viking armies. If the Crippled King finds our ships, we are doomed." He cut another strip of lamb and offered it to Rognvald, who took it with a bow. "But when will Bjorn arrive? For we are outnumbered without his crews."

"He said to expect him a week behind our own travels," Einar answered. "We have sailed to Frankia, Avaldsnes, and Vanylven in that time, so he should arrive any day with twenty ships of Ragnarsson warriors."

"Then we should wait for Bjorn. No sense in attacking or searching until then. We are too outnumbered without him."

"Wait where?" asked Gunnr. "We can't stay here. The Scots won't take kindly to us eating their sheep."

"Victory depends on many things. Bravery, weapons, war skill. But also on numbers, food supplies and the availability of water or ale. I have been without food on campaign, and there is no quicker way to rust an army's will to fight. We have enough supplies for two, perhaps three days. So, wherever we go, we must raid and take what we need until Bjorn arrives. I say we sail for Mann, take a piece of Finn Ivarsson's island, fortify it, beach out ships behind those fortifications, and wait. They'll have to attack us to drive us out, and we can retreat to our ships whenever we choose."

"Unless he sends his fleet to block our escape," said Rognvald.

"Which is what a clever man would do. But he can't block us in from both land and sea unless he crews his ships with only men to sail them, not to fight on board. Wherever we fight, it must be on a field of our choosing. We stop at every fishing village from here to Eyrrspollr and take their oil. We gather anything we can burn. We dig gulleys and knee-high trenches on the field of battle and make the bastards come to us. If an army appears at our camp, we can retreat and fight our way past his ships. If the ships appear without the army, then the warriors are all onboard. In which case, we march inland and destroy the Crippled King's fortress, steal his silver, and take the island."

"Finn won't leave his fortress and treasure unguarded," Einar replied. "The silver he makes from his markets funds his army; without it, he has nothing."

"We are here to kill the Crippled King. If he sends his fleet against us, we can take his fortress without Bjorn. If the army comes, then we must hold them until Ironside arrives. I fancy we could take the Crippled King's fortress with two crews if his army and ships come to kill us. We keep two ships with full crews just off the coast.

When they come, the two ships sail about their flank. Burn his temple, sack his fortress, steal his treasure. Give the bastard something to think about. His men will shit their trews when they see we have stolen the silver the Crippled King hoped to pay them with."

"I had heard you were a man of deep cunning, Jarl Haesten," declared Rognvald, raising his ale to the older man. "For once, the bards sang true."

"We'll see about that when we get to Mann. Words are just words until the axes come, or a storm sends our ships off course, or the Crippled King does not do what we want him to do. So we go to war and hope the gods bring us luck. Then we shall see who is cunning and who lies dead."

TWENTY-SEVEN

Hundr watched from the heights as hundreds of warriors marched along a river at the bottom of a shallow valley. The river, which was little more than a brook, wound northeast from the high peaks at the island's centre. Hundr, Erik and Hermoth stood on a cleft on one of those mountains, which spread south across the island like a green, rolling sea.

"The Crippled King's men march towards another force in the distance," said Hermoth, hand over his eyes to shield them from the sun. "I can see their spears."

"So that's where the bastards are going," said Erik cheerfully. "I thought they were leading us on a merry dance away from Eyrrspollr."

Hundr's good eye could see nothing but haze

beyond the valley, but he trusted his son's younger eyes. They had decided to use the mountains as cover and march towards Finn's fortress at Eyrrspollr but had stumbled across the force of enemy warriors marching north and followed them. Orm Eysteinsson led them, riding a white horse, and Hundr could not pass up the chance to attack his enemy beyond the reach of Finn's larger army.

"We'll track them and kill them tonight after nightfall," said Hundr. He stared at Orm's horse, picking its way slowly through reeds ahead of a long column of warriors marching with spears resting on their shoulders and shields slung across their backs. Hate made his heart quicken. There was the man who had burned the Seaworm and taken the fingers from his left hand. He glanced at Hermoth, expecting a challenge from his son, an argument to take the course of action which made the most sense.

"Wait until they are out of the valley," Hermoth suggested, "and we can follow their trail until they camp. The moon wanes, so there will be little light tonight. We'll kill them whilst they snore."

"I expected you to recommend that we keep to the hills and look for a smaller warband to fight," said Hundr.

"We are here to kill Orm, Father. There is risk

in war, I know very well. I seek only to make the right decisions. We are here for vengeance, and we'll kill Orm tonight."

They waited until the sun came down close to the western sea and followed the scar Orm's men left upon the land. Their heavy boots left a brown smear as though a great serpent had slithered through the valley, and it was simple to track their path northwards. Orm led his men towards a force on Mann's northern shore, but all Hundr could make out in the darkness were their campfires. It was not uncommon for Vikings to camp for the night on islands or coastlines. Jarls brought their men ashore to make fires and eat, safe from the risk of sea storms, and the newly arrived force would likely be gone at first light. But Orm Eysteinsson had come with one hundred warriors to make sure the landed men did not cause problems for his Crippled King, and that gave Hundr a chance to strike at the man who had taken his fingers, burned his ship, and killed his crew.

Orm's men halted for the night behind the foot of one of the island's mountains. They lit a fire, posted guards, and would spend the night warm without fear of the visitors seeing their flames beyond the hills. Or so they thought. Hundr waited until the campfire petered out, its flames turning to little more than an orange glow beneath the stars. Then, when he was sure that

Orm and his men had fallen asleep, he, Erik, and Hermoth led the Bloodaxe men towards their snoring enemies.

Yazi the Easterner took his recurved bow and loped in a wide arc around the camp. Orm's guards were as good as dead, for Yazi was a skilled hunter, tracker, and killer, and Hundr had no fear of those men raising the alarm before he was amongst Orm's inner circle. Hundr wore his buckler shield strapped to his left arm and carried the Ulfberht sword in his right hand. He wore Veggr's *brynjar* with a thick sword belt to take most of the weight from his shoulders, and he crept through the heather beside his son and the prince of Norway. The wind rustled through the wild grasses, and the first of Orm's men died in his sleep. Hermoth cut the snoring warrior's throat, and Erik killed the next man in the same way. The iron tang of blood mixed with the smell of the campfire as the rest of Erik's men moved through the camp like deadly wraiths. They slit throats, stabbed and cut Orm's men so that in twenty heartbeats, thirty men were dead, dunging Mann's soil with their lifeblood.

A terror-stricken scream tore through the night air as one of Orm's men woke to find a blood-soaked blade coming for his throat. Hundr winced at the sound because the rest of Orm's men snapped into wakefulness.

"We're under attack!" shouted one in Scotsaccented Norse.

"Arm yourselves!" called another in an Irish accent.

A warrior grabbed the spear lying next to him and then died with Hundr's sword in his chest. Hundr wrenched the blade free, and the night around him turned to chaos. Erik's warriors howled with blood lust as they hacked and chopped, and Orm's men ran in terror. Some tried to stand, clutching their weapons, but the Bloodaxe men advanced on them in a wall of blades and ruthless efficiency. Hundr ran through the carnage, swerving away from spear points and leaping over the dying.

"Orm!" Hundr roared, hate and fury driving him on. "Orm!"

Three of Orm's men reared up as Hundr reached the embers of their campfire, and without breaking stride, Hundr kicked the burning logs and faggots at them, showering them with orange embers and flame. A horse whickered on his blind side. There was only one horse with the enemy force, and it was Orm's mount. Hundr veered toward it, deflecting an axe swing before slashing his sword across the attacker's belly. Through the fray, he spotted the white horse and a warrior scrambling onto its back. Hundr broke free from the skirmish and charged at the mounted figure – a hulking man who turned and flashed him a wicked grin. Orm Eysteinsson.

"Another time, dog," he growled and drove his heels into the horse's flanks. "I'll come for you and kill you this time!" Orm shouted over his shoulder as the horse's hooves tossed up clods of earth and lurched into a gallop. Hundr ran after him, but the horse sped away. He had missed a chance to kill his enemy, and Hundr slumped to his knees, struggling to contain the rage inside him.

"Father, look," said Hermoth, striding from the fight with his axe pointed north. Torches came from the unknown camp, bobbing in the dark like fireflies, dozens of them.

"Finish this scum off, and then we'll see who approaches."

Erik's men killed eighty of Orm's fighters, and twenty fled for the hills, disappearing into the darkness with their weapons and pride left on the battlefield. Hundr found Yazi crouched on the hillside, staring out towards the approaching torches.

"He got away," said Yazi, standing as Hundr drew close.

"For now," Hundr replied. "How many?" He jutted his chin in the direction of the new arrivals.

"Five score – maybe more coming behind them."

"Well," beamed Erik cheerfully as he cleaned blood from his axe blade. "Let's see what they want."

The torches drew closer, and holding them came warriors in shining mail. Hundr raised a hand in greeting and then began to laugh.

"What amuses you?" Erik asked, chuckling himself at Hundr's absurd reaction to an oncoming force of warriors.

"I'd know those men anywhere, even in the pits of Niflheim. It's Einar."

TWENTY-EIGHT

Twenty-six crews of Norse warriors waited on a flat meadow in sight of Eyrrspollr's settlement. Hundr's one eye stung from lack of sleep, but his heart was swollen with pride. Einar had come, and with an army of heroes at his back. Standards flapped in the morning wind. Leather creaked, and hundreds of voices rumbled as men shifted positions.

"At least you saved the prow," said Einar, standing beside Hundr at the centre of their battle line. "That's something." He had not taken the news of the Seaworm's burning well and had mentioned it repeatedly as their army marched south through the night. "How did you keep it safe through all that you have endured?"

Hundr shrugged. "It wasn't that heavy," he lied.

"Hermoth has grown. He's a fine warrior."

"He is, and we shall need his axe today. I thought Haesten was with you?"

Einar smiled. "He has a little surprise for the Crippled King."

"More surprises?"

"I think that's the lot," Jarl Rognvald called, striding towards them with a grin splitting his face. He wore a simple green tunic above leather trews and looked as though he was visiting a friend for supper, not preparing to fight a battle.

"It's done?" asked Einar.

"It was a long night, but we finished the trench and spread the oil on the heather."

"Will it burn?"

"It's a hot summer morning, and it hasn't rained for a week." Rognvald stamped his boot down on the dry grass. "It will burn. But we are still outnumbered without Bjorn Ironside."

"Bjorn is coming?" Hundr asked

"He said he would," Einar replied. "With his sons Refil and Erik and twenty ships."

"You must have sailed halfway across Midgard."

"We did. You have many friends, and they have all come to fight for you. Though I don't know why. You have always been a miserable bastard. And I don't like what you've done with your hair. You look like a drowned rat."

Hundr smiled, unable to express the depth of gratitude he owed to Einar and to all who joined the fight. Movement on the walls sent a stir through the army. Spear points within Eyrrspollr caught the morning sun as it rose, tinged with red beyond the eastern sea. Scores of warriors appeared at the waist-high outer walls and stared at the army facing them. Hundr's army had appeared as if from nowhere, waiting silently as though the gods had placed them there whilst the Crippled King's forces slept with the prayers of Loki still ringing in their ears.

"What are they waiting for?" huffed Erik Bloodaxe, striding from the ranks in his *brynjar*, thumbs flicking against the hafts of the two axes at his belt.

"They'll come," said Hundr.

Erik paced before the army, and Gunnr arranged the ranks of her Valkyrie, but Finn Ivarsson did not come.

"Are we going to have our war this morning?" said Rognvald. "Or have we come all this way for nothing?"

Hundr drew the Ulfberht sword. "I'd better pick a fight. We grow impatient." He marched through the heather until he could see the whites of the warriors' eyes staring back at him. They were there to guard the settlement wall in case Hundr led his men in a wild charge. Finn and Orm held their greater force further within the snarl of houses, barns and hovels, ready to counter that charge in a slaughter through the streets and lanes of Eyrrspollr. The army Einar had assembled did not have the numbers for such a fight. It had to be a battle beyond the walls. The battle Hundr and Einar had prepared for.

"Finn Ivarsson!" Hundr shouted and held his sword aloft. "I am The Man with the Dog's Name, and I come to kill you like I killed your nithing father and your witch mother!" He wanted to poke Finn, to goad his hate and bring the Crippled King's army forth to fight. "Orm Eysteinsson! You burned my ship, and I have returned to kill you. Are you brave enough to fight the Champion of the North, or do you cower behind your walls?"

Hundr waited, pacing back and forth like a prowling beast. Spears inside the town shifted, and the gate creaked open. Two men came out on horseback – Orm Eysteinsson on his white mare and Finn Ivarsson on a gelding as black as a moonless night.

"I am glad that you are alive," Orm snarled, leaning across his saddle. His huge neck muscles twitched as he glowered down at Hundr. He reached slowly to his hip and tapped his fingers on the hilt of Battle Fang, the blade he had taken from Hundr, along with two fingers of his left hand. "You don't look like the Champion of the North. You look like a scourged beggar. Have you come to beg? I burned your ship and killed your men. I laughed as it burned, and I took your sword. I think I am the champion now. How is your hand?" He pointed at Hundr's maimed left hand and laughed.

Hundr held his left hand up for Orm to see. He hated the young warrior, and seeing his old blade at Orm's side made Hundr's shoulders shiver with rage. "Healed. Soon, you will both die. I have brought Odin's Valkyrie to cast you down, Finn. Your Loki talk will cost you your life. There will be no Ragnarök. Only defeat."

Finn wore a long black cloak with the hood pulled up so that it hid his face in shadow. He slowly raised his arm and held it there silently. A raven cawed and flew from Eyrrspollr, wings flapping and eyes shining. It flew in a circle about Hundr's army and then perched upon Finn's outstretched arm. The Valkyrie clutched their Gungnir pendants as one, but Hundr felt no fear of Finn and his evil *seiðr*, for he had once faced and defeated the Witch-Queen of Vedrafjord.

"Loki told me of your coming," Finn growled from beneath his hood. He wore a long silver chain with his mother's remaining bones set into a cross piece resting upon his chest. "Long have I waited for this moment. You shall all drown in blood. Your defeat only hastens the loosing of the chained one. When we crush Odin's priestesses, we shall weaken his power. The Ragnarök is upon us all."

Finn's raven flew away, and at that moment, drums beat from within the town. Deep drums pounding, the sound thrumming inside Hundr's chest. Finn spoke his last words loud enough for his men to hear, and Hundr wondered if he believed his own Loki *seiðr*.

Boom. Boom. Boom, ba-boom. Boom. Boom. Boom, ba-boom.

Three thousand warriors marched from Eyrrspollr's gates and formed up in ranks. They were Irishmen with plaid cloaks thrown over one shoulder, Saxons with long hair and short beards, tattooed Norsemen, Orm's shield-gnashing berserkers and Finn's own hearth troop of Novgorod Rus. Hundr stood there and watched every one of them line up behind their Crippled King. He wanted them to see him, to see his sword and his scarred face and know who they fought that summer morning. Einar joined him with Prince Erik, Gunnr, and Rognvald. The drums beat their rhythmic war song, and Hundr returned to his ranks only when the enemy army was fully formed.

"Looks like we will have our fight after all," chirped Rognvald, rubbing his hands together. "Time for Bavlos, I think."

"The Sami shaman is here?" asked Einar, peering over the heads of the warriors in search of King Harald's small but powerful shaman.

"Just so. My *Úlfhéðnar* will be ready."

Finn Ivarsson turned his horse and rode slowly through the ranks of his army. They knelt as he rode, falling like scythed wheat as Finn passed by, malevolent, hooded and hunched on his mount. The drums continued, their relentless rhythm heightening the hold Finn wielded over his men – a power that left Hundr in awe. When their king had gone, the warriors rose, and Orm rode before the front line, brandishing Battle Fang. His cloak whipped behind him as he bellowed, stoking the men's bloodlust into a furious pitch.

"It's time," Hundr said. He reached inside his *brynjar* and touched his fingers against the small crucifix Thatchulf had pressed into his hand before he had died. Hundr thought of The Crow, Gunnulfr, Arne, and the rest of the Seaworm men he had led to their deaths in the fight against Finn and Orm. It was time for blood, time to punish their enemies with iron and war fury. "Fall back fifty paces."

Each of the leaders left to join their own contingents. Hundr's army then shuffled back fifty paces and presented their shields to the enemy. Hundr stood before them, the Ulfberht sword still in his hand. The enemy roared and cheered, and Orm's berserkers took their place at the centre of their ranks. They howled like madmen, froth in their beards, and Orm dismounted to take his place amongst them.

"We're ready," Einar said. He clapped Hundr on the shoulder. "Let's finish the bastards."

Orm led his men forward. They came quickly, eager for the fight. Hundr counted their steps, his own force remaining calm and ready behind their shields.

"Light them up!" Hundr called when the enemy had marched twenty paces, reaching the ground prepared by Hundr and Einar's men in the dark of night.

Hildr blew onto smoking kindling she'd kept ready for this moment. She lit an arrow wrapped in an oiled cloth, and the tip sprang aflame.

"Give them the fire they worship so much, my love," Einar said. Hildr set the crackling arrow to her bow and drew the string. She released the arrow with a twang of her bow. It flew high into the sunny morning sky and then fell like a dead bird into the enemy's massed ranks. The arrow landed in the dry grass soaked in fish oil, igniting the crisp heather as if struck by Surtr's fiery sword. In a flash, the flames whooshed across the field like dragon fire, and the tortured screams from Finn's burning warriors were enough to chill a man's soul.

"Fall back another fifty paces," Hundr ordered. Fastbjorn Brokenspear lowered the spear he carried, from which the one-eye banner fluttered in the breeze. The leaders knew the signal, and the army shuffled back even further. Flame and smoke swirled into the morning sky, snatched away by the wind. "They have their Loki fire!" Hundr roared to his men and lifted his sword high. "Wait for the signal, and then we send them to hel!"

Hundr and Einar's army made their new battle line beyond a knee-high trench the men had dug during the night. It was only as wide as a furrow but enough for the next part of their battle plan. Orm led his warriors, surging around the flames, howling like beasts in their desperation to avenge their fallen, scorched comrades. Hundr tightened his three-fingered grip on his buckler.

"Still so many," gasped a man behind him. Hundr, Einar, Erik, Rognvald, Haesten, and Gunnr had hoped the fire would terrorise the enemy ranks, but still, they came on. Three thousand warriors arrayed on the field beyond Eyrrspollr against half that number in Hundr's army.

Where is Bjorn?

Orm rode before the enemy lines, waving Battle Fang as he ordered men into positions, bellowing at them to ignore the fire at their backs. The screams of the burned died down, and the fires receded. Enemy war drums beat again.

Boom. Boom. Boom, ba-boom. Boom. Boom. Boom, ba-boom.

Orm dismounted and sent his horse running to the rear. The enemy roared their war cries and charged, a cacophony of sound and fury. Behind Hundr, a wave of fear surged through his warriors – a primal terror that grips every man as an enemy army bears down upon him. Shields, spears, axes, and swords gleamed with lethal edges, ready to rip and tear flesh. These warriors came to kill, and each man in Hundr's ranks felt that roiling, blistering dread deep in his gut. Hundr felt it, too, though he welcomed it, inhaling the stench of fire and ash. The fear churned within him, rising through his body like molten fire, and as the enemy closed in, that fear transformed into fury.

"Who do you fight for?" Hundr roared at his men,

"The Man with the Dog's Name!" they shouted back at him.

"Death to our enemies! Death to the Crippled King!"

"Death! Death! Death!"

Einar, Erik, and Gunnr called to the warriors, but the sound of their war fury became lost as Hundr focused on the snarling, spitting faces charging towards him.

"Shield wall!" Hundr called, and the wall came together; hundreds of linden wood shields bossed and rimmed with iron clattering together, overlapping to make an impenetrable wall held fast by warriors' strength and will.

The enemy came on in a wild charge, and Hundr held his buckler between Sigvarth's and Toki's shields. Einar, Amundr, Thorgrim, and Hildr were further along the battle line, with Gunnr and the Valkyrie on the right flank. Rognvald waited in the rear with his *Úlfhéðnar*, preparing themselves with Bavlos' potions and ancient *seiðr*. The charge grew in noise until it filled Midgard with howls, stomping boots and clattering shields.

"Hold fast!" Hundr shouted as the enemy came within twenty paces. They advanced so rapidly that the Crippled King's army did not notice the small trench and their first rank stepped into it. Four hundred warriors plunged forward like children running on unsteady feet, though not all of them fell. Some managed to leap over the furrow, but those who tumbled encumbered the rankers behind them, and suddenly, that wild charge turned into blundered disarray.

"Kill the bastards!" Einar roared, and the battle truly began.

Hundr darted forward. A fallen enemy warrior stared up at him, teeth clenched so hard in terror that they cracked and splintered in his mouth. Hundr stabbed the Ulfberht sword into that man's chest and slashed open the throat of another. Toki stabbed his spear into a sprawling man's spine. The unfallen enemy hammered into Hundr's shield wall, but he stood firm, resolute in his determination to defeat all who dared to oppose him.

TWENTY-NINE

A spear scraped over the rim of Einar's shield, and the blade nicked his neck. The stink of blood and the voided bowels of dying men replaced the fire smell. Einar fought with the ferocity of a man half his age, drawing on every ounce of battle experience from his weary mind. He tilted his shield, cut beneath the rim with his axe, stamped on feet, and aimed for eyes and throats. The battle raged until the shield walls crumbled, yielding to chaotic combat as the two armies, fatigued by the relentless heave and counter-push, let their front-rank champions break away to clash with weapons sharpened to lethal edges. Einar killed a young man with bright eyes and battered down another foe with the edge of his shield. Amundr was just ten paces away, surrounded by the bodies of slain warriors.

Two men charged at Einar, shields raised and axes swinging. He met them head-on with his shield, rapidly severing the legs of the leftmost attacker with his axe. Another enemy surged into the space, driving Einar backwards with his shield. Einar staggered but managed to raise his shield just in time to block an axe aimed at his skull. Thorgrim charged into the fray, his double-bladed axe splintering a shield into kindling. A Vanylven man fell with a spear lodged in his throat while two Irishmen hacked another enemy to death. Einar hurled himself at the opposition, yet their numbers continued to force him back.

"We cannot hold!" screamed Gunnr from the flank, though Einar could not see her. He ducked beneath a spear and chopped his axe through the attacker's wrist. All about him, men died or screamed in agony from terrible wounds. The ground at his feet was no longer grass and heather but a morass of mud, soaked with offal and blood churning about his boots like *Nástrǫnd,* the corpse shore.

"Einar!" Hildr screamed. Panic flooded Einar's senses as he scanned the fray, desperate to find his wife. With a mighty shove, he pushed a man aside with his shield and caught sight of her in the gap. Four foes surrounded Hildr, three Vanylven men dead at their feet. A dozen enemies lay between Einar and his beloved Hildr, and though she tried to fend them off with her axe and shield, blood showed from cuts to her arm and thigh. He could not help her, and Einar howled with impotent rage. Amundr's monstrous frame appeared in the melee, and he was closer to Hildr, though still surrounded by ferocious enemies.

"Amundr!" Einar bellowed so loud that it burned his throat. He caught an axe on his shield and heaved the enemy away from him. Amundr glanced at him, face hidden by his helmet. Einar pointed his axe at Hildr, and Amundr set off like a lumbering bear.

Two enemies tried to block the giant's path. He drove his axe through the first man's shield with such power that he sliced through boards, rivets, and iron rims to cleave the man's arm off and chop its blade into the chest of the next man. Amundr left the axe, embedded as it was in bone and muscle, and continued his charge. He took a spear thrust to the shoulder and ignored the blow. Amundr shouldered two burly Irishmen out of his way and reached Hildr just as her attacker drove her to her knees. Amundr was weaponless, so he tore his precious helmet from his head and smashed it into the face of the first enemy and then again into the back of the next man's head. He beat Hildr's attackers with his helmet, using it like a club until they fell back from his fury. Three warriors died beneath his rage, and when the helmet was little more than a crushed lump of blood-soaked metal, Amundr threw it at them. He scooped Hildr up into his muscled arms and carried her away from the carnage. Einar had never been so relieved. He laughed for joy, sheer joy, because Hildr was alive, and he loved brave Amundr so much his heart could burst.

More enemies loomed, a fresh rank of unblooded foes. Einar gathered his men about him and prepared to meet their onslaught. Prince Erik and Hermoth joined him, and they made new battle lines, retreating further into the field.

"We're losing too many men!" Hermoth called above the battle din. "We can't hold them much longer."

Einar peered about him and saw that was true. The Crippled King's ranks had bowed around Einar and Hundr's army so that they were half surrounded. Einar's men were bloody, wounded, and exhausted. His shield had been bashed and broken in three places. But they had to hold; they had to fight.

Finn Ivarsson came forth from his warriors, limping and terrible in his black hooded cloak, staff in one hand, and his raven perched on one shoulder. He threw back his hood, revealing his horribly scarred face, and his dark eyes glowered at Einar across the bloody battlefield. Einar realised then that the battle was all but over. The enemy outnumbered and outmatched his men. Finn still had half of his force to unleash, and Einar's heart sank because victory seemed impossible. Too many had died, and more moaned and suffered beyond the rear rank from injuries taken in battle. Einar's shoulders sagged. He wiped the sweat from his brow on the back of his hand and turned to Hermoth.

"If we are going to die, then at least we are all together. We won't die easy, lad. Every one of us they take will cost them dearly," Einar said.

Erik grinned maniacally and readied his axes for the last charge. Finn Ivarsson capered in front of his men, glorying in his victory over enemies he hated with the utmost intensity. His raven flew about them as Finn invoked the will of Loki and raged about the Ragnarök and the end of days. Einar caught Hundr's one eye further along the front rank, and he nodded to his old friend. Hundr returned the gesture, and Einar gripped his axe and shield firmly.

A horn blared, long and loud. The sound was melodious and distant. Every man on the battlefield turned their heads, searching for the source of so beautiful a call. It came again, like the song of the Aesir from the heavens, like Heimdall's Gjallarhorn. Einar wondered if it was a sign from Odin to say that he approved of this last stand, of the end of Einar's long life devoted to *drengskapr.* But then figures appeared to the east. First, a large figure crested a hill – a big man with an axe slung over his shoulder, silhouetted against the sun. Following him was a battle standard, a massive square of black cloth fluttering in the morning breeze. More men appeared on the hilltop – hundreds of them, shields in hand. They kept coming, a relentless tide until one and a half thousand warriors filled the hillside.

"The Raven Banner!" a man called.

Einar squinted, and his old eyes saw the white raven standing proudly on the enormous black war banner. Einar shouted jubilantly. He clashed his axe against his shield and laughed like a drunkard. A huge man led the new army, a man who came bellowing and shaking his axe towards the battlefield. Tears of joy rolled down Einar's face because Bjorn Ironside, the last surviving son of Ragnar Lothbrok, had come to war.

THIRTY

Something caught Hundr's eye as the warriors gaped at Bjorn's Ragnarsson army. A flicker, a spark of something beyond the enemy lines. Hundr turned, peering over the Crippled King and his swooping raven. Men swirled around the Loki temple, men bearing firebrands. A heartbeat later, the temple glowed as though Loki himself had emerged from his fetters to bring his malice to the battlefield. But then Hundr realised it was not Loki; it was Haesten. The old fox strode from the temple with his four hundred warriors at his back.

"Yazi?" Hundr said to the bowman who stood behind him. "Bring that bird down."

The wooden Loki temple burned like a beacon. Its wood, parched by the hot weather, ate the flames like a starving beggar. The Crippled King's army stared in horror, looking from Bjorn to the inferno that had been their temple. Yazi's arrow struck the raven soaring high above Finn's troops. The bird squawked in alarm before plummeting to the ground, prompting gasps of dread from the Crippled King's warriors – an ominous sign of their king's waning fortune.

"No!" Finn Ivarsson screamed. He ran, limping, towards his burning temple, waving his staff, his raven dead, and his Loki religion crumbling around him. Finn stumbled, rose, and fell again. His mysterious aura fled from him, leaving only a lame, desperate man screaming at the sky. Bjorn Ironside's men let out a roar to shake Mann's very roots and broke into an all-out charge. Finn's army backed away, unsure of what to do. The lesser amongst them, the hired hands, turned and ran. Some followed their king towards where Haesten's men waited; others formed ranks to face Bjorn's newly arrived army.

Orm Eysteinsson appeared from the heaving mass of Finn's army. He held his two swords, and his berserkers capered about him with rolling eyes and frothing mouths. Gunnr, the Valkyrie leader, lay dead before him, her *brynjar* slashed and bloody. Orm pointed his swords at Hundr and smiled. His berserkers ran at Hundr, sixty men out of their minds with berserk fury. Hundr braced himself to meet their blood-mad charge, as did the surrounding warriors. But there was no need because Rognvald and his

Úlfhéðnar wolf warriors came, full of their own *berserkergang*. They howled and snarled like wild beasts, rushing between Hundr's men, stripped almost naked. Rognvald himself went with them, as mad as the rest, and he killed two of Orm's berserkers in a wild, axe-swinging rage.

Erik Bloodaxe and Hermoth led their men in a charge at the centre of Finn's crumbling army, and Bjorn's fighters smashed into the enemy like an implacable tidal wave. The wind kissed Hundr's shorn head, and he sighed. His Odin luck had turned. He flexed his hand around the Ulfberht sword and walked calmly towards Rognvald and his men, who were transforming Orm's warriors into carrion. He found Orm Eysteinsson staring dumbfounded at the onslaught, and the son of his old enemy turned to him with wide eyes and a gaping mouth. Hundr prepared himself, buckler and sword ready. Orm's face contorted into a mask of hatred as he charged at Hundr, swinging his two swords. Hundr sidestepped the wild assault and flicked his wrist, allowing the tip of his blade to carve a deep gash into Orm's shoulder. The dwarven-forged steel sliced through the links of Orm's *brynjar*, and the son of Eystein Longaxe stared in horror at his wound.

Roaring incoherently, Orm launched himself at Hundr once more, consumed by rage and hatred. He believed he was facing the same

Hundr he had battled aboard the burning warship Seaworm. But Hundr had been injured then, weakened and not himself. Now leaner but healed, his sword flashed with the speed and skill he had once possessed.

Hundr caught a sword blow with his buckler and a lunge of Orm's second sword with his own blade. He stepped into Orm and headbutted him savagely in the face. As the colossal man reeled from the blow, face pulped and bloody, Hundr crashed the buckler into his midriff and cut his sword deftly in a half lunge, just enough to cut off Orm's ear. Orm staggered, blood gushing down his head and shoulder. He raised one sword arm to touch the injured side of his head, and Hundr darted forward again, feinting low and then chopping his sword blade into Orm's hand. Fingers fell to the blood-churned mud, and Orm's mangled hand dropped Battle Fang. He staggered away from Hundr, shaking his head in horror and pain.

"You burned my ship and killed my men," Hundr growled. Orm found his courage again and surged at Hundr, but Hundr met the charge and crashed his buckler into Orm's face. The small shield crushed cheekbone and lips, and Orm spat out a mouthful of blood and broken teeth. He fell to his knees, shaking his head in disbelief. His had been a hard life. A child of war, Orm had risen fuelled by hate to become a great warrior like his father, and now he had found death at the hand of his most hated of enemies. Still, Hundr felt no pity – all men who choose that life know the risks. He shouted in defiance, leapt, and drove the Ulfberht sword overhand. The point pierced Orm's gullet and stabbed down deep inside his torso, piercing his chest and organs, cold steel slicing his life away. Hundr ripped the blade free and stared at Battle Fang and the mangled corpse of his enemy.

Live. Survive and rise to fight again. Finn must die. Orm must die.

Those words had kept him alive, and now, Hundr would kill the last of his enemies. The Crippled King of Mann. He followed Erik and Hermoth as they cut through Finn's warriors as though they were barely there. The Mann army had broken. They had seen their temple burn and their champion, Orm, killed. Hildr led the Valkyrie in a crushing charge into the enemy flank, and Finn's warriors fled like frightened sheep. The Valkyrie formed up with their bows and loosed arrow after deadly arrow into the enemy until their will and their courage broke. Erik Bloodaxe fought with his red hair unbound, and he killed with wild abandon. Hermoth followed, controlled, efficient and deadly. Toki and Sigvarth flanked Hundr and cut down any of the enemy fighters who tried to block his path. They found Finn Ivarsson with his hearth troop before the burning ruins of his Loki temple. Thirty Rus warriors stood with their drooping moustaches and heavy *brynjars.* They formed two ranks in front of their king, who seemed suddenly small and hunched as the embers of his burning dreams died around him.

"Where's Haesten?" asked Erik.

Hundr shrugged. "Kill the Rus, leave the Crippled King for me."

Erik grinned and led his warriors in a furious charge against the last of Finn's army. That fight lasted only a few heartbeats. The Rus warriors died protecting their lord, but the will and fury of Erik, Hermoth, and their warriors was too much, even for the hardened warriors of Novgorod. Hundr stalked through the dead and dying and found Finn waiting for him, kneeling, the hood covering his scarred face.

"It's over," Hundr said. He raised his sword, using the bloody tip to lift Finn's chin. The head came up, and the hood fell back to reveal a tortured face, darkened by ash and stained with tears.

"You took everything from me," Finn hissed. "Everything my life could have been... should have been. I curse you, Hundr, I curse you."

"Too late for that." Hundr had known suffering himself. Monumental suffering. Sigrid,

Sigurd. So much death, so much regret. He wondered for a fleeting moment what might have been if Finn's mother, Saoirse, had run away with him that night long ago in Jorvik when he was a boy full of pride and love for a beautiful princess. He had scaled the walls of the Minster to ask her to run away with him. She was Ivar's prisoner then, betrothed to his son. Saoirse had refused, and so their lives had intertwined to become the Norns' playthings. Could he have lived a quiet life in a wooded valley somewhere? Raised a family? Given up his dreams of reputation and glory?

"I won't let you kill me," Finn screeched. "I give myself to Loki. I am the master of my destiny!" Finn wailed in a high-pitched, dreadful tone. A blade flashed from the folds of his cloak, and he drove a long knife into his own belly. Finn wrenched at the blade, sawing at himself. He collapsed over the weapon, covered and dying in the folds of his cloak.

"So ends the Crippled King," said Hermoth. Hundr sighed and sheathed his sword. It was over.

THIRTY-ONE

Einar found Bjorn Ironside amongst his men. They stood against the last two hundred of Finn's warriors, the champions – the core of his front rankers who would not die and would never surrender. Bjorn's shield wall faced them, but Bjorn himself lay upon a shield between a dozen of his warriors. A plethora of wounds slashed his *brynjar*, and he coughed a gout of blood into his beard.

"Get me up, I said," Bjorn wheezed.

"Bjorn, old friend," said Einar. He knelt and grabbed Bjorn's hand and pulled the son of Ragnar to his feet.

"It's my time, Einar, time for me to meet my brothers in Valhalla."

"Aye," nodded Einar, looking with pride and respect upon the great king. Bjorn's men let go of their lord and Bjorn took up an axe in each of his great fists. Einar helped him walk to the front of his men, where the hardest of the enemy waited.

"Valhalla, Valhalla, Valhalla," Bjorn muttered under his breath as his eyes blazed. Another river of blood slopped from his mouth into his beard.

"We said we would seek Odin's hall together."

"We did. I told you I would come, Einar. My sons Refil and Erik are here. They will lead my kingdom now. I go to join my father and my brothers. Come with me, Einar. We shall travel the Bifrost together and share our first horns of ale with the heroes beside Valhalla's great hearth fire."

Einar searched for Hildr but could not see her. A calm came over him. He was ready. Einar gripped his axe and smiled at Bjorn. Together, they roared like bears and charged at the enemy. Bjorn hacked into them, killing an enormous man with a sweep of his axe. Einar cut the legs from one and parried a slash from another. A spear stabbed Bjorn in the chest, and a sword pierced his belly. The rings of his *brynjar* shattered. Bjorn killed the swordsman with his axe, and he fell to the battleground. Bjorn smiled at the heavens, eyes shining as though his mighty brothers reached out to accept him. The enemy ceased their attack, as did every warrior who had fought that day. The

Ragnarsson banner dipped, for one of the great Viking heroes, the last son of Lothbrok, had died. No blade had touched Einar in that last charge. Bjorn had gone, and Einar remained. Valhalla had eluded him once again.

Einar found Hildr in the aftermath. She was with Amundr, watching whilst the giant plucked and examined helmets from amongst the piles of weapons retrieved from the battlefield. Einar and Hildr walked together towards the sea. Einar held her close, glad that she was alive, and despite missing his chance to join the Einherjar, overjoyed that he would get to spend more time with his beloved wife. They looked out together on the glistening sea. Both exhausted, both solemn. Six ships sailed from Eyrrspollr, sails filled by the wind as they crashed through the whitecaps. In the prow of the first *drakkar,* an old man waved to Einar with a wolfish grin on his hatchet-hard face.

"That's Haesten," said Hildr.

"It is," Einar replied, laughing.

"He's stolen the Crippled King's hoard of silver from Eyrrspollr, hasn't he?"

"He has. But he played his part well." Einar waved and shook his head at the old rogue's cunning.

Einar returned to the battlefield and found

Hundr before the burned temple. Men tended to the wounded, and an eerie silence fell over the island. Rage fell from the warriors, leaving them only with sorrow for their dead comrades and the groans and suffering of the wounded. The warriors would feast and celebrate their victory later, but the time following battle was a time of sorrow and relief, of limbs trembling with exhaustion and searching through the corpses for missing friends and brothers.

"Finn," Hildr gasped, and she knelt beside the crumpled form of Finn Ivarsson.

Einar knelt with her. He turned the body over, cradling Finn in his arms. He saw the boy he had once loved in the open but dead brown eyes. A single tear rolled down Einar's cheek as Hildr sagged, sobbing against his shoulder. Einar lay Finn down carefully and rose, bringing Hildr into a powerful embrace.

"I'm sorry," murmured Hundr, appearing from a group of warriors. Rognvald, Erik, and Hermoth flanked him, along with Refil and Erik Bjornsson.

"What for?" Einar asked.

"For everything. The warp and weft my luck brought to your life. Finn, Saoirse, Sigrid, and Sigurd. For Sten, Ragnhild, Hrist, Bush, Kolo, Bjorn, and all the friends and loves we have lost on our journey together."

"This is the life we chose, brother. Do not be sorry. We have lived lives most men would envy."

"I have the Seaworm prow. We shall fit her onto one of the captured ships. Make a new Seaworm."

"Then back to the Whale Road?"

"To the Whale Road, Einar. What else is there for men like us?"

Einar did not reply. He held Hildr close. It had been a long road full of fast ships, desperate battles, reputation, and glory. All he craved now was Vanylven and his hearth fire, where he and Hildr could see out their days together. But there was a gleam in Hundr's one eye, one Einar had not thought to see again. It was the same look which had first caught his attention twenty years ago when a young waif begged him for a berth aboard the Seaworm. A boy with a dog's name and nothing but a heart full of warrior pride and a gift of breath-taking sword skill. The memory stirred something deep inside Einar, a thing at the core of his very being. The fire in his belly, the essence of his very soul. *Drengskapr*. The way of the warrior. Perhaps there would be another voyage one day. Another chance to sail to battle again aboard the warship Seaworm...

AUTHOR MAILING LIST

If you enjoyed this book, why not join the authors mailing list and receive updates on new books and exciting news. No spam, just information on books. Every sign up will receive a free download of one of Peter Gibbons' historical fiction novels.

https://petermgibbons.com

ABOUT THE AUTHOR

Peter Gibbons

Peter is the winner of the 2022 Kindle Storyteller Literary Award, and an author based in Kildare in Ireland, with a passion for Historical Fiction, Fantasy, Science Fiction, and of course writing!

Peter was born in Warrington in the UK and studied Law at Liverpool John Moores University, before taking up a career in Financial Services and is now a full time author.

Peter currently lives in Kildare Ireland, and is married with three children. Peter is an avid reader of both Historical Fiction and Fantasy novels, particularly those of Bernard Cornwell, Steven Pressfield, David Gemmell, and Brandon Sanderson.

Peter's books include the Viking Blood and Blade Saga and The Saxon Warrior Series. You can visit

Peter's website at www.petermgibbons.com.

Printed in Great Britain
by Amazon